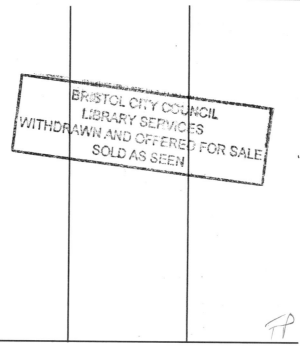
Please return/renew this item by the last date shown on this label, or on your self-service receipt.

To renew this item, visit **www.librarieswest.org.uk** or contact your library.

Your Borrower number and PIN are required.

Electric Monkey books by David Levithan

*Another Day*
*How They Met and Other Stories*
*Marly's Ghost*
*Two Boys Kissing*

Written with Rachel Cohn
*Naomi and Ely's No Kiss List*
*Nick and Norah's Infinite Playlist*

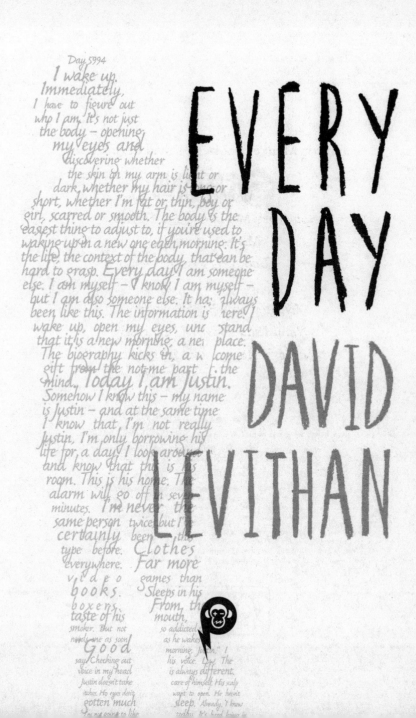

# EVERY DAY

## DAVID LEVITHAN

Day 5994

I wake up.

Immediately, I have to figure out who I am. It's not just the body – opening my eyes and discovering whether the skin on my arm is light or dark, whether my hair is long or short, whether I'm fat or thin, boy or girl, scarred or smooth. The body is the easiest thing to adjust to, if you're used to waking up in a new one each morning. It's the life, the context of the body, that can be hard to grasp. Every day I am someone else. I am myself – I know I am myself – but I am also someone else. It has always been like this. The information is here. I wake up, open my eyes, understand that it is a new morning, a new place. The biography kicks in, a welcome gift from the not-me part of the mind. Today I am Justin. Somehow I know this – my name is Justin – and at the same time I know that I'm not really Justin, I'm only borrowing his life for a day. I look around and know that this is his room. This is his home. The alarm will go off in seven minutes. I'm never the same person twice, but I've certainly been this type before. Clothes everywhere. Far more video games than books. Sleeps in his boxers. From the taste of his mouth, smoker. But not so addicted that he needs one as soon as he wakes. Good morning, Justin. I say. Checking out his voice. Low. The voice in my head is always different. Justin doesn't take care of himself. His scalp itches. His eyes don't want to open. He hasn't gotten much sleep. Already, I know I'm not going to like today. It's hard being in

First published in the USA in 2012
by Alfred A Knopf,
an imprint of Random House Children's Books,
a division of Random House Inc, New York
First published in Great Britain in 2013
by Electric Monkey, an imprint of Egmont UK Limited
The Yellow Building, 1 Nicholas Road, London W11 4AN

Text copyright © 2012 David Levithan

The moral rights of the author have been asserted

ISBN 978 1 4052 6442 6

www.egmont.co.uk

A CIP catalogue record for this title is available from the British Library

Typeset by Avon Dataset Ltd, Bidford on Avon, Warwickshire
Printed and bound in Great Britain by CPI Group

52981/10

Please note: Any website addresses listed in this book are correct at the time of going to print.
However, Egmont cannot take responsibility for any third party content or advertising.
Please be aware that online content can be subject to change and websites can contain content
that is unsuitable for children. We advise that all children are supervised when using the internet.

*For Paige*
*(May you find happiness every day)*

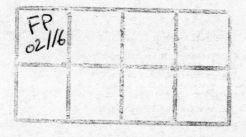

# DAY 5994

I wake up.

Immediately, I have to figure out who I am. It's not just the body – opening my eyes and discovering whether the skin on my arm is light or dark, whether my hair is long or short, whether I'm fat or thin, boy or girl, scarred or smooth. The body is the easiest thing to adjust to, if you're used to waking up in a new one each morning. It's the life, the context of the body, that can be hard to grasp.

Every day I am someone else. I am myself – I know I am myself – but I am also someone else.

It has always been like this.

The information is there. I wake up, open my eyes, understand that it is a new morning, a new place. The biography kicks in, a welcome gift from the not-me part of the mind. Today I am Justin. Somehow I know this – my name is Justin – and at the same time I know that I'm not really Justin, I'm only borrowing his life for a day. I look around and know that this is his room. This is his home. The alarm will go off in seven minutes.

I'm never the same person twice, but I've certainly been this type before. Clothes everywhere. Far more

1

video games than books. Sleeps in his boxers. From the taste of his mouth, a smoker. But not so addicted that he needs one as soon as he wakes up.

"Good morning, Justin," I say. Checking out his voice. Low. The voice in my head is always different.

Justin doesn't take care of himself. His scalp itches. His eyes don't want to open. He hasn't gotten much sleep.

Already, I know I'm not going to like today.

It's hard being in the body of someone you don't like, because you still have to respect it. I've harmed people's lives in the past, and I've found that every time I slip up, it haunts me. So I try to be careful.

From what I can tell, every person I inhabit is the same age as me. I don't hop from being sixteen to being sixty. Right now, it's only sixteen. I don't know how this works. Or why. I stopped trying to figure it out a long time ago. I'm never going to figure it out, any more than a normal person will figure out his or her own existence. After a while, you have to be at peace with the fact that you simply *are*. There is no way to know why. You can have theories, but there will never be proof.

I can access facts, not feelings. I know this is Justin's room, but I have no idea if he likes it or not. Does he want to kill his parents in the next room? Or would he be lost without his mother coming in to make sure he's

2

awake? It's impossible to tell. It's as if that part of me replaces the same part of whatever person I'm in. And while I'm glad to be thinking like myself, a hint every now and then of how the other person thinks would be helpful. We all contain mysteries, especially when seen from the inside.

The alarm goes off. I reach for a shirt and some jeans, but something lets me see that it's the same shirt he wore yesterday. I pick a different shirt. I take the clothes with me to the bathroom, dress after showering. His parents are in the kitchen now. They have no idea that anything is different.

Sixteen years is a lot of time to practise. I don't usually make mistakes. Not anymore.

I read his parents easily: Justin doesn't talk to them much in the morning, so I don't have to talk to them. I have grown accustomed to sensing expectation in others, or the lack of it. I shovel down some cereal, leave the bowl in the sink without washing it, grab Justin's keys and go.

Yesterday I was a girl in a town I'd guess to be two hours away. The day before, I was a boy in a town three hours farther than that. I am already forgetting their details. I have to, or else I will never remember who I really am.

Justin listens to loud and obnoxious music on a loud

3

and obnoxious station where loud and obnoxious DJs make loud and obnoxious jokes as a way of getting through the morning. This is all I need to know about Justin, really. I access his memory to show me the way to school, which parking space to take, which locker to go to. The combination. The names of the people he knows in the halls.

Sometimes I can't go through these motions. I can't bring myself to go to school, maneuver through the day. I'll say I'm sick, stay in bed and read a few books. But even that gets tiresome after a while, and I find myself up for the challenge of a new school, new friends. For a day.

As I take Justin's books out of his locker, I can feel someone hovering on the periphery. I turn, and the girl standing there is transparent in her emotions – tentative and expectant, nervous and adoring. I don't even have to access Justin to know that this is his girlfriend. No one else would have this reaction to him, so unsteady in his presence. She's pretty, but she doesn't see it. She's hiding behind her hair, happy to see me and unhappy to see me at the same time.

Her name is Rhiannon. And for a moment – just the slightest beat – I think that, yes, this is the right name for her. I don't know why. I don't know her. But it feels right.

This is not Justin's thought. It's mine. I try to ignore it. I'm not the person she wants to talk to.

4

"Hey," I say, keeping it casual.

"Hey," she murmurs back.

She's looking at the floor, at her inked-in Converse. Something's happened between her and Justin, and I don't know what it is. It's probably not something that Justin even recognized at the time.

"Are you okay?" I ask.

I see the surprise on her face, even as she tries to cover it. This is not something that Justin normally asks.

And the strange thing is: I want to know the answer. The fact that he wouldn't care makes me want it more.

"Sure," she says, not sounding sure at all.

I find it hard to look at her. I know from experience that beneath every peripheral girl is a central truth. She's hiding hers away, but at the same time she wants me to see it. That is, she wants *Justin* to see it. And it's there, just out of my reach. A sound waiting to be a word.

She is so lost in her sadness that she has no idea how visible it is. I think I understand her – but then, from within this sadness, she surprises me with a brief flash of determination. Bravery, even.

Shifting her gaze away from the floor, her eyes matching mine, she asks, "Are you mad at me?"

I can't think of any reason to be mad at her. If anything, I am mad at Justin, for making her feel so diminished. It's there in her body language. When she is around him, she makes herself small.

"No," I say. "I'm not mad at you at all."

I tell her what she wants to hear, but she doesn't trust it. I feed her the right words, but she suspects they're threaded with hooks.

This is not my problem; I know that. I am here for one day. I cannot solve anyone's boyfriend problems. I should not change anyone's life.

I turn away from her, get my books out, close the locker. She stays in the same spot, anchored by the profound, desperate loneliness of a bad relationship.

"Do you still want to get lunch today?" she asks.

The easy thing would be to say no. I often do this: sense the other person's life drawing me in, and run in the other direction.

But there's something about her – the cities on her shoes, the flash of bravery, the unnecessary sadness – that makes me want to know what the word will be when it stops being a sound. I have spent years meeting people without ever knowing them, and on this morning, in this place, with this girl, I feel the faintest pull of wanting to know. And in a moment of either weakness or bravery on my own part, I decide to follow it. I decide to find out more.

"Absolutely," I say. "Lunch would be great."

Again I read her. What I've said is too enthusiastic. Justin is never enthusiastic.

"No big deal," I add.

She's relieved. Or at least, as relieved as she'll allow herself to be, which is a very guarded form of relief, the relief of being in the eye of a hurricane and knowing the other wall is probably coming quick. By accessing, I know she and Justin have been together for over a year. That's as specific as it gets. Justin doesn't remember the exact date.

She reaches out and takes my hand. I am surprised by how good this feels.

"I'm glad you're not mad at me," she says. "I just want everything to be okay."

I nod. If there's one thing I've learned, it's this: we all want everything to be okay. We don't even wish so much for fantastic or marvelous or outstanding. We will happily settle for okay, because most of the time, okay is enough.

The first bell rings.

"I'll see you later," I say.

Such a basic promise. But to Rhiannon, it means the world.

At first it was hard to go through each day without making any lasting connections, leaving any life-

7

changing effects. When I was younger, I craved friendship and closeness. I would make bonds without acknowledging how quickly and permanently they would break. I took other people's lives personally. I felt their friends could be my friends, their parents could be my parents. But after a while, I had to stop. It was too heartbreaking to live with so many separations.

I am a drifter, and as lonely as that can be, it is also remarkably freeing. I will never define myself in terms of anyone else. I will never feel the pressure of peers or the burden of parental expectation. I can view everyone as pieces of a whole, and focus on the whole, not the pieces. I have learned how to observe, far better than most people observe. I am not blinded by the past or motivated by the future. I focus on the present, because that is where I am destined to live.

I learn. Sometimes I am taught something I have already been taught in dozens of other classrooms. Sometimes I am taught something completely new. I am often given information but have no context. I have to access the body, access the mind, see what information it's retained. And when I do, I learn. Knowledge is the only thing I take with me when I go.

I know so many things that Justin doesn't know, that he will never know. I sit there in his math class, open his notebook and write down phrases he has never heard.

Shakespeare and Kerouac and Dickinson. Tomorrow, or some day after tomorrow, or never, he will see these words in his own handwriting, and he won't have any idea where they came from, or even what they are.

That is as much interference as I allow myself.

Everything else must be done cleanly.

Rhiannon stays with me. Her details. Flickers from Justin's memories. Small things, like the way her hair falls, the way she bites her fingernails, the determination and resignation in her voice. Random things. I see her dancing with Justin's grandfather, because he's said he wants a dance with a pretty girl. I see her covering her eyes during a scary movie, peering between her fingers, enjoying her fright. These are the good memories. I don't look at any others.

I only see her once in the morning, a brief passing in the halls between first and second period. I find myself smiling when she comes near, and she smiles back. It's as simple as that. Simple and complicated, as most true things are. I find myself looking for her after second period, and then again after third and fourth. I don't even feel in control of this. I want to see her. Simple. Complicated.

By the time we get to lunch, I am exhausted. Justin's body is worn down from too little sleep and I, inside of it, am worn down from restlessness and too much thought.

I wait for her at Justin's locker. The first bell rings. The second bell rings. No Rhiannon. Maybe I was supposed to meet her somewhere else. Maybe Justin's forgotten where they always meet.

If that's the case, she's used to Justin forgetting. She finds me right when I'm about to give up. The halls are nearly empty, the cattle call has passed. She comes closer than she did before.

"Hey," I say.

"Hey," she says.

She is looking to me. Justin is the one who makes the first move. Justin is the one who figures things out. Justin is the one who says what they're going to do.

It depresses me.

I have seen this too many times before. The unwarranted devotion. Putting up with the fear of being with the wrong person because you can't deal with the fear of being alone. The hope tinged with doubt, and the doubt tinged with hope. Every time I see these feelings in someone else's face, it weighs me down. And there's something in Rhiannon's face that's more than just the disappointments. There is a gentleness there. A gentleness that Justin will never, ever appreciate. I see it right away, but nobody else does.

10

I take all my books and put them in the locker. I walk over to her and put my hand lightly on her arm.

I have no idea what I'm doing. I only know that I'm doing it.

"Let's go somewhere," I say. "Where do you want to go?"

I am close enough now to see that her eyes are blue. I am close enough now to see that nobody ever gets close enough to see how blue her eyes are.

"I don't know," she replies.

I take her hand.

"Come on," I tell her.

This is no longer restlessness – it's recklessness. At first we're walking hand in hand. Then we're running hand in hand. That giddy rush of keeping up with one another, of zooming through the school, reducing everything that's not us into an inconsequential blur. We are laughing, we are playful. We leave her books in her locker and move out of the building, into the air, the real air, the sunshine and the trees and the less burdensome world. I am breaking the rules as I leave the school. I am breaking the rules as we get into Justin's car. I am breaking the rules as I turn the key in the ignition.

"Where do you want to go?" I ask again. "Tell me, truly, where you'd love to go."

I don't initially realize how much hinges on her answer.

11

If she says, *Let's go to the mall*, I will disconnect. If she says, *Take me back to your house*, I will disconnect. If she says, *Actually, I don't want to miss sixth period*, I will disconnect. And I should disconnect. I should not be doing this.

But she says, "I want to go to the ocean. I want you to take me to the ocean."

And I feel myself connecting.

It takes us an hour to get there. It's late September in Maryland. The leaves haven't begun to change, but you can tell they're starting to think about it. The greens are muted, faded. Color is right around the corner.

I give Rhiannon control of the radio. She's surprised by this, but I don't care. I've had enough of the loud and the obnoxious, and I sense that she's had enough of it too. She brings melody to the car. A song comes on that I know, and I sing along.

*And if I only could, I'd make a deal with God . . .*

Now Rhiannon goes from surprised to suspicious. Justin never sings along.

"What's gotten into you?" she asks.

"Music," I tell her.

"Ha."

"No, really."

She looks at me for a long time. Then smiles.

12

"In that case," she says, flipping the dial to find the next song.

Soon we are singing at the top of our lungs. A pop song that's as substantial as a balloon, but lifts us in the same way when we sing it.

It's as if time itself relaxes around us. She stops thinking about how unusual it is. She lets herself be a part of it.

I want to give her a good day. Just one good day. I have wandered for so long without any sense of purpose, and now this ephemeral purpose has been given to me – it feels like it has been given to me. I only have a day to give – so why can't it be a good one? Why can't it be a shared one? Why can't I take the music of the moment and see how long it can last? The rules are erasable. I can take this. I can give this.

When the song is over, she rolls down her window and trails her hand in the air, introducing a new music into the car. I roll down all the other windows and drive faster, so the wind takes over, blows our hair all around, makes it seem like the car has disappeared and we are the velocity, we are the speed. Then another good song comes on and I enclose us again, this time taking her hand. I drive like that for miles, and ask her questions. I ask her how her parents are doing. What it's like now that her sister's off at college. If she thinks school is different at all this year.

It's hard for her. Every single answer starts with the phrase *I don't know*. But most of the time she *does* know, if I give her the time and the space in which to answer. Her mother means well; her father less so. Her sister isn't calling home, but Rhiannon can understand that. School is school – she wants it to be over, but she's afraid of it being over, because then she'll have to figure out what comes next.

She asks me what I think, and I tell her, "Honestly, I'm just trying to live day to day."

It isn't enough, but it's something. We watch the trees, the sky, the signs, the road. We sense each other. The world, right now, is only us. We continue to sing along. And we sing with the same abandon, not worrying too much if our voices hit the right notes or the right words. We look at each other while we're singing; these aren't two solos, this is a duet that isn't taking itself at all seriously. It is its own form of conversation – you can learn a lot about people from the stories they tell, but you can also know them from the way they sing along, whether they like the windows up or down, if they live by the map or by the world, if they feel the pull of the ocean.

She tells me where to drive. Off the highway. The empty back roads. This isn't summer; this isn't a weekend. It's the middle of a Monday, and nobody but us is going to the beach.

"I should be in English class," Rhiannon says.

"I should be in bio," I say, accessing Justin's schedule.

We keep going. When I first saw her, she seemed to be balancing on edges and points. Now the ground is more even, welcoming.

I know this is dangerous. Justin is not good to her. I recognize that. If I access his memories of her, I see tears, fights and remnants of passable togetherness. She is always there for him, and he must like that. His friends like her, and he must like that too. But that's not the same as love. She has been hanging on to the hope of him for so long that she doesn't realize there isn't anything left to hope for. They don't have silences together; they have noise. Mostly his. If I tried, I could go deep into their arguments. I could track down whatever shards he's collected from all the times he's destroyed her. If I were really Justin, I would find something wrong with her. Right now. Tell her. Yell. Bring her down. Put her in her place.

But I can't. I'm not Justin. Even if she doesn't know it.

"Let's just enjoy ourselves," I say.

"Okay," she replies. "I like that. I spend so much time thinking about running away – it's nice to actually do it. For a day. It's good to be on the other side of the window. I don't do this enough."

There are so many things inside of her that I want to know. And at the same time, with every word we speak, I feel there may be something inside of her that I already know. When I get there, we will recognize each other. We will have that.

I park the car and we head to the ocean. We take off our shoes and leave them under our seats. When we get to the sand, I lean over to roll up my jeans. While I do, Rhiannon runs ahead. When I look back up, she is spinning around the beach, kicking up sand, calling my name. Everything, at that moment, is lightness. She is so joyful, I can't help but stop for a second and watch. Witness. Tell myself to remember.

"C'mon!" she cries. "Get over here!"

*I'm not who you think I am,* I want to tell her. But there's no way. Of course, there's no way.

We have the beach to ourselves, the ocean to ourselves. I have her to myself. She has me to herself.

There is a part of childhood that is childish, and a part that is sacred. Suddenly we are touching the sacred part – running to the shoreline, feeling the first cold burst of water on our ankles, reaching into the tide to catch at shells before they ebb away from our fingers. We have returned to a world that is capable of glistening, and we are wading deeper within it. We stretch our arms wide, as if we are embracing the wind. She splashes me mischievously and I mount a counterattack. Our pants, our shirts get wet, but we don't care. We are carefree.

She asks me to help her build a sand castle, and as I do, she tells me about how she and her sister would never work on sand castles together – it was always a competition, with her sister going for the highest possible mountains while Rhiannon paid attention to detail, wanting each castle to be the dollhouse she was never allowed to have. I see echoes of this detail now, as she makes turrets bloom from her cupped hands. I myself have no memories of sand castles, but there must be some sense memory attached, because I feel I know how to do this, how to shape this.

When we are done, we walk back down to the water to wash off our hands. I look back and see the way our footsteps intermingle to form a single path.

"What is it?" she asks, seeing me glance backward, seeing something in my expression.

How can I explain this? The only way I know is to say, "Thank you."

She looks at me as if she's never heard the phrase before.

"For what?" she asks.

"For this," I say. "For all of it."

17

This escape. The water. The waves. Her. It feels like we've stepped outside of time. Even though there is no such place.

There's still a part of her that's waiting for the twist, the moment when all of this pleasure will jackknife into pain.

"It's okay," I tell her. "It's okay to be happy."

The tears come to her eyes. I take her in my arms. It's the wrong thing to do. But it's the right thing to do. I have to listen to my own words. Happiness is so rarely a part of my vocabulary, because for me it's so fleeting.

"I'm happy," she says. "Really, I am."

Justin would be laughing at her. Justin would be pushing her down into the sand, to do whatever he wanted to do. Justin would never have come here.

I am tired of not feeling. I am tired of not connecting. I want to be here with her. I want to be the one who lives up to her hopes, if only for the time I'm given.

The ocean makes its music; the wind does its dance. We hold on. At first we hold on to one another, but then it starts to feel like we are holding on to something even bigger than that. Greater.

"What's happening?" Rhiannon asks.

"Shhh," I say. "Don't question it."

She kisses me. I have not kissed anyone in years. I have not allowed myself to kiss anyone for years. Her

18

lips are soft as flower petals, but with an intensity behind them. I take it slow, let each moment pour into the next. Feel her skin, her breath. Taste the condensation of our contact, linger in the heat of it. Her eyes are closed and mine are open. I want to remember this as more than a single sensation. I want to remember this whole.

We do nothing more than kiss. We do nothing less than kiss. At times, she moves to take it further, but I don't need that. I trace her shoulders as she traces my back. I kiss her neck. She kisses beneath my ear. The times we stop, we smile at each other. Giddy disbelief, giddy belief. She should be in English class. I should be in bio. We weren't supposed to come anywhere near the ocean today. We have defied the day as it was set out for us.

We walk hand-in-hand down the beach as the sun dips in the sky. I am not thinking about the past. I am not thinking about the future. I am full of such gratitude for the sun, the water, the way my feet sink into the sand, the way my hand feels holding hers.

"We should do this every Monday," she says. "And Tuesday. And Wednesday. And Thursday. And Friday."

"We'd only get tired of it," I tell her. "It's best to have it just once."

"Never again?" She doesn't like the sound of that.

"Well, never say never."

"I'd never say never," she tells me.

There are a few more people on the beach now, mostly older men and women taking an afternoon walk. They nod to us as we walk past, and sometimes they say hello. We nod back, return their hellos. Nobody questions why we're here. Nobody questions anything. We're just a part of the moment, like everything else.

The sun falls farther. The temperature drops alongside it. Rhiannon shivers, so I stop holding her hand and put my arm around her. She suggests we go back to the car and get the "make-out blanket" from the trunk. We find it there, buried under empty beer bottles, twisted jumper cables and other guy crap. I wonder how often Rhiannon and Justin have used the make-out blanket for that purpose, but I don't try to access the memories. Instead I bring the blanket back out onto the beach and put it down for both of us. I lie down and face the sky, and Rhiannon lies down next to me and does the same. We stare at the clouds, breathing distance from one another, taking it all in.

"This has to be one of the best days ever," Rhiannon says.

Without turning my head, I find her hand with my hand.

"Tell me about some of the other days like this," I ask.

"I don't know . . ."

"Just one. The first one that comes to mind."

Rhiannon thinks about it for a second. Then she shakes her head. "It's stupid."

"Tell me."

She turns to me and moves her hand to my chest. Makes lazy circles there. "For some reason, the first thing that comes to mind is this mother-daughter fashion show. Do you promise you won't laugh?"

I promise.

She studies me. Makes sure I'm sincere. Continues.

"It was in fourth grade or something. Renwick's was doing a fundraiser for hurricane victims, and they asked for volunteers from our class. I didn't ask my mother or anything – I just signed up. And when I brought the information home – well, you know how my mom is. She was terrified. It's enough to get her out to the supermarket. But a fashion show? In front of strangers? I might as well have asked her to pose for *Playboy*. God, now there's a scary thought."

Her hand is now resting on my chest. She's looking off to the sky.

"But here's the thing: She didn't say no. I guess it's only now that I realize what I put her through. She didn't make me go to the teacher and take it back. No, when the day came, we drove over to Renwick's and went where they told us to go. I had thought they would put us in matching outfits, but it wasn't like that. Instead, they basically told us we could wear whatever we wanted from the store. So there we were, trying all these things on. I went for the gowns, of course – I was so much more of a girl then. I ended up with this light blue dress – ruffles all over the place. I thought it was so sophisticated."

"I'm sure it was classy," I say.

She hits me. "Shut up. Let me tell my story."

I hold her hand on my chest. Lean over and kiss her quickly.

"Go ahead," I say. I am loving this. I never have people tell me their stories. I usually have to figure them out myself. Because I know that if people tell me stories, they will expect them to be remembered. And I cannot guarantee that. There is no way to know if the stories stay after I'm gone. And how devastating would it be to confide in someone and have the confidence disappear? I don't want to be responsible for that.

But with Rhiannon I can't resist.

She continues. "So I had my wannabe prom dress. And then it was Mom's turn. She surprised me, because she went for the dresses too. I'd never really seen her all dressed up before. And I think that was the most amazing thing to me: It wasn't me who was Cinderella. It was her.

"After we picked out our clothes, they put on makeup and everything. I thought Mom was going to flip, but she was actually enjoying it. They didn't really do much with her – just a little more color. And that was all it took. She was pretty. I know it's hard to believe, knowing her now. But that day, she was like a movie star. All the other moms were complimenting her. And then it was time for the actual show, and we paraded out there and people applauded. Mom and I were both smiling, and it was real, you know?

"We didn't get to keep the dresses or anything. But I remember on the ride home, Mom kept saying how great I was. When we got back to our house, Dad looked at us like we were aliens, but the cool thing is, he decided to play along. Instead of getting all weird, he kept calling us his supermodels, and asked us to do the show for him in our living room, which we did. We were laughing so much. And that was it. The day ended. I'm not sure Mom's worn makeup since. And it's not like I turned out to be a supermodel. But that day reminds me of this one. Because it was a break from everything, wasn't it?"

"It sounds like it," I tell her.

"I can't believe I just told you that."

"Why?"

"Because. I don't know. It just sounds so silly."

"No, it sounds like a good day."

"How about you?" she asks.

"I was never in a mother-daughter fashion show," I joke. Even though, as a matter of fact, I've been in a few.

She hits me lightly on the shoulder. "No. Tell me about another day like this one."

I access Justin and find out he moved to town when he was twelve. So anything before that is fair game, because Rhiannon won't have been there. I could try to find one of Justin's memories to share, but I don't want to do that. I want to give Rhiannon something of my own.

"There was this one day when I was eleven." I try to remember the name of the boy whose body I was in, but it's lost to me. "I was playing hide-and-seek with my friends. I mean, the brutal, tackle kind of hide-and-seek. We were in the woods, and for some reason I decided that what I had to do was climb a tree. I don't think I'd ever climbed a tree before. But I found one with some low branches and just started moving. Up and up. It was as natural as walking. In my memory, that tree was hundreds of feet tall. Thousands. At some point, I crossed the tree line. I was still climbing, but there weren't any other trees around. I was all by myself, clinging to the trunk of this tree, a long way from the ground."

I can see shimmers of it now. The height. The town below me.

"It was magical," I say. "There's no other word to describe it. I could hear my friends yelling as they were caught, as the game played out. But I was in a completely different place. I was seeing the world from above, which is an extraordinary thing when it happens for the first time. I'd never flown in a plane. I'm not even sure I'd been in a tall building. So there I was, hovering above everything I knew. I had made it somewhere special, and I'd gotten there all on my own. Nobody had given it to me. Nobody had told me to do it. I'd climbed and climbed and climbed, and this was my reward. To watch over the world, and to be alone with myself. That, I found, was what I needed."

Rhiannon leans into me. "That's amazing," she whispers.

"Yeah, it was."

"And it was in Minnesota?"

In truth, it was in North Carolina. But I access Justin and find that, yes, for him it would've been Minnesota. So I nod.

"You want to know another day like this one?" Rhiannon asks, curling closer.

I adjust my arm, make us both comfortable. "Sure."

"It was our second date."

*But this is only our first,* I think. Ridiculously.

"Really?" I ask.

"Remember?"

I check to see if Justin remembers their second date. He doesn't.

"Dack's party?" she prompts.

Still nothing.

"Yeah . . ." I hedge.

"I don't know – maybe it doesn't count as a date. But it was the second time we hooked up. And, I don't know, you were just so . . . sweet about it. Don't get mad, all right?"

I wonder where this is going.

"I promise, nothing could make me mad right now," I tell her. I even cross my heart to prove it.

She smiles. "Okay. Well, lately – it's like you're always in a rush. Like, we have sex, but we're not really . . . intimate. And I don't mind. I mean, it's fun. But every now and then, it's good to have it be like this. And at Dack's party – it was like this. Like you had all the time in the world, and you wanted us to have it together. I loved that. It was back when you were really looking at me. It was like – well, it was like you'd climbed up that tree and found me there at the top. And we had that together. Even though we were in someone's back yard. At one point – do you remember? – you made me move over a little so I'd be in the moonlight. 'It makes your skin glow,' you said. And I felt like that. Glowing. Because you were watching me, along with the moon."

Does she realize that right now she's lit by the warm orange spreading from the horizon, as not-quite-day becomes not-quite-night? I lean over and become that shadow. I kiss her once, then we drift into each other, close our eyes, drift into sleep. And as we drift into sleep, I feel something I've never felt before. A closeness that isn't merely physical. A connection that defies the fact that we've only just met. A sensation that can only come from the most euphoric of feelings: belonging.

What is it about the moment you fall in love? How can such a small measure of time contain such enormity? I suddenly realize why people believe in déjà vu, why people believe they've lived past lives, because there is no way the years I've spent on this earth could possibly encapsulate what I'm feeling. The moment you fall in love feels like it has centuries behind it, generations – all of them rearranging themselves so that this precise, remarkable intersection could happen. In your heart, in your bones, no matter how silly you know it is, you feel that everything has been leading to this, all the secret arrows were pointing here, the universe and time itself have crafted this long ago, and you are just now realizing it, you are just now arriving at the place you were always meant to be.

We wake an hour later to the sound of her phone.

I keep my eyes closed. Hear her groan. Hear her tell her mother she'll be home soon.

The water has gone deep black and the sky has gone ink blue. The chill in the air presses harder against us as we pick up the blanket, provide a new set of footprints.

She navigates, I drive. She talks, I listen. We sing some more. Then she leans into my shoulder and I let her stay there and sleep for a little longer, dream for a little longer.

I am trying not to think of what will happen next.

I am trying not to think of endings.

I never get to see people while they're asleep. Not like this. She is the opposite of when I first met her. Her vulnerability is open, but she's safe within it. I watch the rise and fall of her, the stir and rest of her. I only wake her when I need her to tell me where to go.

The last ten minutes, she talks about what we're going to do tomorrow. I find it hard to respond.

"Even if we can't do this, I'll see you at lunch?" she asks.

I nod.

"And maybe we can do something after school?"

"I think so. I mean, I'm not sure what else is going on. My mind isn't really there right now."

This makes sense to her. "Fair enough. Tomorrow is tomorrow. Let's end today on a nice note."

Once we get to town, I can access the directions to her house without having to ask her. But I want to get lost, anyway. To prolong this. To escape this.

"Here we are," Rhiannon says as we approach her driveway.

I pull the car over. I unlock the doors.

She leans over and kisses me. My senses are alive with the taste of her, the smell of her, the feel of her, the sound of her breathing, the sight of her as she pulls her body away from mine.

"That's the nice note," she says. And before I can say anything else, she's out the door and gone.

I don't get a chance to say goodbye.

I guess, correctly, that Justin's parents are used to him being out of touch and missing dinner. They try to yell at him, but you can tell that everyone's going through the motions, and when Justin storms off to his room, it's just the latest rerun of an old show.

I should be doing Justin's homework – I'm always pretty conscientious about that kind of thing, if I'm able to do it – but my mind keeps drifting to Rhiannon.

Imagining her at home. Imagining her floating from the grace of the day. Imagining her believing that things are different, that Justin has somehow changed.

I shouldn't have done it. I know I shouldn't have done it. Even if it felt like the universe was telling me to do it.

I agonize over it for hours. I can't take it back. I can't make it go away.

I fell in love once, or at least until today I thought I had. His name was Brennan, and it felt so real, even if it was mostly words. Intense, heartfelt words. I stupidly let myself think of a possible future with him. But there was no future. I tried to navigate it, but I couldn't.

That was easy compared to this. It's one thing to fall in love. It's another to feel someone else falling in love with you, and to feel a responsibility toward that love.

There is no way for me to stay in this body. If I don't go to sleep, the shift will happen anyway. I used to think that if I stayed up all night, I'd get to remain where I was. But instead I was ripped from the body I was in. And the ripping felt exactly what you would imagine being ripped from a body would feel like, with every single nerve experiencing the pain of the break, and then the pain of being fused into someone new. From then on, I went to sleep every night. There was no use fighting it.

*

I realize I have to call her. Her number's right there in his phone. I can't let her think tomorrow is going to be like today.

"Hey!" she answers.

"Hey," I say.

"Thank you again for today."

"Yeah."

I don't want to do this. I don't want to ruin it. But I have to, don't I?

I continue, "But about today?"

"Yeah? Are you going to tell me that we can't cut class every day? That's not like you."

Not like me.

"Yeah," I say, "but, you know, I don't want you to think every day is going to be like today. Because they're not going to be, all right? They can't be."

There's a silence. She knows something's wrong.

"I know that," she says carefully. "But maybe things can still be better. I know they can be."

"I don't know," I tell her. "That's all I wanted to say. I don't know. Today was something, but it's not, like, everything."

"I know that."

"Okay."

"Okay."

I sigh.

There's always a chance that, in some way, I will have brushed off on Justin. There's always a chance that his life will in fact change – that he will change. But I have no way of knowing. It's rare that I get to see a body after I've left it. And even then, it's usually months or years later. If I recognize it at all.

I want Justin to be better to her. But I can't have her expecting it.

"That's all," I say. It feels like a Justin thing to say.

"Well, I'll see you tomorrow."

"Yeah, you will."

"Thanks again for today. No matter what trouble we get into tomorrow for it, it was worth it."

"Yeah."

"I love you," she says.

And I want to say it. I want to say *I love you too*. Right now, right at this moment, every part of me would mean it. But that will only last for a couple more hours.

"Sleep well," I tell her. Then I hang up.

There's a notebook on his desk.

*Remember that you love Rhiannon,* I write in his handwriting.

I doubt he'll remember writing it.


I go on to his computer. I open up my own email account, then type out her name, her phone number, her email address, as well as Justin's email and password. I write about the day. And I send it to myself.

As soon as I'm through, I clear Justin's history.

This is hard for me.

I have gotten so used to what I am, and how my life works.

I never want to stay. I'm always ready to leave.

But not tonight.

Tonight I'm haunted by the fact that tomorrow he'll be here and I won't be.

I want to stay.

I pray to stay.

I close my eyes and wish to stay.

# DAY 5995

I wake up thinking of yesterday. The joy is in remembering; the pain is in knowing it was yesterday.

I am not there. I am not in Justin's bed, not in Justin's body.

Today I am Leslie Wong. I have slept through the alarm, and her mother is mad.

"Get up!" she yells, shaking my new body. "You have twenty minutes, and then Owen leaves!"

"Okay, Mom," I groan.

"Mom! If your mother was here, I can't imagine what she'd say!"

I quickly access Leslie's mind. Grandmother, then. Mom's already left for work.

As I stand in the shower, trying to remind myself I have to make it a quick one, I lose myself for a minute in thoughts of Rhiannon. I'm sure I dreamt of her. I wonder: If I started dreaming when I was in Justin's body, did he continue the dream? Will he wake up thinking sweetly of her?

Or is that just another kind of dream on my part?

"Leslie! Come on!"

I get out of the shower, dry off and get dressed quickly. Leslie is not, I can tell, a particularly popular girl. The few photos of friends she has around seem half-hearted, and her clothing choices are more like a thirteen-year-old's than a sixteen-year-old's.

I head into the kitchen and the grandmother glares at me.

"Don't forget your clarinet," she warns.

"I won't," I mumble.

There's a boy at the table giving me an evil look. Leslie's brother, I assume – and then confirm it. Owen. A senior. My ride to school.

I have gotten very used to the fact that most mornings in most homes are exactly the same. Stumbling out of the bed. Stumbling into the shower. Mumbling over the breakfast table. Or, if the parents are still asleep, the tiptoe out of the house. The only way to keep it interesting is to look for the variations.

This morning's variation comes care of Owen, who lights up a joint the minute we get into the car. I'm assuming this is part of his morning routine, so I make sure Leslie doesn't seem as surprised as I am.

Still, Owen hazards a "Don't say a word" about three minutes into the ride. I stare out the window. Two minutes later, he says, "Look, I don't need your judgment, okay?" The joint is done by then; it doesn't make him any mellower.

*

I prefer to be an only child. In the long term, I can see how siblings could be helpful in life – someone to share family secrets with, someone of your own generation who knows if your memories are right or not, someone who sees you at eight and eighteen and forty-eight all at once, and doesn't mind. I understand that. But in the short term, siblings are at best a hassle and at worst a terror. Most of the abuse I have suffered in my admittedly unusual life has come from brothers and sisters, with older brothers and older sisters being, by and large, the worst offenders. At first, I was naïve, and assumed that brothers and sisters were natural allies, instant companions. And sometimes, the context would allow this to happen – if we were on a family trip, for example, or if it was a lazy Sunday where teaming up with me was my sibling's only form of entertainment. But on ordinary days, the rule is competition, not collaboration. There are times when I wonder whether brothers and sisters are, in fact, the ones who sense that something is off with whatever person I'm inhabiting, and move to take advantage. When I was eight, an older sister told me we were going to run away together – then abandoned the "together" part when we got to the train station, leaving me to wander there for hours, too scared to ask for help – scared that she would find out and berate me for ending our game. As a boy, I've had brothers – both older and younger – wrestle me, hit me, kick me, bite me, shove me, and call me more names than I could ever catalog.

The best I can hope for is a quiet sibling. At first I have Owen pegged as one of those. In the car, it appears I am wrong. But then, once we get out at school, it appears I am right again. With other kids around, he retreats into invisibility, keeping his head down as he makes his way inside, leaving me completely behind. No goodbye, no have-a-nice-day. Just a quick glance to see that my door is closed before he locks the car.

"What are you looking at?" a voice asks from over my left shoulder as I watch him enter school alone.

I turn around and do some serious accessing.

Carrie. Best friend since fourth grade.

"Just my brother."

"Why? He's such a waste of space."

Here's the strange thing: I am fine thinking the same words myself, but hearing them come out of Carrie's mouth makes me feel defensive.

"Come on," I say.

"Come on? Are you kidding me?"

Now I think: *She knows something I don't.* I decide to keep my mouth shut.

She seems relieved to change the subject.

"What did you do last night?" she asks.

Flashes of Rhiannon rise in my mind's eye. I try to tamp them down, but they're not that easy to contain. Once you experience enormity, it lingers everywhere you look, and wants to be every word you say.

"Not much," I push on, not bothering to access Leslie. This answer always works, no matter what the question. "You?"

"You didn't get my text?"

I mumble something about my phone dying.

"That explains why you haven't asked me yet! Guess what. Corey IM'd me! We chatted for, like, almost an hour."

"Wow."

"Yeah, isn't it?" Carrie sighs contently. "After all this time. I didn't even know he knew my screen name. You didn't tell him, did you?"

More accessing. This is the kind of question that can really trip a person up. Maybe not right away. But in the future. If Leslie claims she wasn't the one who told Corey, and Carrie finds out she was, it could throw their friendship off balance. Or if Leslie claims she was, and Carrie finds out she wasn't.

Corey is Corey Handlemann, a junior who Carrie's had a crush on for at least three weeks. Leslie doesn't know him well, and I can't find a memory of giving a screenname to him. I think it's safe.

"No," I say, shaking my head. "I didn't."

"Well, I guess he really had to work hard to find it," she says. (*Or*, I think, *he just saw it on your Facebook profile*.)

I immediately feel guilty for my snarky thoughts. This is the hard part about having best friends that I feel no attachment to – I don't give them any benefit of the doubt. And being best friends is always about the benefit of the doubt.

Carrie is very excited about Corey, so I pretend to be very excited for her. It's only after we separate for homeroom that I feel an emotion kicking at me, one I thought I had under control: jealousy. Although I am not articulating it to myself in as many words, I am feeling jealous that Carrie can have Corey while I can never have Rhiannon.

*Ridiculous*, I chastise myself. *You are being ridiculous*.

When you live as I do, you cannot indulge in jealousy. If you do, it will rip you apart.

Third period is band class. I tell the teacher that I left my clarinet at home, even though it's in my locker. Leslie gets marked down and has to take the class as a study hall, but I don't care.

I don't know how to play the clarinet.

Word about Carrie and Corey travels fast. All of our friends are talking about it, and mostly they're pleased. I can't tell, though, whether they're pleased because it's a perfect match or because now Carrie will shut up about it.

When I see Corey at lunchtime, I am unsurprised by how unremarkable he is. People are rarely as attractive in reality as they are in the eyes of the people who are in love with them. Which is, I suppose, as it should be. It's almost heartening to think that the attachment you have can define your perception as much as any other influence.

Corey comes over at lunch to say hi, but he doesn't stay to eat with us, even though we make room for him at our table. Carrie doesn't seem to notice this; she's just giddy that he's come by, that she didn't dream the whole IM exchange, that chatting has escalated into speaking . . . and who knows what will happen next? As I suspected, Leslie does not move in a fast crowd. These girls are thinking of kissing, not sex. The lips are the gates of their desire.

I want to run away again, to skip the second half of the day again.

But it wouldn't be right, without her.

It feels like I am wasting time. I mean, that's always the case. My life doesn't add up to anything.

40

Except, for an afternoon, it did.

Yesterday is another world. I want to go back there.

Early sixth period, right after lunch, my brother is called down to the principal's office.

At first, I think I might have heard it wrong. But then I see other people in class looking at me, including Carrie, who has pity in her eyes. So I must have heard it right.

I am not alarmed. I figure if it was something really bad, they would have called us both. Nobody in my family has died. Our house hasn't burned down. It's Owen's business, not mine.

Carrie sends me a note. *What happened?*

I send a shrug in her direction. How am I supposed to know?

I just hope I haven't lost my ride home.

Sixth period ends. I gather my books and head to English class. The book is *Beowulf*, so I'm completely prepared. I've done this unit plenty of times.

I'm about ten steps away from the classroom when someone grabs me.

I turn, and there's Owen.

Owen, bleeding.

"Shh," he says. "Just come with me."

"What happened?" I ask.

"Just shh, okay?"

He's looking around like he's being chased. I decide to go along. After all, this is more exciting than *Beowulf*.

We get to a supply closet. He motions me in.

"Are you kidding me?" I say.

"*Leslie*."

There's no arguing. I follow him in. I find the light switch easily.

He's breathing hard. For a moment, he doesn't say anything.

"You were going to tell me what happened?" I say.

"I think I might be in trouble."

"Duh. I heard you called to the principal's office. Why aren't you down there?"

"I *was* down there. I mean, before the announcement. But then I . . . left."

"You bolted from the principal's office?"

"Yeah. Well, the waiting room. They went to check my locker. I'm sure of it."

The blood is coming from a cut above his eye.

"Who hit you?" I ask.

"It doesn't matter. Just shut up and listen to me, okay?"

"I'm listening, but you're not saying anything!"

I don't think Leslie usually talks back to her older brother. But I don't care. He isn't really paying attention to me, anyway.

"They're going to call home, okay? I need you to back me up." He hands me his keys. "Just go home after school and see what the situation is. I'll call you."

Luckily, I know how to drive.

When I don't argue, he takes it as acquiescence.

"Thanks," he tells me.

"Are you going to the principal's office now?" I ask him.

He leaves without an answer.

Carrie has the news by the end of the day. Whether it's the truth doesn't really matter. It's the news that's going around, and she's eager to report it to me.

"Your brother and Josh Wolf got into a fight out by the field, during lunch. They're saying it had to do with drugs, and that your brother is a dealer or something. I mean, I knew he was into pot and everything, but I had no idea he *dealt*. He and Josh were dragged down to the principal's office, but Owen decided to run. Can you believe it? They were paging him to come back. But I don't think he did."

"Who'd you hear it from?" I ask. She's giddy with excitement.

"From Corey! He wasn't out there, but some of the guys he hangs out with saw the fight and everything."

I see now that the fact that Corey told her is the

43

bigger news here. She's not so selfish that she wants me to congratulate her, not with my brother in trouble. But it's clear what her priority is.

"I've got to drive home," I say.

"Do you want me to come with you?" Carrie asks. "I don't want you to have to walk in there alone."

For a second, I'm tempted. But then I imagine her giving Corey the blow-by-blow account of what goes down, and even if that's not a fair assumption to make, it's enough to make me realize I don't want her there.

"It's okay," I say. "If anything, this is really going to make me look like the good daughter."

Carrie laughs, but more out of support than humor.

"Tell Corey I say hi," I say playfully as I close my locker.

She laughs again. This time, out of happiness.

"Where is he?"

I haven't even stepped through the kitchen door and the interrogation begins.

Leslie's mother, father and grandmother are all there, and I don't need to access her mind to know this is an unusual occurrence at three in the afternoon.

"I have no idea," I say. I'm glad he didn't tell me; this way, I don't have to lie.

"What do you mean, you have no idea?" my father

asks. He's the lead inquisitor in this family.

"I mean, I have no idea. He gave me the keys to the car, but he wouldn't tell me what was going on."

"And you let him walk away?"

"I didn't see any police chasing after him," I say. Then I wonder if there are, in fact, police chasing after him.

My grandmother snorts in disgust.

"You always take his side," my father intones. "But not this time. This time you are going to tell us everything."

He doesn't realize he's just helped me. Now I know that Leslie always takes Owen's side. So my instinct is correct.

"You probably know more than I do," I say.

"Why would your brother and Josh Wolf have a fight?" my mother asks, genuinely bewildered. "They're such good friends!"

My mental image of Josh Wolf is of a ten-year-old, leading me to believe that at one point, my brother probably *was* good friends with Josh Wolf. But not anymore.

"Sit down," my father commands, pointing to a kitchen chair.

I sit down.

"Now . . . where is he?"

"I genuinely don't know."

"She's telling the truth," my mother says. "I can tell when she's lying."

Even though I have way too many control issues to do drugs myself, I am starting to get a sense why Owen likes to get stoned.

"Well, let me ask this, then," my father continues. "Is your brother a drug dealer?"

This is a very good question. My instinct is *no*. But a lot depends on what happened on the field with Josh Wolf.

So I don't answer. I just stare.

"Josh Wolf says the drugs in his jacket were sold to him by your brother," my father prods. "Are you saying they weren't?"

"Did they find any drugs on Owen?" I ask.

"No," my mother answers.

"And in his locker? Didn't they search his locker?" My mother shakes her head.

"And in his room? Did you find any in his room?"

My mother actually looks surprised.

"I *know* you looked in his room," I say.

"We haven't found anything," my father answers. "Yet. And we also need to take a look in that car. So if you will please give me the keys . . ."

I am hoping that Owen was smart enough to clear out the car. Either way, it's not up to me. I hand over the keys.

Unbelievably, they've searched my room too.

"I'm sorry," my mother says from the hallway, tears in her eyes now. "He thought your brother might have hidden the drugs in here. Without you knowing."

"It's fine," I say, more to get her out of the room than anything else. "I'm just going to clean up now."

But I'm not quick enough. My phone rings. I hold it so my mom can't see Owen's name on the display.

"Hi, Carrie," I say.

Owen is at least smart enough to keep his voice down so it won't be overheard.

"Are they mad?" he whispers.

I want to laugh. "What do you think?"

"That bad?"

"They've ransacked his room, but they haven't found anything. They're looking in his car now!"

"Don't tell her that!" my mother says. "Get off the phone."

"Sorry – Mom's here, and not happy about me talking to you about this. Where are you? Are you at home? Can I call you back?"

"I don't know what to do."

"Yeah, he really does have to come home eventually, doesn't he?"

"Look . . . meet me in a half-hour at the playground, okay?"

"I really have to go. But, yes, I'll do that."

I hang up. My mother is still looking at me.

"I'm not the one you're mad at!" I remind her.

Poor Leslie will have to clean up the mess in her room tomorrow morning – I can't be bothered to figure out where everything goes. That would take too much accessing, and the priority is finding which playground Owen means. There's one at an elementary school about four blocks from the house. I assume that's the place.

It's not easy to sneak out of the house. I wait until the three of them return to Owen's room to tear it apart again, then skulk out the back door. I know this is a risky maneuver – the minute they realize I'm gone, there will be hell to pay. But if Owen comes back with me, that'll all be forgotten.

I know I should be focusing on the matter at hand, but I can't help but think of Rhiannon. School's now over for her too. Is she hanging out with Justin? If so, is he treating her well? Did anything about yesterday rub off on him?

I hope, but never expect.

Owen's nowhere to be found, so I head to the swings

and hang in the air for a while. Eventually he appears on the sidewalk and heads over to me.

"You always pick that swing," he says, sitting down on the swing next to mine.

"I do?" I say.

"Yeah."

I wait for him to say something else. He doesn't.

"Owen," I finally say. "What happened?"

He shakes his head. He's not going to tell me.

I stop swinging and plant my feet on the ground.

"This is stupid, Owen. You have five seconds to tell me what happened, or I'm going to head right back home, and you'll be on your own for whatever happens next."

Owen is surprised. But I figure the circumstances can justify Leslie's anger.

"What do you want me to say? Josh Wolf gets me my pot. Today we got into a fight over it – he was saying I owed him, when I didn't. He started pushing me around, so I pushed him back. And we got caught. He had the drugs, so he said I'd just dealt them to him. Real smooth. I said that was totally wrong, but he's in all AP classes and everything, so who do you think they're going to believe?"

He has definitely convinced himself it's the truth. But whether it started out being the truth or not, I can't tell.

49

"Well," I say, "you have to come home. Dad's trashed your room, but they haven't found any drugs yet. And they didn't find any in your locker, and I'm guessing they didn't find any in the car or I would've heard about it. So right now, it's all okay."

"I'm telling you, there aren't any drugs. I used the weed up this morning. That's why I needed more from Josh."

"Josh, your former best friend."

"What are you talking about? I haven't been friends with him since we were, like, eight."

I am sensing that this was the last time Owen had a best friend.

"Let's go," I tell him. "It's not the end of the world."

"Easy for you to say."


I am not expecting our father to hit Owen. But as soon as he sees him in the house, he decks him.

I think I am the only one who is truly stunned.

"What have you done?" my father is yelling. "What stupid, stupid thing have you done?"

Both my mother and I move to stand between them. Grandma just watches from the sidelines, looking mildly pleased.

"I haven't done anything!" Owen protests.

"Is that why you ran away? Is that why you are being

expelled? Because you haven't done anything?"

"They won't expel him until they hear his side of the story," I point out, fairly sure this is true.

"Stay out of this!" my father warns.

"Why don't we all sit down and talk this over?" my mother suggests.

The anger rises off my father like heat. I feel myself receding in a way that I'm guessing is not unusual for Leslie when she's with her family.

It is during moments like this that I become nostalgic for that first waking moment of the morning, back before I had any idea what ugliness the day would bring.

We sit down this time in the den. Or, rather, Owen, our mother and I sit down – Owen and me on the couch, our mother in a nearby chair. Our father hovers over us. Our grandmother stays in the doorway, as if she's keeping lookout.

"You are a *drug dealer*!" our father yells.

"I am *not* a drug dealer," Owen answers. "For one, if I were a drug dealer, I'd have a lot more money. And I'd have a stash of drugs that you would've found by now!"

Owen, I think, needs to shut up.

"Josh Wolf was the drug dealer," I volunteer. "Not Owen."

"So what was your brother doing – *buying from him*?"

Maybe, I think, I'm the one who needs to shut up.

51

"Our fight had nothing to do with drugs," Owen says. "They just found them on him afterward."

"Then what were you and Josh fighting about?" our mother asks, as if the fact that these two boyhood chums fought is the most unbelievable thing that's occurred.

"A girl," Owen says. "We were fighting about a girl."

I wonder if Owen thought this one out ahead of time, or whether it's come to him spontaneously. Whatever the case, it's probably the only thing he could have possibly said that would have made our parents momentarily . . . *happy* might be overstating it. But less angry. They don't want their son to be buying or selling drugs, being bullied or bullying anyone else. But fighting over a girl? Perfectly acceptable. Especially since, I'm guessing, it's not like Owen's ever mentioned a girl to them before.

Owen sees he's gained ground. He pushes further. "If she found out – oh God, she can't find out. I know some girls like it when you fight over them, but she definitely doesn't."

Mom nods her approval.

"What's her name?" Dad asks.

"Do I have to tell you?"

"Yes."

"Natasha. Natasha Lee."

Wow, he's even made her Chinese. Amazing.

"Do you know this girl?" Dad asks me.

"Yes," I say. "She's awesome." Then I turn to Owen and shoot him fake daggers. "But Romeo over here never told me he was into her. Although now that he says it, it's starting to make sense. He has been acting very weird lately."

Mom nods again. "He has."

*Eyes bloodshot,* I want to say. *Eating a lot of Cheetos. Staring into space. Eating more Cheetos. It must be love. What else could it possibly be?*

What was threatening to be an all-out war becomes a war council, with our parents strategizing what the principal can be told, especially about the running away. I hope for Owen's sake that Natasha Lee is in fact a student at the high school, whether he has a crush on her or not. I can't access any memory of her. If the name rings a bell, the bell's in a vacuum.

Now that our father can see a way of saving face, he's almost amiable. Owen's big punishment is that he has to go clean up his room before dinner.

I can't imagine I would have gotten the same reaction if I'd beaten up another girl over a boy.

I follow Owen up to his room. When we're safely inside, door closed, no parents around, I tell him, "That was kinda brilliant."

He looks at me with unconcealed annoyance and

says, "I don't know what you're talking about. Get out of my room."

This is why I prefer to be an only child.

I have a sense that Leslie would let it go. So I should let it go. That's the law I've set down for myself – don't disrupt the life you're living in. Leave it as close to the same as you can.

But I'm pissed. So I diverge a little from the law. I think, perversely, that Rhiannon would want me to. Even though she has no idea who Owen or Leslie are. Or who I am.

"Look," I say, "you lying little pothead bitch. You are going to be nice to me, okay? Not only because I am covering your butt, but because I am the one person in the world right now who is being decent to you. Is that understood?"

Shocked, and maybe a little contrite, Owen mumbles his assent.

"Good," I say, knocking a few things off his shelves. "Now happy cleaning."

Nobody talks at dinner.

I don't think this is unusual.

I wait until everyone is asleep before I go on the computer. I retrieve Justin's email and password from my own email, then log in as him.

There's an email from Rhiannon, sent at 10:11p.m.

J –

i just don't understand. was it something I did?
yesterday was so perfect, and today you are mad at
me again. if it's something I did, please tell me, and
I'll fix it. I want us to be together. I want all our days to
end on a nice note. not like tonight.

with all my heart,

r

I reel back in my seat. I want to hit reply, I want to
reassure her that it will be better – but I can't. *You're not
him anymore*, I have to remind myself. *You're not there.*
And then I think: *What have I done?*

I hear Owen moving around in his room. Hiding
evidence? Or is fear keeping him awake?

I wonder if he'll be able to pull it off tomorrow.

There's no way for me to know.

I want to get back to her. I want to get back to yesterday.

# DAY 5996

All I get is tomorrow.

As I fell asleep, I had a glint of an idea. But I as I wake up, I realize the glint has no light left in it.

Today I'm a boy. Skylar Smith. Soccer player, but not a star soccer player. Clean room, but not compulsively so. Video-game console in his room. Ready to wake up. Parents asleep.

He lives in a town that's about a four hour drive from where Rhiannon lives.

This is nowhere near close enough.

It's an uneventful day, as most are. The only suspense comes from whether I can access things fast enough.

Soccer practice is the hardest part. The coach keeps calling out names, and I have to access like crazy to figure out who everyone is. It's not Skylar's best day at practice, but he doesn't embarrass himself.

I know how to play most sports, but I've also learned my limits. I found this out the hard way when I was eleven. I woke up in the body of some kid who was in the middle of a ski trip. I thought that, hey, skiing had always looked fun. So I figured I'd try. Learn it as I went.

How hard could it be?

The kid had already graduated from the bunny slopes, and I didn't even know there was such a thing as a bunny slope. I thought skiing was like sledding – one hill fits all.

I broke the kid's leg in three places.

The pain was pretty bad. And I honestly wondered if, when I woke up the next morning, I would still feel the pain of the broken leg, even though I was in a new body. But instead of the pain, I felt something just as bad – the fierce, living weight of terrifying guilt. Just as if I'd rammed him with a car, I was consumed by the knowledge that a stranger was lying in a hospital bed because of me.

And if he'd died . . . I wondered if I would have died too. There is no way for me to know. All I know is that, in a way, it doesn't matter. Whether I die or just wake up the next morning as if nothing happened, the fact of the death will destroy me.

So I'm careful. Soccer, baseball, field hockey, football, softball, basketball, swimming, track – all of those are fine. But I've also woken up in the body of an ice hockey player, a gymnast, a horse jumper, and once, recently, a volunteer firefighter.

I've sat all those out.

If there's one thing I'm good at, it's video games. It's a universal presence, like TV or the internet. No matter where I am, I usually have access to these things, and video games especially help me calm my mind.

After soccer practice, Skylar's friends come over to play *World of Warcraft*. We talk about school and talk about girls (except for his friends Chris and David, who talk about boys.) This, I've discovered, is the best way to waste time, because it isn't really wasted – surrounded by friends, talking crap and sometimes talking for real, with snacks around and something on a screen.

I might even be enjoying myself, if I could only unmoor myself from the place I want to be.

# DAY 5997

It's almost eerie how well the next day works out.

I wake up early – six in the morning.

I wake up as a girl.

A girl with a car. And a licence.

In a town only an hour away from Rhiannon's.

I apologize to Amy Tran as I drive away from her house, a half hour after waking up. What I'm doing is, no doubt, a strange form of kidnapping.

I strongly suspect that Amy Tran wouldn't mind. Getting dressed this morning, the options were black, black, or . . . black. Not in a Goth sense – none of the black came in the form of lace gloves – but more in a rock 'n' roll sense. The mix in her car stereo puts Janis Joplin and Brian Eno side by side, and somehow it works.

I can't rely on Amy's memory here – we're going somewhere she's never been. So I did some Google mapping right after my shower, typed in the address of Rhiannon's school and watched it pop up in front of me. That simple. I printed it out, then cleared the history.

I have become very good at clearing histories.

I know I shouldn't be doing this. I know I'm poking a wound, not healing it. I know there's no way to have a future with Rhiannon.

All I'm doing is extending the past by a day.

Normal people don't have to decide what's worth remembering. You are given a hierarchy, recurring characters, the help of repetition, of anticipation, the firm hold of a long history. But I have to decide the importance of each and every memory. I only remember a handful of people, and in order to do that, I have to hold tight, because the only repetition available – the only way I am going to see them again – is if I conjure them in my mind.

I choose what to remember, and I am choosing Rhiannon. Again and again, I am choosing her, I am conjuring her, because to let go for an instant will allow her to disappear.

The same song that we heard in Justin's car comes on – *And if I only could, I'd make a deal with God* . . .

I feel the universe is telling me something. And it doesn't even matter if it's true or not. What matters is that I feel it, and believe it.

The enormity rises within me.

The universe nods along to the songs.

*

I try to hold on to as few mundane, everyday memories as possible. Facts and figures, sure. Books I've read or information I need to know. The rules of soccer, for instance. The plot of *Romeo and Juliet*. The phone number to dial if there's an emergency. I remember those.

But what about the thousands of everyday memories, the thousands of everyday reminders, that every person accumulates? The place you keep your house keys. Your mother's birthday. The name of your first pet. The name of your current pet. Your locker combination. The location of the silverware drawer. The channel number for MTV. Your best friend's last name.

These are the things I have no need for. And, over time, my mind has rewired itself so all this information falls away as soon as the next morning comes.

Which is why it's remarkable – but not surprising – that I remember exactly where Rhiannon's locker is.

I have my cover story ready: If anyone asks, I am checking out the school because my parents might be moving to town.

I don't remember if there are assigned parking spaces, so just in case, I park far from the school. Then I simply walk in. I am just another random girl in the halls – the freshmen will think I'm a senior, and the seniors will think I'm a freshman. I have Amy's school bag with me – black with anime details, filled with books that won't really apply here. I look like I have a destination. And I do.

If the universe wants this to happen, she will be there at her locker.

I tell myself this, and there she is. Right there in front of me.

Sometimes memory tricks you. Sometimes beauty is best when it's distant. But even from here, thirty feet away, I know that the reality of her is going to match my memory.

Twenty feet away.

Even in the crowded hallway, there is something in her that radiates out to me.

Ten.

She is carrying herself through the day, and it's not an easy task.

Five.

I can stand right here and she has no idea who I am. I can stand right here and watch her. I can see that the sadness has returned. And it's not a beautiful sadness – beautiful sadness is a myth. Sadness turns our features to clay, not porcelain. She is dragging.

"Hey," I say, my voice thin, a stranger here.

At first, she doesn't understand that I'm talking to her. Then it registers.

"Hey," she says back.

Most people, I've noticed, are instinctively unkind to strangers. They expect every approach to be an attack, every question to be an interruption. But not Rhiannon. She doesn't have any idea who I am, but she's not going to hold that against me. She is not going to assume the worst.

"Don't worry – you don't know me," I quickly say. "It's just – it's my first day here. I'm checking the school out. And I really like your skirt and your bag. So I thought, you know, I'd say hello. Because, to be honest, I am completely alone right now."

Again, some people would be scared by this. But not Rhiannon. She offers her hand, introduces herself as we shake, and asks me why there isn't someone showing me around.

"I don't know," I say.

"Well, why don't I take you to the office? I'm sure they can figure something out."

I panic. "No!" I blurt out. Then I try to cover for myself, and prolong my time with her. "It's just . . . I'm not here officially. Actually, my parents don't even know I'm doing this. They just told me we're moving here, and I . . . I wanted to see it and decide whether I should be freaking out or not."

Rhiannon nods. "That makes sense. So you're

cutting school in order to check school out?"

"Exactly."

"What year are you?"

"A junior."

"So am I. Let's see if we can pull this off. Do you want to come around with me today?"

"I'd love that."

I know she's just being nice. Irrationally, I also want there to be some kind of recognition. I want her to be able to see behind this body, to see me inside here, to know that it's the same person she spent an afternoon with on the beach.

I follow her. Along the way, she introduces me to a few of her friends, and I am relieved to meet each one, relieved to know that she has more people in her life than Justin. The way she includes me, the way she takes this total stranger and makes her feel a part of this world, makes me care about her even more. It's one thing to be love-worthy when you are interacting with your boyfriend; it's quite another when you act the same way with a girl you don't know. I no longer think she's just being nice. She's being kind. Which is much more a sign of character than mere niceness. Kindness connects to who you are, while niceness connects to how you want to be seen.

Justin makes his first appearance between second

and third period. We pass him in the hall; he barely acknowledges Rhiannon and completely ignores me. He doesn't stop walking, just nods at her. She's hurt – I can tell – but she doesn't say anything about it to me.

By the time we get to math class, fourth period, the day has turned into an exquisite form of torture. I am right there next to her, but I can't do a thing. As the teacher reduces us to theorems, I must remain silent. I write her a note, just as an excuse to touch her shoulder, to pass her some words. But they are inconsequential. They are the words of a guest.

I want to know if I changed her. I want to know if that day changed her, if only for a day.

I want her to see me, even though I know she can't.


He joins us at lunch.

As strange as it is to see Rhiannon again, and to have her measure so well against my memory, it is even stranger to be sitting across from the jerk whose body I inhabited just three days ago. Mirror images do no justice to this sensation. He is more attractive than I thought, but also uglier. His features are attractive, but what he does with them is not. He wears the superior scowl of someone who can barely hide his feelings of inferiority. His eyes are full of scattershot anger, his posture one of defensive bravado.

65

I must have rendered him unrecognizable.

Rhiannon explains to him who I am, and where I come from. He makes it clear that he couldn't care less. He tells her he left his wallet at home, so she goes and buys him food. When she gets back to the table with it, he says thanks, and I'm almost disappointed that he does. Because I'm sure that a single thank you will go a long way in her mind.

I want to know about three days ago, about what he remembers.

"How far is it to the ocean?" I ask Rhiannon.

"It's so funny you should say that," she tells me. "We were just there the other day. It took about an hour or so."

I am looking at him, looking for some recognition. But he just keeps eating.

"Did you have a good time?" I ask him.

She answers. "It was amazing."

Still no response from him.

I try again. "Did you drive?"

He looks at me like I'm asking really stupid questions, which I suppose I am.

"Yes, I drove" is all he'll give me.

"We had such a great time," Rhiannon goes on. And it's making her happy – the memory is making her happy. Which only makes me sadder.

I should not have come here. I should not have tried this. I should just go.

But I can't. I am with her. I try to pretend that this is what matters.

I play along.

I don't want to love her. I don't want to be in love.

People take love's continuity for granted, just as they take their body's continuity for granted. They don't realize that the best thing about love it its regular presence. Once you can establish that, it's an added foundation to your life. But if you cannot have that regular presence, you only have the one foundation to support you, always.

She is sitting right next to me. I want to run my finger along her arm. I want to kiss her neck. I want to whisper the truth in her ear.

But instead I watch as she conjugates verbs. I listen as the air is filled with a foreign language, spoken in haphazard bursts. I try to sketch her in my notebook, but I am not an artist, and all that comes out are the wrong shapes, the wrong lines. I cannot hold on to anything that's her.

The final bell rings. She asks me where I've parked, and I know that this is it, this is the end. She is writing her email address on a piece of paper for me. This is goodbye. For all I know, Amy Tran's parents have called the police. For all I know, there's a manhunt going on, an hour away. It is cruel of me, but I don't care. I want Rhiannon to ask me to go to a movie, to invite me over to her house, to suggest we drive to the beach. But then Justin appears. Impatient. I don't know what they are going to do, but I have a bad feeling. He wouldn't be so insistent if sex weren't involved.

"Walk me to my car?" I ask.

She looks at Justin for permission.

"I'll get my car," he says.

We have a parking lot's length of time left with each other. I know I need something from her, but I'm not sure what.

"Tell me something nobody else knows about you," I say.

She looks at me strangely. "What?"

"It's something I always ask people – tell me something about you that nobody else knows. It doesn't have to be major. Just something."

Now that she gets it, I can tell she likes the challenge of the question, and I like her even more for liking it.

"Okay," she says. "When I was ten, I tried to pierce my own ear with a sewing needle. I got it halfway through, and then I passed out. Nobody was home, so nobody found me. I just woke up, with this needle halfway in my ear, drops of blood all over my shirt. I pulled the needle out, cleaned up, and never tried it again. It wasn't until I was fourteen that I went to the mall with my mom and got my ears pierced for real. She had no idea. How about you?"

There are so many lives to choose from, although I don't remember most of them.

I also don't remember whether Amy Tran has pierced ears or not, so it won't be an ear-piercing memory.

"I stole Judy Blume's *Forever* from my sister when I was eight," I say. "I figured if it was by the author of *Superfudge*, it had to be good. Well, I soon realized why she kept it under her bed. I'm not sure I understood it all, but I thought it was unfair that the boy would name his, um, organ, and the girl wouldn't name hers. So I decided to give mine a name."

Rhiannon is laughing. "What was its name?"

"*Helena*. I introduced everyone to her at dinner that night. It went over really well."

We're at my car. Rhiannon doesn't know it's my car, but it's the farthest car, so it's not like we can keep walking.

"It was great to meet you," she says. "Hopefully I'll see you around next year."

"Yeah," I say, "it was great to meet you too."

I thank her about five different ways. Then Justin drives over and honks.

Our time is up.

Amy Tran's parents haven't called the police. They haven't even gotten home yet. I check the house phone's voicemail, but the school hasn't called.

It's the one lucky thing that's happened all day.

# DAY 5998

Something is wrong the minute I wake up the next morning. Something chemical.

It's barely even morning. This body has slept until noon. Because this body was up late, getting high. And now it wants to be high again. Right away.

I've been in the body of a pothead before. I've woken up still drunk from the night before. But this is worse. Much worse.

There will be no school for me today. There will be no parents waking me up. I am on my own, in a dirty room, sprawled on a dirty mattress with a blanket that looks like it was stolen from a child. I can hear other people yelling in other rooms of the house.

There comes a time when the body takes over the life. There comes a time when the body's urges, the body's needs, dictate the life. You have no idea you are giving the body the key. But you hand it over. And then it's in control. You mess with the wiring and the wiring takes charge.

I have only had glimpses of this before. Now I really feel it. I can feel my mind immediately combating the body. But it's not easy. I cannot sense pleasure. I have to cling to the memory of it. I have to cling to the

71

knowledge that I am only here for one day, and I have to make it through.

I try to go back to sleep, but the body won't let me. The body is awake now, and it knows what it wants.

I know what I have to do, even though I don't really know what's going on. Even though I have not been in this situation before, I have been in situations before where it's been me against the body. I have been ill, seriously ill, and the only thing to do is to power through the day. At first, I thought there was something I could do within a single day that could make everything better. But very soon I learned my own limitations. Bodies cannot be changed in a day, especially not when the real mind isn't in charge.

I don't want to leave the room. If I leave the room, anything and anyone can happen. Desperately, I look around for something to help me through. There is a decrepit bookshelf, and on it is a selection of old paperbacks. These will save me, I decide. I open up an old thriller and focus on the first line. *Darkness had descended on Manassas, Virginia . . .*

The body does not want to read. The body is alive with electric barbed wire. The body is telling me there is only one way to fix this, only one way to end the pain, only one way to feel better. The body will kill me if I don't listen to it. The body is screaming. The body demands its own form of logic.

I read the next sentence.

I lock the door.

I read the third sentence.

The body fights back. My hand shakes. My vision blurs.

I am not sure I have the strength to resist this.

I have to convince myself that Rhiannon is on the other side. I have to convince myself that this isn't a pointless life, even though the body is telling me it is.

The body has obliterated its memories in order to hone its argument. There isn't much for me to access. I must rely on my own memories, the ones that are separate from this.

I must remain separate from this.

I read the next sentence, then the next sentence. I don't even care about the story. I am moving from word to word, fighting the body from word to word.

It's not working. The body makes me feel like it wants to defecate and vomit. First in the usual way. Then I feel I want to defecate through my mouth and vomit through the other end. Everything is being mangled. I want to claw at the walls. I want to scream. I want to punch myself repeatedly.

I have to imagine my mind as something physical,

something that can control the body. I have to picture my mind holding the body down.

I read another sentence.

Then another.


There is pounding on the door. I scream that I'm reading.

They leave me alone.

I don't have what they want in this room.

They have what I want outside this room.

I must not leave this room.

I must not let the body out of this room.

I imagine her walking the hallways. I imagine her sitting next to me. I imagine her eyes meeting mine.

Then I imagine her getting in his car, and I stop.


The body is infecting me. I am getting angry. Angry that I am here. Angry that this is my life. Angry that so many things are impossible.

Angry at myself.

*Don't you want it to stop?* the body asks.

I must push myself as far away from the body as I can.

Even as I'm in it.


I have to go to the bathroom. I really have to go to the bathroom.

Finally, I pee in a soda bottle. It splashes all over.

But it's better than leaving this room.

If I leave the room, I will not be able to stop the body from getting what it wants.

I am ninety pages into the book. I can't remember any of it.

Word by word.

The fight is exhausting the body.

I am winning.

It is a mistake to think of the body as a vessel. It is as active as any mind, as any soul. And the more you give yourself to it, the harder your life will be. I have been in the body of starvers and purgers, gluttons and addicts. They all think their actions make their lives more desirable. But the body always defeats them in the end.

I just need to make sure the defeat doesn't take place on my watch.

I make it to sundown. Two-hundred sixty-five pages gone. I am shivering under the filthy blanket. I don't know if it's the temperature in the room or if it's me.

*Almost there,* I tell myself.

*There is only one way out of this,* the body tells me.

At this point, I don't know if it means drugs or death.
The body might not even care, at this point.

Finally, the body wants to sleep.
I let it.

# DAY 5999

My mind is thoroughly wrung out, but I can tell Nathan Daldry has gotten a good night's sleep.

Nathan is a good guy. Everything in his room is in order. Even though it's only Saturday morning, he's already done his homework for the weekend. He's set his alarm for eight o'clock, not wanting the day to go to waste. He was probably in bed by ten.

I go on his computer and check my email, making sure to write myself some notes about the last few days, so I can remember them. Then I log in to Justin's email and find out there's a party tonight at Steve Mason's house. Steve's address is only a Google search away. When I map out the distance between Nathan's house and Steve's, I find it's only a ninety-minute drive.

It looks like Nathan might be going to a party tonight.

First, I must convince his parents.

His mother interrupts me when I'm back on my own email, rereading what I wrote about the day with Rhiannon. I very quickly shut the window, and oblige when she tells me that today is not a computer day, and that I am to come down for breakfast.

I very quickly discover that Nathan's parents are

a very nice couple who make it very clear that their niceness shouldn't be challenged or pressed.

"Can I borrow the car?" I ask. "The school musical is tonight, and I would like to go see it."

"Have you done your homework?"

I nod.

"Your chores?"

"I will."

"And you'll be back by midnight?"

I nod. I decide not to mention to them that if I'm not back by midnight, I'll be ripped from my current body. I don't think they'd find that reassuring.

It's clear to me that they won't need the car tonight. They are the type of parents who don't believe in having a social life. They have television instead.

I spend most of the day doing chores. After I'm done with them and have had a family dinner, I'm good to go.

The party's supposed to start at seven, so I know I have to wait until nine to show up, so there will be enough people there to hide my presence. If I get there and it ends up being open to only a dozen kids, I'll have to turn back around. But that doesn't strike me as Justin's kind of party.

Nathan's kind of party, I'm guessing, involves board

games and Dr Pepper. As I drive back to Rhiannon's town, I access some of his memories. I am a firm believer that every person, young or old, has at least one good story to tell. Nathan's, however, is pretty hard to find. The only tremor of emotion I can find in his life was when he was nine and his dog April died. Ever since then, nothing seems to have disturbed him too much. Most of his memories involve homework. He has friends, but they don't do very much outside of school. When Little League was over, he gave up sports. He has never, from what I can tell, sipped anything stronger than a beer, and even that was during a Father's Day barbecue, at his uncle's prodding.

Normally, I would take these as parameters. Normally, I would stay within the Nathan's safe zone.

But not today. Not with a chance of seeing Rhiannon again.

I remember yesterday, and how the trail that got me through the darkness seemed to be attached in some way to her. It's as if when you love someone, they become your reason. And maybe I've gotten it backward, maybe it's just because I need a reason that I find myself falling in love with her. But I don't think that's it. I think I would have continued along, oblivious, if I hadn't happened to meet her.

Now I'm letting my life hijack these other lives for a

day. I am not staying within their parameters. Even if that's dangerous.

I'm at Steve Mason's house by eight, but Justin's car is nowhere in sight. In fact, there aren't that many cars out in front. So I wait and watch. After a while, people start arriving. Even though I've just spent a day and a half at their school, I don't recognize any of them. They were all peripheral.

Finally, just after nine-thirty, Justin's car pulls up. Rhiannon is with him, as I'd hoped she'd be. As they head in, he walks a little bit in front, her a little behind. I get out of my car and follow them inside.

I'm worried there will be someone at the door, but the party's already spiraled into its own form of chaos. The early guests are well past the point of drunkenness, and everyone else is quickly catching up. I know I look out of place – Nathan's wardrobe is more suited to a debate tournament than a Saturday night house party. But nobody really cares; they're too caught up in each other or themselves to notice a random geek in their midst.

The lights are dim, the music is loud, and Rhiannon is hard to find. But just the fact that I am in the same place as her has me nervously exhilarated.

Justin is in the kitchen, talking with some guys. He

looks at ease, in his element. He finishes one beer and immediately goes for another.

I push past him, push through the living room and find myself in the den. The instant I step in the room, I know she's here. Even though the music's blaring from a laptop connected to some speakers, she's over by the CD collection, thumbing through cases. Two girls are talking nearby, and I have a sense that at one point she was a part of their conversation, then decided to drop out.

I walk over and see that one of the CDs she's looking at has a song we listened to on our car ride.

"I really like them," I say, gesturing to the CD. "Do you?"

She startles, as if this is a quiet room and I am a sudden noise. *I notice you,* I want to say. *Even when no one else does, I do. I will.*

"Yeah," she says. "I like them too."

I start to sing the song, the one from the car. Then I say, "I like that one in particular."

"Do I know you?" she asks.

"I'm Nathan," I say, which isn't a no or a yes.

"I'm Rhiannon," she says.

"That's a beautiful name."

"Thanks. I used to hate it, but I don't so much anymore."

"Why?"

"It's just a pain to spell." She looks at me closely. "Do you go to Octavian?"

"No. I'm just here for the weekend. Visiting my cousin."

"Who's your cousin?"

"Steve."

This is a dangerous lie, since I have no idea which of the guys is Steve, and I have no way of accessing the information.

"Oh, that explains it."

She is starting to drift away from me, just as I imagine she drifted away from the girls talking next to us.

"I hate my cousin," I say.

This gets her attention.

"I hate the way he treats girls. I hate the way he thinks he can buy all his friends by throwing parties like this. I hate the way that he only talks to you when he needs something. I hate the way he doesn't seem capable of love."

I realize I'm now talking about Justin, not Steve.

"Then why are you here?" Rhiannon asks.

"Because I want to see it fall apart. Because when this party gets busted – and if it stays this loud, it *will* be busted – I want to be a witness. From a safe distance away, of course."

"And you're saying he's incapable of loving Stephanie?

They've been going out for over a year."

With a silent apology to Stephanie and Steve, I say, "That doesn't mean anything, does it? I mean, being with someone for over a year can mean that you love them . . . but it can also mean you're trapped."

At first I think I've gone too far. I can feel Rhiannon taking in my words, but I don't know what she's doing with them. The sound of words as they're said is always different from the sound they make when they're heard, because the speaker hears some of the sound from the inside.

Finally she says, "Speaking from experience?"

It's laughable to think that Nathan – who, from what I can tell, hasn't gone on a date since eighth grade – would be speaking from experience. But she doesn't know him, which means I can be more like me. Not that I'm speaking from experience either. Just the experience of observing.

"There are many things that can keep you in a relationship," I say. "Fear of being alone. Fear of disrupting the arrangement of your life. A decision to settle for something that's okay, because you don't know if you can get any better. Or maybe there's the irrational belief that it will get better, even if you know he won't change."

"'He'?"

"Yeah."

"I see."

At first I don't understand what she sees – clearly, I was talking about her. Then I get where the pronoun has led her.

"That cool?" I ask, figuring it will make Nathan even less threatening if he's gay.

"Completely."

"How about you?" I ask. "Seeing anyone?"

"Yeah," she says. Then, deadpan, "For over a year."

"And why are you still together? Fear of being alone? A decision to settle? An irrational belief that he'll change?"

"Yes. Yes. And yes."

"So . . ."

"But he can also be incredibly sweet. And I know that, deep down, I mean the world to him."

"Deep down? That sounds like settling to me. You shouldn't have to venture deep down in order to get to love."

"Let's switch the topic, okay? This isn't a good party topic. I liked it more when you were singing to me."

I'm about to make reference to another song we heard on our car ride – hoping that maybe I'll register in some way – when Justin's voice comes from over my shoulder, asking, "So who's this?" If he was relaxed when I saw him in the kitchen, now he's annoyed.

"Don't worry, Justin," Rhiannon says. "He's gay."

"Yeah, I can tell from the way he's dressed. What are you doing here?"

"Nathan, this is Justin, my boyfriend. Justin, this is Nathan."

I say hi. He doesn't respond.

"You seen Stephanie?" he asks Rhiannon. "Steve's looking for her. I think they're at it again."

"Maybe she went to the basement."

"Nah. They're dancing in the basement."

Rhiannon likes this news, I can tell.

"Want to go down there and dance?" she asks Justin.

"Hell no! I didn't come here to dance. I came here to *drink*."

"Charming," Rhiannon says, more (I think) for my benefit than his. "Do you mind if I go dance with Nathan?"

"You sure he's gay?"

"I'll sing you show tunes if you want me to prove it," I volunteer.

Justin slaps me on the back. "No, dude, don't do that, okay? Go dance."

So that's how it comes to pass that Rhiannon is leading me to Steve Mason's basement. As we hit the stairs, we can feel the bass under our feet. It's a different soundtrack here – a tide of pulse and beat. Only a few red lights are on, so all we can see are the outlines of bodies as they meld together.

"Hey, Steve!" Rhiannon calls out. "I like your cousin!"

A guy who must be Steve looks at her and nods. Whether he can't hear what she's said or whether he's trashed, I can't tell.

"Have you seen Stephanie?" he yells.

"No!" Rhiannon yells back.

Then we're in with the dancers. The sad truth is that I have about as much experience on a dance floor as Nathan does. I try to lose myself in the music, but that doesn't work. Instead, I need to lose myself in Rhiannon. I have to give myself over entirely to her – I must be her shadow, her compliment, the other half of this conversation of bodies. As she moves, I move with her. I touch her back, her waist. She comes in closer.

By losing myself to her, I gain her. The conversation is working. We have found our rhythm and we are riding it. I find myself singing along, singing to her, and she loves it. She transforms once again into someone carefree, and I transform into someone whose only care is her.

"You're not bad!" she shouts over the music.

"You're amazing!" I shout back.

I know that Justin is not coming down here. She is safe with Steve Mason's gay cousin, and I am safe knowing that nobody else will interfere with this moment. The songs collide into one long song – as if one singer is taking over when the previous one stops, all of them taking turns to give us this. The sound waves push us into each other, wrap around us like colors. We are paying attention to each other and we are paying attention to the enormity. The room has no ceiling; the room has no walls. There is only the open field of our excitement, and we run across it in small movements, sometimes without our feet leaving the ground. We go for what feels like hours and also feels like no time at all. We go until the music stops, until someone turns on the lights and says the party is ending, that the neighbors have complained and the police are probably coming.

Rhiannon looks as disappointed as I feel.

"I have to find Justin," she says. "Are you going to be okay?"

*No*, I want to tell her. *I won't be okay until you can come with me to wherever it is that I'm going next.*

I ask her for her email address, and when she raises an eyebrow, I tell her again not to worry, that I'm still gay.

"That's too bad," she says. I want her to say more, but then she's giving me her email address, and in response

I'm giving her a fake email address that I'll have to set up as soon as I get home.

People are starting to run from the house. Sirens can be heard in the distance, probably waking up as many people as the party has. Rhiannon leaves me to find Justin, promising me that she'll be the one to drive. I don't see them as I run to my car. I know it's late, but I don't know how late it is until I turn on the car and look at the clock.

11:15.

There's no way I'll get there in time.

Seventy miles an hour.

Eighty miles an hour.

Eighty-five.

I drive as fast as I can, but it's not fast enough.

At 11:50, I pull over to the side of the road. If I close my eyes, I should be able to fall asleep before midnight. That is the blessing of what I have to go through – I am able to fall asleep in minutes.

Poor Nathan Daldry. He is going to wake up on the side of an interstate, an hour away from his home. I can only imagine how terrified he will be.

I am a monster for doing this to him.

But I have my reason.

# DAY 6000

It's time for Roger Wilson to go to church.

I quickly dress myself in his Sunday best, which either he or his mother conveniently left out the night before. Then I go downstairs and have breakfast with his mother and his three sisters. There's no father in sight. It doesn't take much accessing to know he left just after the youngest daughter was born, and it's been a struggle for their mom ever since.

There's only one computer in the house, and I have to wait until Roger's mother is getting the girls ready to go before I can quickly boot it up and create the email address I gave Rhiannon last night. I can only hope that she hasn't tried to get in touch with me already.

Roger's name is being called – it's church time. I sign off, clear the history, and join my sisters in the car. It takes me a few minutes to get their names straight – Pam is eleven, Lacey is ten and Jenny is eight. Only Jenny seems excited about going to church.

When we get there, the girls head off to Sunday school while I join Roger's mother in the main congregation. I prepare myself for a Baptist service, and try to remember what makes it different from the other church services I've been to.

I have been to many religious services over the years. Each one I go to only reinforces my general impression that religions have much, much more in common than they like to admit. The beliefs are almost always the same; it's just that the histories are different. Everybody wants to believe in a higher power. Everybody wants to belong to something bigger than themselves, and everybody wants company in doing that. They want there to be a force of good on earth, and they want an incentive to be a part of that force. They want to be able to prove their belief and their belonging, through rituals and devotion. They want to touch the enormity.

It's only in the finer points that it gets complicated and contentious, the inability to realize that no matter what religion or gender or race or geographic background, we all have about 98 percent in common with each other. Yes, the differences between male and female are biological, but if you look at the biology as a matter of percentage, there aren't a whole lot of things that are different. Race is different purely as a social construction, not as an inherent difference. And religion – whether you believe in God or Yahweh or something else, odds are that at heart you want the same things. For whatever reason, we like to focus on the 2 percent that's different, and most of the conflict in the world comes from that.

The only way I can navigate through my life is because of the 98 percent every life has in common.

I think of this as I go through the rituals of a Sunday morning at church. I keep looking at Roger's mother, who is so tired, so taxed. I feel as much belief in her as I do in God – I find faith in human perseverance, even as the universe throws challenge after challenge our way. This might be one of the things I saw in Rhiannon, too – her desire to persevere.

After church, we head to Roger's grandmother's house for Sunday dinner. There's no computer, and even if it weren't a four-hour drive away, there wouldn't be any way for me to get to Rhiannon. So I take it as a day of rest. I play games with my sisters and make a ring of hands with the rest of my family when it's time to say grace.

The only discord comes when we're driving home and a fight breaks out in the backseat. As sisters, they probably have closer to 99 percent in common, but they're not about to recognize that. They'd rather fight over what kind of pet they're going to get . . . even though I'm not sensing any indication from their mother that a pet is in their near future. It's an argument for its own sake.

When we get home, I bide my time before asking if I can use the computer. It's in a very public place, and I will need everyone to be in another room in order to check my email. While the three girls run around, I retire to Roger's room and do his weekend homework the best that I can. I am banking on the fact that Roger has a later bedtime than his sisters, and in this I am correct. After Sunday supper, the girls get an hour of television in the same room as the computer. Then Roger's mother tells them it's time to get ready for bed. There's much protest, but it falls on deaf ears. This is its own kind of ritual, and mom always wins.

While Roger's mother is getting them into their pajamas and getting out their clothes for tomorrow, I have a few minutes on my own. I quickly check the email I set up in the morning, and there's no message from Rhiannon yet. I decide it can't hurt to be proactive here, so I type in her address and start an email before I can stop myself.

Hi Rhiannon,

I just wanted to say that it was lovely meeting you and dancing with you last night. I'm sorry the police came and separated us. Even though you're not my type, gender-wise, you're certainly my type, person-wise. Please keep in touch.

N.

That seems safe enough to me. Clever, but not self-congratulatorily so. Sincere, but not overbearing. It's only a few lines, but I reread it at least a dozen times before I hit send. I let go of the words and wonder what words will come back. If any.

Bedtime seems to be taking a while – it sounds like there's some argument about which chapter their read-aloud left off on – so I load up my personal email.

Such an ordinary gesture. One click, and the instant appearance of the inbox, in all its familiar rows.

But this time, it's like walking into a room and finding a bomb right in the middle of it.

There, under a bookstore newsletter, is an incoming message from none other than Nathan Daldry.

The subject line is WARNING.

I read:

I don't know who you are or what you are or what
you did to me yesterday, but I want you to know you
won't get away with it. I will not let you possess me
or destroy my life. I will not remain quiet. I know what
happened and I know you must be in some way
responsible. Leave me alone. I am not your host.

"Are you okay?"

I turn and find Roger's mother in the doorway.

"I'm fine," I say, positioning myself in front of the screen.

"All right, then. You have ten minutes more, then I want you to help me unload the dishwater and head to bed. We have a long week ahead of us."

"Okay, Mom. I'll be there in ten minutes."

I turn back to the email. I don't know how to respond, or if I should respond. I have a vague recollection of Nathan's mother interrupting me while I was on the computer – I must have closed the window without clearing the history. So when Nathan loaded up his email, it must have been my address that popped up. But he doesn't know my password, so the account itself should be safe. Just in case, though, I know I need to change my password and move all my old emails, quick.

*I will not remain quiet.*

I wonder what this means.

I can't forward all my old emails in the ten minutes that I have, but I start to make a dent in them.

"Roger!"

Roger's mother calls me and I know I have to go. But clearing the history and turning off the computer can't stop my thoughts. I think about Nathan waking up on the side of the road. I try to imagine what he must have felt. But the truth is, I don't know. Did he feel like it was something he had gotten himself into? Or did he immediately know that something was wrong, that someone else had been in control? Was he sure of this when he went to his computer and saw my email address?

Who does he think I am?

*What* does he think I am?

I head into the kitchen and Roger's mother gives me another look of concern. She and Roger are close, I can tell. She knows how to read her son. Over the years, they've been there for each other. He's helped raise his sisters. And she's raised him.

If I really were Roger, I could tell her everything. If I really were Roger, no matter how hard it was to understand, she would be on my side. Fiercely. Unconditionally.

But I am not really her son, or anyone's son. I can't disclose what's bothering Roger today, because it doesn't have much bearing on who he'll be tomorrow. So I brush off his mother's concern, tell her it's no big deal, then help her take the dishes out of the dishwasher. We work in quiet camaraderie until the task is done and sleep calls.

For a while, though, I can't go to sleep. I lie in bed, stare at the ceiling. This is the irony: Even though I wake

95

up in a different body every morning, I've always felt in some way that I am in control.

But now I don't feel in control at all.

Now there are other people involved.

# DAY 6001

The next morning, I am even farther from Rhiannon.

I'm four hours away, and in the body of Margaret Weiss. Luckily, Margaret has a laptop that I can check before we go to school.

There's an email waiting from Rhiannon.

Nathan!

I'm so glad you emailed, because I lost the slip of paper that I wrote your email on. It was wonderful talking and dancing with you, too. How dare the police break us up! You're my type, person-wise, too. Even if you don't believe in relationships that last longer than a year. (I'm not saying you're wrong, btw. Jury's still out.) I never thought I'd say this, but I hope Steve has another party soon. If only so you can bear witness to its evil.

Love,
Rhiannon

I can imagine her smiling when she wrote this, and this makes me smile too.

Then I open my other account, and there's another email from Nathan.

I have given the police this email address. Don't think
you can get away with this.

The police?
Quickly, I type Nathan's name into a search engine. A news item comes up, dated this morning.

## THE DEVIL MADE HIM DO IT
### *Local boy, pulled over by police, claims demonic possession*

When police officers found Nathan Daldry, 16, of 22 Arden Lane, sleeping in his vehicle along the side of Route 23 early Sunday morning, they had no idea the story he would tell. Most teenagers would blame their condition on alcohol use, but not Daldry: He claimed no knowledge of how he had gotten where he was. The answer, he said, was that he must have been possessed by a demon.

"It was like I was sleepwalking," Daldry tells the *Crier*. "The whole day, this thing was in charge of my body. It made me lie to my parents and drive to a party in a town I've never been. I don't really remember the details. I only know it wasn't me."

To make matters more mysterious, Daldry says that when he returned home, someone else's email was on his computer.

"I wasn't myself," he says.

Officer Lance Houston of the State Police says that because there was no sign of alcohol use and because the car wasn't reported stolen, Daldry was not being charged with any offense.

"Look, I'm sure he has reasons for saying what he's saying. All I can tell you is that he didn't do anything illegal."

But that's not enough for Daldry.

"If anyone else has experienced this, I want them to come forward," he says. "I can't be the only one."


It's a local paper's website, nothing to worry too much about. And the police don't seem to feel it's a particularly pressing case. But still, I'm worried. In all of my years, I've never had someone do this to me before.

It's not that I can't imagine how it happened: Nathan is woken up on the side of the road by a police officer tapping on his window. Maybe there are even flashing lights bathing the darkness in red and blue. Within seconds, Nathan realizes what kind of trouble he's in –

it's well past midnight and his parents are going to kill him. His clothes smell like cigarettes and alcohol, and he has no way of remembering whether or not he was drunk or high. He is a blank – a sleepwalker waking up. Only . . . he has a sense of me. Some lone memory of not being himself. When the officer asks him what's going on, he says he doesn't know. When the officer asks him where he's been, he says he doesn't know. The officer gets him out of the car, makes him take a Breathalizer test. Nathan proves to be stone-cold sober. But the officer still wants answers, so Nathan tells him the truth – that his body was taken over. Only, he can't imagine anyone who takes over bodies except for the devil. This is going to be his story. He is a good kid – he knows that everybody will back him up on that. They're going to believe him.

The officer just wants him to get home safely. Maybe he even escorts Nathan home, calling ahead to his parents. They're awake when Nathan gets there. They're angry and concerned. He repeats his story to them. They don't know what to believe. Meanwhile, some reporter hears the officer talking about it on the shortwave, or maybe it gets around the station. The teenager who snuck off to a party and then tried to blame it on the devil. The reporter calls the Daldry home on Sunday, and Nathan decides to talk. Because that will make it more real, won't it?

I feel both guilty and defensive. Guilty because I did this to Nathan, whatever my intentions. Defensive because I certainly didn't force him to react in this way, which will only make it worse for him, if not me.

In the one-in-a-million chance that Nathan can convince someone to trace my emails, I realize I can't check this account from people's homes anymore. Because if he can do that, he'll be able to chart most of the houses I've been in over the past two or three years . . . which would lead to a lot of confusing conversations.

Part of me wants to write back to him, to explain. But I'm not sure any explanation will be enough. Especially because I don't have most of the answers. I gave up on figuring out why a long time ago. I am guessing Nathan won't give up as easily.

Margaret Weiss's boyfriend, Sam, likes to kiss her. A lot. Public, private – it doesn't matter. If he gets a chance to make a move, he does.

I am not in the mood.

Margaret quickly comes down with a cold. The kissing stops, and the doting begins. Sam is rather smitten, and he surrounds Margaret with the sweet quicksand of his love. From recent memories, I can tell that Margaret is usually just as willing to do the same. Everything comes second to being with Sam. It's a miracle that she still has friends.

There's a quiz in science. Judging from my accessing, it appears that I know more about the subject than Margaret does. It's her lucky day.

I am dying to get on one of the school computers, but I have to get rid of Sam first. Even though I've separated them at the lips, I can't seem to get Sam and Margaret separated at the hips. At lunch, he puts one of his hands in her back pocket while he eats, and then pouts when Margaret doesn't do the same thing. They then have study hall together, and he spends all of it stroking her and talking to her about the movie they saw last night.

Eighth period is the only class they don't have together, so I decide to run with it. As soon as Sam drops her off at the classroom door, I have her go to the teacher, say she's going to the nurse, and head straight to the library.

First, I finish forwarding all my emails from my old account. All that remains are the two emails from Nathan. I can't bring myself to delete them, just as I can't bring myself to delete the account. For some reason, I want him to be able to contact me. I feel that much responsibility.

I load up the new email account, with the intention of writing Rhiannon back. Much to my surprise, there's already another email from her. Giddy, I open it.

Nathan,

Apparently, Steve doesn't have a cousin Nathan, and
none of his cousins were at his party. Care to explain?

Rhiannon

I don't deliberate. I don't weigh my options. I just
type and hit send.

Rhiannon,

I can indeed explain. Can we meet up? It's the kind of
explanation that needs to be done in person.

Love,
Nathan

It's not that I'm planning to tell the truth. I just want
to give myself time to thing of the best lie.

The last bell rings, and I know Sam will be looking
for Margaret soon. When I find him at his locker, he
acts as if we haven't seen each other in weeks. When I
kiss him, I pretend I am practising for Rhiannon. When
I kiss him, it feels almost disloyal to Rhiannon. When I
kiss him, my mind is hours away, with her.

# DAY 6002

The universe, it seems, is on my side the next morning, because when I wake up in the body of Megan Powell, I also wake up a mere hour away from Rhiannon.

Then, when I check my email, there's a message from her.

Nathan,

This better be a good explanation. I'll meet you in the coffee shop at The Clover Bookstore at 5.

Rhiannon

To which I reply:

Rhiannon,

I'll be there. Although not in a way you might expect. Bear with me and hear me out.

A

Megan Powell is going to have to leave cheerleading

104

practice a little early today. I go through her closet and pick an outfit that most looks like something Rhiannon would wear; I've found that people tend to trust other people who dress like them. And whatever I do, I am going to need all the trust I can get.

The whole day, I think about what I'm going to say to her, and what she's going to say. It feels entirely dangerous to tell her the truth. I have never told anyone the truth. I have never come close.

But none of the lies fit well. And the more I stumble through possible lies, I realize I am heading in the direction of telling her everything. I am learning that a life isn't real unless someone else knows its reality. And I want my life to be real.

If I've gotten used to my life, could somebody else?

If she believes in me, if she feels the enormity like I do, she will believe in this.

And if she doesn't believe in me, if she doesn't feel the enormity, then I will simply seem like one more crazy person let loose on the world.

There's not much to lose in that.

But, of course, it will feel like losing everything.

I manufacture a doctor's appointment for Megan, and at four o'clock, I'm on the road to Rhiannon's town.

There's some traffic, and I get a little lost, so I'm ten minutes late to the bookstore. I look in the café window and see her sitting there, flipping through a magazine, looking up at the door every now and then. I want to keep her like this, hold her in this moment. I know everything is about to change, and I fear that one day I will long for this minute before anything is said, that I will want to travel back in time and undo what's coming next.

Megan is not, of course, who Rhiannon's looking for. So she's a little startled when I come over to her table and sit down.

"I'm sorry – that seat's taken," she says.

"It's okay," I tell her. "Nathan sent me."

"He sent you? Where is he?" Rhiannon is looking around the room, as if he's hiding somewhere behind a bookshelf.

I look around too. There are other people near us, but none of them seem to be within earshot. I know I should ask Rhiannon to take a walk with me, that there shouldn't be any people around when I tell her. But I don't know why she'd go with me, and it would probably scare her if I asked. I will have to tell her here.

"Rhiannon," I say. I look in her eyes, and I feel it again. That connection. That feeling of so much beyond us. That recognition.

106

I don't know if she feels it too, not for sure, but she stays where she is. She returns my glance. She holds the connection.

"Yes?" she whispers.

"I need to tell you something. It's going to sound very, very strange. What I need is for you to listen to the whole story. You will probably want to leave. You might want to laugh. But I need you to take this seriously. I know it will sound unbelievable, but it's the truth. Do you understand?"

There is fear in her eyes now. I want to reach out my hand and hold hers, but I know I can't. Not yet.

I keep my voice calm. True.

"Every morning, I wake up in a different body. It's been happening since I was born. This morning, I woke up as Megan Powell, who you see right in front of you. Three days ago, last Saturday, it was Nathan Daldry. Two days before that, it was Amy Tran, who visited your school and spent the day with you. And last Monday, it was Justin, your boyfriend. You thought you went to the ocean with him, but it was really me. That was the first time we ever met, and I haven't been able to forget you since."

I pause.

"You're kidding me, right?" Rhiannon says. "You have to be kidding."

I press on. "When we were on the beach, you told me about the mother-daughter fashion show that you and your mother were in, and how it was probably the last time you ever saw her in makeup. When Amy asked you to tell her about something you'd never told anyone else, you told her about trying to pierce your own ear when you were ten, and she told you about reading Judy Blume's *Forever*. Nathan came over to you as you were sorting through CDs, and he sang a song that you and Justin sang during the car ride to the ocean. He told you he was Steve's cousin, but he was really there to see you. He talked to you about being in a relationship for over a year, and you told him that deep down Justin cares a lot about you, and he said that deep down isn't good enough. What I'm saying is that . . . all of these people were me. Just for a day. And now I'm Megan Powell, and I want to tell you the truth before I switch again. Because I think you're remarkable. Because I don't want to keep meeting you as different people. I want to meet you as myself."

I look at the disbelief on her face, searching for one small possibility of belief. I can't find it.

"Did Justin put you up to this?" she says, disgust in her voice. "Do you really think this is funny?"

"No, it's not funny," I say. "It's true. I don't expect you to understand right away. I know how crazy it sounds. But it's true. I swear, it's true."

"I don't understand why you're doing this. I don't even know you!"

"Listen to me. Please. You know it wasn't Justin with you that day. In your heart, you know. He didn't act like Justin. He didn't do things Justin does. That's because it was me. I didn't mean to do it. I didn't mean to fall in love with you. But it happened. And I can't erase it. I can't ignore it. I have lived my whole life like this, and you're the thing that has made me wish it could stop."

The fear is still there in her face, in her body. "But why me? That makes no sense."

"Because you're amazing. Because you're kind to a random girl who just shows up at your school. Because you also want to be on the other side of the window, living life instead of just thinking about it. Because you're beautiful. Because when I was dancing with you in Steve's basement on Saturday night, it felt like fireworks. And when I was lying on the beach next to you, it felt like perfect calm. I know you think that Justin loves you deep down, but I love you through and through."

"Enough!" Rhiannon's voice breaks a little as she raises it. "It's just – enough, okay? I think I understand what you're saying to me, even though it makes *no sense whatsoever.*"

"You know it wasn't him that day, don't you?"

"*I don't know anything!*" This is loud enough that a few people look our way. Rhiannon notices, and lowers her voice again. "I don't know. I really don't know."

She's near tears. I reach out and take her hand. She doesn't like it, but she doesn't pull away.

"I know it's a lot," I tell her. "Believe me, I know."

"It's not possible," she whispers.

"It is. I'm the proof."

When I pictured this conversation in my head, I could imagine it going in two ways: revelation or revulsion. But now we're stuck somewhere in between. She doesn't think I'm telling the truth – not to the point that she can believe it. And at the same time, she hasn't stormed out, she hasn't maintained that it's just a sick joke someone is playing on her.

I realize: I am not going to convince her. Not like this. Not here.

"Look," I say, "what if we met here again tomorrow at the same time? I won't be in the same body, but I'll be the same person. Would that make it easier to understand?"

She's skeptical. "But couldn't you just tell someone else to come here?"

"Yes, but why would I? This isn't a prank. This isn't a joke. It's my life."

"You're insane."

"You're just saying that. You know I'm not. You can sense that much."

Now it's her turn to look me in the eye. Judge me. See what connection she can find.

"What's your name?" she asks.

"Today I'm Megan Powell."

"No. I mean your real name."

My breath catches. Nobody has ever asked me this before. And I've certainly never offered it.

"A," I say.

"Just A?"

"Just A. I came up with it when I was a little kid. It was a way of keeping myself whole, even as I went from body to body, life to life. I needed something pure. So I went with the letter A."

"What do you think about my name?"

"I told you the other night. I think it's beautiful, even if you once found it hard to spell."

She stands up from her chair. I stand up too.

She holds there. I can tell there are lots of thoughts she's considering, but I have no idea what they are. Falling in love with someone doesn't mean you know any better how they feel. It only means you know how you feel.

"Rhiannon," I say.

She holds up her hand for me to stop.

"No more," she tells me. "Not now. Tomorrow. I'll give you tomorrow. Because that's one way to know, isn't it? If what you say is happening is really happening – I mean, I need more than a day."

"Thank you," I tell her.

"Don't thank me until I show up," she says. "This is all really confusing."

"I know."

She puts on her jacket and starts heading for the door. Then she turns around to me one last time.

"The thing is," she says, "I didn't really feel it was him that day. Not completely. And ever since then, it's like he wasn't there. He has no memory of it. There are a million possible explanations for that, but there it is."

"There it is," I agree.

She shakes her head.

"Tomorrow," I say.

"Tomorrow," she says, a little less than a promise, and a little more than a chance.

# DAY 6003

I am not alone when I wake up the next morning.

I am sharing the room with two other boys – my brothers Paul and Tom. Paul is a year older than me. Tom is my twin. My name is James.

James is big – a football player. Tom is about the same size. Paul is even bigger.

The room is clean, but even before I know what town I'm in, I know we're not in the nice part of it. This is a big family in a small house. There is not going to be a computer here. James is not going to have a car.

It's Paul's job – self-appointed or otherwise – to get us up and out. Our father's not home from the night shift yet, and our mother's already on the way to her job. Our two sisters are about done with the bathroom. We're next.

I access and find that I'm in the town next to Nathan's, over an hour from Rhiannon's.

This is going to be a hard day.

The bus ride to school takes forty-five minutes. When we get there, we head to the cafeteria for free breakfast. I am amazed at James's appetite – I pile on pancake after pancake, and he's still hungry. Tom matches him bite for bite.

Luckily, I have study hall first period. Unluckily, there's still homework that James needs to do. I push through that as quick as I can, and have about ten minutes of computer time left at the end.

There's a message from Rhiannon, written at one in the morning.

A,

I want to believe you, but I don't know how.

Rhiannon

I write back:

Rhiannon,

You don't need to know how. You just make up your mind and it happens. I am in Laurel right now, over an hour away. I am in the body of a football player named James. I know how strange that sounds. But, like everything I've told you, it's the truth.

Love, A

There's just enough time for me to check my other email address. There's another email from Nathan.

> You can't avoid my questions forever. I want to know who you are. I want to know why you do what you do.

> Tell me.

Again, I leave him unanswered. I have no idea whether I owe him an explanation or not. I probably owe him something. But I'm not sure it's an explanation.

I make it through to lunch. I want to go immediately to the library to check the computers again. But James is hungry, and Tom is with him, and I am afraid that if he doesn't get his lunch now, there won't be anything for him to eat until dinnertime. I checked, and there are only about three dollars in his wallet, including change.

So I get the free lunch and eat it quickly. Then I excuse myself to the library, which inspires no shortage of taunts from Tom, who claims that, "libraries are for girls." A true brother, I shoot back with, "Well, that explains why you never find any." A wrestling match ensues. All of this takes away time from what I need to do.

When I get to the library, all the computers are taken. I have to loom large over a freshman for about two minutes before he freaks out enough to give me his space. Quickly, I check out public transportation and find out I'll need to take three buses in order to make it to Rhiannon's town. I'm ready to do it, but when I check my email, there's another message from Rhiannon, dated just two minutes ago.

A,

Do you have a car? If not, I can come to you. There's a Starbucks in Laurel. I'm told that nothing bad ever happens in a Starbucks. Let me know if you want to meet there.

Rhiannon

I type:

Rhiannon,

I would appreciate it if you could come here. Thank you.

A

Two minutes later, a new email from her:

A,

I'll be there at 5. Can't wait to see what you look like today.

(Still not believing this.)
Rhiannon

My nerves are jangling with possibility. She's had time to think about it, and that hasn't turned her against me. It's more than I could ask for. I am careful not to be too grateful, lest it be taken away.

The rest of the school day is unexceptional . . . except for a moment in seventh period. Mrs French, the bio teacher, is hectoring a kid who hasn't done his homework. It's a lab assignment and he's come up blank.

"I don't know what got into me," the slacker says. "I must have been possessed by the devil!"

The rest of the class laughs, and even Mrs French shakes her head.

"Yeah, I was possessed by the devil too," another guys says. "After I drank seven beers!"

"Okay, class," Mrs French intones. "Enough of that."

It's the way they say it – I know Nathan's story must be spreading.

"Hey," I say to Tom as we head to football practice, "did you hear about that kid in Monroeville who says he was possessed by the devil?"

"Dude," he replies, "we were just talking about that yesterday. It was all over the news."

"Yeah, I mean, did you hear anything more about it today?"

"What more is there to say? Kid got caught in a crazy lie, and now the religious crazies want to make him a poster child. I almost feel sorry for him."

This, I think, is not good.

Our coach has to go to his wife's Lamaze class, which he bitches about to us in detail, but it forces him to end practice early. I tell Tom that I'm going to make a Starbucks run, and he looks at me like I have been totally, irredeemably girlified. I was counting on his disgust and am relieved to get it.

She's not there when I arrive, so I get a small black coffee – pretty much the only thing I can afford – and sit and wait for her. It's crowded, and I have to look my most brutish in order to keep the other chair at my table unoccupied.

Finally, about twenty minutes after five, she shows up. She scans the crowd and I wave. Even though I told her I was a football player, she's still a little startled. She comes over anyway.

"Okay," she says, sitting down. "Before we say another word, I want to see your phone." I must look confused, because she adds, "I want to see every single call you've made in the past week, and every single call you received. If this isn't some big joke, then you have nothing to hide."

I hand over James's phone, which she knows how to work better than I do.

After a few minutes of searching, she appears satisfied.

"Now, I quiz you," she says, handing back the phone. "First, what was I wearing on the day that Justin took me to the beach?"

I try to picture it. I try to grab hold of those details. But they've already eluded me. I remember her, not what she was wearing.

"I don't know," I say. "Do you remember what Justin was wearing?"

She thinks about it for a second. "Good point. Did we make out?"

I shake my head. "We used the make-out blanket, but we didn't make out. We kissed. And that was enough."

"And what did I say to you before I left the car?"

"'That's the nice note.'"

"Correct. Quick, what's Steve's girlfriend's name?"

"Stephanie."

"And what time did the party end?"

"Eleven-fifteen."

"And when you were in the body of that girl who I took to all of my classes, what did the note you passed me say?"

"Something like, 'The classes here are just as boring as in the school I'm going to now.'"

"And what were the buttons on your backpack that day?"

"Anime kittens."

"Well, you're either an excellent liar, or you switch bodies every day. I have no idea which one is true."

"It's the second one."

I see, over Rhiannon's shoulder, a woman looking at us quizzically. Has she overheard what we're saying?

"Let's go outside," I whisper. "I feel we may be getting an unintended audience."

Rhiannon looks skeptical. "Maybe if you were a petite cheerleader again. But – I'm not sure if you fully realize this – you're a big, threatening dude today. My mother's voice is very loud and clear in my head: 'No dark corners.'"

I point out the window, to a bench along the road.

"Totally public, only without people listening in."

"Fine."

As we head out, the woman who was eavesdropping

120

seems disappointed. I realize how many people sitting around us have open laptops and open notebooks and hope that none of them have been taking notes.

When we get to the bench, Rhiannon lets me sit down first, so she can determine the distance that we'll sit apart, which is significant.

"So you say you've been like this since the day you were born?"

"Yes. I can't remember it being any different."

"So how did that work? Weren't you confused?"

"I guess I got used to it. I'm sure that, at first, I figured it was just how everybody's lives worked. I mean, when you're a baby, you don't really care much about who's taking care of you, as long as someone's taking care of you. And as a little kid, I thought it was some kind of a game, and my mind learned how to access – you know, look at the body's memories – naturally. So I always knew what my name was, and where I was. It wasn't until I was six or seven that I started to realize I was different, and it wasn't until I was nine or ten that I really wanted it to stop."

"You did?"

"Of course. Imagine being homesick, but without having a home. That's what it was like. I wanted friends, a mom, a dad, a dog – but I couldn't hold on to any of them more than a single day. It was brutal. There are nights I remember screaming and crying, begging my parents not to make me go to bed. They could never figure out what I was afraid of. They thought it was a monster under the bed, or a ploy to get a few more bedtime stories. I could never really explain, not in a way that made sense to them. I didn't want to say goodbye, and they'd assure me it wasn't goodbye. It was just goodnight. I'd tell them it was the same thing, but they thought I was being silly.

Eventually I came to peace with it. I had to. I realized that this was my life and there was nothing I could do about it. I couldn't fight the tide, so I decided to float along."

"How many times have you told this story?"

"None. I swear. You're the first."

This should make her feel special – it's meant to make her feel special – but instead it seems to worry her.

"You have to have parents, don't you? I mean, we all have parents."

I shrug. "I have no idea. I would think so. But it's not like there's anyone I can ask. I've never met anyone else like me. Not that I would necessarily know."

It's clear from her expression that she thinks this is a sad story I'm telling her – a very sad story. I don't know how to convey to her that it hasn't all been sad.

"I've glimpsed things," I say. Then I stop. I don't know what's next.

"Go on," she tells me.

"It's just – I know it sounds like an awful way to live, but I've seen so many things. It's so hard when you're in one body to get a sense of what life is really like. You're so grounded in who you are. But when who you are changes every day – you get to touch the universal more. Even the most mundane details. You see how cherries taste different to different people. Blue looks different. You see all the strange rituals boys have to show affection without admitting it. You learn that if a parent reads to you at the end of the day, it's a good sign that it's a good parent, because you've seen so many other parents who don't make the time. You learn how much a day is truly worth, because they're all so different. If you ask most people what the difference was between Monday and Tuesday, they might tell you what they had for dinner each night. Not me. By seeing the world from so many angles, you get more of a sense of its dimensionality."

"But you never get to see things over time, do you?" Rhiannon asks. "I don't mean to cancel out what you just said. I think I understand that. But you've never had a friend that you've known day-in and day-out for ten years. You've never watched a pet grow older. You've never seen how messed up a parent's love can be over time. And you've never been in a relationship for more than a day, not to mention for more than a year."

I should have known it would come back to that.

"But I've seen things," I tell her. "I've observed. I know how it works."

"From the outside? I don't think you can know from the outside."

"I think you underestimate how predictable some things can be in a relationship."

"I love him," she says. "I know you don't understand, but I do."

"You shouldn't. I've seen him from the inside. I know."

"For a day. You saw him for a day."

"And for a day, you saw who he could be. You fell more in love with him when he was me."

I reach out again for her hand, but this time she says, "No. Don't."

I freeze.

"I have a boyfriend," she says. "I know you don't like him, and I'm sure there are moments when I don't like him either. But that's the reality. Now, I'll admit, you have me actually thinking that you are, in fact, the same person who I've met now in five different bodies. All this means is that I'm probably as insane as you are. I know you say you love me, but you don't really know me. You've known me a week. And I need a little more than that."

"But didn't you feel it that day? On the beach? Didn't everything seem right?"

There it is again – the pull of the ocean, the song of the universe. A better liar would deny it. But some of us don't want to live out our lives as liars. She bites her lip and nods.

"Yes. But I don't know who I was feeling that for. Even if I believe it was you, you have to understand that my history with Justin plays into it. I wouldn't have felt that way with a stranger. It wouldn't have been so perfect."

"How do you know?"

"That's my point. I don't."

She looks at her phone, and whether or not she truly needs to leave, I know this is the sign that she's going to.

"I have to make it back for dinner," she says.

"Thanks for driving all this way," I tell her.

It's awkward. So awkward.

"Will I see you again?" I ask.

She nods.

"I'm going to prove it to you," I tell her. "I'm going to show you what it really means."

"What?"

"Love."

Is she scared by this? Embarrassed? Hopeful?

I don't know. I'm not close enough to tell.

Tom gives me no small amount of grief when I get home – partly because I went to Starbucks, and partly because I then had to walk two miles to get back home and was late for dinner, which our father roundly chewed me out over.

"I hope whoever she was, she was worth it," Tom taunts.

I look at him blankly.

"Dude, don't try to tell me you were just going for the coffee or the folk tunes they play on the speakers. I know you better than that."

I remain silent.

I am assigned to wash all the dishes. While doing so, I turn on the radio, and when the local news comes on, Nathan Daldry comes with it.

"So tell us, Nathan, what you experienced last Saturday," the interviewer says.

"I was possessed. There's no other word for it. I wasn't in control of my own body. I consider myself lucky to be alive. And I want to ask anyone else who's ever been possessed like this, just for a day, to contact me. Because, I'll be honest with you, Chuck, a lot of people think I'm crazy. Other kids at school are making fun of me constantly. But I know what happened. And I know I'm not the only one."

*I know I'm not the only one.*

This is the sentence that haunts me. I wish I felt the same certainty.

I wish I weren't the only one.

# DAY 6004

The next morning I wake up in the same room.

In the same body.

I can't believe it. I don't understand. After all these years.

I look at the wall. My hands. The sheets.

And then I look to my side and see James sleeping there in his bed.

James.

And I realize: I'm not in the same body. I'm not on the same side of the room.

No, this morning I'm his twin, Tom.

I have never had this chance before. I watch as James emerges from sleep, emerges from a day away from his old body. I am looking for the traces of that oblivion, the bafflement of that waking. But what I get is the familiar scene of a football player stretching himself into the day. If he feels at all strange, at all different, he's not showing it.

"Dude, what are you staring at?"

This doesn't come from James, but from our other brother, Paul.

"Just getting up," I mumble.

But really, I don't take my eyes off James. Not through the ride to school. Not at breakfast. He seems a little out of it now, but nothing that couldn't be explained by a bad night's sleep.

"How're you doing?" I ask him.

He grunts. "Fine. Thanks for caring."

I decide to play dumb. He expects me to be dumb, so it shouldn't be much of a stretch.

"What did you do after practice yesterday?" I ask.

"I went to Starbucks."

"Who with?"

He looks at me like I've just sung the question to him in falsetto.

"I just wanted coffee, okay? I wasn't *with* anyone."

I study him, trying to see if he's trying to cover his conversation with Rhiannon. I don't think, though, that such duplicity would be anything but obvious on him.

He really doesn't remember seeing her. Talking to her. Being with her.

"Then why'd it take so long?" I ask him.

"What, were you timing it? I'm *touched*."

"Well, who were you emailing at lunch?"

"I was just checking my email."

"Your own email?"

"Who else's email would I be checking? You're asking

129

seriously weird questions, dude. Isn't he Paul?"

Paul chews on some bacon. "I swear, whenever you two talk, I just tune it right out. I have no idea what you're saying."

Paradoxically, I wish I were still in James's body, so I could see exactly what his memories of yesterday are. From where I sit, it appears that he recalls the places he was, but has somehow concocted an alternate version of events, one that fits closer to his life. Has his mind done this, some kind of adaptation? Or did my mind, right before it left, leave behind this storyline?

James does not feel like he was possessed by the devil.

He thinks yesterday was just another day.

Again, the morning becomes a search to find a few minutes' worth of email access.

*I should have given her my phone number*, I think.

Then I stop myself. I stand there right in the middle of the hallway, shocked. It's such a mundane, ordinary observation – but that's what stops me. In the context of my life, it's nonsensical. There was no way for me to give her a phone number. I know this. And yet, the ordinary thought crept in, made me trick myself for a moment into thinking that I too was ordinary.

I have no idea what this means, but I suspect it's dangerous.

At lunch, I tell James I'm going to the library.

"Dude," he says, "libraries are for girls."

There aren't any new messages from Rhiannon, so I write to her instead.

Rhiannon,

You'd actually recognize me today. I woke up as James's twin. I thought this might help me figure things out, but so far, no luck.

I want to see you again.

A

There isn't anything from Nathan either. I decide to type his name into a search engine again, figuring there might be a few more articles about what he's saying.

I find over two-thousand results. All from the past three days.

Words is spreading. Mostly from evangelical Christian sites, which have bought Nathan's devil claims wholesale. He is, for them, just another example of the world going to H-E-double-hockey-sticks.

From what I can recall, none of the many versions I heard as a child of *The Boy Who Cried Wolf* spent that much time pondering the emotional state of the boy, especially after the wolf finally showed up. I want to know what Nathan is thinking, if he really believes what he's saying. None of the articles and blogs are any help – he's saying the same thing in all of them, and people are either painting him as a freak or an oracle. Nobody's sitting him down and treating him like a sixteen-year-old boy. They are missing the real questions in order to ask the sensational ones.

I open up his last email.

You can't avoid my questions forever. I want to know who you are. I want to know why you do what you do.

Tell me.

But how can I respond without confirming at least part of the story he's created? I feel that he's right – in some way, I can't avoid his questions forever. They will start to dig into me. They will follow me wherever I wake up. But to give him any answer will give him a reassurance I know I shouldn't give. It will keep him on his path.

My best bet is for him to start feeling that he is, indeed, crazy. Which is an awful thing to wish upon someone. Especially when he's not crazy.

I want to ask Rhiannon what to do. But I can imagine what she'd say. Or maybe I'm just projecting my better self onto her. Because I know the answer: Self-preservation isn't worth it if you can't live with the self you're preserving.

I am responsible for his situation. So he's become my responsibility.

I know this, even as I hate it.

I know enough not to write immediately. I need to give it some thought. I need to help him without confirming anything.

Finally, by last period, I think I have it.

I know who you are. I've seen your story on the news.
It doesn't have anything to do with me – you must
have made a mistake.

Still, it appears to me that you're not considering all the
possibilities. I'm sure what happened to you was very
stressful. But blaming the devil is not the answer.

I send it off quickly before football practice.
I also check for an email from Rhiannon.
Nothing.

The rest of the day is uneventful. And I find myself wondering once again when I started to think my days would contain actual events. Up until now, I have lived for the uneventfulness, and have found the smaller satisfaction in the art of getting by. I resent that the hours seem boring now, emptier. Going through the motions gives you plenty of time to examine the motions. I used to find this interesting. Now it has taken on the taint of meaninglessness.

I practise football. I get a ride home. I do some homework. I eat some dinner. I watch TV with my family.

This is the trap of having something to live for:

Everything else seems lifeless.


James and I go to bed first. Paul is in the kitchen, talking to our mother about his work schedule for the weekend. James and I don't say anything as we change into our sleep clothes, as we parade to the bathroom and back.

I get in bed and he turns out the light. I expect to hear him getting into bed next, but instead he hovers in the middle of the room.

"Tom?"

"Yeah?"

"Why did you ask me about what I was up to yesterday?"

I sit up. "I don't know. You just seem

"I just thought it was strange. You ask

He heads to his bed now. I hear his weig
mattress.

"So nothing seemed off to you?" I ask, ho[p] that
there will be something – anything – that rises to the
surface.

"Not that I can think of. I thought it was pretty funny
that Snyder had to end practice so he could go, like,
learn how to help his babymama breathe. But I think
that was the highlight. It's just . . . do I seem off today
too?"

The truth is that I haven't been paying that much
attention, not since breakfast.

"Why do you ask?"

"No reason. I feel fine. I just don't, you know, want to
look like there's something wrong when there's nothing
wrong."

"You seem fine," I assure him.

"Good," he says, shifting his body, getting into the
right position with his pillow.

I want to say more, but don't know what the words
are supposed to be. I feel such a tenderness for these
vulnerable night-time conversations, the way words take
a different shape in the air when there's no light in the
room. I think of the rare jackpot nights when I ended

...e day at a sleepover, or even sharing the room with a sibling or a friend I genuinely liked. Those conversations could trick me into believing I could say anything, even though there was so much I was holding back. Eventually the night would take its hold, but it would always feel like fading to sleep rather than falling.

"Goodnight," I say to James. But what I really feel is goodbye. I am leaving here, leaving this family. It's only been two days, but that's twice what I'm used to. It's just a hint – the smallest hint – of what it would be like to wake up in the same place every morning.

I have to let that go.

# DAY 6005

Some people think mental illness is a matter of mood, a matter of personality. They think depression is simply a form of being sad, that OCD is a form of being uptight. They think the soul is sick, not the body. It is, they believe, something that you have some choice over.

I know how wrong this is.

When I was a child, I didn't understand. I would wake up in a new body and wouldn't understand why things felt muted, dimmer. Or the opposite – I'd be supercharged, unfocussed, like a radio at top volume flipping quickly from station to station. Since I didn't have access to the body's emotions, I assumed the ones I was feeling were my own. Eventually, though, I realized these inclinations, these compulsions, were as much a part of the body as its eye color or its voice. Yes, the feelings themselves were intangible, amorphous, but the cause of the feelings was a matter of chemistry, biology.

It is a hard cycle to conquer. The body is working against you. And because of this, you feel even more despair. Which only amplifies the imbalance. It takes uncommon strength to live with these things. But I have seen that strength over and over again. When I fall into the life of someone grappling, I have to mirror their

137

strength, and sometimes surpass it, because I am less prepared.

I know the signs now. I know when to look for the pill bottles, when to let the body take its course. I have to keep reminding myself – *this is not me*. It is chemistry. It is biology. It is not who I am. It is not who any of them are.

Kelsea Cook's mind is a dark place. Even before I open my eyes, I know this. Her mind is an unquiet one, words and thoughts and impulses constantly crashing into each other. My own thoughts try to assert themselves within this noise. The body responds by breaking into a sweat. I try to remain calm, but the body conspires against that, tries to drown me in distortion.

It is not usually this bad, first thing in the morning. If it's this bad now, it must be pretty bad at all times.

Underneath the distortion is a desire for pain. I open my eyes and see the scars. Not just on the body, although those are there – the hairline fractures across the skin, the web you create to catch your own death. The scars are in the room as well, across the walls, along the floor. The person who lives here no longer cares about anything. Posters hang half-ripped. The mirror is cracked. Clothes lay abandoned. The shades are drawn. The books sit crooked on shelves like rows of neglected teeth. At one point she must have broken open a pen and spun it around, because if you look closely, you can see small, dried drops of ink all over the walls and the ceiling.

I access her history and am shocked to realize that she's gotten this far without any notice, without any diagnosis. She has been left to her own devices, and those devices are broken.

It is five in the morning. I have woken up without any alarm. I have woken up because the thoughts are so loud, and none of them mean me well.

I struggle to get back to sleep, but the body won't let me.

Two hours later, I get out of bed.

Depression has been likened to both a black cloud and a black dog. For someone like Kelsea, the black cloud is the right metaphor. She is surrounded by it, immersed within it, and there is no obvious way out. What she needs to do is try to contain it, get it into the form of the black dog. It will still follow her around wherever she goes; it will always be there. But at least it will be separate, and will follow her lead.

I stumble into the bathroom and start the shower.

"What are you doing?" a male voice calls. "Didn't you shower last night?"

I don't care. I need the sensation of water hitting my body. I need this prompt to start my day.

When I leave the bathroom, Kelsea's father is in the hallway, glaring at me.

"Get dressed," he says with a scowl. I hold my towel tighter around me.

Once I've got my clothes on, I gather my books for school. There's a journal in Kelsea's backpack, but I don't have time to read it. I also don't have time to check my email. Even though he's in the other room, I can sense Kelsea's father waiting.

It's just the two of them. I access and find Kelsea's lied to him in order to be driven to school – she said that the route had been redrawn, but really she doesn't want to be trapped in the bus with other kids. It's not that she's bullied – she's too busy bullying herself to notice. The problem is the confinement, the inability to leave.

Her father's car isn't much better, but at least there's only one other person she has to deal with. Even when we're moving, he doesn't stop exuding impatience. I am always amazed by people who know something is wrong, but still insist on ignoring it, as if that will somehow make it go away. They spare themselves the confrontation, but end up boiling in resentment anyway.

*She needs your help,* I want to say. But it's not my

place to say it, especially because I'm not sure he'll react in the right way.

So Kelsea remains silent the whole drive. From her father's reaction to this silence, I can imagine this is how their mornings always go.

Kelsea has email access on her phone, but I'm still worried about anything being traced, especially after my slip-up with Nathan.

So I walk the halls and go to classes, waiting for my chance. I have to push harder to get Kelsea through the day. Any time I let it, the weight of living creeps in and starts to drag her down. It would be too easy to say that I feel invisible. Instead I feel painfully visible, and entirely ignored. People talk to her, but it feels like they are outside a house, talking through the walls. There are friends, but they are people to spend time with, not people to share time with. There's a false beast that takes the form of instinct and harps on the pointlessness of everything that happens.

The only person who tries to engage me is Kelsea's lab partner, Lena. We're in physics class, and the assignment is to set up a pulley system. I've done this before, so it doesn't strike me as hard. Lena, however, is surprised by Kelsea's involvement. I realize I've overstepped – this is not the kind of thing Kelsea would get excited about. But Lena doesn't let me back down. When I try to mumble apologies and step away, she insists I keep going.

"You're good at this," she says. "Much better than I am."

While I arrange things, adjusting inclines and accounting for various forms of friction, Lena talks to me about a dance that's coming up, asks me if I have any weekend plans, and tells me she might be going to DC with her parents. She seems hypersensitive to my reaction, and I'm guessing the conversation usually gets shut down long before this point. But I let her talk, let her voice counter the unspoken, insistent ones that emanate from my wiring.

Then the period is over, and we go our separate ways. I don't see her again for the rest of the day.

I spend lunchtime in the library at the computer. I don't imagine anyone at lunch will miss me – but maybe that's just what Kelsea would think. Part of growing up is making sure your sense of reality isn't entirely grounded in your own mind; I feel Kelsea's mind isn't letting her to get anywhere near that point, and I wonder how much of my own thoughts are getting stuck there as well.

Logging into my own email is a nice jolt to remind me that I am in fact me, not Kelsea. Even better, there is word from Rhiannon – the sight of which cheers me up, until I read what the email says.

A,

So, who are you today?

What a strange question to ask. But I guess it makes sense. If any of this makes sense.

Yesterday was a hard day. Justin's grandmother is sick, but instead of admitting he's upset about it, he just lashes out at the world more. I'm trying to help him, but it's hard.

I don't know if you want to hear this or not. I know how you feel about Justin. If you want me to keep that part of my life hidden from you, I can. But I don't think that's what you want.

Tell me how your day is going.

Rhiannon

I reply and tell her a little about what Kelsea is up against. Then I end with this:

I want you to be honest with me. Even if it hurts.
Although I would prefer for it not to hurt.

Love,
A


Next, I switch accounts and find a reply from Nathan.

I know I haven't made a mistake. I know what you are.
And I will find out who you are. The reverend says he
is working on that.

You want me to doubt myself. But I am not the only
one. You will see.

Confess now, before we find you.


I stare at the screen for a minute, trying to reconcile
the tone of this email with the Nathan I knew for a
day. It feels like two very different people. I wonder if
it's possible that someone else has taken over Nathan's
account. I wonder who "the reverend" is.

The bell rings, marking the end of the lunch period.
I return to class and the black cloud takes hold. I find
it hard to concentrate on what's being said. I find it
hard to see how any of this is important. Nothing I'm

144

being taught here will make life less painful. None of the people in this room will make life less painful. I attack my cuticles with merciless precision. It is the only sensation that feels genuine.

Kelsea's father is not going to pick her up after school; he's still at work. Instead, she walks home, in order to avoid the bus. I am tempted to break this pattern, but it's been so long since she's ridden the bus that she has no memory of which bus is hers. So I start to walk.

Again, I find myself wishing for the mundane possibility of calling Rhiannon on the phone, for filling the next empty hour with the sound of her voice.

But instead, all I am left with is Kelsea and her damaged perceptions. The walk home is a steep one, and I wonder if it's yet another way she punishes herself. After about a half-hour, with another half-hour in front of me, I decide to stop at a playground I'm about to pass. The parents there give me wary looks because I am not a parent or a little kid, so I steer clear of the jungle gym, the swings and the sandbox, and end up on the outer ring, on a seesaw that looks like it's been banished from everything else for bad behavior.

There's homework I could do, but Kelsea's journal calls out to me instead. I'm a little afraid of what I'll find inside, but mostly I'm curious. If I can't access the

145

things she's felt, I will at least be able to read the partial transcript.

But it's not a journal in the traditional sense. That becomes apparent after a page or two. There are no musings about boys or girls. There are no revisited scenes of discord with her father or her teachers. There are no secrets shared or injustices vented.

Instead there are ways to kill yourself, listed with extraordinary detail

Knives to the heart. Knives to the arm. Belts around the neck. Plastic bags. Hard falls. Death by burning. All of them methodically researched. Examples given. Illustrations provided – rough illustrations where the test case is clearly Kelsea. Self-portraits of her own demise.

I flip to the end, past pages of dosages and special instructions. There are still blank pages at the back, but before them is a page that reads *DEADLINE*, followed by a date that's only six days away.

I look through the rest of the notebook, trying to find other, failed deadlines.

But there's only the one.

I get off the seesaw, back away from the park. Because now I feel like I am the thing the parents are afraid of, I am the reality they want to avoid. No, not just avoid – *prevent*. They don't want me anywhere near their children, and I don't blame them. It feels as if everything I touch will turn to harm.

I don't know what to do. There's no threat in the present – I am in control of the body, and as long as I am in control of the body, I will not allow it to hurt itself. But I am only here for one day. I will not be in control six days from now.

I know I am not supposed to interfere. It is Kelsea's life, not mine. It is unfair of me to do something that limits her choices, that makes up her mind for her.

My childish impulse is to wish I hadn't opened the journal.

But I have.

I try to access any memory of Kelsea giving a cry for help. But the thing about a cry for help is that someone else needs to be around to hear it. And I am not finding a moment of that in Kelsea's life. Her father sees what he wants to see, and she doesn't want to dispel this fiction with fact. Her mother left years ago. Other relatives are distant. Friends all exist far outside the black cloud. Just because Lena was nice in physics class doesn't mean she should be burdened with this, or would know what to do.

I make it back to Kelsea's empty house, sweaty and exhausted. I turn on her computer and everything I need to know is there in her history – the sites where these plans come from, where this information can be gleaned. Right there, one click away for everyone to see. Only no one is looking.

I decide that in one way what I need and what Kelsea needs are the same thing: We both need to talk to someone.

I email Rhiannon.

> I really need to speak to you right now. The girl whose body I'm in wants to kill herself. This is not a joke.

I give her Kelsea's home phone number, figuring there will be no obvious record of it, and that it can always be discounted as a wrong number.

Ten minutes later, she calls.

"Hello?" I answer.

"Is that you?" she asks.

"Yeah." I've forgotten that she doesn't know the sound of my voice. "It's me."

"I got your email. Wow."

"Yeah, wow."

"How do you know?"

I tell her briefly about Kelsea's journal.

"That poor girl," Rhiannon says. "What are you going to do?"

"I have no idea."

"Don't you have to tell someone?"

"There was no training for this, Rhiannon. I really don't know."

All I know is that I need her. But I'm afraid to say it. Because saying it might scare her away.

"Where are you?" she asks.

I tell her the town.

"That's not far. I can be there in a little while. Are you alone?"

"Yeah. Her father doesn't get home until around seven."

"Give me the address."

I do.

"I'll be right there," she says.

I don't even need to ask. It means more that she just knows.

I wonder what would happen if I straightened up Kelsea's room. I wonder what would happen if she woke up tomorrow morning and found everything in its right place. Would it give her some unexpected calm? Would it make her understand that her life did not have to be chaos? Or would she just take one look and destroy it again? Because that's what her chemistry, her biology would tell her to do.

*

149

The doorbell rings. I have spent the past ten minutes staring at the ink stains on the walls, hoping they will rearrange themselves into an answer, and knowing they never will.

The black cloud is so thick at this point that not even Rhiannon's presence can send it away. I am happy to see her in the doorway, but that happiness feels more like resigned gratitude than pleasure.

She blinks, takes me in. I have forgotten that she is not used to this, that she is not expecting a new person every day. It's one thing to acknowledge it theoretically, and quite another thing to have a thin, shaky girl standing on the other side of the precipice.

"Thank you for coming," I say.

It's a little after five, so we don't have much time before Kelsea's father comes home.

We head to Kelsea's room. Rhiannon sees the journal sitting on Kelsea's bed and picks it up. I watch and wait until she's done reading.

"This is serious," she says. "I've had . . . thoughts. But nothing like this."

She sits down on the bed. I sit down next to her.

"You have to stop her," she says.

"But how can I? And is that really my right? Shouldn't she decide that for herself?"

"So, what? You just let her die? Because you didn't want to get involved?"

I take her hand.

"We don't know for sure that the deadline's real. This could just be her way of getting rid of the thoughts. Putting them on paper so she doesn't do them."

She looks at me. "But you don't believe that, do you? You wouldn't have called me if you believed that."

She looks down at our hands.

"This is weird," she says.

"What?"

She squeezes once, then pulls her hand away. "This."

"What do you mean?"

"It's not like the other day. I mean, it's a different hand. You're different."

"But I'm not."

"You can't say that. Yes, you're the same person inside. But the outside matters too."

"You look the same, no matter what eyes I'm seeing you through. I feel the same."

It's true, but it doesn't really address what she's saying.

"You never get involved in the people's lives? The ones you're inhabiting."

I shake my head.

"You try to leave the lives the way you found them."

"Yeah."

"But what about Justin? What made that so different?"

"You," I say.

Just one word and she finally understands. Just one word and the door to the enormity is finally unlocked.

"That makes no sense," she says.

And the only way to show her how it makes sense, the only way to make the enormity real, is for me to lean over and kiss her. Like last time, but not at all like last time. Not our first kiss, but also our first kiss. My lips feel different against hers, our bodies fit differently. And there is also something else that surrounds us, the black cloud as well as the enormity. I am not kissing her because I want to, and I am not kissing her because I need to – I am kissing her for a reason that transcends want and need, that feels elemental to our existence, a molecular component on which our universe will be built. It is not our first kiss, but is the first kiss where she knows me, and that makes it more of a first kiss than the first kiss ever was.

I find myself wishing that Kelsea could feel this too. Maybe she does. It's not enough. It's not a solution. But it does lessen the weight for a moment.

Rhiannon is not smiling when we pull away from each other. There is none of the giddiness of the earlier kiss.

"This is definitely weird," she says.

"Why?"

"Because you're a girl? Because I still have a boyfriend? Because we're talking about someone else's suicide?"

"In your heart, does any of that matter?" In my heart, it doesn't.

"Yes. It does."

"Which part?"

"All of it. When I kiss you, I'm not actually kissing you, you know. You're inside there somewhere. But I'm kissing the outside part. And right now, although I can feel you underneath, all I'm getting is the sadness. I'm kissing her, and I want to cry."

"That's not what I want," I tell her.

"I know. But that's what there is."

She stands up and looks around the room, searching for clues to a murder that has yet to happen.

"If she were bleeding in the street, what would you do?" she asks.

"That's not the same situation."

"If she were going to kill someone else?"

"I would turn her in."

"So how is this different?"

"It's her own life. Not anyone else's."

"But it's still killing."

153

"If she really wants to do it, there's nothing I can do to stop it."

Even as I say this, it feels wrong.

"Okay," I continue, before Rhiannon can correct me. "Putting up obstacles can help. Getting other people involved can help. Getting her to the proper doctors can help."

"Just like if she had cancer, or was bleeding in the street."

This is what I need. It's not enough to hear these things in my own voice. I need to hear them told to me by somebody I trust.

"So who do I tell?"

"A guidance counselor, maybe?"

I look at the clock. "School's closed. And we only have until midnight, remember."

"Who's her best friend?"

I shake my head.

"Boyfriend? Girlfriend?"

"No."

"A suicide hotline?"

"If we call one, they'd only be giving me advice, not her. We have no way of knowing if she'll remember it tomorrow, or if it will have any effect. Believe me, I've thought about these options."

"So it has to be her father. Right?"

"I think he checked out a while ago."

"Well, you need to get him to check back in."

She makes it sound so easy. But both of us know it's not easy.

"What do I say?"

"You say, 'Dad, I want to kill myself.' Just come right out and say it."

"And if he asks me why?"

"You tell him you don't know why. Don't commit to anything. She'll have to work that out starting tomorrow."

"You've thought this through, haven't you?"

"It was a busy drive over."

"What if he doesn't care? What if he doesn't believe her?"

"Then you grab his keys and drive to the nearest hospital. Bring the journal with you."

Hearing her say it, it all makes sense.

She sits back down on the bed.

"Come here," she says. But this time we don't kiss. Instead, she hugs my frail body.

"I don't know if I can do this," I whisper.

"You can," she tells me. "Of course you can."


I am alone in Kelsea's room when her father comes home. I hear him throw down his keys, take something out of the refrigerator. I hear him walk to his bedroom, then come back out. He doesn't call out a hello. I don't even know if he realizes I'm here.

Five minutes pass. Ten minutes. Finally, he calls out, "Dinner!"

I haven't heard any activity in the kitchen, so I'm not surprised to find a KFC bucket on the table. He's already started on a drumstick.

I can guess how this usually works. He takes his dinner into the den, in front of the TV. She takes hers back to her room. And that marks the rest of the night for them.

But tonight is different. Tonight she says, "I want to kill myself."

At first, I don't think he's heard me.

"I know you don't want to hear this," I say. "But it's the truth."

He drops his hand to his side, still holding the drumstick.

"What are you saying?" he asks.

"I want to die," I tell him.

"C'mon now," he says. "Really?"

If I were Kelsea, I'd probably leave the room in disgust. I'd give up.

"You need to get me help," I say. "This is something

156

I've been thinking about for a long time." I put the journal on the table, shove it over to him. This might ultimately be my biggest betrayal of Kelsea. I feel awful, but then I conjure Rhiannon's voice in my ear, telling me I am doing the right thing.

Kelsea's father puts down the drumstick, picks up the journal. Starts reading it. I try to decode his expression. He doesn't want to be seeing this. Resents that it's happening. Hates it, even. But not her. He keeps reading because even if he hates the situation, he doesn't hate her.

"Kelsea . . ." he chokes out.

I wish she could see how it hits him. The look on his face, his life caving in. Because then maybe she'd realize, if only for a split second, that even though the world doesn't matter to her, she matters to the world.

"This isn't just some . . . thing?" he asks.

I shake my head. It's a stupid question, but I'm not going to call him on it.

"So what do we do?"

There. I have him.

"We need to get help," I tell him. "Tomorrow morning, we need to find a counselor who's open on Saturday and we need to see what we have to do. I probably need medication. I definitely need to talk to a doctor. I have been living this for so long."

"But why didn't you tell me?"

*Why didn't you see?* I want to ask back. But now's not the time for that. He'll get there on his own, if he's not there already.

"That doesn't matter. We need to focus on now. I am asking for help. You need to get me help."

"Are you sure it can wait until morning?"

"I'm not going to do anything tonight. But tomorrow you have to watch me. You have to force me if I change my mind. I might change my mind. I might pretend that this whole conversation didn't happen. Keep that notebook. It's the truth. If I fight you, fight me back. Call an ambulance."

"An ambulance?"

"That's how serious this is, Dad."

It's the last word that really brings it home to him. I don't think Kelsea uses it that often.

He's crying now. We just stay there, looking at each other.

Finally, he says, "Have some dinner."

I take some chicken from the bucket, then take it back to my room. I've said everything I've needed to say.

Kelsea will have to tell him the rest.

I hear him pacing throughout the house. I hear him on the phone to someone, and I hope it's someone who can help him the way Rhiannon helped me. I hear him stop outside the door, afraid to open it but still listening in. I make small stirring noises, so he knows I'm awake, alive.

I fall asleep to the sound of his concern.

# DAY 6006

The phone rings.

I reach for it, thinking it's Rhiannon.

Even though it can't be.

I look at the name on the screen. *Austin.*

My boyfriend.

"Hello?" I answer.

"Hugo! This is your nine a.m. wake-up call. I will be there in an hour. Go make yourself purdy."

"Whatever you say," I mumble.

There's a lot I have to do in an hour.

First, there's the usual getting up, getting showered and getting dressed. In the kitchen, I can hear my parents talking loudly in a language I don't know. It sounds like Spanish but isn't Spanish, so I'm guessing it's Portuguese. Foreign languages throw me – I have a beginner's grasp of a few of them, but I can't really access a person's memory fast enough to pretend to be fluent in any of them. I access and find that Hugo's parents are from Brazil. But that's not going to help me understand them better. So I steer clear of the kitchen.

Austin is picking Hugo up to go to a gay pride parade in Annapolis. Two of their friends, William and

Nicolas, will be coming along. It's marked on Hugo's calendar as well as his mind.

Luckily, Hugo has a laptop in his room. I quickly open my email and find something that Rhiannon sent only ten minutes ago.

A,

I hope it went well yesterday. I called her house just now and no one was home – do you think they're getting help? I'm trying to take it as a good sign.

Meanwhile, here's a link you need to see. It's out of control.

Where are you today?

R

I click on the link beneath her initial and am taken to the home page of a big Baltimore tabloid website. The headline blares:

**THE DEVIL AMONG US!**

It's Nathan's story, but it's not only Nathan's story. This time there are five or six other people from the area claiming to have been possessed by the devil. Much to my relief, none of them besides Nathan are familiar to me. All of them are older than I am. Most claim to have been possessed for a time much longer than a single day.

I would think the reporter would have been more skeptical, but she buys the stories uncritically. She even links to other stories of demonic possession – death-row criminals who claimed they were under the influence of satanic forces, politicians and preachers who were caught in compromising positions and said that something very uncharacteristic had come over them. It all sounds very convenient.

I quickly run Nathan through a search engine and find more coverage. The story, it seems, is going wide. In article after article, there is one person quoted. Essentially, he says the same thing every time:

*"I have no doubt that these are cases of demonic possession," says Reverend Anderson Poole, who has been counseling Dalrdry. "These are textbook examples. The devil is nothing if not predictable."*

*"These possessions should come as no surprise," says Poole. "We as a society have been leaving the door wide open. Why wouldn't the devil walk right in?"*

People are believing this. The articles and posts in the comments sections are legion – all from people who see the devil's work in everything.

Even though I should know better, I shoot off a quick email to Nathan.

I am not the devil.

I hit send, but I don't feel any better.

I email Rhiannon, telling her how it went with Kelsea's father. I also let her know that I'm going to be in Annapolis for the day, and tell her what T-shirt I'm wearing and what I look like.

There's a honk outside, and I see a car that must be Austin's. I race through the kitchen and say a hurried goodbye to Hugo's parents. Then I pile in the car – the boy in the passenger seat (William) moves into the back with the other boy (Nicolas) so I can be sitting next to my boyfriend. For his part, Austin takes one look at my outfit and *tsk-tsks*, "You're wearing *that* to Pride?" But he's joking. I think.

There is conversation around me the whole car ride, but I'm not really a part of it. My mind is completely elsewhere.

I shouldn't have sent Nathan that email.

One simple line, but it admits too much.

*

From the moment we hit Annapolis, Austin is in his element.

"Isn't this *fun*?" he keeps asking.

William, Nicolas and I nod, agree. In truth, the Annapolis Pride events aren't that elaborate – in many ways it feels like the Navy has turned gay and lesbian for the day, and a ragtag assortment of people have come along to cheer it on. The weather is sunny and cool, and that seems to cheer everyone further. Austin likes to hold my hand and swing it like we're walking down the yellow brick road. Ordinarily, I'd be charmed. He has every right to be proud, to enjoy this day. It's not his fault I'm so distracted.

I'm looking for Rhiannon in the crowd. I can't help it. Every now and then, Austin catches me.

"See someone you know?" he asks.

"No," I say truthfully.

She's not here. She hasn't made it. And I feel foolish for expecting her to. She can't just drop her life every time I'm available. Her day is no less important than mine.

We come to a corner where there are a few people protesting the festivities. I don't understand this at all. It's like protesting the fact that some people are red-haired.

In my experience, desire is desire, love is love. I have never fallen in love with a gender. I have fallen for individuals. I know this is hard for people to do, but I don't understand why it's so hard, when it's so obvious.

I remember Rhiannon's hesitation to kiss me longer when I was Kelsea. I am hoping this reason was nowhere near the heart of it. There were so many other reasons in that moment.

One of the protestor's signs catches my eye. HOMOSEXUALITY IS THE DEVIL'S WORK, it says. And once again I think about how people use the devil as an alias for the things they fear. The cause and effect is backward. The devil doesn't make anyone do anything. People just do things and blame the devil after.

Predictably, Austin stops to kiss me in front of the protestors. I try to oblige. Philosophically, I am with him. But I'm not inside the kiss. I cannot manufacture the intensity.

He notices. He doesn't say anything, but he notices.

I want to check my email on Hugo's phone, but Austin isn't letting me out of his sight. When William and Nicolas make a move to get some lunch, Austin says he and I are going to go our own way for a little while.

I assume we're going to get lunch too, but instead he pulls me into a hip clothing store and spends the next

165

hour trying things on, with me giving my outside-the-changing-room opinion. At one point, he pulls me into the changing room to steal some kisses, and I oblige. But at the same time, I'm thinking that if we're inside, there's no way Rhiannon is going to find me.

While Austin debates whether the skinny jeans are skinny enough, I find myself wondering what Kelsea is doing at this moment. Is she unburdening herself, going along with it, or is she defiant, denying that she ever wanted help in the first place? I picture Tom and James in their rec room, playing video games, not having any sense that their week was disrupted. I think of Roger Wilson later tonight, preparing his clothes for church tomorrow morning.

"What do you think?" Austin asks.

"They're great," I say.

"You didn't even look."

I can't argue this. He's right. I didn't.

I look at him now. I need to pay more attention.

"I like them," I tell him.

"Well, I don't," he says. Then he storms back into the changing room.

I haven't been a good guest in Hugo's life. I access his memories and discover that he and Austin first became boyfriends at this very celebration, a year ago this weekend. They'd been friends for a little while, but they'd never talked about how they felt. They were each afraid of ruining the friendship, and instead of making it better, their caution made everything awkward. So finally, as a pair of twentysomething men passed by holding hands, Austin said, "Hey, that could be us in ten years."

And Hugo said, "Or ten months."

And Austin said, "Or ten days."

And Hugo said, "Or ten minutes."

And Austin said, "Or ten seconds."

Then they each counted to ten, and held hands for the rest of the day.

The start of it.

Hugo would have remembered this.

But I didn't.


Austin senses something has changed. He comes back from the dressing room without any clothes in his arms, looks at me, and makes a decision.

"Let's get out of here," he says. "I don't want to have this conversation in this particular store."

He leads me down to the water, away from the celebration, away from the crowds. He finds a somewhat secluded bench and I follow him there. Once we sit down, it all comes out.

"You haven't been with me once this whole day," he

says. "You aren't listening to a word I say. You keep looking around for someone else. And kissing you is like kissing a block of wood. And today, of all days. I thought you said you were going to give it a chance. I thought you said you were snapping out of whatever it is that's been afflicting you the past couple of weeks. I am *sure* I recall you saying there wasn't anyone else. But maybe I'm mistaken. I was willing to bend over backward, Hugo. But I can't bend over backward and walk around at the same time. I can't bend over backward and have a conversation. I guess when it all comes down to it, I'm just not that damn flexible."

"Austin, I'm sorry," I say.

"Do you even love me?"

I have no idea if Hugo loves him or not. If I tried, I'm sure I could access moments when he loved him and moments when he didn't. But I can't answer his question and be sure I'm being truthful. I'm caught.

"My feelings haven't changed," I say. "I'm just a little off today. It has nothing to do with you."

Austin laughs. "Our anniversary has nothing to do with me?"

"That's not what I said. I mean my mood."

Now Austin is shaking his head.

"I can't do this, Hugo. You know I can't do this."

"Are you breaking up with me?" I ask, genuine fear in

my voice. I can't believe I'm doing this to both of them.

Austin hears the fear, looks at me and maybe sees something worth keeping.

"This isn't the way I want today to go," he says. "But I have to believe that it isn't the way you want it to go either."

I can't imagine that Hugo was planning to break up with Austin today. And if he was, he can always do it tomorrow.

"Come here," I say. Austin moves in to me and I lean into his shoulder. We sit like that for a moment, looking at the ships on the bay. I take his hand. When I turn to look at him, he's blinking back tears.

This time when I kiss him, I know there's something in it. When he feels it, it may come across as love. It is my thanks to him for not ending it. It is my thanks to him for giving it at least one day more.


We stay out until late, and I am a good boyfriend the whole time. Eventually I lose myself a little in his life, dancing along with Austin, William, Nicolas, and a few hundred other gays and lesbians when the parade organizers blast the Village People's "In the Navy".

I keep looking for Rhiannon, but only when Austin is distracted. And at a certain point, I give up.

*

When I get home, there's an email from her:

A,

Sorry I couldn't make it to Annapolis – there were
some things I had to do.

Maybe tomorrow?
R

I wonder what the "things I had to do" were. I have to
assume they involve Justin, because otherwise, wouldn't
she have told me what they were?

I'm pondering this when Austin texts me to say he
ended up having a great day. I text him back and say
I had a great day too. I can only hope that's the way
Hugo remembers it, because now Austin has proof if he
denies it.

Hugo's mother comes in and says something to me in
Portuguese. I only get about half of it.

"I'm tired," I tell her in English. "I think it's time for
bed."

I don't think I've addressed her questions, but she
just shakes her head – I am a typical, unforthcoming
teenager – and heads back to her room.

Before I go to sleep, I decide to see if Nathan has written me back.

He has.

Two words.

Prove it.

# DAY 6007

I wake up the next morning in Beyoncé's body.

Not the real Beyoncé. But a body remarkably like hers. All the curves in all the right places.

I open my eyes to a blur. I reach for the glasses on the nightstand, but they're not there. So I stumble into the bathroom and put in my contact lenses.

Then I look in the mirror.

I am not pretty. I am not beautiful.

I'm top-to-bottom gorgeous.


I am always happiest when I am just attractive enough. Meaning: Other people won't find me unattractive. Meaning: I make a positive impression. Meaning: My life is not defined by my attractiveness, because that brings its own perils as well as its own rewards.

Ashley Ashton's life is defined by her attractiveness. Beauty can come naturally, but it's hard to be stunning by accident. A lot of work has gone into this face, this body. I'm sure there's a complete morning regimen that I'm supposed to undergo before heading into the day.

I don't want to have any part of it though. With girls like Ashley, I just want to shake them, and tell them that no matter how hard they fight it, these teenage looks aren't going to last forever, and that there are much better foundations to build a life upon than how attractive you are. But there's no way for me to get that message across. My only course of rebellion is to leave her eyebrows unplucked for the day.

I access where I am and discover I'm only about fifteen minutes away from Rhiannon.

A good sign.

I log onto my email and find a message from her.

A,

I'm free and have the car today. I told my mom I have errands.

Want to be one of my errands?

R

I tell her yes. A million times yes.

Ashley's parents are away for the weekend. Her older brother, Clayton, is in charge. I worry he's going to give me a hassle, but he's got his own things to do, as he tells me repeatedly. I tell him I won't stand in his way.

"You're going out in that?" he asks.

Normally, when an older brother asks this, it means a skirt is too short, or too much cleavage is showing. But in this case, I think he's saying I'm still dressed as the private Ashley, not the public one.

I don't really care, but I have to respect the fact that Ashley would care – probably very much. So I go back and change, and even put on some makeup. I'm fascinated by the life Ashley must lead, being such a knockout. Like being very short or very tall, it must change your whole perspective on the world. If other people see you differently, you'll end up seeing them differently too.

Even her brother defers to her in a way I bet he wouldn't if she were normal looking. He doesn't blink when I tell him I'm going out for the day with my friend Rhiannon.

If your beauty is unquestioned, so many other things can go unquestioned as well.

The minute I get into the car, Rhiannon bursts out laughing.

"You've got to be kidding me," she says.

"What?" I say. Then I get it.

"*What?*" she mocks me. I'm happy she feels comfortable enough to do it, but I'm still being mocked.

"You have to understand – you're the first person to

ever know me in more than one body. I'm not used to this. I don't know how you're going to react."

This makes her a little more serious.

"I'm sorry. It's just that you're this super hot black girl. It makes it very hard for me to have a mental image of you. I have to keep changing it."

"Picture me however you want to picture me. Because odds are, that'll be more true than any of the bodies you see me in."

"I think my imagination needs a little more time to catch up to the situation, okay?"

"Okay. Now where to?"

"Since we've already been to the ocean, I figured today we'd go to a forest."

So off we go, into the woods.

It's not like last time. The radio is on, but we're not singing along. We're sharing the same space, but our thoughts are spreading outside of it.

I want to hold her hand, but I sense it wouldn't work. I know she's not going to reach for my hand, not unless I need it. This is the problem with being so beautiful – it can render you untouchable. And this is the problem with being in a new body each day – the history is there, but it's not visible. It has to be different from last time, because I am different.

We talk a little about Kelsea; Rhiannon called her house yesterday, just to see what would happen. Kelsea's father answered, and when Rhiannon introduced herself as a friend, he said that Kelsea had gone away to deal with some things, and left it at that. Both Rhiannon and I decide to take this as a good sign.

We talk some more, but not about anything that matters. I want to cut through the awkwardness, have Rhiannon treat me like her boyfriend or girlfriend again. But I can't. I'm not.

We get to the park and navigate ourselves away from the other weekenders. Rhiannon finds us a secluded picnic area, and surprises me by taking a feast from the trunk.

I watch as she picks everything out of the picnic hamper. Cheeses. French bread. Hummus. Olives. Salads. Chips. Salsa.

"Are you a vegetarian?" I ask, based on the evidence in front of me.

She nods.

"Why?"

"Because I have this theory that when we die, every animal that we've eaten has a chance at eating us back. So if you're a carnivore and you add up all the animals you've eaten – well, that's a long time in purgatory, being chewed."

"Really?"

She laughs. "No. I'm just sick of the question. I mean, I'm vegetarian because I think it's wrong to eat other sentient creatures. And it sucks for the environment."

"Fair enough." I don't tell her how many times I've accidentally eaten meat while I've been in a vegetarian's body. It's just not something I remember to check for. It's usually the friends' reactions that alert me. I once made a vegan really, really sick at a McDonald's.

Over lunch, we make more small talk. It's not until we've put away the picnic and are walking through the woods that the real words come out.

"I need to know what you want," she says.

"I want us to be together." I say it before I can think it over.

She keeps walking. I keep walking alongside her.

"But we can't be together. You realize that, don't you?"

"No. I don't realize that."

Now she stops. Puts her hand on my shoulder.

"You need to realize it. I can care about you. You can care about me. But we can't be together."

It's so ridiculous, but I ask, "Why?"

"Why? Because one morning you could wake up on the other side of the country. Because I feel like I'm meeting a new person every time I see you. Because you can't be there for me. Because I don't think I can like you no matter what. Not like this."

"Why can't you like me like this?"

"It's too much. You're too perfect right now. I can't imagine being with someone like . . . you."

"But don't look at her – look at me."

"I can't see beyond her, okay? And there's also Justin. I have to think of Justin."

"No, you don't."

"*You don't know*, okay? How many waking hours were you in there? Fourteen? Fifteen? Did you really get to know everything about him while you were in there? Everything about me?"

"You like him because he's a lost boy. Believe me, I've seen it happen before. But do you know what happens to girls who love lost boys? They become lost themselves. Without fail."

"You don't know me –"

"But I know how this works! I know what he's like. He doesn't care about you nearly as much as you care about him. He doesn't care about you nearly as much as I care about you."

"Stop! Just stop."

But I can't. "What do you think would happen if he met me in this body? What if the three of us went out? How much attention do you think he'd pay you? Because he doesn't care about who you are. I happen to think you are about a thousand times more attractive than Ashley is. But do you really think he'd be able to keep his hands to himself if he had a chance?"

"He's not like that."

"Are you sure? Are you really sure?"

"Fine," Rhiannon says. "Let me call him."

Despite my immediate protests, she dials his number and, when he answers, says she has a friend in town that she wants him to meet. Maybe we could all go for dinner? He says fine, but not until Rhiannon says it'll be her treat.

Once she hangs up, we just hang there.

"Happy?" she asks.

"I have no idea," I tell her honestly.

"Me either."

"When are we meeting him?"

"Six."

"Okay," I say. "In the meantime, I want to tell you everything, and I want you to tell me everything in return."

It's so much easier when we're talking about things that are real. We don't have to remind ourselves what the point is, because we're right there in it.

She asks me when I first knew.

"I was probably four or five. Obviously, I knew before that about changing bodies, having a different mom and

179

dad each day. Or grandmother or babysitter or whoever. There was always someone to take care of me, and I assumed that was just what living was – a new life every morning. If I got something wrong – a name, a place, a rule – people would correct me. There was never that big a disturbance. I didn't think of myself as a boy or a girl – I never have. I would just think of myself as a boy or a girl for a day. It was like a different set of clothes.

"The thing that ended up tripping me up was the concept of tomorrow. Because after a while, I started to notice – people kept talking about doing things tomorrow. Together. And if I argued, I would get strange looks. For everyone else, there always seemed to be a tomorrow together. But not for me. I'd say, 'You won't be there,' and they'd say, 'Of course I'll be there.' And then I'd wake up, and they wouldn't be. And my new parents would have no idea why I was so upset.

"There were only two options – something was wrong with everyone else, or something was wrong with me. Because either they were tricking themselves into thinking there was a tomorrow together, or I was the only person who was leaving."

Rhiannon asks, "Did you try to hold on?"

I tell her, "I'm sure I did. But I don't remember it now. I mean, do you remember a lot about when you were five?"

She shakes her head. "Not really. I remember my

mom bringing me and my sister to the shoe store to get new shoes before kindergarten started. I remember learning that green light meant go and red meant stop. I remember coloring them in, and the teacher being a little confused about how to explain yellow. I think she told us to treat it the same as red."

"I learned my letters quickly," I tell her. "I remember the teachers being surprised that I knew them. I imagine they were just as surprised the next day, when I'd forgotten them."

"A five-year-old probably wouldn't notice taking a day off."

"Probably. I don't know."

"I keep asking Justin about it, you know. The day you were him. And it's amazing how clear his fake memories are. He doesn't disagree when I say we went to the beach, but he doesn't really remember it either."

"James, the twin, was like that too. He didn't notice anything wrong. But when I asked him about meeting you for coffee, he didn't remember it at all. He remembered he was at Starbucks – his mind accounted for the time. But it wasn't what actually happened."

"Maybe they remember what you want them to remember."

"I've thought about that. I wish I knew for sure."

We walk farther. Circle a tree with our fingers.

181

"What about love?" she asks. "Have you ever been in love?"

"I don't know that you'd call it love," I say. "I've had crushes, for sure. And there have been days where I've really regretted leaving. There were even one or two people I tried to find, but that didn't work out. The closest was this guy Brennan."

"Tell me about him."

"It was about a year ago. I was working at a movie theater, and he was in town, visiting his cousins, and when he went to get some popcorn, we flirted a little, and it just became this . . . spark. It was this small, one-screen movie theater, and when the movie was running, my job was pretty slow. I think he missed the second half of the movie, because he just came back out and started talking to me more. I ended up having to tell him what happened, so he could pretend he'd been in there most of the time. At the end, he asked for my email, and I made up this email address."

"Like you did for me."

"Exactly like I did for you. And he emailed me later that night, and left the next day back home to Maine, and that proved to be ideal, because then the rest of our relationship could be online. I'd been wearing a nametag, so I had to give him that first name, but I made up a last name, and then I made up an online profile using some of the photos from the real guy's profile. I think his name was Stephen."

"Oh – so you were a boy?"

"Yeah," I say. "Does that matter?"

"No," she tells me. "I guess not." But I can tell it does. A little. Again, her mental picture needs adjustment.

"So we'd email almost every day. We'd even chat. And while I could tell him what was really happening – I emailed him from some very strange places – I still felt like I had something out there in the world that was consistently mine, and that was a pretty new feeling. The only problem was, he wanted more. More photos. Then he wanted to Skype. Then, after about a month of these intense conversations, he started talking about visiting again. His aunt and uncle had already invited him back, and summer was coming."

"Uh-oh."

"Yup – uh-oh. I couldn't figure out a way around it. And the more I tried to dodge it, the more he noticed. All of our conversations became about us. Every now and then, a tangent would get in there, but he'd always drag it back. So I had to end it. Because there wasn't going to be a tomorrow for us."

"Why didn't you tell him the truth?"

"Because I didn't think he could take it. Because I didn't trust him enough, I guess."

"So you called it off."

"I told him I'd met someone else. I borrowed photos from the body I was in at the time. I changed my fake profile's relationship status. Brennan never wanted to talk to me again."

"Poor guy."

"I know. After that, I promised myself I wouldn't get into any more virtual entanglements, as easy as they might seem to be. Because what's the point of something virtual if it doesn't end up being real? And I could never give anyone something real. I could only give them deception."

"Like impersonating their boyfriends," Rhiannon says.

"Yeah. But you have to understand – you were the exception to the rule. Because you were exceptional. And I didn't want it to be based on deception. Which is why you're the first person I've ever told."

"The funny thing is, you say it like it's so unusual that you've only done it once. But I bet a whole lot of people go through their lives without ever telling the truth, not really. And they wake up in the same body and the same life every single morning."

"Why? What aren't you telling me?"

Rhiannon looks me in the eye. "If I'm not telling you something, it's for a reason. Just because you trust me, for whatever reason, it doesn't mean I have to automatically trust you. Trust doesn't work like that."

"That's fair."

"I know it is. But enough of that. Tell me about – I don't know – third grade."

The conversation continues. She learns the reason I now have to access information about allergies before eating anything (after having been nearly killed by a strawberry when I was nine), and I learn the origin of her fear of bunny rabbits (a particularly malevolent creature named Swizzle who liked to escape its cage and sleep on people's faces). She learns about the best mom I ever had (a water park is involved) and I learn about the highs and lows of living with the same mother for your entire life, about how no one can make you angrier, but how you can't really love anyone more. She learns that I haven't always been in Maryland, but only move great distances when the body I'm in moves great distances. I learn that she's never been on an airplane.

She still keeps a physical space between us – there will be no leaning on shoulders or holding hands right now. But if our bodies keep apart, our words do not. I don't mind that.

We return to the car and pick at the remains of the picnic. Then we walk around and talk some more. I am astonished at the number of lives I can remember to tell Rhiannon about, and she is amazed that her single life bears as many stories as my multiple one. Because her normal existence is so foreign to me, so intriguing to me, it starts to feel a little more interesting to her as well.

I could go on like this until midnight. But at five-fifteen, Rhiannon looks at her phone and says, "We better get going. Justin will be waiting for us."

Somehow, I'd managed to forget.

It should be a foregone conclusion. I am a seriously attractive girl. Justin is a typically horny boy.

I am hoping that Rhiannon's theory is right, and that Ashley will only remember what I want her to remember, or what her mind wants her to remember. Not that I'm going to take this far – all I need is confirmation of Justin's willingness, not actual contact. Ashley should be safe.

Rhiannon's picked a clam house off the highway. True to form, I confirm that Ashley doesn't have any shellfish allergies. In truth, Ashley has tricked herself into thinking she's "allergic" to a number of things, as a way of narrowing down her diet. But shellfish never hit that particular watch list.

When she walks into the room, heads actually turn. Most of them are attached to men a good thirty years older than her. I'm sure she's used to it, but it freaks me out.

Even though Rhiannon was concerned about Justin having to wait for us, he ends up coming ten minutes after we do. The look on his face when he first sees me is priceless – when Rhiannon said she had a friend in town, Ashley was *not* what he pictured. He gives Rhiannon her hello, but he's gaping at me when he does.

We take our seats. At first I'm so focused on his reaction that I don't notice Rhiannon's. She's retreating into herself, suddenly quiet, suddenly timid. I can't tell whether it's Justin's presence that's making this happen, or whether it's the combination of his presence and mine.

We've been so wrapped up in our own day that we haven't really prepared for this. So when Justin starts asking the obvious questions – how do Rhiannon and I know each other, and how come he hasn't heard about me before? – I have to jump into the breach. For Rhiannon, fabrication is a ruminative act. For me, lying is a part of my necessary nature, born out of a reality too strange to be believed.

I tell him that my mother and Rhiannon's mother were best friends in high school. I'm now living in Los Angeles (why not?), auditioning for TV shows (because I can). My mother and I are visiting the east coast for a week, and she wanted to check in on her old friend. Rhiannon and I have seen each other off and on through the years, but this is the first time in a while.

Justin appears to be hanging on my every word, but he isn't listening at all. I brush his leg "accidentally" under the table. He pretends he doesn't notice. Rhiannon pretends too.

I'm brazen, but careful with my brazenness. I touch Rhiannon's hand a few times when I'm making a point, so it doesn't seem so unusual when I do it to Justin. I mention a Hollywood star that I once kissed at a party, but make it clear that it was no big deal.

I want Justin to flirt back, but he appears incapable. Especially once there's food in front of him. Then the order of attention goes: food, then Ashley, then Rhiannon. I dip my crab cakes in tartar sauce, and imagine Ashley yelling at me for doing so.

When the food is finished, he focuses back on me. Rhiannon comes alive a little and tries to mimic my movements, first by holding his hand. He doesn't move away, but he also doesn't seem all that into it; he acts like she's embarrassing him. I figure this is a good sign.

Finally, Rhiannon says she has to go to the ladies room. This is my chance to get him to do something irredeemable, get her to see who he truly is.

I start with the leg move. This time, with Rhiannon gone, he doesn't move his leg away.

"Hello there," I say.

"Hello," he says back. And smiles.

"What are you doing after this?" I ask.

"After dinner?"

"Yeah, after dinner."

"I don't know."

"Maybe we should do something," I suggest.

"Yeah. Sure."

"Maybe just the two of us."

*Click.* He finally gets it.

I move in. Touch his hand. Say, "I think that would be fun."

I need him to lean in to me. I need him to give in to what he wants. I need him to take it one step further. All it takes is a yes.

He looks around, to see if Rhiannon is near, and to see if the other guys in the room are seeing this happen.

"Whoa," he says.

"It's okay," I tell him. "I really like you."

He sits back. Shakes his head. "Um . . . no."

I've been too forward. He needs it to be his idea.

"Why not?" I ask.

He looks at me like I'm a complete idiot.

"Why not?" he says. "How about Rhiannon? Jeez."

I'm trying to think of a comeback for that, but there isn't one. And it doesn't even matter, because at this point, Rhiannon returns to the table.

"I don't want this," she says. "Stop."

Justin, fool that he is, thinks he's talking to her.

"I'm not doing anything!" he says, his leg firmly back on his side of the booth now. "Your friend here is a little out of control."

"I don't want this," she repeats.

"It's okay," I say. "I'm sorry."

"You should be!" Justin yells. "God, I don't know how they do things in California, but here, you don't act like that." He stands up. I steal a glance at his groin and see that despite his denials, my flirtation did have at least one effect. But I can't really point it out to Rhiannon.

"I'm gonna go," he says. Then, as if to prove something, he kisses Rhiannon right in front of me. "Thanks, baby," he says. "I'll see you tomorrow."

He doesn't bother saying goodbye to me.

Rhiannon and I sit back down.

"I'm sorry," I tell her again.

"No, it's my fault. I should've known."

I'm waiting for the "I told you so" . . . and then it comes.

"I told you that you don't understand. You can't understand us," she says.

The check comes. I try to pay, but she waves me off.

"It's not your money," she says. And that hurts just as much as anything else.

I know she wants the night to end. I know she wants to drop me off at home, just so she can call Justin and apologize, and make everything right with him again.

# DAY 6008

I go to the computer as soon as I wake up the next morning. But there's no email from Rhiannon. I send her another apology. I send her more thanks for the day. Sometimes when you hit send, you can imagine the message going straight into the person's heart. But other times, like this time, it feels like the words are merely falling into a well.

I head to the social networking sites, searching for something more. I see that Austin and Hugo still list their relationship status as being together – a good sign. Kelsea's page is locked to non-friends. So there's proof of one thing I managed to save, and another where saving is possible.

I have to remind myself it's not all bad.

Then there's Nathan. The coverage of him continues. Reverend Poole is getting more testimony by the day, and the news sites are eating it up. Even the *Onion* is getting into the act, with a headline: WILLIAM CARLOS WILLIAMS TO REVEREND POOLE: 'THE DEVIL MADE ME EAT THE PLUM.' If smart people are parodying it, that's a sure sign that some less smart people are believing it.

But what can I do? Nathan wants his proof, but I'm

not sure I have any to give. All I have is my word, and what kind of proof is that?

Today, I'm a boy named AJ. He has diabetes, so I have a whole other layer of concerns on top of my usual ones. I've been diabetic a couple of times, and the first time was harrowing. Not because diabetes isn't controllable, but because I had to rely on the body's repetitive memories to tell me what to look out for, and how to manage it. I ended up pretending I wasn't feeling well, just so my mother would stay at home and monitor my health with me. Now I feel I can handle it, but I am very attentive to what the body is telling me, much more so than I usually am.

AJ is full of idiosyncrasies that probably don't seem all that idiosyncratic to him anymore. He's a sports fanatic – he plays soccer on the JV squad, but his real love is baseball. His head is full of statistics, facts and figures extrapolated into thousands of different combinations and comparisons. In the meantime, his room is a shrine to the Beatles, and it appears that George is by far his favorite. It isn't hard to figure out what he's going to wear, because his entire wardrobe is blue jeans and different variations of the same button-down shirt. There are also more caps than I can imagine anyone needing, but I figure he's not allowed to wear those to school.

It's a relief, in many ways, to be a guy who doesn't mind riding the bus, who has friends waiting for him when he gets on, who doesn't have to deal with anything more troubling than the fact that he ate breakfast and is still hungry.

It's an ordinary day, and I try to lose myself in that.

But between third and fourth periods, I'm dragged right back. Because there, right in the hall, is Nathan Daldry.

At first I think I might be mistaken. There are plenty of kids who could look like Nathan. But then I see the way the other kids in the hall are reacting to him, as if he's this walking joke. He's trying to make it seem like he doesn't notice the laughter, the snickers, the snarky comments. But he can't hide how uncomfortable he is.

I think: *He deserves this. He didn't have to say a word. He could've just let it slide.*

And I think: *It's my fault. I'm the one who did this to him.*

I access AJ and find out that he and Nathan were good friends in elementary school, and are still friendly now. So it makes sense that when he passes by me, I say hello. And that he says hello back.

I sit with my friends at lunch. Some of the guys ask me about the game last night, and I answer vaguely, accessing the whole time.

Out of the corner of my eye, I see Nathan sit down at his own table, eating alone. I don't remember him being friendless, just dull. But it looks as if he's friendless now.

"I'm going to go talk to Nathan," I tell my friends.

One of them groans. "Really? I'm so sick of him."

"I hear he's doing talk shows now," another chimes in.

"You would think the devil would have more important things to do than take a Subaru for a joyride on a Saturday night."

"Seriously."

I pick up my tray before the conversation can go any further and tell them I'll see them later.

Nathan sees me coming over, but still seems surprised when I sit down with him.

"Do you mind?" I ask.

"No," he says. "Not at all."

I don't know what I'm doing. I think of his last email – *PROVE IT* – and half-expect those words to flash from his eyes, for there to be some challenge that I will have to meet. I am the proof. I am right in front of him. But he doesn't know that.

"So how are you doing?" I ask, picking up a fry, trying to act like this is a normal lunchtime conversation between friends.

"Okay, I guess." I get a sense that for all the attention

people have been giving him, not many people have been asking him how he's doing.

"So what's new?"

He glances over my shoulder. "Your friends are looking at us."

I turn around, and everyone from my old table suddenly looks anywhere but here.

"Whatever," I say. "Don't pay attention to them. To any of them."

"I'm not. They don't understand."

"I understand. I mean, I understand that they don't understand."

"I know."

"It must be pretty overwhelming, though, having everyone so interested. And all the blogs and stuff. And this reverend."

I wonder if I've pushed too far. But Nathan seems happy to talk. AJ is a good guy.

"Yeah, he really gets it. He knew people would give me grief. But he told me I had to be stronger. I mean, having people laugh is nothing compared to surviving a possession."

*Surviving a possession.* I have never thought about what I do in those terms. I never thought my presence was something that anyone would have to survive.

Nathan sees me thinking. "What?" he asks.

"I'm just curious – what do you remember from that day?"

Now a wariness creeps into his expression.

"Why are you asking?"

"Curiosity, I guess. I'm not doubting you. Not at all. I just feel like, in all the things I've read and all the things people have said, I never really got to hear your side. It's all been second hand and third hand and probably seventh or eighth hand, so I figured I'd just come and ask you first hand."

I know I'm on dangerous ground here. I can't make AJ too much of a confidant, because tomorrow will come and he might not remember anything that's been said, and that might make Nathan suspicious. But at the same time, I want to know what he remembers.

Nathan wants to talk. I can see it. He knows he's stepped off his own map. And while he won't pull back, he also regrets it a little. I don't think he ever meant for it to take over his life.

"It was a pretty normal day," he tells me. "Nothing unusual. I was home with my parents. I did chores, that kind of thing. And then – I don't know. Something must have happened. Because I made up this story about a school musical and borrowed their car for the night. I don't remember the musical part – they told me that later. But there I was, driving around. And I had these

197

. . . urges. Like I was being drawn somewhere."

He pauses.

"Where?" I ask.

He shakes his head. "I don't know. This is the weird part. There are a few hours there that are completely blank. I have this sense of not being in control of my body, but that's it. I have flashes of a party, but I have no idea where, or who else was there. Then suddenly I'm being woken up by a policeman. And I haven't drunk a sip. I haven't done any drugs. They tested for that, you know."

"What if you had a seizure?"

"Why would I borrow my parents' car to have a seizure? No, there was something else in control. The reverend says I must have wrestled with the devil. Like Jacob. I must have known my body was being used for something evil, and I fought it. And then, when I won, the devil left me by the side of the road."

He believes this. He genuinely believes this.

And I can't tell him it's not true. I can't tell him what really happened. Because if I do, AJ will be in danger. I will be in danger.

"It didn't have to be the devil," I say.

Nathan becomes defensive. "I just know, okay? And I'm not the only one. There are lots of people out there who've experienced the same thing. I've chatted with a few of them. It's scary how many things we have in common."

"Are you afraid it will happen again?"

"No. I'm prepared this time. If the devil is anywhere near me, I'll know what to do."

I sit right there across from him and listen.

He doesn't recognize me.

*I am not the devil.*

This thought is what echoes through my mind the rest of the day.

*I am not the devil, but I could be.*

Looking at it from afar, looking at it from a perspective like Nathan's, I can see how scary it could be. Because what's to stop me from doing harm? What punishment would there be if I took the pencil in my hand and gauged it into the eye of the girl sitting next to me in chem class? Or worse. I could easily get away with the perfect crime. The body that committed the murder would inevitably get caught, but the murderer would go free. Why haven't I thought of this before?

I have the potential to be the devil.

But then I think, *Stop.* I think, *No.* Because, really, does that make me any different from everyone else? Yes, I have more likelihood of getting away with it, but certainly we all have the potential to commit the crime.

We choose not to. Every single day, we choose not to. I am no different than that.

I am not the devil.

There is still no word from Rhiannon. Whether her silence is coming from her confusion or coming from a desire to be rid of me, I have no way of knowing.

I write to her and say, simply:

I have to see you again.

A

# DAY 6009

There's still no word from her the next morning.

I get in the car and drive.

The car belongs to Adam Cassidy. He should be in school. But I call the office pretending to be his father and say he has a doctor's appointment.

It may last the entire day.

It's a two-hour drive. I know I should spend it getting to know Adam Cassidy, but he seems incidental to me right now. I used to inhabit lives like this all the time – testing the bare minimum I needed to know in order to get through the day. I got so good at it that I made it through a few days without accessing once. I'm sure these were very blank days for the bodies I was in, because they were extraordinarily blank days for me.

Most of the drive, I think about Rhiannon. How to get her back. How to keep in her graces. How to make this work.

It's the last part that's the hardest.

When I get to her school, I park where Amy Tran parked. The school day is already in full swing, so when I open the doors, I jump right into the fray. It's between periods, and I have all of two minutes to find her.

I don't know where she is. I don't even know what period's starting. I just push through the halls, looking for her. People brush by, tell me to watch where I'm going. I don't care. There is everyone else, and there is her. I am only focused on her.

I let the universe tell me where to go. I rely purely on instinct, knowing that instinct comes from somewhere other than me, somewhere other than this body.

She is turning into a classroom. But she stops. Looks up. Sees me.

I don't know how to explain it. I am an island in the hall, as people push around me. She is another island. I see her, and she knows exactly who I am. There is no way for her to know this. But she knows.

She walks away from the classroom, walks toward me. Another bell rings and the rest of the people drain out of the hall, leaving us alone together.

"Hey," she says.

"Hey," I say.

"I thought you might come."

"Are you mad?"

"No, I'm not mad." She glances back at the classroom. "Although Lord knows you're not good for my attendance record."

"I'm not good for anybody's attendance record."

202

"What's your name today?"

"A," I tell her. "For you, it's always A."

She has a test next period that she can't skip, so we stay on the school grounds. When we start to encounter other kids – kids without classes this period, kids also cutting – she grows a little more cautious.

"Is Justin in class?" I ask, to give her fear a name.

"Yeah. If he decided to go."

We find an empty classroom and go inside. From all the Shakespearean paraphernalia hanging on the walls, I'm guessing we're in an English classroom. Or drama.

We sit in the back row, out of sight of the window in the door.

"How did you know it was me?" I have to ask.

"The way you looked at me," she says. "It couldn't have been anyone else."

This is what love does: It makes you want to rewrite the world. It makes you want to choose the characters, build the scenery, guide the plot. The person you love sits across from you, and you want to do everything in your power to make it possible, endlessly possible. And when it's just the two of you, alone in a room, you can pretend that this is how it is, this is how it will be.

*

I take her hand and she doesn't pull away. Is this because something between us has changed, or is it only because my body has changed? Is it easier for her to hold Adam Cassidy's hand?

The electricity in the air is muted. This is not going to lead to anything more than an honest conversation.

"I'm sorry about the other night," I say again.

"I deserve part of the blame. I never should have called him."

"What did he say? Afterward?"

"He kept calling you 'that black bitch'."

"Charming."

"I think he sensed it was a trap. I don't know. He just knew something was off."

"Which is probably why he passed the test."

Rhiannon pulls away. "That's not fair."

"I'm sorry."

I wonder why it is that she's strong enough to say no to me, but not strong enough to say no to him.

"What do you want to do?" I ask her.

She matches my glance perfectly. "What do you want me to do?"

"I want you to do whatever you feel is best for you."

"That's the wrong answer," she tells me.

"Why is it the wrong answer?"

"Because it's a lie."

*You are so close,* I think. *You are so close, and I can't reach you.*

"Let's go back to my original question," I say. "What do you want to do?"

"I don't want to throw everything away for something uncertain."

"What about me is uncertain?

She laughs. "Really? Do I have to explain it to you?"

"Besides that. You know you are the most important person I've ever had in my life. That's certain."

"In just two weeks. That's uncertain."

"You know more about me than anyone else does."

"But I can't say the same for you. Not yet."

"You can't deny that there's something between us."

"No. There is. When I saw you today – I didn't know I'd been waiting for you until you appeared. And then all of that waiting rushed through me in a second. That's something . . . but I don't know if it's certainty."

*I know what I'm asking of you,* I want to say. But I stop myself. Because I realize that would be another lie. And she'd call me on it.

She looks at the clock. "I have to get ready for my test. And you have another life to get back to."

I can't help myself. I ask, "Don't you want to see me?"

She holds there for a moment. "I do. And I don't. You

205

would think it would make things easier, but it actually makes them harder."

"So I shouldn't just show up here?"

"Let's stick to email for now. Okay?"

And just like that, the universe goes wrong. Just like that, all the enormity seems to shrink into a ball and float away from my reach.

I feel it, and she doesn't.

Or I feel it, and she won't.

# DAY 6010

I am four hours away from her.

I'm a girl named Chevelle, and I can't stand the idea of going to school today. So I feign sickness, get permission to stay home. I try to read, play video games, surf the web, do all the things I used to do to fill the time.

None of them works. The time still feels empty.

I keep checking my email.

Nothing from her.

Nothing.

Nothing.

# DAY 6011

I am only thirty minutes away from her.

I am woken at dawn by my sister shaking me, shouting my name, Valeria.

I think I'm late for school.

But no. I'm late for work.

I am a maid. An underage, illegal maid.

Valeria doesn't speak English, so all of the thoughts I have to access are in Spanish. I barely know what's happening. It takes me time to translate what's going on.

There are four of us in the apartment. We put on our uniforms and a van comes to pick us up. I am the youngest, the least respected. My sister speaks to me, and I nod. I feel like my insides are twisting, and at first I think it's just because of the shock of the situation. Then I realize they really are twisting. Cramps.

I find the words and tell my sister this. She understands, but I'm still going to have to work.

More women join us in the van. And another girl my age. Some people chat, but my sister and I don't say a word to any of them.

The van starts dropping us off at people's homes. Always at least two of us per house, sometimes three or four. I am paired with my sister.

I am in charge of bathrooms. I must scrub the toilets. Remove the hairs from the shower. Shine the mirrors until they gleam.

Each of us is in our own room. We do not talk. We don't play music. We just work.

I am sweating in my uniform. The cramps will not go away. The medicine cabinets are full, but I know that I am here to clean, not to take. Nobody would miss two Midol, but it's not worth the risk.

When I get to the master bathroom, the woman of the house is still in her bedroom, talking on the phone. She doesn't think I can understand a word she says. What a shock it would be were Valeria to stomp right in and start talking to her about the laws of thermodynamics, or the life of Thomas Jefferson, in flawless English.

After two hours, we are done with the house. I think that will be it, but there are four more houses after that. By the end, I can barely move, and my sister, seeing this, does the bathrooms with me. We are a team, and that kinship gives the day its only memory worth keeping.

By the time we get home, I can barely speak. I force myself to have dinner, but it's a silent meal. Then I head to bed, leaving room for my sister beside me.

Email is not an option.

# DAY 6012

I am an hour away from her.

I open Sallie Swain's eyes and search her room for a computer. Before I'm fully awake, I am loading up my email.

> A,
>
> I'm sorry I didn't get to write to you yesterday. I meant to, but then all these other things happened (none of them important, just time-consuming). Even though it was hard to see you, it was good to see you. I mean it. But taking a break and thinking things out makes sense.
>
> How was your day? What did you do?
>
> R

Does she really want to know, or is she just being polite? I feel as if she could be talking to anybody. And while I once thought what I wanted from her was this normal, everyday tone, now that I have it, the normalcy disappoints.

I write her back and tell her about the last two days. Then I tell her I have to go – I can't skip school today, because Sallie Swain has a big cross-country meet, and it wouldn't be fair for her to miss it.

I run. I am made for running. Because when you run, you could be anyone. You hone yourself into a body, nothing more or less than a body. You respond as a body, to the body. If you are racing to win, you have no thoughts but the body's thoughts, no goals but the body's goals. You obliterate yourself in the name of speed. You negate yourself in order to make it past the finish line.

# DAY 6013

I am an hour and a half away from her, and I am part of a happy family.

The Stevens family does not let Saturdays go to waste. No, Mrs Stevens wakes Daniel up at nine o'clock on the dot and tells him to get ready for a drive. By the time he's out of the shower, Mr Stevens has loaded the car and Daniel's two sisters are raring to go.

First stop is the art museum in Baltimore for a Winslow Homer exhibit. Then there's lunch at Inner Harbor, followed by a long trip to the aquarium. Then an IMAX version of a Disney movie, for the girls, and dinner at a seafood restaurant that's so famous they don't feel the need to put the word *famous* in their name.

There are brief moments of tension – a sister who is bored by the dolphins, a spot where Dad gets frustrated about the lack of available parking spaces. But for the most part, everyone remains happy. They are so caught up in their happiness that they don't realize I'm not really a part of it. I am wandering along the periphery. I am like the people in the Winslow Homer paintings, sharing the same room with them but not really there. I am like the fish in the aquarium, thinking in a different language, adapting to a life that's not my natural habitat. I am the people in the other cars, each with his or her own story, but passing too quickly to be noticed or understood.

It is a good day, and that certainly helps me more than a bad day. There are moments when I don't think about her, or even think about me. There are moments I just sit in my frame, float in my tank, ride in my car and say nothing, think nothing that connects me to anything at all.

# DAY 6014

I am forty minutes away from her.

It's Sunday, so I decide to see what Reverend Poole is up to.

Orlando, the boy whose body I'm in, rarely wakes before noon on Sunday, so if I keep my typing quiet, his parents will leave me alone.

Reverend Poole has set up a website for people to tell their stories of possession. Already there are hundreds of posts and videos.

Nathan's post is perfunctory, as if it's been summarized from his earlier statements. He has not made a video. I don't learn anything new.

Other stories are more elaborate. Some are clearly the work of nutjobs – clinically paranoid people who need professional help, not arenas in which to vent their hyperbolic conspiracy theories. Other testimonials, however, are almost painfully sincere. There's a woman who genuinely feels that Satan struck her at the checkout line in the supermarket, filling her with the urge to steal. And there's a man whose son killed himself, who believes that the son must have been possessed by real demons, rather than fighting the more metaphorical ones inside.

Since I only inhabit people around my age, I look for the teenagers. Poole must screen each and every thing that appears on the site, because there's no parody, no sarcasm. So teenagers are few and far between. There is one, however, from Montana, whose story makes me shiver. He says he was possessed, but only for one day. Nothing major happened, but he knows he wasn't in control of his body.

I have never been to Montana. I'm sure of it.

But what he's describing is a lot like what I do.

There is a link on Poole's site:

**IF YOU BELIEVE THE DEVIL IS WITHIN YOU,**
**CLICK HERE OR CALL THIS NUMBER.**

But if the devil is truly within you, why would he click or call?

I go on my old email and find that Nathan's tried to get in touch with me again.

No proof, then?

Get help.

He even attaches the link to Poole's page. I want to

write back to him and point out that he and I talked just the other day. I want him to ask his friend AJ how his Monday was. I want him to fear that I could be there at any moment, in any person.

*No*, I think. *Don't feel that way.*

It was so much easier when I didn't want anything.

Not getting what you want can make you cruel.

I check my other email and find another message from Rhiannon. She tells me vaguely about her weekend and asks me vaguely about my weekend.

I try to sleep for the rest of the day.

# DAY 6015

I wake up, and I'm not four hours away from her, or one hour, or even fifteen minutes.

No, I wake up in her house.

In her room.

In her body.

At first I think I'm still asleep, dreaming. I open my eyes, and I could be in any girl's room – a room she's lived in for a long time, with Madame Alexander dolls sharing space with eyeliner pencils and fashion magazines. I am sure it is only a dreamworld trick when I access my identity and find it's Rhiannon who appears. Have I had this dream before? I don't think so. But in a way, it makes sense. If she's the thought, the hope, the concern under my every waking moment, then why wouldn't she permeate my sleeping hours as well?

But I'm not dreaming. I am feeling the pressure of the pillow against my face. I am feeling the sheets around my legs. I am breathing. In dreams, we never bother to breathe.

I instantly feel like the world has turned to glass. Every moment is delicate. Every movement is a risk. I know she wouldn't want me here. I know the horror she would be feeling right now. The complete loss of control.

Everything I do could break something. Every word I say. Every move I make.

I look around some more. Some girls and boys obliterate their rooms as they grow older, thinking they have to banish all their younger incarnations in order to convincingly inhabit a new one. But Rhiannon is more secure with her past than that. I see pictures of her and her family when she is three, eight, ten, fourteen. A stuffed penguin still keeps watch over her bed. J D Salinger sits next to Dr Seuss on her bookshelf.

I pick up one of the photographs. If I wanted to, I could try to access the day it was taken. It looks like she and her sister are at a country fair. Her sister is wearing some kind of prize ribbon. It would be so easy for me to find out what it is. But then it wouldn't be Rhiannon telling me.

I want her here next to me, giving me the tour. Now I feel like I've broken in.

The only way to get through this is to live this day as Rhiannon would want me to. If she knows I was here – and I have a feeling she will – I want her to be certain that I didn't take any advantage. I know instinctively that this is not the way I want to learn anything. This is not the way I want to gain anything.

Because of this, it feels like all I can do is lose.

This is how it feels to raise her arm.

This is how it feels to blink her eyes.

This is how it feels to turn her head.

This is how it feels to run her tongue over her lips, to put her feet on the floor.

This is the weight of her. This is the height of her. This is the angle from which she sees the world.

"Hello."

This is what her voice sounds like from the inside.

This is what her voice sounds like when she's by herself.

Her mother shuffles past me in the hallway, awake but not by her own choice. It has been a long night for her, leading into a short morning. She says she's going to try to go back to sleep, but adds that it's not likely.

Rhiannon's father is in the kitchen, about to leave for work. His "good morning" holds less complaint. But he's in a rush, and I have a sense that those two words are all Rhiannon's going to get. I get some cereal as he searches for his keys, then say a goodbye echo to his own quick goodbye.

I decide not to take a shower, or even to change out

of last night's underwear. I feel naked enough looking in the mirror and seeing Rhiannon's face. I can't push it any further than that. Brushing her hair is already too intimate. Putting on makeup. Even putting on shoes. To experience her body's balance within the word, the sensation of her skin from the inside, touching her face and receiving the touch from both sides – it's unavoidable and incredibly intense. I try to think only as me, but I can't stop feeling that I'm her.

I have to access to find my keys, then find my way to school. Maybe I should stay home, but I'm not sure I could bear being alone as her for that long without any distractions. The radio station is tuned to the news, which is unexpected. Her sister's graduation tassel hangs from the rearview mirror.

I look to the passenger seat, expecting Rhiannon to be there, looking at me, telling me where to go.

I am going to try to avoid Justin. I go early to my locker, get my books, then head directly to my first class. As friends trickle into the classroom, I make as much conversation as I can. Nobody notices any difference – not because they don't care, but because it's early in the morning, and nobody's expected to be fully there. I've been so hung up on Justin that I haven't realized how much Rhiannon's friends are part of her life. I realize that until now, the most I've really seen of her full life has been when I was Amy Tran, visiting the school for the day. Because she doesn't spend her day alone. These friends are not what she wants to escape when she makes her escape.

"Did you get to all the bio?" her friend Rebecca asks. At first I think she's asking to copy my homework, but then I realize she's offering hers. Sure enough, Rhiannon has a few problems left to do. I thank Rebecca and start copying away.

When class begins and the teacher starts to lecture, all I need to do is listen and take notes.

*Remember this*, I tell Rhiannon. *Remember how ordinary it is*.

I can't help but get glimpses of things I've never seen before. Doodles in her notebook of trees and mountains. The light imprint her socks leave on her ankles. A small red birthmark at the base of her left thumb. These are probably things she never notices. But because I'm new to her, I see everything.

This is how it feels to hold a pencil in her hand.

This is how it feels to fill her lungs with air.

This is how it feels to press her back against the chair.

This is how it feels to touch her ear.

This is what the world sounds like to her. This is what she hears every day.

*

I allow myself one memory. I don't choose it. It just rises, and I don't cut it off.

Rhiannon's friend Rebecca is sitting next to me, chewing gum. At one point in class, she's so bored that she takes it out of her mouth and starts playing with it between her fingers. And I remember a time she did this in sixth grade. The teacher caught her, and Rebecca was so surprised at being caught that she startled, and the gum went flying from her hand and into Hannah Walker's hair. Hannah didn't know what had happened at first, and all the kids started laughing at her, making the teacher more furious. I was the one who leaned over to her and told her there was gum in her hair. I was the one who worked it out with my fingers, careful not to get it knotted further in. I got it all out. I remember I got it all out.

I try to avoid Justin at lunch, but I fail.

I'm in a hallway nowhere near either of our lockers or the lunchroom, and he ends up being there too. He's not happy to see me or unhappy to see me; he regards my presence as a fact, no different than the bell between periods.

"Wanna take it outside?" he asks.

"Sure," I say, not really knowing what I'm agreeing to.

In this case, "outside" means a pizza place two blocks from the school. We get slices and Cokes. He pays for himself, but makes no offer to pay for me. Which is fine.

He's in a talkative mood, focusing on what I imagine is his favorite theme: the injustices perpetrated against him by everyone else, all the time. It's a pretty wide conspiracy, involving everything from his car's faulty ignition to his father's nagging about college to his English teacher's "gay way of talking". I'm barely following his conversation, and *following* very much feels like the right word, because this conversation is designed for me to be at least five steps behind. He doesn't want my opinion. Any time I offer something, he just lets it sit there on the table between us, doesn't pick it up.

As he goes on about what a bitch Stephanie is being to Steve, and keeps shoving pizza into his face, and looks at the table much more than he looks at me, I must struggle against the palpable temptation to do something drastic. Although he doesn't realize it, the power is all mine. All it would take is a minute – less – to break up with him. All it would take are a few well-chosen words to cut the tether. He could counterattack with tears or rage or promises, and I could withstand every single one.

It is so much what I want, but I don't open my mouth. I don't use this power. Because I know that this kind of ending would never lead to the beginning I want. If I end things like this, Rhiannon will never forgive me. Not only might she undo it all tomorrow, she would also define me by my betrayal for as long as I remained in her life, which wouldn't be long.

I hope she realizes: the whole time, Justin never notices. She can see me in whatever body I'm in, but he can't see she's missing. He's not looking that closely.

Then he calls her Silver. Just a simple, "Let's go, Silver," when we're done. I think maybe I've heard him wrong. So I access, and there it is. A moment between them. They've been reading *The Outsiders* for English class, lying on his bed side by side with the same book open, she a little farther along. She thinks the book's a relic from when weepy gang boys bonded over *Gone with the Wind*, but she quiets herself when she sees how much it's affecting him. She stays there after she's finished, starts reading the beginning again until he's done. The he closes the book and says, "Wow. I mean, nothing gold can stay. How true is that?" She doesn't want to break the moment, doesn't want to question what it means. And she's rewarded when he smiles and says, "I guess that means we'll have to be silver." When she leaves that night, he calls out, "So long, Silver!" And it stays.

*

When we head back to school, we don't hold hands, or even talk. When we part, he doesn't wish me a good afternoon or thank me for the time we just had together. He doesn't even say he'll see me soon. He just assumes it.

I am hyperaware – as he leaves me, as I am surrounded by other people – of the perilous nature of what I am attempting, of the butterfly effect that threatens to flutter its wings with every interaction. If you think about it hard enough, if you trace potential reverberations long enough, every step can be a false step, any move can lead to an unintended consequence.

Who am I ignoring that I shouldn't be ignoring? What am I not saying that I should be saying? What won't I notice that she would absolutely notice? While I'm out in the public hallways, what private languages am I not hearing?

When we look at a crowd, our eyes naturally go to certain people, whether we know them or not. But my glance right now is blank. I know what I see, but not what she'd see.

The world is still glass.

This is how it feels to read words through her eyes.

This is how it feels to turn a page with her hand.

This is how it feels when her ankles cross.

This is how it feels to lower her head so her hair hides her eyes from view.

This is what the handwriting looks like. This is how it is made. This is one of the marks she makes that marks her as an individual. This is how she signs her name.


There's a quiz in English class. It's *Tess of the D'Urbervilles*, which I've read. I think Rhiannon does okay.

I access enough to know she doesn't have any plans after school. Justin finds her before last period and asks her if she wants to do something. It's clear to me what this something will be, and I can't see much benefit to it.

"What do you want to do?" I ask.

He looks at me like I'm an imbecile puppy.

"What do you think?"

"Homework?"

He snorts. "Yeah, we can call it that, if you want."

I need a lie. Really, what I want to do is say yes and then blow him off. But there could be repercussions for that tomorrow. So instead I tell him I have to take my mom to some doctor for her sleep problems. It's a real drag, but they'll be drugging her up and she probably won't be able to drive herself home.

"Well, as long as they give her plenty of pills," he

says. "I love your mom's pills."

He leans in for a kiss and I have to do it. Amazing how it's the same two bodies as three weeks ago, but the kiss couldn't be more different. Before, when our tongues touched, it felt like another form of intimate conversation. Now it feels like he's shoving something alien and gross into my mouth.

"Go get some pills," he says when we break apart.

I hope my mom has some extra birth control I can slip him.

We have been to an ocean together, and a forest. So today I decide we should go to a mountain.

A quick search shows me the nearest place to climb. I have no idea if Rhiannon's ever been here, but I'm not sure that matters.

She's not really dressed for hiking – her Converse don't have a whole lot of tread left in them. I plunge forward nonetheless, taking a water bottle and a phone with me, and leaving everything else in the car.

Again it's a Monday, and the trails are largely clear. Every now and then I'll pass another hiker on his or her way down, and we'll nod or say hello, in the way that people surrounded by acres of silence do. The paths are haphazardly marked, or perhaps I'm just not attentive enough. I can feel the incline as it's measured by Rhiannon's leg muscles, can feel her breath shift into more challenging air. I keep going.

For our afternoon, I've decided to attempt to give Rhiannon the satisfaction of being fully alone. Not the lethargy of lying on the couch or the dull monotony of drifting off in math class. Not the midnight wandering in a sleeping house or the pain of being left in a room after the door has been slammed shut. This alone is not a variation of any of those. This alone is its own being. Feeling the body, but not using it to sidetrack the mind. Moving with purpose but not in a rush. Conversing not with the person next to you, but with all of the elements. Sweating and aching and climbing and making sure not to slip, not to fall, not to get too lost, but lost enough.

And at the end, the pause. At the top, the view. Grappling with the last steep incline, the final turns of the path, and finding yourself above it all. It's not that there's a spectacular view. It's not that we've reached the peak of Everest. But here we are, at the highest point the eye can see, not counting the clouds, the air, the lazy sun. I am eleven again; we are atop that tree. The air feels cleaner because when the world is below us, we allow ourselves to breathe fully. When no one else is around, we open ourselves to the quieter astonishments that enormity can offer.

*Remember this,* I implore Rhiannon as I look out over the trees, as I catch her breath. *Remember this sensation. Remember that we were here.*

I sit down on a rock and drink down some water. I know I am in her body, but it feels very much like she is here with me. Like we are two separate people, together, sharing this.

I have dinner with her parents. When they ask me what I did today, I tell them. I'm sure I tell them more than Rhiannon would, more than the day usually allows.

"That sounds wonderful," her mother says.

"Just be careful out there," her father adds. Then he changes the conversation to something that happened at work, and my day, briefly registered, becomes solely my own again.

I do her homework as best as I can. I don't check her email, afraid that there will be something there that she wouldn't want me to see. I don't check my own email, because she's the only person I'd want to hear from. There's a book on her night table, but I don't read from it, for fear that she won't remember what I've read, and will have to read it again anyway. I thumb through some magazines.

Finally, I decide to leave her a note. It's the only

way she'll know for sure that I've been here. Another palpable temptation is to pretend that none of this has happened, to deny any accusation she makes based on whatever remnant of memory remains. But I want to be truthful. The only way this will work is if we are entirely truthful.

So I tell her. At the very beginning of my letter, I ask her to try to remember the day as much as possible before she reads on, so the contents won't taint what is really left in her mind. I explain that I never would have chosen to be in her body, that it isn't something I have control over. I tell her I tried to respect her day as much as I knew how, and that I hoped not to have caused any disruption in her life. Then, in her own handwriting, I map out our day for her. It is the first time I've ever written to the person whose life I've occupied, and it feels both strange and comfortable, knowing that Rhiannon will be the reader of these words. There are so many explanations I can leave unsaid. The fact that I am writing the letter at all is an expression of faith – faith both in her and in the belief that trust can lead to trust, and truth can lead to truth.

This is how it feels as her eyelids close.

This is how sleep will taste to her.

This is how night touches her skin.

This is how the house noises sing her to bed.

This is the goodbye she feels every night. This is how her day ends.

I curl up in bed, still wearing my clothes. Now that the day is almost done, the world of glass recedes, the butterfly threat diminishes. I imagine that we're both here in this bed, that my invisible body is nestled against hers. We are breathing at the same pace, our chests rising and falling in unison. We have no need to whisper, because at this distance, all we need is thought. Our eyes close at the same time. We feel the same sheets against us, the same night. Our breath slows together. We split into different versions of the same dream. Sleep takes us at the exact same time.

# DAY 6016

A,

I think I remember everything. Where are you today?
Instead of writing a long email, I want to talk.

R

I am roughly two hours away from her when I read
this email, in the body of a boy named Dylan Cooper.
He's a hardcore design geek, and his room is an orchard
of Apple products. I access him enough to know that
when he really, really likes a girl, he creates a font and
names it after her.

I write back to Rhiannon and tell her where I am. She
writes back immediately – she must be waiting by her
computer – and asks me if I can meet her after school.
We arrange to meet at the Clover Bookstore.

Dylan is a charmer. He also, from what I can tell, has
crushes on three different girls at the same time. I spend
the day trying not to commit him any closer to any of
them. He will have to figure out for himself which font
he prefers.

I am a half hour early to the bookstore, but I'm too nervous to read anything but the faces of the people around me.

She walks in the door, also early. I don't need to stand or wave. She looks around the room, sees me and the way I'm looking at her, and knows.

"Hey," she says.

"Hey," I say back.

"It feels like the morning after," she tells me.

"I know," I say.

She's gotten us coffee, and we sit there at the table with the cups sheltered in our hands.

I see some of the things I noticed yesterday – the birthmark, the scattering of pimples on her forehead. But they don't matter to me nearly as much as the complete picture.

She doesn't seem freaked out. She doesn't seem angry. If anything, she seems at peace with what's happened. When the shock wears off, you always hope there's understanding underneath. And with Rhiannon, it seems as if the understanding has already arrived. Any vestige of doubt has been swept away.

"I woke up and I knew something was different," she tells me. "Even before I saw your letter. It wasn't the usual disorientation. But I didn't feel like I'd missed

233

a day. It was like I woke up and something had been
. . . added. Then I saw your letter and started reading,
and immediately I knew it was true. It had actually
happened. I stopped when you told me to stop, and
tried to remember everything about yesterday. It was
all there. Not the things I'd usually forget, like waking
up or brushing my teeth. But climbing that mountain.
Having lunch with Justin. Dinner with my parents. Even
writing the letter itself – I had a memory of that. Even
though it shouldn't make sense – why would I write a
letter to myself for the next morning? But in my mind, it
makes sense."

"Do you feel me there? In your memories."

She shakes her head. "No. Not in the way you'd
think. I don't feel you in control of things, or in my
body, or anything. I feel like you were with me. Like, I
can feel your presence there, but it's outside of me."

She stops. Starts again. "It's insane that we're having
this conversation."

But I want to know more.

"I wanted you to remember everything," I tell her.
"And it sounds like your mind went along with that. Or
maybe it wanted you to remember everything too."

"I don't know. I'm just glad I do."

We talk more about the day, more about how strange

this is. Finally, she says, "Thank you for not messing up my life. And for keeping my clothes on. Unless, of course, you don't want me to remember that you sneaked a peek."

"No peeks were sneaked."

"I believe you. Amazingly, I believe you about everything."

I can tell there's something else she wants to say.

"What?" I ask.

"It's just – do you feel you know me more now? Because the weird thing is . . . I feel I know you more. Because of what you did, and what you didn't do. Isn't that strange? All this time, I assumed it would be the other way around, that you would find out more about me . . . but I'm not sure that's true."

"I got to meet your parents," I say.

"And what was your impression?"

"I think they both care about you, in their own way."

She laughs. "Well said."

"Well, it was nice to meet them."

"I'll be sure to remember that when you really meet them. 'Mom and Dad, this is A. You think you're meeting him for the first time, but actually, you've met him before, when he was in my body.'"

"I'm sure that'll go over well."

Of course, we both know it won't go over at all. There's no way for me to meet her parents. Not as myself.

I don't say it, and neither does she. I don't even know if she's thinking it in the pause that ensues. But I am.

"It can never happen again, right?" she eventually asks. "You're never the same person twice."

"Correct. It will never happen again."

"No offense, but I'm relieved I don't have to go to sleep wondering if I'm going to wake up with you in control. Once, I guess I can deal with. But don't make a habit of it."

"I promise – I want to make a habit of being with you, but not that way."

And there it is: I had to go and bring up the issue of where we go from here. We got through the past, are enjoying the present, but now I push it and we stumble on the future.

"You've seen my life," she says. "Tell me a way you think this can work."

"We'll find a way," I tell her.

"That's not an answer. It's a hope."

"Hope's gotten us this far. Not answers."

She gives me a hint of a grin. "Good point." She takes a sip of coffee, and I can tell another question's coming. "I know this is weird, but . . . I keep wondering. Are you really not a boy or a girl? I mean, when you were in my body, did you feel more . . . at home than you would in the body of a boy?"

It's interesting to me that this is the thing she's hung up on.

"I'm just me," I tell her. "I always feel at home and I never feel at home. That's just the way it is."

"And when you're kissing someone?"

"Same thing."

"And during sex?"

"Is Dylan blushing?" I ask. "Right now, is he blushing?"

"Yeah," Rhiannon says.

"Good. Because I know I am."

"No one?"

"It wouldn't be fair of me to –"

"No one!"

"I am so glad you find this funny."

"Sorry."

"There was this one girl."

"Really?"

"Yeah. Yesterday. When I was in your body. Don't you remember? I think you might have gotten her pregnant."

"That's not funny!" she says. But she's laughing.

"I only have eyes for you," I say.

Just six words and the conversation turns serious again. I can feel it like a shift in the air, like when a cloud moves over the sun. The laughter stops and we sit there in the moment after it's faded away.

"A —" she starts. But I don't want to hear it. I don't want to hear about Justin or impossibilities or any of the other reasons why we can't be together.

"Not now," I say. "Let's stay on the nice note."

"Okay," she says. "I can do that."

She asks me about more of the things I noticed when I was in her body, and I tell her about the birthmark, about different people I noticed in her classes, about her parents' concern. I share the Rebecca memory, but don't tell her my observations about Justin, because she already knows those things, whether or not she admits them to me or herself. And I don't mention the slight wrinkles around her eyes or her pimples, because I know they would bother her, when really they add something real to her beauty.

Both of us have to be home for dinner, but the only way I'm willing to let her leave is to extract a promise that we'll share time together soon. Tomorrow. Or if not tomorrow, the next day.

"How can I say no?" she says. "I'm dying to see who you'll be next."

I know it's a joke, but I have to tell her, "I'll always be A."

She stands up and kisses me on the forehead.

"I know," she says. "That's why I want to see you."

We leave on a nice note.

# DAY 6017

I have gone two days without thinking about Nathan, but it's clear that Nathan hasn't gone two days without thinking about me.

7:30 p.m., MONDAY
I still want proof.

8:14 p.m., MONDAY
Why aren't you talking to me?

11:43 p.m., MONDAY
You did this to me. I deserve an explanation.

6:13 a.m., TUESDAY
I can't sleep anymore. I wonder if you're going to come back. I wonder what you'll do to me. Are you mad?

2:30 p.m., TUESDAY
You have to be the devil. Only the devil would leave me like this.

2:12 a.m., WEDNESDAY
Do you have any idea what it's like for me now?

240

The burden I feel is the burden of responsibility, which is a tricky one to deal with. It makes me slower, heavier. But at the same time, it prevents me from floating away into meaninglessness.

It is six in the morning; Vanessa Martinez has gotten up early. After reading Nathan's emails, I think about what Rhiannon said, what Rhiannon feared. Nathan deserves no less of a response from me.

> It will never happen again. That is an absolute. I can't explain much more than that, but this much I know: it only happens once. Then you move on.

He writes me back two minutes later.

> Who are you? How am I supposed to believe you?

I know that any response I give runs the risk of being posted on Reverend Poole's website within seconds. I don't want to give him my real name. But I feel if I give him a name, it will make it less likely he sees me as the devil, and more likely he will see me for what I am: just a person like him.

> My name is Andrew. You need to believe me because I am the only person who truly understands what happened to you.

Not surprisingly, he replies with:

Prove it.

I tell him:

You went to a party. You didn't drink. You chatted with a girl there. Eventually, she asked you if you wanted to go dance in the basement. You did. And for about an hour, you danced. You lost track of time. You lost track of yourself. And it was one of the most fantastic moments of your life. I don't know if you remember it, but there will probably come a time when you are dancing like that again, and it will feel familiar, you will know you've done it before. That will be the day you forgot. That's how you'll get that part of it back.

This isn't enough.

But why was I there?

I try to keep it simple.

You were there to talk to the girl. For just that one day, you wanted to talk to that girl.

He asks:

What is her name?

I can't get her involved. I can't explain the whole
story. So I choose to evade.

That's not important. The important thing is that for a
short time, it was worth it. You were having so much
fun that you lost track of time. That's why you were at
the side of the road. You didn't drink. You didn't crash.
You just ran out of time.

I'm sure it was scary. I'm positive it's hard to
comprehend. But it will never happen again.

Answerless questions can destroy you. Move on.

It's the truth, but it's not enough.

That would be easy for you, right? If I moved on.

Every chance I give him, every truth I tell him,
lightens the weight of my responsibility that much more.
I sympathize with his confusion, but I feel nothing
toward his hostility.

243

Nathan, what you do or don't do is no concern of mine. I'm just trying to help. You're a good guy. I am not your enemy. I never have been. Our paths just happened to cross. Now they've diverged.

I'm going to go now.

I close the window, then open a new one to see if Rhiannon will appear in it. I realize I haven't yet determined how far away I am from her and am disheartened to find she's nearly four hours away. I break the news to her in an email, and an hour later she says that it was going to be hard to meet up today anyway. So we aim for tomorrow.

In the meantime, there's Vanessa Martinez to contend with. She runs at least two miles every morning and I am already late for the routine. She has to make do with a single mile, and I can almost hear her chiding me for it. At breakfast, though, nobody else says anything – Vanessa's parents and sister seem genuinely afraid of her.

This is my first tipoff to something I will see evidenced again and again throughout the day: Vanessa Martinez is not a nice person.

It's there when she meets up with her friends at the start of school. They too are afraid of her. They're not dressed identically, but it's clear they've all dressed within the same sartorial guidelines, dictated by you-know-who.

She has a poison personality and I feel that even I am susceptible to it. Every time there's something mean to be said, everyone looks to her for a comment. Even the teachers. And I find myself stuck in those silences, with words on the venomous tip of my tongue. I see all the girls who aren't dressed within the parameters, and see how easy it would be to tear them all apart.

*Is that a backpack that Lauren has on? I guess she's acting like she's in third grade until her chest fills in. And, oh my God, why is Felicity wearing those socks? Are those kittens? I thought only convicted child molesters were allowed to wear those. And Kendall's top? I don't think there's anything sadder than an unsexy girl trying to dress sexy. We should have a fund-raiser for her, it's so sad. Like, tornado victims would look at her and say, "No, really, we don't need the money – give it to that unfortunate girl."*

I don't want these thoughts anywhere near my mind. The weird thing is that when I withhold them, when I don't let Vanessa say them out loud, I don't sense relief from any of the people around me. I sense disappointment. They're bored. And their boredom is the thing that the meanness feeds on.

Vanessa's boyfriend, a jock named Jeff, thinks it's

her time of the month. Her best friend and number one acolyte, Cynthia, asks her if someone died. They know something's off, but will never guess the real reason. They certainly won't think she's been taken over by the devil. If anything, they're suspicious that the devil's taken a day off.

I know it would be foolish of me to try to change her. I could run off this afternoon and sign her up to volunteer in a soup kitchen, but I'm sure when she arrived there tomorrow, she'd only make fun of the homeless people's clothes, and the quality of the soup. The best I could probably do would be to get Vanessa into a compromising position that someone could blackmail her about. (*Did you all see the video of Vanessa Martinez walking through the hallway in her thong underwear, singing songs from* Sesame Street? *And then she ran into the girls room and flushed her own head in a toilet?*) But that would be stooping to her level, and I'm sure that using her own poison against her would cause at least a little of it to fall back inside me as well.

So I don't try to change her. I simply stop her ire for a single day.

It's exhausting, trying to make a bad person act good. You can see why it's so much easier for them to be bad.

I want to tell Rhiannon all about it. Because when something happens, she's the person I want to tell. The most basic indicator of love.

I have to resort to email, and email is not enough. I am starting to get tired of relying on words. They are full of meaning, yes, but they lack sensation. Writing to her is not the same as seeing her face as she listens. Hearing back from her is not the same as hearing her voice. I have always been grateful for technology, but now it feels as if there's a little hitch of separation woven into any technological interaction. I want to be there, and this scares me. All of my usual disconnected comforts are being taken away, now that I see the greater comfort of presence.

Nathan also emails me, as I knew he would.

You can't leave now. I have more questions.

I don't have the heart to tell him that's the wrong way to think about the world. There will always be more questions. Every answer leads to more questions.

The only way to survive is to let some of them go.

# DAY 6018

The next day, I am a boy named George and I am only forty-five minutes away from Rhiannon. She emails me and says she'll be able to leave school at lunch.

I, however, am going to have a harder time, because today I am homeschooled.

George's mother and father are stay-at-home parents, and George and his two brothers stay at home with them each and every day. The room that in most homes would be called the rec room is instead called "the schoolhouse" by George's family. The parents have even set up three desks for them, which seem to have been left over from a one-room schoolhouse at the turn of the last century.

There is no sleeping late here. We're all woken at seven, and there's a protocol about who showers when. I manage to sneak a few minutes at the computer to read Rhiannon's message and send her one of my own, saying we'll have to see how the day plays out. Then, at eight, we're promptly at our desks, and while our father works at the other end of the house, our mother teaches us.

By accessing, I learn that George has never been in a

classroom besides this one, because of a fight his parents had with his older brother's kindergarten teacher about her methods. I can't imagine what kindergarten methods would be shocking enough to pull a whole family out of school forever, but there's no way to access information about this event – George has no idea. He's only dealt with the repercussions.

I have been homeschooled before, by parents who were engaged and engaging, who made sure their kids had room to explore and grow. This is not the case here. George's mother is made of stern, unyielding material, and she also happens to be the slowest speaker I've ever heard.

"Boys . . . we're going to talk . . . about . . . the events . . . leading up . . . to . . . the Civil . . . War."

The brothers are all resigned to this. They stare forward at all times, a pantomime of paying perfect attention.

"The president . . . of the . . . South . . . was . . . a man . . . named . . . Jefferson . . . Davis."

I refuse to be held hostage like this – not when Rhiannon will soon be waiting for me. So after an hour, I decide to take a page from Nathan's playbook.

I start asking questions.

What was the name of Jefferson Davis's wife?

Which states were in the Union?

How many people actually died in Gettysburg?

Did Lincoln write the Gettysburg address all by himself?

And about three dozen more.

My brothers look at me like I'm on cocaine, and my mother gets flustered with each question, since she has to look up each answer.

"Jefferson Davis . . . was married . . . twice. His first wife . . . Sarah . . . was the daughter of . . . President . . . Zachary Taylor. But Sarah . . . died . . . of malaria . . . three months after . . . they . . . were . . . married. He remarried . . ."

This goes on for another hour. Then I ask her if I can go to the library, to get some books on the subject.

She tells me yes, and offers to drop me off herself.

It's the middle of a school day, so I'm the only kid in the library. The librarian knows me, though, and knows where I'm coming from. She is nice to me but abrupt with my mother, leading me to believe that the kindergarten teacher isn't the only person in town who my mother doesn't think is doing her job right.

I find a computer and email my location to Rhiannon. Then I take a copy of *Feed* off the shelves and try to remember where I left off reading it, a number of bodies ago. I sit at a carrel by a window and keep being drawn to the traffic, even though I know it's still a couple of hours until Rhiannon will show up.

I shed my borrowed life for an hour and put on the borrowed life of the book I'm reading. Rhiannon finds me like that, in the selfless reading space that the mind loans out, when she arrives. I don't even notice her standing there at first.

"Ahem," she says.

"Hey," I say.

"I figured you were the only kid in the building, so it had to be you."

It's too easy – I can't resist.

"Excuse me?" I say somewhat abruptly.

"It's you, right?"

I make George look as confused as possible. "Do I know you?"

Now she starts to doubt herself. "Oh, I'm sorry. I just, uh, am supposed to meet somebody."

"What does he look like?"

"I don't, um, know. It's, like, an online thing."

I grunt. "Shouldn't you be in school?"

"Shouldn't *you* be in school?"

"I can't. There's this really amazing girl I'm supposed to meet."

She looks at me hard. "You jerk."

"Sorry, it was just –"

"You jerky . . . jerk."

She's seriously pissed; I've seriously messed up.

I stand up from my carrel.

"Rhiannon, I'm sorry."

"You can't do that. It's not fair." She is actually backing away from me.

"I will never do it again. I promise."

"I can't believe you just did that. Look me in the eyes and say it again. That you promise."

I look her in the eyes. "I promise."

It's enough, but not really. "I believe you," she says. "But you're still a jerk until you prove otherwise."

We wait until the librarian is distracted, then sneak out the door. I'm worried there's some law about reporting homeschooled kids when they go AWOL. I know George's mother is coming back in two hours, so we don't have much time.

We head to a Chinese restaurant in town. If they think we should be in school, they keep it to themselves. Rhiannon tells me about her uneventful morning – Steve and Stephanie got into another fight, but then made up by second period – and I tell her about being in Vanessa's body.

"I know so many girls like that," Rhiannon says when I'm done. "The dangerous ones are the ones who are actually good at it."

"I suspect she's very good at it."

"Well, I'm glad I didn't have to meet her."

*But you didn't get to see me,* I think. I keep it to myself.

We press our knees together under the table. My hands find hers and we hold them there. We talk as if none of this is happening, as if we can't feel life pulse through all the spots where we're touching.

"I'm sorry for calling you a jerk," she says. "I just – this is hard enough as it is. And I was so sure I was right."

"I was a jerk. I'm taking for granted how normal this all feels."

"Justin sometimes does that. Pretends I didn't tell him something I just told him. Or makes up this whole story then laughs when I fall for it. I hate that."

"I'm sorry –"

"No, it's okay. I mean, it's not like he was the first one. I guess there's something about me that people love to fool. And I'd probably do it – fool people – if it ever occurred to me."

I take all of the chopsticks out of their holder and put them on the table.

"What are you doing?" Rhiannon asks.

I use the chopsticks to outline the biggest heart possible. Then I use the Sweet'N Low packets to fill it in. I borrow some from two other tables when I run out.

When I'm done, I point to the heart on the table.

"This," I say, "is only about one ninety-millionth of how I feel about you."

She laughs.

"I'll try not to take it personally," she says.

"Take what personally?" I say. "You should take it very personally."

"The fact that you used artificial sweetener?"

I take a Sweet'N Low packet and fling it at her.

"Not everything is a symbol!" I shout.

She picks up a chopstick and brandishes it as a sword. I pick up another chopstick in order to duel.

We are doing this when the food arrives. I'm distracted and she gets a good shot in at my chest.

"I die!" I proclaim.

"Who has the moo shu chicken?" the waiter asks.

The waiter continues to indulge us as we laugh and banter our way through lunch. He's a real pro, the kind of waiter who refills your water glass when it's half empty, without you noticing he's doing it.

He delivers us our fortune cookies at the end of the meal. Rhiannon breaks hers neatly in half, checks out the slip of paper, and frowns.

"This isn't a fortune," she says, showing it to me.

"No. *You will have a nice smile* – that would be a fortune," I tell her.

"I'm going to send it back."

I raise an eyebrow . . . or at least try to. I'm sure I look like I'm having a stroke.

"Do you often send back fortune cookies?"

"No. This is the first time. I mean, this is Chinese restaurant –"

"Malpractice."

"Exactly."

Rhiannon flags the waiter down, explains the predicament, and gets a nod. When he returns to our table, he has a half-dozen more fortune cookies for her.

"I only need one," she tells him. "Wait one second."

The waiter and I are both paying close attention as Rhiannon cracks open her second fortune cookie. This time, it gets a nice smile.

She shows it to both of us.

<br>

ADVENTURE IS AROUND THE CORNER

"Well done, sir," I tell the waiter.

Rhiannon prods me to open mine. I do, and find it's the exact same fortune as hers.

I don't send it back.

We return to the library with about a half-hour to spare. The librarian catches us walking back in, but doesn't say a word.

"So," Rhiannon asks me, "what should I read next?"

I show her *Feed*. I tell her all about *The Book Thief*. I drag her to find *Destroy All Cars* and *First Day on Earth*. I explain to her that these have been my companions all these years, the constants from day to day, the stories I can always return to even if mine is always changing.

"What about you?" I ask her. "What do you think I should read next?"

She takes my hand and leads me to the children's section. She looks around for a second, then heads over to a display at the front. I see a certain green book sitting there and panic.

"No! Not that one!" I say.

But she isn't reaching for the green book. She's reaching for *Harold and the Purple Crayon*.

"What could you possibly have against *Harold and the Purple Crayon*?" she asks.

"I'm sorry. I thought you were heading for *The Giving Tree*."

Rhiannon looks at me like I'm an insane duck. "I absolutely HATE *The Giving Tree*."

I am so relieved. "Thank goodness. That would've been the end of us, had that been your favorite book."

"Here – take my arms! Take my legs!"

"Take my head! Take my shoulders!"

"Because that's what love's about!"

"That kid is like the jerk of the century," I say, relieved that Rhiannon will know what I mean.

"The biggest jerk in the history of all literature," Rhiannon ventures. Then she puts down *Harold* and moves closer to me.

"Love means never having to lose your limbs," I tell her, moving in for a kiss.

"Exactly," she murmurs, her lips soon on mine.

It's an innocent kiss. We're not about to start making out in the beanbag chairs offered by the children's room. But that doesn't stop the ice-water effect when George's mother calls out his name, shocked and angry.

"What do you *think* you're *doing*?" she demands. I assume she's talking to me, but when she gets to us, she pummels right into Rhiannon. "I don't know who your parents are, but I did not raise *my* son to hang out with *whores*."

"Mom!" I shout. "Leave her alone."

"Get in the car, George. Right this minute."

I know I'm only making it worse for George, but I don't care. I am not leaving Rhiannon alone with her.

257

"Just calm down," I tell George's mother, my voice squeaking a little as I do. Then I turn to Rhiannon and tell her I will talk to her later.

"You most certainly will not!" George's mother proclaims. I take some satisfaction out of the fact that I'm only under her supervision for another eight hours or so.

Rhiannon gives me a kiss goodbye and whispers that she's going to figure out a way to run away for the weekend. George's mother actually grabs him by the ear and pulls him outside.

I laugh, and that only makes things worse.

It's like Cinderella in reverse. I've danced with the prince and now I'm back home, cleaning the toilets. That is my punishment – every toilet, every tub, every garbage pail. This would be bad enough, but every few minutes, George's mother stops in to give me a lecture about "the sins of the flesh". I hope that George doesn't internalize her scare tactics. I want to dispute her, tell her that "sins of the flesh" is just a control mechanism – if you demonize a person's pleasure, then you can control his or her life. I can't say how many times this tool has been wielded against me, in a variety of forms. But I see no sin in a kiss. I only see sin in the condemnation.

I don't say any of this to George's mother. If she were

my full-time mother, I would. If I were the one who would shoulder the aftermath, I would. But I can't do that to George. I've messed up his life already. Hopefully for the better, but maybe for the worse.

Emailing Rhiannon is out of the question. It will just have to wait until tomorrow.

After all the toil is done, after George's father has weighed in with a speech of his own, seemingly dictated by his wife, I head to bed early, take advantage of having the silence of a room all to myself. If my time as Rhiannon is any proof, I can construct the memories that I will leave George with. So as I lie there in his bed, I conjure an alternate truth. He will remember heading to the library, and he will remember meeting a girl. She will be a stranger to town, dropped off at the library while her mother visited an old colleague. She asked him what he was reading, and a conversation began. They went for Chinese food together and had a good time. He was really into her. She was really into him. They went back to the library, had the same conversation about *The Giving Tree*, and moved in to kiss. That's when his mother arrived. That's what his mother disrupted. Something unexpected, but also something wonderful.

The girl disappeared. They never told each other their names. He has no idea where she lives. It was all just there for a moment, and then the moment unraveled.

I am leaving him with longing. Which may be a cruel thing to do, but I'm hoping he will use this longing to get out of this small, small house.

# DAY 6019

I am much luckier the next morning, when I wake up in the body of Surita, whose parents are away and who is being watched over by her ninety-year-old grandmother, who doesn't seem to care what Surita does, as long as it doesn't interfere with her programs on the Game Show Network. I'm only about an hour away from Rhiannon, and in the interest of her not being called to the principal for repeated attendance violations, I meet her back at the Clover Bookstore after school is out.

She is full of plans.

"I told everyone I was visiting my grandmother for the weekend, and I told my parents I would be at Rebecca's, so I'm a free agent. I'm actually staying at Rebecca's tonight, but I was thinking tomorrow night we could . . . go somewhere."

I tell her I like that plan.

We head to a park, walking around and playing on the jungle gym and talking. I notice she's less affectionate with me when I'm in a girl's body, but I don't call her on it. She's still with me and she's still happy, and that's something.

We don't talk about Justin. We don't talk about the fact that we have no idea where I'll be tomorrow. We

don't talk about how to make things work.
We block all this out and enjoy ourselves.

# DAY 6020

Xavier Adams could not have imagined his Saturday was going to turn in this direction. He's supposed to go to play practice at noon, but as soon as he leaves his house, he calls his director and tells him he has a bad flu bug – hopefully the twenty-four-hour kind. The director is understanding – the play is *Hamlet* and Xavier is playing Laertes, so there are plenty of scenes that can be run without him there. So Xavier is free . . . and immediately heads toward Rhiannon.

She's left me directions, but she hasn't told me what the ultimate destination is. I drive for almost two hours, west into the hinterlands of Maryland. Eventually, the directions lead me to a small cabin hidden in the woods. If Rhiannon's car wasn't in front, I'm sure I'd think I was hopelessly lost.

She's waiting in the doorway by the time I get out of the car. She looks happy-nervous. I still have no idea where I am.

"You're really cute today," she observes as I get closer.

"French Canadian dad, Creole mom," I say. "But I don't speak a word of French."

"Your mom isn't going to show up this time, is she?"

"Nope."

263

"Good. Then I can do this without being killed."

She kisses me hard. I kiss her hard back. And suddenly we're letting our bodies do the talking. We are inside the doorway, inside the cabin. But I'm not looking at the room – I am feeling her, tasting her, pressing against her as she's pressing against me. She's pulling off my coat and we're kicking off our shoes and she's directing me backward. The edge of the bed kicks the back of my legs, and then we are awkwardly, enjoyably stumbling over, me lying down, her pinning my shoulders, us kissing and kissing and kissing. Breath and heat and contact and shirts off and skin on skin and smiles and murmurs and the enormity revealing itself in the tiniest of gestures, the most delicate sensations.

I pull back from a kiss and look at her. She stops and looks at me.

"Hey," I say.

"Hey," she says.

I trace the contours of her face, her collarbone. She runs her fingers along my shoulders, my back. Kisses my neck, my ear.

For the first time, I look around. It's a one-room cabin – the bathroom must be out back. There are deer heads on the wall, staring down at us with glass eyes.

"Where are we?" I ask.

"It's a hunting cabin my uncle uses. He's in California now, so I figured it was safe to break in."

I search for broken windows, signs of forced entry. "You broke in?"

"Well, with the spare key."

Her hand moves to the patch of hair at the center of my chest, then to my heartbeat. I rest one of my hands on her side, glide lightly over the smoothness of the skin there.

"That was quite a welcome," I tell her.

"It's not over yet," she says. And, just like that, we're pressed together again.

I am letting her take the lead. I am letting her unbutton the top of my jeans. I am letting her pull the zipper down. I am letting her remove her bra. I am following along, but with each step the pressure builds. How far is this going? How far should this go?

I know our nakedness means something. I know our nakedness is as much a form of trust as it is desire. This is what we look like when we are completely open to each other. This is where we go when we no longer want to hide. I want her. I want this. But I am afraid.

We move as if we're in a fever, then we slow down and move as if we're in a dream. There's no clothing now, just sheets. This is not my body, but it's the body she wants.

I feel like a pretender.

This is the source of the pressure. This is the cause of my hesitation. Right now I am here with her completely. But tomorrow I might not be. I can enjoy this today. It can feel right now. But tomorrow, I don't know. Tomorrow I might be gone.

I want to sleep with her. I want to sleep with her so much.

But I also want to wake up next to her the next morning.

The body is ready. The body is close to bursting with sensation. When Rhiannon asks if I want to, I know what the body would answer.

But I tell her no. I tell her we shouldn't. Not yet. Not right now.

Even though it was a genuine question, she's surprised by the answer. She pulls away to look at me.

"Are you sure? I want to. If you're worried about me, don't be. I want to. I . . . prepared."

"I don't think we should."

"Okay," she says, pulling farther away.

"It's not you," I tell her. "And it's not that I don't want to."

"So what is it?" she asks.

"It feels wrong."

She looks hurt by this answer.

"Let me worry about Justin," she says. "This is you and me. It's different."

"But it's not just you and me," I tell her. "It's also Xavier."

"Xavier?"

I gesture to my body. "Xavier."

"Oh."

"He's never done it before," I tell her. "And it just feels wrong . . . for him to do it for the first time, and not know it. I feel like I'm taking something from him if I do that. It doesn't seem right."

I have no idea if this is true or not, and I'm not going to access to find out. Because it is an acceptable reason to stop – acceptable because it shouldn't hurt her pride.

"Oh," Rhiannon says again. Then she moves back closer and nestles in next to me. "Do you think he would mind this?"

The body relaxes. Enjoys itself in a different way.

"I set an alarm," Rhiannon says. "So we can sleep."

We drift together, naked in the bed. My heart is still racing, but as it slows, it slows in pace with hers. We have entered the safest cocoon our affections can make, and we lie there, and we luxuriate in the wealth of the moment, and we gently fall into each other, fall into sleep.

*

It is not the alarm that wakes us. It is the sound of a flock of birds outside the window. It is the sound of the wind hitting the eaves.

I have to remind myself that normal people feel this way too: The desire to take a moment and make it last forever. The desire to stay like this for much longer than it will really last.

"I know we don't talk about it," I say. "But why are you with him?"

"I don't know," she tells me. "I used to think I did. But I don't know anymore."

"Who was your favorite?" she asks.

"My favorite?"

"Your favorite body. Your favorite life."

"I was once in the body of a blind girl," I tell her. "When I was eleven. Maybe twelve. I don't know if she was my favorite, but I learned more from being her for a day than I'd learn from most people over a year. It showed me how arbitrary and individual it is, the way we experience the world. Not just that the other senses were sharper. But that we find ways to navigate the world as it is presented to us. For me, it was this huge challenge. But for her, it was just life."

"Close your eyes," Rhiannon whispers.

I close my eyes, and she does the same.

We experience each other's bodies in a different way.

The alarm goes off. I don't want to be reminded of time.

We have not turned on the lights, so as the air turns to dusk, the cabin turns to dusk as well. Haze of darkness, remnant of light.

"I'm going to stay here," she says.

"I'm going to come back tomorrow," I promise.

"I would end it," I tell her. "I would end all the changing if I could. Just to stay here with you."

"But you can't end it," she says. "I know that."

Time itself becomes the alarm. I can't look at the clock without knowing it's past the hour for me to go. Play rehearsal is over. Even if Xavier goes out with friends after, he's going to have to be home soon. And definitely by midnight.

"I'll wait for you," she tells me.

I leave her in the bed. I put on my clothes, pick up my keys and close the door behind me. I turn back. I keep turning back to see her. Even when there are walls between us. Even when there are miles between us. I keep turning back. I keep turning in her direction.

# DAY 6021

I wake up, and for at least a minute I can't figure out who I am. All I can find is the body, and the body is pounding with pain. There's a hazy blur to my thoughts, a vice compressing my head. I open my eyes and the light nearly kills me.

"Dana," a voice outside of me says. "It's noon."

I don't care that it's noon. I don't care about anything at all. I just want the pounding to go away.

Or not. Because when the pounding briefly stops, the rest of my body chimes in with nausea.

"Dana, I'm not going to let you sleep all day. Being grounded does not mean you get to sleep all day."

It takes three more attempts, but I manage to open my eyes and keep them open, even if the bedroom light feels like it has the same wattage of the sun.

Dana's mother stares down at me with as much sorrow as anger.

"Dr P is coming in a half hour," she tells me. "I think you need to see him."

I am accessing like crazy, but it's as if my synapses have been dipped in tar.

"After all we've been through, the fact that you would pull such a stunt last night . . . it's beyond words. We

271

have done nothing but care about you. And this is how you repay us? This is what you do? Your father and I have had enough. No more."

What did I do last night? I can remember being with Rhiannon. I can remember going home as Xavier. Talking to his friends on the phone. Hearing about play practice. But I can't reach Dana's memories. She is too hungover for them to be there.

Is this what it's like for Xavier this morning? A complete blank?

I hope not, because this is awful.

"You have half an hour to shower and get dressed. Don't expect any help from me."

Dana's mother slams the door shut and the echo of the slam spreads through my whole body. As I start to move, it feels like I am trapped twenty miles under water. And when I start to rise, I get a bad case of the bends. I actually have to steady myself against my bed post, and nearly miss it when I reach out.

I don't really care about Dr P or Dana's parents. As far as I'm concerned, Dana must have done this to herself, and she deserves the grief she gets. It must have taken *a lot* of drinking to get in this state. She is not the reason I get up. I get up because somewhere near here, Rhiannon is alone in a hunting cabin, waiting for me. I have no idea how I'm going to get out of here, but I have to.

I trudge through the hallway to the shower. I turn it on, then stand there for at least a minute, forgetting entirely why I am standing there. The water is just background music to the horror of my body. Then I remember, and I step in. The water wakes me up a little more, but I stagger through the waking. I could easily collapse into the tub, and fall asleep with the water running over me, my foot against the drain.

When I get back to Dana's room, I let the towel drop and leave it there, then put on whatever clothes are nearest. There's no computer in the room, no phone. No way to get in touch with Rhiannon. I know I should search the house, but just the thought of it takes too much energy. I need to sit down. Lie down. Close my eyes.

"Wake up!"

The command is as abrupt as the earlier door slam, and twice as close. I open my eyes and find Dana's very angry father.

"Dr P is here," Dana's mother chimes in from behind him, with a slightly more conciliatory tone. Maybe she's feeling bad for me. Or maybe she just doesn't want her husband to kill me in front of a witness.

I wonder if what I'm feeling isn't entirely a hangover, if a doctor is making a house call. But when Dr P sits down next to me, there's not a medical bag in sight. Just a notebook.

"Dana," she says gently.

I look at her. Sit up, even as my head howls.

She turns to my parents.

"It's okay. Why don't you leave us now?"

They don't need to be told twice.

Accessing is still hard. I know the facts are there, but they're behind a murky wall.

"Do you want to tell me what happened?" Dr P asks.

"I don't know," I say. "I don't remember."

"It's that bad?"

"Yeah. It's that bad."

She asks me if my parents have given me any Tylenol, and I tell her no, not since I woke up. She leaves for a second and comes back with two Tylenol and a glass of water.

I don't get the Tylenol down on the first try, and I'm embarrassed by the chalky gag that results. The second time is better, and I gulp down the rest of the water. Dr P goes out and refills the glass, giving me time to think. But the thoughts in my head are still clumsy, dull.

When she returns, she begins with, "You can understand why your parents are upset, can't you?"

I feel so stupid, but I can't pretend.

"I really don't know what I did," I say. "I'm not lying. I wish I did."

"You were at Cameron's party." She looks as me, seeing if this registers. When it doesn't, she continues. "You snuck out to go there. And when you got there, you started drinking. A lot. Your friends were concerned, for obvious reasons. But they didn't stop you. They only tried to stop you when you went to drive home."

It's as if I'm in a room at the end of a long, long house, and my memory of this is in a room on the other side. I know it's there. I know she's telling me the truth. But I can't see it.

"I drove?"

"Yes. Even though you weren't supposed to. You stole your father's keys."

"I stole my father's keys." I say it out loud, hoping it will spark an image.

"When you went to drive home, some of your friends tried to stop you. But you insisted. They tried to . . . stop you. You lashed out at them. Called them awful things. And when Cameron tried to take your keys away . . ."

"What did I do?"

"You bit him on the wrist. And you ran."

This must have been how Nathan felt. The morning after.

Dr P continues. "Your friend Lisa called your parents.

They rushed over. When your father got to you, you were already in the car. He went to stop you and you nearly ran him over."

*I nearly ran him over?*

"You didn't get far. You were too drunk to back out of the driveway. You ended up in the neighbor's yard. You crashed into a basketball net. Luckily, no one was hurt."

I exhale. I am pushing inside Dana's mind, trying to find any of this.

"What we want to know, Dana, is why you would do such a thing. After what happened with Anthony, why would you do this?"

*Anthony.* That name is a knife that cuts right through the confusion. He is the fact that is too bright to hide. My body convulses in pain. Pain is all I can feel.

Anthony. My brother.

My dead brother.

My brother who died next to me.

My brother who died next to me, in the passenger seat.

Because I crashed.

Because I was drunk.

Because of me.

"Oh my god," I cry out. "Oh my god."

I am seeing him now. His bloody body. I am screaming.

"It's okay," Dr P says. "It's okay now."

But it's not.

It's not.

Dr P gives me something stronger than Tylenol. I try to resist, but it's no use.

"I have to tell Rhiannon," I say. I don't mean to say it. It just comes out.

"Who's Rhiannon?" Dr P asks.

My eyelids close. I give in before she can get an answer.

It starts to come back to me while I'm asleep, and when I wake again, I remember more of it. Not the end – I genuinely can't remember getting in the car, almost running over my father, hitting the basketball net. I must have checked out by then. But before that, I can remember being at the party. Drinking anything anyone offered. Feeling better because of it. Feeling lighter. Flirting with Cameron. Drinking some more. Not thinking. After so much thinking, blocking it all out.

I'm like Dana's parents, or Dr P – I want to ask her why. Even from the inside, I can't figure it out. Because the body can't answer that.

My limbs are heavy, wooden. But I prop myself up. I

edge myself out of bed. I need to find a computer or a phone.

Why I get to the door, I find it's locked. There should be a key that lets me out, but somebody's taken it.

I'm trapped in my own room.

Now that they know I remember at least some of it, they are letting me stew in my own guilt.

And the worst part is: it's working.

I am out of water. I call out that I need more water. Within a minute, my mother is at the door with a glass. She looks like she's been crying. She is shattered. I have shattered my mother.

"Here," she says.

"Can I come out?" I ask. "There are some things I need to look up for school."

She shakes her head. "Maybe later. After dinner. For now, Dr P would like you to write down everything you're feeling."

She leaves and locks the door behind her. I find a piece of paper and a pen.

*What I feel is helplessness,* I write.

But then I stop. Because I'm not writing as Dana. I'm writing as me.

*

The headache and nausea are subsiding. Although every time I imagine Rhiannon alone in the cabin, I feel sick again.

I promised her. Even though I knew the risk, I promised her.

And now I'm proving to her that it's too risky to accept my promises.

I am proving to her that I won't be able to come through.

Dana's mother brings me lunch on a tray, as if I'm an invalid. I thank her for it. And then I find the words I should have been using all along.

"I'm sorry," I tell her. "I'm really, really sorry."

She nods, but I can tell it's not enough.

I must have told her I was sorry too many times before. At some point – maybe last night – she must have stopped believing it.

When I ask her where my father is, she tells me he's getting the car fixed.

They decide that I will have to go to school tomorrow, and that I will have to make amends to my friends then. They say I can use the computer for my homework, but then sit there behind me as I make up things to research.

Emailing Rhiannon is out of the question.

And they show no signs of giving me back my phone.

The previous night's events never come back to me. I spend the rest of the night staring into that blank space. And I can't help but feel it staring right back.

# DAY 6022

My plan is to wake up early – around six – and email Rhiannon with a full explanation. I expect she gave up on me after a while.

But my plan is foiled when I'm shaken awake a little before five.

"Michael, it's time to wake up."

It's my mother – Michael's mother – and unlike Dana's mother, there's only apology in her voice.

I figure it's time for swim practice, or something else I have to do before school. But when I get out of bed, my foot hits a suitcase.

I hear my mom in the other room, waking up my sisters.

"It's time to go to Hawaii!" she says cheerily.

Hawaii.

I access and find that, yes, we are leaving for Hawaii this morning. Michael's older sister is getting married there. And Michael's family has decided to take a weeklong vacation.

Only for me it won't be a week. Because in order to get back, I'd have to wake up in the body of a sixteen-year-old who was heading home to Maryland that day. It could take weeks. Months.

It might never happen.

"The car's coming in forty-five minutes!" Michael's dad calls up.

Under no circumstances can I go.

Michael's wardrobe consists mostly of T-shirts for heavy metal bands. I throw one on, as well as jeans.

"You're just asking homeland security to give you a full cavity search," one of my sisters says as I pass her in the halls.

I am still trying to figure out what to do.

Michael doesn't have his licence, and I don't think it would help for me to steal one of his parents' cars. His older sister's wedding isn't until Friday, so at least I'm not jeopardizing his attendance there. But who am I kidding? Even if the wedding were this evening, I wouldn't get on that plane.

I know I am going to get Michael in a huge amount of trouble. I apologize to him profusely as I write my note and leave it on the kitchen table.

*I can't go today. I am so sorry. I will be back later tonight. Go without me. I'll get there somehow by Thursday.*

While everyone else is upstairs, I walk out the back door.

I could call a cab, but I'm afraid his parents will call the local cab companies to see if they've picked up any metalhead teens lately. I am at least two hours away from Rhiannon. I take the nearest bus I can find and ask the driver the best way to get to her town. He laughs and says, "By car." I tell him that's not an option, and in return he tells me I'll probably have to head to Baltimore and then back out again.

It takes about seven hours.

School isn't out yet when I get there, having walked about a mile from the center of town. Again, nobody stops me, even though I'm a big, hairy, sweaty guy in a Metallica T-shirt storming up the steps.

I try to remember Rhiannon's schedule from when I was inside her head and have a vague recollection that this period is gym. I check the gymnasium and find it empty. The natural next stop is the fields, which are behind the school. When I walk out, I find a softball game in action. Rhiannon is at third base.

She sees me out of the corner of her eye. I wave. It's unclear whether she recognizes me as me or not. I feel too out in the open, to much in the line of the gym teachers' sights. So I retreat back to the school, by the door. Just another slacker, taking a smokeless smoke break.

Rhiannon walks over to one of the teachers and says

something. The teacher looks sympathetic and puts another student on third base. Rhiannon starts heading toward the school. I step back inside and wait for her in the empty gym.

"Hey," I say once she steps inside.

"Where the hell were you?" she replies.

I've never seen her this angry before. It's the kind of anger that comes from when you feel betrayed by not just a single person, but the universe.

"I was locked in my room," I tell her. "It was awful. There wasn't even a computer."

"I waited for you," she tells me. "I got up. Made the bed. Had some breakfast. And then I waited. My reception on my phone went on and off, so I figured that had to be it. I started reading old issues of *Field & Stream*, because that's the only reading material up there. Then I heard footsteps. I was so excited. When I heard someone at the door, I ran to it.

"Well, it wasn't you. It was this eighty-year-old guy. And he had this dead deer with him. I don't know who was more surprised. I just screamed when I saw him. And he nearly had a heart attack. I wasn't naked, but I was close. I was so ashamed of myself. He wasn't even sweet about it. He said I was trespassing. I told him Artie was my uncle, but he wasn't believing me. I think the only thing that saved me was that me and Artie have the same last name. I was there in my underwear, showing this guy my ID. There was blood on his hands. And he said there were other guys coming. He just assumed my car was one of theirs.

"The problem was – I still thought you were coming. So I couldn't leave. I put on my clothes and had to sit there as they came back and gutted that poor deer. I waited there after they left. I waited there until dark. The cabin smelled like blood, A. But I stayed there. And you never came."

I tell her about Dana. Then I tell her about Michael, and running out of his house.

It's something. But it's not enough.

"How are we supposed to do this?" she asks me. "How?"

I want there to be an answer. I want to have an answer.

"Come here," I say. And I hold her close. I hold her because that's the only answer I have.

We stand like that for a minute, each not knowing what comes next. When the door to the gym opens, we pull away from each other. But we're too late. I figure it's one of the gym teachers, or another girl from class. But it's not even that door. It's the door from the school side, and it's Justin who's walked through.

"What the hell?" he says. "What. The. Hell?"

Rhiannon tries to explain. "Justin –" she begins. But he cuts her off.

"Lindsay texted me to say you weren't feeling well. So I was going to see if you were okay. Well, I guess you're real okay. Don't let me interrupt."

"Stop it," Rhiannon says.

"Stop what, you bitch?" he asks. He's on us now.

"Justin," I say.

He turns to me. "You're not even allowed to speak, bro."

I'm about to say something else, but he's already punching me. His fist crashes right against the bridge of my nose. I'm knocked down to the ground.

Rhiannon screams and moves to help me up. Justin pulls at her arm.

"I always knew you were a slut," Justin says.

"Stop it!" Rhiannon cries out.

Justin lets go of her and comes back over to me. He starts kicking my body.

"This your new boyfriend?" Justin yells. "You love him?"

"I don't love him!" Rhiannon yells back. "But I don't love you either."

The next time he kicks, I grab his leg and pull him down. He crashes on the gym floor. I think this will stop him, but he jabs his boot out again and gets me in

286

the chin. My teeth rattle.

At this point, some whistle must blow outside, because within thirty seconds, girls from softball are streaming into the gym. When they see the carnage, they cluck and gasp. One girl runs over to Rhiannon to make sure she's okay.

Justin gets up and kicks me again, just so everyone can see it. It barely grazes me, and I use the momentum of dodging the blow to stand up. I want to hit him so it hurts, but I honestly don't know how.

Plus, I have to leave. It will be easy enough to discover that I don't go to this school. And even though I'm the clear loser of this fight, they can still call the police on me for trespassing and brawling in the first place.

I teeter over to Rhiannon. Her friend makes a move to shield her from me, but Rhiannon gestures her off.

"I have to go," I tell her. "Meet me at the Starbucks where we first met. When you can."

I feel a hand on my shoulder. Justin, pulling me around. He won't hit me with my back turned.

I know I should face him. Hit him if I can. But instead I duck out of his grip and I run. He's not going to follow me. He will bask instead in the victory of me running.

It is not my intention to leave Rhiannon crying, but that is exactly what I do.

*

I make my way back to the bus stop, then use a nearby phone booth to call a cab. Nearly fifty dollars later, I am at the Starbucks. If before I was a big, hairy, sweaty guy in a Metallica T-shirt, now I am a big, hairy, sweaty guy in a Metallica T-shirt who's beaten, bruised and bleeding. I order a venti black coffee and leave twenty dollars in the tip jar. Now they'll let me stay as long as I want, no matter how scary I look.

I clean myself up some in the bathroom. Then I sit down and wait.

And wait.

And wait.

She doesn't arrive until a little after six.

She doesn't apologize. She doesn't explain why it took her so long. She doesn't even come to my table right away. She stops at the counter and gets a coffee first.

"I really need this," she says as she sits down. I know she's talking about the coffee, not anything else.

I'm on my fourth coffee and second scone.

"Thank you for coming," I tell her. It sounds too formal.

"I thought about not coming," she says. "But I didn't seriously consider it." She looks at my face, my bruises. "You okay?"

"I'm fine."

"Remind me – what's your name today?"

"Michael."

She looks me over again. "Poor Michael."

"This is not how I imagine he thought the day would go."

"That makes two of us."

I feel we're each standing a good hundred feet from the real subject. I have to move us closer.

"Is it over now? With the two of you?"

"Yes. So I guess you got what you wanted."

"That's an awful way to put it," I say. "Don't you want it too?"

"Yes. But not like that. Not in front of everybody like that."

I reach up to touch her face, but she flinches. I lower my hand back down.

"You're free of him," I tell her.

She shakes her head. I've said yet another thing wrong.

"I forget how little you know about these things," she says. "I forget how inexperienced you are. I'm not free of him, A. Just because you break up with someone, it doesn't mean you're free of him. I'm still attached to Justin in a hundred different ways. We're just not dating anymore. It's going to take me years to be free of him."

*But at least you've started,* I want to say. *At least you've cut that one attachment.* I remain silent though.

This might be what she knows, but it's not what she wants to hear.

"Should I have gone to Hawaii?" I ask.

She softens to me then. It's such an absurd question, but she knows what I mean.

"No, you shouldn't have. I want you here."

"With you?"

"With me. When you can be."

I want to promise more than that, but I know I can't.

We both stay there, on our tightrope. Not looking down, but not moving either.

We use her phone to check the local flights to Hawaii, and when we're sure there's no way Michael's family can get him on a plane, Rhiannon drives me home.

"Tell me more about the girl you were yesterday," she asks. So I do. And when I'm done, and a sadness fills the car, I decide to tell her about other days, other lives. Happier. I share with her memories of being sung to sleep, memories of meeting elephants at zoos and circuses, memories of first kisses and near-first kisses in rec-room closets and Boy Scout sleepovers and scary movies. It's my way of telling her that even though I haven't experienced so many things, I have managed to have a life.

*

We get closer and closer to Michael's house.

"I want to see you tomorrow," I say.

"I want to see you too," she says. "But I think we both know it's not just a matter of want."

"I'll hope it then," I tell her.

"And I'll hope it too."

I want to kiss her goodnight, not goodbye. But when we get there, she makes no move to kiss me. I don't want to push it and make the first move. And I don't want to ask her, for fear that she'll say no.

So we leave with me thanking her for the ride, and so much else going unspoken.

I don't go straight into the house. I walk around to run out the clock more. It's ten o'clock when I am at the front door. I access Michael to find out where the spare key is kept, but by the time I've found it, the door has opened and Michael's father is there.

At first, he doesn't say a word. I stand there in the lamplight, and he stares.

"I want to beat the crap out of you," he says, "but it looks like someone else got there first."

My mother and sisters have been sent ahead to Hawaii. My father has stayed back for me.

In order to apologize, I have to give him some kind of explanation. I come up with one that's as pathetic as I feel – there was a concert I had to go to, and there was just no way to tell him ahead of time. I feel awful messing up Michael's life to such a degree, and this awfulness must come through as I speak, because Michael's father is much less hostile than he has every right to be. I'm in no way off the hook: the change fee for the tickets will be coming out of my allowance for the next year, and when we're in Hawaii, I may be grounded from doing anything that isn't wedding-related. I will be getting guilt for this for the rest of my life. The only saving grace is that there were tickets available for the next day.

That night, I create a memory of the best concert Michael will ever go to. It is the only thing I can think to give him to make any of it worth it.

# DAY 6023

Even before I open my eyes, I like Vic. Biologically female, gendered male. Living within the definition of his own truth, just like me. He knows who he wants to be. Most people our age don't have to do that. They stay within the realm of the easy. If you want to live within the definition of your own truth, you have to choose to go through the painful process of finding it.

It's supposed to be a busy day for Vic. There's a history test and a math test. There's band practice, which is the thing he looks forward to the most in the day. There's a date with a girl named Dawn.

I get up. I get dressed. I get my keys and get in my car.

But when I get to the place where I should turn off for school, I keep driving.

It's just over a three-hour drive from Rhiannon. I've emailed to let her know Vic and I are coming. I didn't give her time to reply, or to say no.

On the drive, I access pieces of Vic's history. There are few things harder than being born into the wrong body. I had to deal with it a lot when I was growing up, but only for a day. Before I became so adaptable – so acquiescent to the way my life worked – I would resist

293

some of the transitions. I loved having long hair, and would resent it when I woke up to find my long hair was gone. There were days I felt like a girl and days I felt like a boy, and those days wouldn't always correspond with the body I was in. I still believed everyone when they said I had to be one or the other. Nobody was telling me a different story, and I was too young to think for myself. I had yet to learn that when it came to gender, I was both and neither.

It is an awful thing to be betrayed by your body. And it's lonely, because you feel you can't talk about it. You feel it's something between you and the body. You feel it's a battle you will never win . . . and yet you fight it day after day, and it wears you down. Even if you try to ignore it, the energy it takes to ignore it will exhaust you.

Vic was lucky in the parents his was given. They didn't care if he wanted to wear jeans instead of skirts, or play with trucks instead of dolls. It was only as he grew older, into his teens, that it gave them some pause. They knew that their daughter liked girls. But it took a while for him to articulate – even to himself – that he liked them as a boy. That he was meant to be a boy, or at least live as a boy, to live in the blur between a boyish girl and a girlish boy.

His father, a quiet man, understood and supported

him in a quiet way. His mother took it harder. She respected Vic's desire to be who she needed to be, but at the same time had a difficult time giving up the fact of having a daughter for the fact of having a son. Some of Vic's friends understood, even at thirteen and fourteen. Others were freaked out – the girls more than the boys. To the boys, Vic had always been the tagalong, the nonsexual friend. This didn't change that.

Dawn was always there in the background. They'd gone to school together since kindergarten, friendly without ever really becoming friends. When they got to high school, Vic was hanging out with the kids who furiously scribbled poems into their notebooks and let them lie there, while Dawn was with the kids who would submit their poems to the literary magazine the minute they were finished. The public girl, running for class treasurer and joining the debate club, and the private boy, the sidekick on 7-Eleven runs. Vic would have never noticed Dawn, would have never thought it was a possibility, if Dawn hadn't noticed him first.

But Dawn did notice him. He was the corner that her eye always strayed toward. When she closed her eyes to go to sleep, it was thoughts of him that would lead her into her dreams. She had no idea what she was attracted to – the boyish girl, the girlish boy – and eventually she decided it didn't really matter. Boy or girl, she was attracted to Vic. And Vic had no idea she existed. Not in that way.

Finally, as Dawn would later recount to Vic, it became unbearable. They had plenty of mutual friends who could have done reconnaissance, but Dawn felt that if she was going to risk it, she was going to risk it first hand. So one day when she saw Vic piling in with some of the other guys for a 7-Eleven run, she jumped into her car and followed them. As she'd hoped, Vic decided to hang out in front while her friends played in the aisles. Dawn walked over and said hello. Vic didn't understand at first why Dawn was talking to him, or why she seemed so nervous, but then he slowly realized what was happening, and that he wanted it to happen too. When the chime of the front door marked his friends' exit, he waved them off and stayed with Dawn, who didn't even remember to pretend she needed something from the store. Dawn would have talked there for hours; it was Vic who suggested they go get coffee, and it all went from there.

There had been ups and downs since, but the heart of it remained: when Dawn looked at Vic, she saw Vic exactly as he wanted to be seen. Whereas Vic's parents couldn't help seeing who he used to be, and so many friends and strangers couldn't help seeing who he didn't want to be anymore, Dawn only saw him. Call it a blur if you want, but Dawn didn't see a blur. She saw a very distinct, very clear person.

As I sift through these memories, as I put together this story, I feel such gratitude and such longing – not Vic's, but my own. This is what I want from Rhiannon. This is what I want to give Rhiannon.

But how can I make her see past the blur, if I'm a body she'll never really see, in a life she'll never really be able to hold?

I arrive the period before lunch and park in my usual spot.

By now, I know which class Rhiannon is in. So I wait outside the door for the bell to ring. When it does, she's in the middle of a crowd, talking to her friend Rebecca. She doesn't see me; she doesn't even look up. I have to follow behind her for a ways, not knowing whether I'm the ghost of her past, present or future. Finally, she and Rebecca head in different directions and I can talk to her alone.

"Hey," I say.

And it's there – a moment's hesitation before she turns. But then she does, and I see that recognition again.

"Hey," she says. "You're here. Why am I not surprised?"

This isn't exactly the welcome I was hoping for, but

it's a welcome I understand. When we're alone together, I'm the destination. When I'm here in her life at school, I'm the disruption.

"Lunch?" I ask.

"Sure," she says. "But I really have to get back afterwards."

I tell her that's okay.

We're silent as we walk. When I'm not focused on Rhiannon, I can sense that people are looking at her differently. Some positive, but more negative.

She sees me noticing.

"Apparently, I'm now a metalhead slut," she says. "Apparently, I've even slept with members of Metallica. It's kind of funny, but also kind of not." She looks me over. "You, however, are something completely different. I don't even know what I'm dealing with today."

"My name's Vic. I'm a biological female, but my gender is male."

Rhiannon sighs. "I don't even know what that means."

I start to explain, but she cuts me off.

"Let's just wait until we're off school grounds, okay? Why don't you walk behind me for a while. I think it'll just make things easier."

I have no choice but to follow.

*

We head to a diner where the average age of the customers is ninety-four, and applesauce seems to be the most popular item on the menu. Not exactly a high school hangout.

Once we've sat down and ordered, I ask her more about the aftermath of the previous day.

"I can't say Justin seems that upset," she says. "And there's no shortage of girls who want to comfort him. It's pathetic. Rebecca's been awesome. I swear, there should be an occupation called Friendship PR – Rebecca would be ace at that. She's getting my half of the story out there."

"Which is?"

"Which is that Justin's a jerk. And that the metalhead and I weren't doing anything besides talking."

The first part is irrefutable, but even to me, the second part sounds weak.

"I'm sorry it had to all go down like that," I say.

"It could've been worse. And we have to stop apologizing to each other. Every sentence can't start with 'I'm sorry'."

There's such resignation in her voice, but I can't tell what she's actually resigned herself to.

"So you're a girl who's a boy?" she says.

"Something like that." I sense she doesn't want to get into it.

"And how far did you drive?"

"Three hours."

"And what are you missing?"

"A couple of tests. A date with my girlfriend."

"Do you think that's fair?"

I'm stuck for a second. "What do you mean?" I ask.

"Look," Rhiannon says, "I'm happy you've come all this way. Really, I am. But I didn't get much sleep last night, and I'm cranky as hell, and this morning when I got your email, I just thought: Is all of this really fair? Not to me or to you. But to these . . . people whose lives you're kidnapping."

"Rhiannon, I'm always careful –"

"I know you are. And I know it's just a day. But what if something completely unexpected was supposed to happen today? What if her girlfriend is planning this huge surprise party for her? What if her lab partner is going to fail out of class if she's not there to help? What if – I don't know. What if there's this huge accident and she's supposed to be nearby to pull a baby to safety?"

"I know," I tell her. "But what if *I'm* the one that something is supposed to happen to? What if I'm supposed to be here, and if I'm not, the world will go the wrong direction? In some infinitesimal but important way."

"But shouldn't her life come above yours?"

300

"Why?"

"Because you're just the guest."

I know this is true, but it's shocking to hear her say it. She immediately moves to temper what sounds like an accusation.

"I'm not saying you're any less important. You know I'm not. Right now, you are the person I love the most in the entire world."

"Really?"

"What do you mean, *really*?"

"Yesterday, you said you didn't love me."

"I was talking about the metalhead. Not you."

Our food arrives, but Rhiannon just stabs the ketchup with her French fries.

"I love you too, you know," I say.

"I know," she tells me. But she doesn't seem any happier.

"We're going to get through this. Every relationship has a hard part at the beginning. This is our hard part. It's not like a puzzle piece where there's an instant fit. With relationships, you have to shape the pieces on each end before they go perfectly together."

"And your piece changes shape every day," she observes.

"Only physically."

"I know." She finally eats one of the fries. "Really, I do. I guess I need to work on my piece more. There's too

301

much going on. And you being here – that adds to the too much."

"I'll go," I say. "After lunch."

"It's not that I want you to. I just think I need you to."

"I understand," I say. And I do.

"Good." She smiles. "Now tell me about this date you're going on tonight. If I don't get to be with you, I want to know who does."

I've texted Dawn to tell her I'm not in school, but the date is still on. We're meeting for dinner after she's done with field hockey practice.

I get back to Vic's house at the usual time he'd come back home from school. Safe in my room, I feel the usual set of pre-date jitters. I see that Vic has a large selection of ties in his closet, leading me to believe that he likes wearing them. So I put together a dapper outfit – maybe a little too dapper, but if what I've accessed about Dawn is true, I know she'll appreciate it.

I whittle away the hours online. There's no new email from Rhiannon, and there are eight new emails from Nathan, none of which I open. Then I go to Vic's playlists and listen to some of the songs he's listened to the most. I often find new music this way.

Finally, it's a little before six and I'm out the door. It's almost strange how much I am looking forward to this.

I want to be a part of something that works, no matter what the challenge.

Dawn does not disappoint. She loves the way Vic looks, using the word *debonair* instead of *dapper*. She is full of news of the day, and full of questions about what I've been up to. This is a delicate area – I don't want him to be caught in a lie later on – so I tell her I simply had the impulse to take the day off. No tests, no hallways, just driving to somewhere I've never been before . . . as long as I was back in time for her. She fully supports this decision, and doesn't even ask why I didn't invite her along. This is, I hope, how Vic will remember the day.

I have to access rapid-fire in order to follow all of Dawn's reference points, but even still, it's a good time. Vic's memory of her is absolutely correct – she sees him so precisely, so wonderfully, so offhandedly. She doesn't broadcast her understanding at all. It's just there.

I know their situation is different from ours. I know I am not Vic, just as Rhiannon is not Dawn. But part of me wants to make the analogy. Part of me wants us to transcend in the same way. Part of me wants love to be that strong, that powerful.

Both Vic and Dawn have their own cars, but at Dawn's request, Vic follows her home, just so he can walk her to the door and they can have a proper goodnight kiss.

I think this is sweet, and go along, walking hand in hand with Dawn up the front steps. I have no idea if her parents are home, but if she doesn't care, neither do I. We get to the screen door and then hang there for a moment, like a courting couple from the 1950s. Then Dawn leans over and kisses me hard, and I kiss her back hard, and it's not the door we're propelled toward but the bushes. She's pushing me back into the darkness, and I am taking all of her in, and it's so intense that I lose my mind, or lose track of Vic's mind so I'm in my own mind completely, and I am kissing her and feeling it and out of my mouth comes the word *Rhiannon*. At first I don't think Dawn's heard it, but she pulls back for a second and asks me what I just said, and I tell her it's like the song – doesn't she know the song? – and I've always wondered what that word meant, but this is what it is, this is what it feels like, and Dawn says she has no idea what song I'm talking about, but it doesn't matter, she's used to my quirks by now, and I tell her I'll play it for her later, but in the meantime there's this and this and this. We are covered in leaves, my tie is caught on a branch, but it's just so full of life that we don't mind. We don't mind any of it.

That night there's an email from Rhiannon.

A,

Today was awkward, but I think that's because it feels like a very awkward time. It isn't about you, and it isn't about love. It's about everything crashing together at once. I think you know what I mean.

Let's try again. But I don't think it can be at school. I think that's too much for me. Let's meet after. Somewhere with no traces of the rest of my life. Only us.

I'm having a hard time imagining how, but I want these pieces to fit.

Love,
R

# DAY 6024

No alarm wakes me the next day. Instead, I awake to find a mother – someone's mother, my mother – sitting at the edge of my bed, watching me. She is sorry to wake me, I can see, but that sorrow is a minor part of a much larger sadness. She touches my leg lightly.

"It's time to wake up," she says quietly, as if she wants the transition from sleep to waking to be the easiest it can be. "I've hung your clothes on the door of the closet. We'll be leaving in about forty-five minutes. Your father is . . . very upset. We all are. But he's taking this particularly hard, so just . . . give him room, okay?"

While she's talking to me, I don't really have the focus to figure out who I am or what's going on. But after she leaves and I see the dark suit hanging on the closet door, I piece it all together.

My grandfather has died and I'm about to go to my first funeral.

I tell my mother I forgot to tell friends to cover me for homework, and get on the computer to tell Rhiannon that it's not likely I'll be able to see her today. From what I can tell, the service is at least two hours away. At least we won't be spending the night.

My father has stayed in my parents' bedroom for most of the morning, but as I'm hitting send on my message to Rhiannon, he emerges. He doesn't just look upset – he looks newly blind. There is such loss in his eyes, and it permeates every other part of his body. A tie hangs feebly from his neck, barely knotted.

"Marc," he says to me. "*Marc*." This is my name, and coming from his lips right now it sounds like both an incantation and a cry of disbelief. I have no idea how to react.

Marc's mother sweeps in.

"Oh, honey," she says, wrapping her arms around her husband for a second, then pulling back to straighten his tie. Then she turns to me and asks me if I'm ready to go.

I clear the history, turn off the computer and tell her I just need to put on my shoes.

The car ride to the funeral is largely silent. The news plays on the radio, but after the third loop, I don't think any of us are listening to it. Instead, I imagine that Marc's mother and father are doing the same thing that I'm doing – accessing memories of Marc's grandfather.

Most of the memories I find are wordless. Silent, strong stretches of sitting together in fishing boats, waiting for a pull on the line. The sight of him sitting at the head of the Thanksgiving table, carving the turkey like it was his birthright to do so. When I was younger, he took me to the zoo – all I can remember is the authority in his voice as he told me about the lions and the bears. I don't remember the lions or the bears themselves, just the sense of them that he created.

There's my grandmother's death, before I really knew what death meant. She is the ghost in the background of all of these memories, but I am sure she is much more prominent in my parents' thoughts. My own thoughts now turn to the last few months, the sight of my grandfather's diminishment, the awkwardness between us as I grew taller than him and he seemed to shrink into himself, into age. His death was still a surprise – we knew it was coming, but not that particular day. My mother was the one to answer the phone. I didn't have to hear her words to know something was wrong. She drove to my father's office to tell him. I wasn't there. I didn't see it.

It is my father who looks diminished now. As if when someone close to us dies, we momentarily trade places with them, in the moment right before. And as we get over it, we're really living their life in reverse, from death to life, from sickness to health.

The fish in all the nearby lakes and rivers will be safe

today, because it seems like every fisherman in the state of Maryland is here at the funeral. There are few suits to be seen, and fewer ties. My extended family is here too – crying cousins, tearful aunts, stoic uncles. My father seems to be taking it the hardest, and he is the magnet for everyone else's condolences. My mother and I stand at his side, and get nods and pats on the shoulder.

I feel like a complete imposter. I am observing, trying to record as much as I can for Marc's memories, because I know he is going to want to have been here, is going to want to remember this.

I am not prepared for the open casket, to have Marc's grandfather right there in front of me when we walk into the chapel. We are in the front row and I can't take my eyes off of it. This is what a body looks like with nothing inside. If I could step out of Marc for a moment – if he did not come back in – this is what he would look like. It's very different from sleeping, no matter how much the undertaker has tried to make it look like sleeping.

Marc's grandfather grew up in this town, and has been a member of this congregation for his whole life. There's a lot to be said, and a lot of emotion in the saying of it. Even the preacher seems moved – so used to saying the words, but not for someone who he's cared about.

Marc's father gets up to speak, and his body seems at war with his sentences – every time he tries to release one, his breath stops, his shoulders seize. Marc's mother goes up and stands next to him. It looks like he's going to ask her to read his words for him, but then he decides against it. Instead, he puts away the speech. He talks. He unspools the memories, and sometimes they have knots in them, and sometimes they are frayed, but they are the things he thinks of when he thinks about his father, and around him, the congregation laughs and cries and nods in recognition.

Tears are welling up in my eyes, streaming down my face. At first I don't understand it, because I don't really know the man they're talking about – I don't know any of the people in this room. I am not a part of this . . . and that is why I'm crying. Because I am not a part of this and will never be a part of something like this. I've known this for a while, but you can know something for years without it really hitting you. Now it's hitting me. I will never have a family to grieve for me. I will never have people feel about me the way they feel about Marc's grandfather. I will not leave the trail of memories that he's left. No one will ever have known me or what I've done. If I die, there will be no body to mark me, no funeral to attend, no burial. If I die, there will be nobody but Rhiannon who will know I've ever been here.

I cry because I am so jealous of Marc's grandfather, because I am jealous of anyone who can make other people care so much.

Even after my father's done speaking, I am sobbing. When my parents sit back down in the pew, they sit on either side of me, comforting me.

I cry for a little while longer, knowing full well that Marc will remember these as tears for his grandfather, that he will never remember I've been here at all.

Such a strange ritual, to return the body to the ground. I am there as they lower him. I am there as we say our prayers. I take my place in the line as the dirt is shoveled onto the coffin.

He will never again have this many people thinking of him at a single time. Even though I never knew him, I wish he were here to see it.

We go back to his house afterwards. Soon enough there will be sorting and dispersing, but now it's the museum backdrop for the exhibition of grief. Stories are told – sometimes the same exact story simultaneously in different rooms. I don't know many of the people here, but that's not a failure of accessing. There were simply more people in Marc's grandfather's life than his grandson could comprehend.

After the food and the stories and the consolation, there's the drinking, and after the drinking, there's the ride home. Marc's mother has stayed sober the whole time, so she's behind the wheel as we make our way back in the darkness. I can't tell if Marc's father is asleep or lost in thought.

"It's been a long day," Marc's mother murmurs. Then we listen to the news wrap around itself, repeat at half-hour intervals until we are finally home.

I try to pretend this is my life. I try to pretend these are my parents. But it all feels hollow, because I know better.

# DAY 6025

The next morning, it's hard to raise my head from the pillow, hard to raise my arms from my sides, hard to raise my body from the bed.

This is because I must weigh at least three hundred pounds.

I have been heavy before, but I don't think I've ever been this heavy. It's as if sacks of meat have been tied to my limbs, to my torso. It takes so much more effort to do anything. Because this is not muscular heaviness. I am not a linebacker. No, I'm fat. Flabby, unwieldy fat.

When I finally take a look around and take a look inside, I'm not very excited about what I see. Finn Taylor has retreated from most of the world; his size comes from negligence and laziness, a carelessness that would be pathological if it had any meticulousness to it. While I'm sure if I access deep enough I will find some well of humanity, all I can see on the surface is the emotional equivalent of a burp.

I trudge to the shower, pick a ball of lint the size of a cat's paw out of Finn's belly button. I have to push hard to get anything done. There must have come a time

313

where it became too exhausting to do anything, and Finn just gave in to it.

Within five minutes of getting out of the shower, I'm sweating.

I don't want to Rhiannon to see me like this. But I have to see Rhiannon – I can't cancel on her for a second day in a row, not when things feel so precarious between us.

I warn her. I say in my email that I am huge today. But I still want to see her after school. I'm close to the Clover Bookstore today, so I propose that as a meeting place.

I pray that she'll come.

There's nothing in Finn's memory that leads me to believe that he'd be upset about missing school, but I go anyway. I'll let him save his absences for when he's actually conscious of them.

Because of the size of this body, I must concentrate much harder than I usually do. Even the small things – my foot on the gas pedal, the amount of space I have to leave around me in the halls – require major adjustment.

And there are the looks I get – such undisguised disgust. Not just from other students. From teachers. From strangers. The judgment flows freely. It's possible that they're reacting to the thing that Finn has allowed himself to become. But there's also something more primal, something more defensive in their disgust. I am what they fear becoming.

I've worn black today, because I've heard so often that it's supposed to be slimming. But instead I am this sphere of darkness submarining through the halls.

The only respite is lunch, where Finn has his two best friends, Ralph and Dylan. They've been best friends since kindergarten. They make fun of Finn's size, but it's clear they don't really care. If he was thin, they'd make fun of him for that too.

I feel I can relax around them.

I go home after school to take another shower and change. As I'm drying myself off, I wonder if I could plant a traumatic memory in Finn's brain, something so shocking that he'd stop eating so much. Then I'm horrified at myself for even thinking such a thing. I remind myself that it's not my business to tell Finn what to do.

I've put on Finn's best clothes – an XXXL button down and some size 46 jeans – to meet up with Rhiannon. I even try a tie, but it looks ridiculous, ski-sloping off my stomach.

The chairs are wobbly underneath me at the bookstore's café. I decide to walk the aisles instead, but they're too narrow and I keep knocking things off the shelves. In the end, I wait for her out front.

She spots me right away; it's not like she can miss me. The recognition's in her eyes, but it's not a particularly happy one.

"Hey," I say.

"Yeah, hey."

We just stand there.

"What's up?" I ask.

"Just taking you all in, I guess."

"Don't look at the package. Look at what's inside."

"That's easy for you to say. I never change, do I?"

*Yes and no*, I think. Her body's the same. But a lot of the time, I feel like I'm meeting a slightly different Rhiannon. As if each mood presents a variation.

"Let's go," I say.

"Where to?"

"Well, we've been to the ocean and to the mountain and to the woods. So I thought this time we'd try . . . dinner and a movie."

This gets a smile.

"That sounds suspiciously like a date," she says.

"I'll even buy you flowers if you'd like."

"Go ahead," she dares. "Buy me flowers."

316

Rhiannon is the only girl in the movie theater with a bouquet of a dozen roses on the seat next to her. She is also the only girl whose companion is spilling over his chair and into hers. I try to make it less awkward by draping my arm around her. But then I'm conscious of my sweat, of how my fleshy arm must feel against the back of her neck. I'm also conscious of my breathing, which wheezes a little if I exhale too much. After the previews are over, I move over a seat. But then I move my hand to the seat in between us, and she takes it. We last like that for at least ten minutes, until she pretends she has an itch, and doesn't return her hand to mine.

I've chosen a nice place for dinner, but that doesn't guarantee that it will be a nice dinner.

She keeps staring at me – staring at Finn.

"What is it?" I finally ask.

"It's just that . . . I can't see you inside. Usually I can. Some glimmer of you in the eyes. But not tonight."

In some way, this is flattering. But the way she says it, it's also disheartening.

"I promise I'm in here."

"I know. But I can't help it. I just don't feel anything. When I see you like this, I don't. I can't."

"That's okay. The reason you're not seeing it is because he's so unlike me. You're not feeling it because I'm not like this. So in a way, it's consistent."

"I guess," she says, spearing some asparagus.

She doesn't sound convinced. And I feel I've already lost if we've gotten to the convincing stage.

It doesn't feel like a date. It doesn't feel like friendship. It feels like something that fell off the tightrope but hasn't yet hit the net.

Our cars are still at the bookstore, so we head back there. Instead of cradling her roses, she dangles them at her side, as if at any moment she might need to use them as a bat.

"What's going on?" I ask her.

"Just an off night, I guess." She holds the roses up to her nose, smells them. "We're allowed to have off nights, right? Especially considering . . ."

"Yeah. Especially considering."

If I were in a different body, this would be the time I would lean down and kiss her. If I were in a different body, that kiss could transform the night from off to on. If I were in a different body, she would see me inside. She would see what she wanted to see.

But now it's awkward.

She holds the roses to my nose. I breathe in the perfume.

"Thanks for the flowers," she says.

And that is our goodbye.

# DAY 6026

I feel guilty by how relieved I am to be a normal size the next morning. I feel guilty because I realize that while before I didn't care what other people thought, or how other people saw me, now I am conscious of it, now I am judging alongside them, now I am seeing myself through Rhiannon's eyes. I guess this is making me more like everyone else, but I feel something is being lost too.

Lisa Marshall looks a lot like Rhiannon's friend Rebecca – dark straight hair, a scattering of freckles, blue eyes. She is not someone you'd go out of your way to notice if you saw her on the street, but you'd definitely notice her if she was sitting next to you in class.

*Rhiannon won't mind me today,* I think. Then I feel guilty for thinking it.

There's an email from her waiting in my inbox . It starts like this:

I really want to see you today.

And I think, *That's good.* But then it continues.

We need to talk.

And I don't know what to think anymore.

The day becomes a waiting game, a countdown, even if I'm not sure what I'm counting down toward. The clock brings me closer. My fears pound louder.

Lisa's friends don't get much out of her today.

Rhiannon's told me to meet her at a park by her school. Since I'm a girl today, I'm guessing that's safe neutral ground. No one from town is going to see the two of us and assume something R-rated. They already think male metalheads are her type.

I'm early, so I sit on a bench with Lisa's copy of an Alice Hoffman novel, stopping every now and then to watch a jogger push by. I'm so lost in the pages that I don't realize Rhiannon's here until she sits down next to me.

I can't help but smile when I see that it's her.

"Hey," I say.

"Hey," she says.

Before she can tell me what she wants to tell me, I ask her about her day, ask her about school, ask her about the weather – anything to avoid the topic of her and me. But this only lasts for about ten minutes.

"A," she says. "There are things that I need to say to you."

I know that this phrase is rarely followed by good things. But still I hope.

Even though she's said *things*, even though she's implied there's more than one, it all comes down to her next sentence.

"I don't think I can do this."

I only pause for a moment. "You don't think you can do it, or you don't *want* to do it?"

"I want to. Really, I do. But how, A? I just don't see how it's possible."

"What do you mean?"

"I mean, you're a different person every day. And I just can't love every single person you are equally. I know it's you underneath. I know it's just the package. But I can't, A. I've tried. And I can't. I want to – I want to be the person who can do that – but I can't. And it's not just that. I've just broken up with Justin – I need time to process that, to put that away. And there are just so many things you and I can't do. We'll never hang out with my friends. I can't even talk about you to my friends, and that's driving me crazy. You'll never meet my parents. I will never be able to go to sleep with you at night and then wake up with you the next morning. Never. And I've been trying to argue myself into thinking these things don't matter, A. Really, I have. But I've lost the argument. And I can't keep having it, when I know what the real answer is."

This is the part where I should be able to say *I'll change*. This is the part where I should be able to assure her that things can be different, show her it's possible. But the best I can do is to give her my deepest fantasy, the one I've been too self-conscious to share.

"It's not impossible," I tell her. "Do you think I haven't been having the same arguments with myself, the same thoughts? I've been trying to imagine how we can have a future together. So what about this? I think one way for me to not travel so far would be if we lived in a city. I mean, there would be more bodies the right age nearby, and while I don't know how I get passed from one body to the next, I do feel certain that the distance I travel is related to how many possibilities there are. So if we were in New York City, I'd probably never leave. There are so many people to choose from. So we could see each other all the time. Be with each other. I know it's crazy. I know you can't just leave home on a moment's notice. But eventually we could do that. Eventually that could be our life. I will never be able to wake up next to you, but I can be with you all the time. It won't be a normal life – I know that. But it will be a life. A life together."

I've pictured us there, having an apartment to ourselves. Me coming home each day, kicking off my shoes, us making dinner together, then crawling into bed, with me tiptoeing out when midnight approached. Growing up together. Knowing more of the world through knowing her.

But she's shaking her head. There are tears becoming possible in her eyes. And that's all it takes for my fantasy to pop. That's all it takes for my fantasy to become another fool's dream.

"That will never happen," she says gently. "I wish I could believe it, but I can't."

"But, Rhiannon –"

"I want you to know, if you were a guy I met – if you were the same guy every day, if the inside was the outside – there's a good chance I could love you forever. This isn't about the heart of you – I hope you know that. But the rest is too difficult. There might be girls out there who could deal with it. I hope there are. But I'm not one of them. I just can't do it."

Now my tears are coming. "So . . . what? This is it? We stop?"

"I want us to be in each other's lives. But your life can't keep derailing mine. I need to be with my friends, A. I need to go to school and go to prom and do all of the things I'm supposed to do. I am grateful – truly grateful – not to be with Justin anymore. But I can't let go of the other things."

I'm surprised by my own bitterness. "You can't do that for me the way I can do that for you?"

"I can't. I'm sorry, but I can't."

We are outside, but the walls are closing in. We are on solid ground, but the bottom has just dropped out.

"Rhiannon . . . " I say. But the words stop there. I can't think of anything else to say. I've run out of my own argument.

She leans over and kisses me on the cheek.

"I should go," she says. "Not forever. But for now. Let's talk again in a few days. If you really think about it, you'll come to the same conclusion. And then it won't be as bad. Then we'll be able to work through it together, and figure out what comes next. I want there to be something next. It just can't be . . ."

"Love?"

"A relationship. Dating. What you want."

She stands up. I am left stranded on the bench.

"We'll talk," she assures me.

"We'll talk," I echo. It sounds empty.

She doesn't want to leave it like this. She will stay until I give some indication of being all right, of surviving this moment.

"Rhiannon, I love you," I say.

"And I love you."

That isn't the question, she's saying.

But it's not the answer either.

I wanted love to conquer all. But love can't conquer anything. It can't do anything on its own.

It relies on us to do the conquering on its behalf.

I get home and Lisa's mother is cooking dinner. It smells amazing, but I can't imagine having to sit at the table and make conversation. I can't imagine talking to a single other person. I can't imagine making it through the next few hours without screaming.

I tell her I'm not feeling well and head upstairs.

I lock myself in Lisa's bedroom and feel that's where I'll always be. Locked inside a room. Trapped with myself.

# DAY 6027

I wake up the next morning with a broken ankle. Luckily, I've had it for a while and the crutches are next to my bed. It's the one thing about me that feels newly healed.

I can't help it – I check my email. But there's no word from Rhiannon. I feel alone. Completely alone. Then I realize there's one other person in the world who vaguely knows who I am. I check to see if he's written me lately.

And indeed he has. There are now twenty unread messages from Nathan, each more desperate than the previous one, ending with:

> All I ask is for an explanation. I will leave you alone
> after that. I just need to know.

I write him back.

> Fine. Where should we meet?

With her broken ankle, Kasey can't exactly drive. And since he's still in trouble for his blanked-out joy ride, Nathan's not allowed to use the car either. So our parents have to drop us off. Even though I don't say it is, mine just assume it's a date.

327

The hitch is that Nathan is expecting me to be a guy named Andrew, since that's who I said I was last time. But if I'm going to tell him the truth, being Kasey will help me illustrate my point.

We're meeting at a Mexican restaurant by his house. I wanted somewhere public, but also somewhere our parents could drop us off without raising eyebrows. I see him walk in, and it's almost like he's dressed for a date too – even if he doesn't look sporty, he's certainly trying to be his best self. I raise one of my crutches and wave to him; he knows I have crutches, just not that I'm a girl. I figured I'd save that for in person.

He looks very confused as he's walking over.

"Nathan," I say when he gets to me. "Have a seat."

"You're . . . Andrew?"

"I can explain. Sit down."

Sensing tension, the waiter swoops in and smothers us with specials. Our water glasses are filled. We give our drink order. Then we're forced to talk to each other.

"You're a girl," he says.

I want to laugh. It freaks him out so much more to think he was possessed by a girl, not a guy. As if that really matters.

"Sometimes," I say. Which only confuses him more.

"*Who are you?*" he asks.

"I'll tell you," I reply. "I promise. But let's order first."

I don't really trust him, but I tell him I do, as a way of inspiring a reciprocal trust. It's still a risk I'm taking, but I can't think of any other way to give him peace of mind.

"Only one other person knows this," I begin. And then I tell him what I am. I tell him how it works. I tell him again what happened the day I was inside his body. I tell him how I know it won't happen another time.

I know that, unlike Rhiannon, he won't doubt me. Because my explanation feels right to him. It fits nicely into his own experience. It's what he's always suspected. Because in some way, I primed him to remember it. I don't know why, but when my mind and his mind concocted our cover story, we left a hole in it. Now I'm filling in that hole.

When I'm done, Nathan doesn't know what to say.

"So . . . whoa . . . I guess . . . so, like, tomorrow, you're not going to be her?"

"No."

"And she'll . . . ?"

"She'll have some other memory of today. Probably that she met a boy for a date, but that it didn't work out. She won't remember it's you. It'll just be this vague idea of a person, so if her parents ask tomorrow how it went, she won't be surprised by the question. She'll never know she wasn't here."

"So why did I know?"

"Maybe because I left you so fast. Maybe I didn't lay the groundwork for a proper memory. Or maybe I wanted you to find me, in some way. I don't know."

Our food, which arrived while I was talking, remains largely untouched on the table.

"This is huge," Nathan says.

"You can't tell anyone," I remind him. "I'm trusting you."

"I know, I know." He nods absently, and starts to eat. "This is between you and me."

At the end of the meal, Nathan tells me it's really helped to talk to me and to know the truth. He also asks if we can meet again the next day, just so he can see the switch for himself. I tell him I can't make any guarantees, but I'll try.

Our parents pick us up. On the drive back home, Kasey's mom asks me how it went.

"Good . . . I think," I tell her.

It's the only truthful thing I tell her the whole ride.

# DAY 6028

The next day, a Sunday, I wake up as Ainsley Mills. Allergic to gluten, afraid of spiders, proud owner of three Scotties, two of which sleep in her bed.

In ordinary circumstances, I would think this was going to be an ordinary day.

Nathan emails me, saying he wants to meet up, and that if I have a car, I can come to his house. His parents are away for the day, so he doesn't have a ride.

Rhiannon doesn't email me, so I go with Nathan.

Ainsley tells her parents she's going shopping with some friends. They don't question her. They give her the keys to her mom's car and tell her not to be back too late. They need her to babysit her sister starting at five.

It's only eleven. Ainsley assures them she'll be back in plenty of time.

Nathan is only fifteen minutes away. I figure I won't have to stay too long. I'll just have to prove to him that I am the same person as yesterday. Then that's it – I don't think I have anything else to offer. The rest is up to him.

He looks surprised when he opens the door and sees

me. I guess he didn't really believe it would be true, and now it is. He looks nervous, and I chalk it up to the fact that I'm here in his house. I recognize it, but already it's started blending into all the other houses I've lived in. If you put me in the main hallway and all the doors were closed, I don't think I could tell you which door led to which room.

Nathan takes me into his living room – this is where guests go, and even if I've been him for a day, I am still a guest.

"So it's really you," he says. "In a different body."

I nod and sit down on the couch.

"Do you want something to drink?" he offers.

I tell him water will be fine. I do not tell him that I plan on leaving soon, and water probably isn't necessary.

As he goes to get it, I study some of the family portraits on display. Nathan looks uncomfortable in each of them . . . just like his father. Only his mother beams.

I hear Nathan come back in and don't look up. So it's a jolt when a voice that isn't Nathan's says, "I'm so glad I have a chance to meet you."

It's a man with silver hair and a gray suit. He's wearing a tie, but it's loose at the neck; this is casual time for him. I stand up, but in Ainsley's slight body, there's no way I can meet him eye to eye.

"Please," Reverend Poole says, "there's no need for you to stand. Let's sit."

He closes the door behind him, then chooses an armchair that's between me and the door. He is probably twice Ainsley's size, so he could stop me if he wanted to. The question is whether he'd really want to. The fact that my instinct is to wonder about these things is a tip-off that there may be cause for alarm.

I decide to come on tough.

"It's Sunday," I say. "Shouldn't you be in church?"

He smiles. "More important things for me here."

This must have been what it was like when the red riding hood first met the big bad wolf. What she felt must have been as much intrigue as terror.

"What do you want?" I ask.

He folds his leg across his knee. "Well, Nathan told me the most interesting story, and I'm wondering if it's indeed true."

There's no use denying it. "Nathan wasn't supposed to tell anyone!" I say loudly, hoping Nathan hears me.

"While for the past month, you've left Nathan hanging, I have been attempting to give him answers. It's natural that he should confide in me when he is told such a thing."

Poole has an angle. That much is clear. I just don't know what it is yet.

"I am not the devil," I say. "I am not a demon. I am not any of the things you want me to be. I am just a person. A person who borrows other people's lives for a day."

"But can't you see the devil at work?"

I shake my head. "No. There was no devil inside of Nathan. There is no devil inside of this girl. There is only me."

"You see," Poole says, "that's where you're wrong. Yes, you are inside of these bodies. But what's inside of you, my friend? Why do you think you are the way you are? Don't you feel it could be the devil's work?"

I speak calmly. "What I do is not the devil's work."

At this, Poole actually laughs.

"Relax, Andrew. Relax. You and I are on the same side."

I stand up. "Good. Then let me go."

I make a move to leave, but as I anticipated, he blocks me. He pushes Ainsley back to the sofa.

"Not so fast," he says. "I'm not finished."

"On the same side, I see."

The grin disappears. And for a moment, I see something in his eyes. I'm not sure what it is, but it paralyzes me.

"I know you so much better than you give me credit for," Poole says. "Do you think this is an accident? Do you think I'm just some religious zealot here to exorcise your demons away? Did you ever ask yourself why I am cataloging such things, what I'm looking for? The answer is you, Andrew. And others like you."

He's fishing. He has to be.

"There are no others like me," I tell him.

His eyes flash again at me. "Of course there are, Andrew. Just because you're different, it doesn't mean you're *unique*."

I don't know what he's saying. I don't want to know what he's saying.

"Look at me," he commands.

And I do. I look into those eyes, and I know. I know what he's saying.

"The amazing thing," he tells me, "is that you still haven't learned how to make it last longer than a single day. You have no idea the power that you possess."

I back away from him. "You're not Reverend Poole," I say, unable to keep the shaking out of Ainsley's voice.

"I am today. I was yesterday. Tomorrow – who knows? I have to judge what best suits me. I wasn't going to miss *this*."

He is taking me beyond another window. But right away, I know that I don't like what's there.

"There are better ways to live your life," he continues. "I can show you."

335

There's recognition in his eyes, yes. But there's also menace. And something else – an entreaty. Almost as if Reverend Poole is inside, trying to warn me.

"Get off of me," I say, standing up.

He seems amused. "I'm not touching you. I am sitting here, having a conversation."

"Get off of me!" I say louder, and start ripping at my own shirt, sending the buttons flying.

"What –"

"GET OFF OF ME!" I scream, and in that scream is a sob, and in that sob is a cry for help, and just as I'd hoped, Nathan hears it, Nathan has been listening, and the door to the living room is flung open, and there he is, just in time to see me screaming and crying, my shirt ripped open, Poole standing now with murder in his eyes.

I am betting everything on the common decency I saw in Nathan, back when I was inside of him, and even though he is clearly terrified, the common decency does rise, because instead of running away or closing the door or listening to what Poole has to say, Nathan yells, "What are you doing?" And he holds the door open for me as I flee, and he blocks the Reverend – or whoever he is inside – from catching me as I run out the front door and into my car. Nathan summons the strength to hold Poole back, buying me those crucial seconds, so by the time Poole is on the lawn, my key is already in the ignition.

"There's no point in running away!" Poole yells. "You're only going to want to find me later! All the others have!"

Trembling, I turn up the radio and drown him out with the sound of the song, and the sound of me driving away.

I don't want to believe him. I want to think he's an actor, a charlatan, a fake.

But when I looked closely at him, I saw someone else inside. I recognized him in the same way that Rhiannon recognized me.

Only, I also saw danger there.

I saw someone who does not play by the same set of rules.

As soon as I'm gone, I wish I'd stayed a few minutes longer, let him talk a little bit more. I have more questions than I've ever had before, and he might have had the answers.

But if I'd stayed just a few more minutes, I don't know if I could have left. And I would have been dooming Ainsley to the same struggle as Nathan, if not worse. I don't know what Poole would have done with her –

what *we* would have done with her, if I'd stayed.

He could be lying. I have to remind myself that he could be lying.

*I am not the only one.*

I cannot wrap my thoughts around this. The fact that there could be others. They may have been in the same school as me, the same room as me, the same family as me. But because we keep our secret so hidden, there'd be no way to know.

I remember the boy in Montana whose story was so similar to mine. Was that true? Or is it just a trap Poole set.

*There are others.*

It can change everything.

Or it can change nothing.

As I drive back to Ainsley's house, I realize it's my choice.

# DAY 6029

Darryl Drake is very distracted the next day.

I guide him through school and say the right things when I have to. But his friends keep commenting that he's lost in space. At track practice, the coach berates him repeatedly for lack of focus.

"What's on your mind?" Darryl's girlfriend, Sasha, asks him when he drives her home.

"I guess I'm not really here today," he tells her. "But I'll be back tomorrow."

I spend the afternoon and the evening on the computer. Darryl's parents are both at work and his brother is in college, so I have the whole house to myself.

My story is front and center on Poole's website – a bastardized account of what I told Nathan, with some errors that either come from Nathan hiding something or from Poole goading me on.

Going outside his own site, I find out everything I can about Reverend Poole, but it's not much. He doesn't seem to have become outspoken about demonic possession until Nathan's story hit. I look at photos from before and from after, trying to tell if there's some difference. But in photographs, he looks the same.

The eyes are hidden by the flatness of the image.

I read all the stories on the site, trying to find myself within them, trying to find other people like me. Again, there are a couple from Montana. And others that could be similar, if what Poole hinted at is true: that the one-day limit is only for newcomers and can be somehow transcended.

It's what I want, of course. To stay in a single body. To lead a single life.

But at the same time, it's not what I want. Because I can't help but think about what would happen to the person whose body I'd stay in. Does he or she just wink out of existence? Or is the original soul then banished to bounce from body to body – basically, are the roles reversed? I can't imagine anything sadder than having once had a single body and then suddenly not being able to stay in any for longer than a day. At least I've had the comfort of never knowing anything else. I would destroy myself if I'd actually had to give something up before leading this traveler's existence.

If there were no one else involved, it would be an easy choice. But isn't that always the case? And there's always someone else involved.

There's an email from Nathan, saying how sorry he is for what happened yesterday. He says that he'd thought

Reverend Poole could help me. Now he's not sure of anything.

I write back to tell him that it isn't his fault, and that he has to get away from Reverend Poole and try to get back to his normal life.

I also tell him this is the last time I will ever email him. I don't explain that it's because I can't trust him. I figure he'll make that connection for himself.

When I'm done, I forward our email chain to my new email address. And then I close my account. Just like that, a few years of my life are over. The only through-line is gone. It's silly to feel nostalgic about an email address, but I do. There aren't many pieces to my past, so I have to mourn at least a little when one falls away.

Later that night, there's an email from Rhiannon.

How are you?

R

That's it.

I want to tell her everything that's happened in the past forty-eight hours. I want to lay the past two days in front of her to see how she reacts, to see if she understands what they mean to me. I want her help.

341

I want her advice. I want her reassurance.

But I don't think that's what she wants. And I don't want to give it to her unless it's what she wants. So I type back:

> It's been a rough two days. Apparently, I may not be the only person out there like this. Which is hard to think about.
>
> A

There are still a few hours left in the night, but she doesn't use any of them to get back to me.

# DAY 6030

I wake up only two towns away from her, in someone else's arms.

I am careful not to wake this girl who enfolds me. Her feather-yellow hair covers her eyes. The beat of her heart presses against my back. Her name is Amelia, and last night she snuck in my window to be with me.

My name is Zara – or at least that's the name I've chosen for myself. I was born Clementine, and I loved that name until I turned ten. Then I started to experiment, with Zara being the name that stuck. Z has always been my favorite letter, and twenty-six is my lucky number.

Amelia stirs under the sheets. "What time is it?" she asks groggily.

"Seven," I tell her.

Instead of getting up, she curls into me.

"Will you be a good scout and check the whereabouts of your mom? I'd rather not leave the way I came in. My morning coordination is so much fuzzier than my night-time coordination, and I'm always much more inspired when I'm approaching the maiden."

"Okay," I say, and in thanks, she kisses my bare shoulder.

The tenderness between two people can turn the air tender, the room tender, time itself tender. As I step out of bed and slip on an oversize shirt, everything around me feels like it's the temperature of happiness. Nothing from the previous night has dissipated. I've woken into the comfort they've created.

I tiptoe into the hallway and listen at my mother's door. The only sound is sleep-breathing, so it appears we're safe. When I get back to my room, Amelia is still in bed, the sheet pulled back so it's just her, her t-shirt and her underwear. I have a feeling that Zara would not let this moment pass without crawling in beside her, but I feel I can't do that in her place.

"She's asleep," I report.

"Like, safe-to-take-a-shower asleep?"

"I think so."

"You want first shower, second shower, or both shower?"

"You can go first."

She gets out of bed and stops to kiss me on the way out. Her hands move under my oversize shirt and I don't resist. I fall right into it, kiss her a little bit longer.

"You sure?" she asks.

"You go first," I tell her.

And then, just like Zara would, I miss her when she's left the room.

I want it to be Rhiannon.

She sneaks out of the house while I'm in my shower. Then, twenty minutes later, she's back at the door, to pick me up for school. My mother is awake now and in the kitchen, and smiles when she sees Amelia heading up the path.

I wonder how much she knows.

We spend most of the day together at school, but not in a way that limits our interactions with other people. If anything, we incorporate our friends into what we have between us. We exist as individuals. We exist as a pair. We exist as parts of trios, quartets, and so on. And it all feels right.

I can't get Rhiannon off my mind. Remembering what she said about how her friends would never know me. How no one else would ever know me. How what we have together will only be us, always.

I am starting to realize what this means, and how sad it would be.

I am already feeling some of the sadness now, and it isn't even happening.

Seventh period, Amelia has study hall in the library while I have gym. When we meet up after, she shows me the books she's taken out for me, because they look like ones I'd like.

Will I ever know Rhiannon this well?

Amelia has basketball practice after school. I usually wait around for her, doing my homework. But she is making me miss Rhiannon too much; I have to do something about it. I ask her if I can borrow her car and run some errands.

She hands over the keys, no questions asked.

It takes me ten minutes to get over to Rhiannon's school. I park in my usual space as most of the cars head in the other direction. Then I find a place to sit and watch the door, hoping she hasn't already left.

I am not going to talk to her. I am not going to start everything again. I just want to see her.

Five minutes after I've arrived, she appears. She is talking to Rebecca and a couple of her other friends. I can't hear what they're saying, but they're all involved in the conversation.

From here, she doesn't look like someone who's recently lost something. Her life seems to be playing on all chords. There's one moment – one small moment – when she looks up and glances around. For that moment, I can believe she's looking for me. But I can't

346

tell you what happens in the moment after, because I quickly turn away, stare at something else. I don't want her to see my eyes.

This is the after for her, and if she's in the after, then I have to be in the after too.

I stop off at a Target on the way back to Amelia. Zara knows all her favorite foods and most of them are of the snack variety. I stock up, and before I go back into the school to find her, I arrange them on the dashboard, spelling her name. It is, I believe, what Zara would want me to do.

I am not fair. I wanted Rhiannon to see me there. Even as I looked away, I wanted her to come right over and treat me just like Amelia would treat Zara after spending three days apart.

I know it's never going to happen. And that knowledge is a flash of light I can't quite see through.

Amelia is delighted by the dashboard display and insists on taking me to dinner. I call home and tell my mother, who doesn't seem to mind.

I can sense that Amelia realizes I'm only half here, but she's going to let me be half elsewhere, because that's where I need to be. Over dinner, she fills the silence with tales from her day, some real and some completely imaginary. She makes me guess which is which.

We've only been together for seven months. Still, as far as the number of memories Zara's collected, it feels like a long time.

*This is what I want,* I think.

And then I can't help it. I add, *This is what I can't have.*

"Can I ask you something?" I say to Amelia.

"Sure. What?"

"If I woke up in a different body every day – if you never knew what I was going to look like tomorrow – would you still love me?"

She doesn't miss a beat, or even act like the question is strange. "Even if you were green and had a beard and a male appendage between your legs. Even if your eyebrows were orange and you had a mole covering your entire cheek and a nose that poked me in the eye every time I kissed you. Even if you weighed seven hundred pounds and had hair the size of a Doberman under your arms. Even then, I would love you."

"Likewise," I tell her.

It's so easy to say, because it never has to be true.

Before we say goodbye, she kisses me with everything she

has. And I try to kiss her back with everything I want.

*This is the nice note,* I can't help but think.

But just like a sound, as soon as the note hits the air, it begins to fade.

When I walk inside, Zara's mother says to her, "You know, you can invite Amelia in."

I tell her I know. Then I rush to my room, because it's too much. So much happiness can only make me sad. I close the door and begin to sob. Rhiannon's right. I know it. I can never have these things.

I don't even check my email. Either way, I don't want to know.

Amelia calls to say goodnight. I have to let it go to voicemail, have to compose myself into the most like Zara I can be, before I answer.

"I'm sorry," I tell her when I call her back. "I was talking to Mom. She says you need to come by more often."

"Is she referring to the bedroom window or the front door?"

"The front door."

"Well, it looks like a little bird called *progress* is now sitting on our shoulder."

I yawn, then apologize for it.

"No need to say you're sorry, sleepyhead. Dream a little dream of me, okay."

"I will."

"I love you," she says.

"I love you," I say.

And then we hang up, because nothing else needs to be said after that.

I want to give Zara her life back. Even if I feel I deserve something like this, I don't deserve it at her expense.

She will remember all of it, I decide. Not my discontent. But the contentment that caused it.

# DAY 6031

I wake up feverish, sore, uncomfortable.

July's mother comes in to check on her. Says she seemed fine last night.

Is it sickness or is it heartbreak?

I can't tell.

The thermometer says I'm normal, but clearly I'm not.

# DAY 6032

An email from Rhiannon. Finally.

> I want to see you, but I'm not sure if we should do that.
> I want to hear about what's going on, but I'm afraid that
> will only start everything again. I love you – I do – but
> I am afraid of making that love too important. Because
> you're always going to leave me, A. We can't deny it.
> You're always going to leave.
>
> R

I don't know how to respond to that. Instead, I try
to lose myself in being Howie Middleton. His girlfriend
picks a fight with him at lunchtime, over the fact that
he never spends time with her anymore. Howie doesn't
have much to say about that. In fact, he stays entirely
silent, which only infuriates her more.

*I have to leave,* I think. If there are things I will never
have here, there are also things I will never find here.
Things I might need to find.

# DAY 6033

I wake up the next morning as Alexander Lin. His alarm goes off, playing a song I really like. This makes waking up much easier.

I also like his room. Plenty of books on the shelves, some of their spines worn down from rereading. There are three guitars in the corner, one electric, the amp still plugged in from the night before. In another corner, there's a lime green couch, and I know immediately this is a place where friends come to crash, this is their home away from home. He has Post-its all over the place with random quotes on them. On top of his computer is something from George Bernard Shaw: *Dance is the perpendicular expression of a horizontal desire.* Some of the Post-its are in his handwriting, but others have been written by friends. *I am the walrus. I'm nobody – who are you? Let all the dreamers wake the nation.*

Even before I've gotten to know him, Alexander Lin has made me smile.

His parents are happy to see him. I have a sense that they're always happy to see him.

"Are you sure you're going to be okay for the weekend?" his mother asks. Then she opens the refrigerator, which looks like it's been stocked for at least a month. "I think there's enough here, but if you need anything, just use the money in the envelope."

I feel something is missing here; there is something I should be doing. I access and discover it's the Lins' anniversary tomorrow. They are going on an anniversary trip. And Alexander's gift for them is up in his room.

"One second," I say. I run upstairs and find it in his closet – a bag festooned with Post-its, each of them filled in with something his parents have said to him over the years, from, *A is for Apple* to *Always remember to check your blind spot*. And this is just the wrapping. When I bring the bag down to Mr and Mrs Lin, they open it to find ten hours of music for their ten-hour drive, as well as cookies Alexander has baked for them.

Alexander's father wraps him in a thankful hug, and Alexander's mother joins in.

For a moment, I forget who I really am.


Alexander's locker is also covered in Post-it quotes, in a rainbow of handwritings. His best friend, Mickey, comes by and offers him half a muffin – the bottom half, because Mickey only likes the tops.

Mickey starts telling me about Greg, a boy he's apparently had a crush on for ages – *ages* meaning at least three weeks. I feel the perverse desire to tell Mickey about Rhiannon, who is actually only two towns away. I access and find that Alexander doesn't have any crushes himself at the moment, but if he did, they'd be female. Mickey doesn't pry too much about this. And quickly other friends find them, and the talk turns to an upcoming Battle of the Bands. Apparently, Alexander is playing in at least three of the entrants, including Mickey's band. He's that kind of guy, always willing to chip in with some music.

As the day progresses, I can't help but feel that Alexander is the kind of person I try to be. But part of what makes his personality work is his ability to stick around, to be there day in and day out for people. His friends rely on him, and he relies on them – the simple balance on which so many lives are built.

I decide to make sure that this is true. I zone out of math class and tune in instead to Alexander's memories. The way I access him, it's like turning on a hundred televisions at the same time, I'm seeing so many parts of him at once. The good memories. The hard memories.

His friend Cara is telling him she's pregnant. He is not the father, but she trusts him more than she does the father. His father doesn't want him to spend so much time on the guitar, tells him music is a dead-end calling. He drinks his third can of Red Bull, trying to finish a paper at four in the morning because he was out with friends until one. He is climbing the ladder of a tree house. He is failing his driver's test and fighting back tears when the instructor tells him. He is alone in his room, playing the same tune over and over again on acoustic guitar, trying to figure out what it means. Ginny Dulles is breaking up with him, saying it's just that she likes him as a friend, when the truth is that she likes Brandon Rogers more. He is on a swing set, six years old, going higher and higher until he is convinced that this is it, this time he will fly. He is slipping money into Mickey's wallet while Mickey isn't looking, so later Mickey will be able to pay his share of the check. He is dressed as the Tin Man on Halloween. His mother has burned her hand on the stove and doesn't know what to do. The first morning he has his licence, he drives to the ocean to watch the sunrise. He is the only one there.

I stop there. I stop at this. I lurch back into myself. I don't know if I can do this.

I can't block out the temptation that Poole offered: If I could stay in this life, would I? Every time I pose the question to myself, I get knocked back into my own life from Alexander's. I get ideas, and once they take hold, I can't stop them.

What if there really was a way to stay?

*

Every person is a possibility. The hopeless romantics feel it most acutely, but even for others, the only way to keep going is to see every person as a possibility. The more I see the Alexander that the world reflects back at him, the more of a possibility he seems. His possibility is grounded in the things that mean the most to me. Kindness. Creativity. Engagement in the world. Engagement in the possibilities of the people around him.

The day is nearly half over. I only have a short time to figure out what to do with Alexander's possibilities.

The clock always ticks. There are times you don't hear it, and there are times that you do.

I email Nathan and ask him for Poole's email address. I get a quick response. I email Poole a few simple questions.

I get another quick response.

I email Rhiannon and tell her I'm going to come by this afternoon.

I say it's important.

She tells me she'll be there.

Alexander has to tell Mickey that he can't make their band practice after school.

"Hot date?" Mickey asks, joking.

Alexander smiles mischievously and leaves it at that.

Rhiannon is waiting for me at the bookstore. It's become our place.

She knows me when I walk through the door. Her eyes follow me as I come closer. She doesn't smile, but I do. I am so grateful to see her.

"Hey," I say.

"Hey," she says.

She wants to be here, but she doesn't think it's a good idea. She is also grateful, but she is sure this gratitude will turn into regret.

"I have an idea," I tell her.

"What?"

"Let's pretend this is the first time we've ever met. Let's pretend you were here to get a book, and I happened to bump into you. We struck up a conversation. I like you. You like me. Now we're sitting down to coffee. It feels right. You don't know that I switch bodies every day. I don't know about your ex or anything else. We're just two people meeting for the first time."

"But why?"

"So we don't have to talk about everything else. So we can just be with each other. Enjoy it."

"I don't see the point –"

"No past. No future. Just present. Give it a chance."

She looks torn. She leans her chin on her fist and looks at me. Finally, she decides.

"It's very nice to meet you," she says. She doesn't understand it yet, but she's going to go with it.

I smile. "It's very nice to meet you as well. Where should we go?"

"You decide," she says. "What's your favorite place?"

I access Alexander, and the answer is right there. As if he's handing it to me.

My smile grows wider.

"I know just the place," I say. "But first, we'll need groceries."

Because this is the first time we've met, I don't have to tell her about Nathan or Poole or anything else that's happened or about to happen. The past and future are what's complicated. It's the present that's simple. And that simplicity is the sensation of it being just her and me.

Even though there are only a few things we need, we get a shopping cart and go down every aisle of the grocery store. It doesn't take long before Rhiannon is standing on the front of it, I'm standing on the back of it, and we are riding as fast as we can.

We set down a rule: every aisle has to have a story. So in the pet food aisle, I learn more about Swizzle, the malevolent bunny rabbit. In the produce aisle, I tell her about the day I went to summer camp and had to be part of a greased watermelon pull, and how I ended up with three stitches after the watermelon shot out of everyone's arms and landed in my eye – the first case of watermelon abuse the hospital had ever seen. In the cereal aisle, we offer autobiographies in the form of the cereals we've eaten over the years, trying to pinpoint the year that the cereal turning the milk blue stopped being cool and started being gross.

Finally, we have enough food for a vegetarian feast.

"I should call my mom and tell her I'm eating at Rebecca's," Rhiannon says, taking out her phone.

"Tell her you're staying over," I suggest.

She pauses. "Really?"

"Really."

But she doesn't make a move to call.

"I'm not sure that's a good idea."

"Trust me," I say. "I know what I'm doing."

"You know how I feel."

"I do. But still, I want you to trust me. I'm not going to hurt you. I will never hurt you."

She calls her mother, tells her she's at Rebecca's. Then she calls Rebecca and makes sure the cover story will be intact. Rebecca asks her what's going on. Rhiannon says she'll tell her later.

"You'll tell her you met a boy," I say once she's hung up.

"A boy I just met?"

"Yeah," I say, "a boy you've just met."

We go back to Alexander's house. There's barely enough room in the refrigerator for the groceries we've bought.

"Why did we bother?" Rhiannon asks.

"Because I didn't notice what was in here this morning. And I wanted to make sure we had exactly what we desired."

"Do you know how to cook?"

"Not really. You?"

"Not really."

"I guess we'll figure it out. But first, there's something I want to show you."

She likes Alexander's bedroom as much as I do. I can tell. She loses herself in reading the Post-it notes, then runs her finger over the spines of the books. Her face is a picture of delight.

Then she turns to me and the fact can't be denied: we're in a bedroom, and there's a bed. But that's not why I brought her here.

"Time for dinner," I say. Then I take her hand and we walk away together.

We fill the air with music as we cook. We move in unison, move in tandem. We've never done this together before, but we establish our rhythm, our division of labor. I can't help but think this is the way it could always be – the easygoing sharing of space, the enjoyable silence of knowing each other. My parents away, and my girlfriend has come over to help cook dinner. There she is, chopping vegetables, unaware of her posture, unaware of the wildness of her hair, even unaware that I am staring at her with so much love. Even outside our kitchen-sized bubble, the night-time sings. I can see it through the window, and also see her reflection mapped out on top of it. Everything is in its right place, and my heart wants to believe this can always be true. My heart wants to make it true, even as something darker tugs it away.

It's past nine by the time we're finished.

"Should I set the table?" Rhiannon asks, gesturing to the dining room.

"No. I'm taking you to my favorite place, remember?"

I find two trays and arrange our meals on them. I even find a dozen candlesticks to take along. Then I lead Rhiannon out the back door.

"Where are we going?" she asks once we're in the yard.

"Look up," I tell her.

At first she doesn't see it – the only light is coming from the kitchen, drifting out to us like the afterglow from another world. Then, as our eyes adjust, it becomes visible to her.

"Nice," she says, walking over so Alexander's tree house looms over us, the ladder at our fingertips.

"There's a pulley system," I say, "for the trays. I'll go up and drop it down."

I grab two of the candles and scurry up the ladder. The inside of the tree house matches Alexander's memories pretty well. It's as much a rehearsal space as a tree house, with another guitar in the corner, as well as notebooks full of lyrics and music. Even though there's an overhead light that could be turned on, I rely on candles. Then I send down the dumbwaiter and raise the trays one by one. As soon as the second tray is safely inside, Rhiannon joins me.

"Pretty cool, isn't it?" I ask as she looks around.

"Yeah."

"It's all his. His parents don't come up here."

"I love it."

There isn't any table and there aren't any chairs, so we sit cross-legged on the floor and eat, facing each other in the candlelight. We don't rush it – we let the taste of the moment sink in. I light more candles and revel in the sight of her. We don't need the moon or the sun in here. She is beautiful in our own light.

"What?" she asks.

I lean over and kiss her. Just once.

"That," I say.

She is my first and only love. Most people know that their first love will not be their only love. But for me, she is both. This will be the only chance I give myself. This will never happen again.

There are no clocks in here, but I am aware of the minutes, aware of the hours. Even the candles conspire, getting shorter as time grows shorter. Reminding me and reminding me and reminding me.

I want this to be the first time we've met. I want this to be two teenagers on a first date.

But there are also other things I have to say, other things I have to do.

When we're finished, she pushes the trays aside. She closes the distance between us. I think she's going to kiss me, but instead she reaches into her pocket. She pulls out one of Alexander's pads of Post-it notes. She pulls out a pen. Then she draws a heart on the top Post-it, peels it off and places it on my heart.

"There," she says.

I look down at it. I look up at her.

"I have to tell you something," I say.

I mean I have to tell her everything.

I tell her about Nathan. I tell her about Poole. I tell her I might not be the only one. I tell her there might be a way to stay in a body longer. There might be a way not to leave.

The candles are burning down. I am taking too much time. It's almost eleven when I'm done.

"So you can stay?" she asks when I'm finished. "Are you saying you can stay?"

"Yes," I answer. "And no."

When first love ends, most people eventually know there will be more to come. They are not through with love. Love is not through with them. It will never be the same as the first, but it will be better in different ways.

I have no such consolation. This is why I cling so hard. This is why this is so hard.

"There might be a way to stay," I tell her. "But I can't. I'll never be able to stay."

Murder. When it all comes down to it, it would be murder to stay. No love can outbalance that.

Rhiannon pulls away from me. Stands up. Turns on me.

"You can't do this!" she yells. "You can't swoop in, bring me here, give me all this – and then say it can't work. That's cruel, A. Cruel."

"I know," I say. "That's why this is a first date. That's why this is the first time we've ever met."

"How can you say that? How can you erase everything else?"

I stand up. Walk over. Wrap my arms around her. At first she resists, wants to pull away. But then she gives in.

"He's a good guy," I say, my voice a broken whisper. I don't want to do this, but I have to do this. "He might even be a great guy. And today's the day you first met. Today's your first date. He's going to remember being in the bookstore. He's going to remember the first time he saw you, and how he was drawn to you not just because you're beautiful, but because he could see your strength. He could see how much you want to be a part of the world. He'll remember talking with you, how easy it was, how engaging. He'll remember not wanting it to end, and asking you if you wanted to do something else. He'll remember you asking him his favorite place, and he'll remember thinking about

366

here, and wanting to show it to you. The grocery store, the stories in the aisles, the first time you saw his room – that will all be there, and I won't have to change a single thing. His heartbeat is my heartbeat. The acceleration is the same. I know he will appreciate who you are the way I appreciate who you are. I just know it."

"But what about you?" Rhiannon asks, her voice breaking too.

"You'll find the things in him that you find in me," I tell her. "Without the complications."

"I can't just switch like that."

"I know. He'll have to prove it to you. Every day, he'll have to prove he's worthy of you. And if he doesn't, that's it. But I think he will."

"Why are you doing this?"

"Because I have to go, Rhiannon. For real this time. I have to go far away. There are things I need to find out. And I can't keep stepping into your life. You need something more than that."

"So this is goodbye?"

"It's goodbye to some things. And hello to others."

I want him to remember how it feels to hold her. I want him to remember how it feels to share the world with her. I want him, somewhere inside, to remember how much I love her. And I want him to learn to love her in his own way, having nothing to do with me.

I had to ask Poole if it was really possible. I had to ask him if he could really teach me.

He promised he could. He told me we could work together.

There was no hesitation. No warning. No acknowledgment of the lives we'd be destroying.

That's when I knew for sure I had to run away.

She holds me. She holds me so hard there's no thought in it for letting go.

"I love you," I tell her. "Like I've never loved anyone before."

"You always say that," she says. "But don't you realize it's the same for me? I've never loved anyone like this either."

"But you will," I say. "You will again."

If you stare at the center of the universe, there is a coldness there. A blankness. Ultimately, the universe doesn't care about us. Time doesn't care about us.

That's why we have to care about each other.

The minutes are passing. Midnight is approaching.

"I want to fall asleep next to you," I whisper.

This is my last wish.

She nods, agrees.

We leave the treehouse, run quickly through the night to get back to the light of the house, the music we've left behind. 11:13. 11:14. We go to the bedroom and take off our shoes. 11:15. 11:16. She gets in the bed and I turn off the lights. I join her there.

I lie on my back and she curls into me. I am reminded of a beach, an ocean.

There is so much to say, but there's no point in saying it. We already know.

She reaches up to my cheek, turns my head. Then she kisses me. Minute after minute after minute, we kiss.

"I want you to remember that tomorrow," she says.

Then we return to breathing. We return to lying there. Sleep approaches.

"I'll remember everything," I tell her.

"So will I," she promises.

I will never have a photograph of her to carry around in my pocket. I will never have a letter in her handwriting, or a scrapbook of everything we've done. I will never share an apartment with her in the city. I will never know if we are listening to the same song at the same time. We will not grow old together. I will not be the person she calls when she's in trouble. She will not be the person I call when I have stories to tell. I will never be able to keep anything she's given to me.

I watch her as she falls asleep next to me. I watch her as she breathes. I watch her as the dreams take hold.

This memory.

I will only have this.

I will always have this.

He will remember this too. He will feel this. He will know it's been a perfect afternoon, a perfect evening.

He will wake up next to her, and he will feel lucky.

Time moves on. The universe stretches out. I take a Post-it of a heart and move it from my body to hers. I see it sitting there.

I close my eyes. I say goodbye. I fall asleep.

# DAY 6034

I wake up two hours away, in the body of a girl named Katie.

Katie doesn't know it, but today she's going far away from here. It will be a total disruption to her routine, a complete twist in the way her life is supposed to go. But she has the luxury of time to smooth it out. Over the course of her life, this day will be a slight, barely noticeable aberration.

But for me it is the change of the tide. For me it is the start of a present that has both a past and a future.

For the first time in my life, I run.

## ACKNOWLEDGMENTS

For most of the novels I've written, there's been a definite starting point – the spark of an idea that turned into the story. Usually I remember it. But for this book, I must admit I don't. But I do remember three pivotal moments that pushed me into writing it. The first was a conversation with John Green while we were on tour. The second was a conversation with Suzanne Collins while *she* was on tour. And the third was an afternoon at Billy Merrell's apartment, where I read him the first chapter (all that had been written at that point) and paid very careful attention to his reaction. I'd like to thank all three of them for giving me fuel for the fire. And I'd like to thank the man who was driving me and John, for keeping his promise not to steal the idea and publish it first.

As always, I must thank my family and my friends. My parents. Adam, Jen, Paige, Matthew and Hailey. My aunts, uncles, cousins and grandparents. My author friends. My Scholastic friends. My school friends. My librarian friends. My Facebook friends. My best friends. And the friends who sat across from me writing their own books while I was working on this one (Eliot, Chris, Daniel, Marie, Donna, Natalie). And the one friend who was painting while I wrote (Nathan).

Huge thanks to my intrepid agent, Bill Clegg, as well as the fantastic team at WMEE, including Alicia Gordon, Shaun Dolan and Lauren Bonner. Thanks to my fantastic home base at Random House, across all the sales, marketing, editorial and art departments. (I would like to give a special shout-out to Adrienne Waintraub, Tracy Lerner and Lisa Nadel, for almost a decade's worth of dinners and booth signings, and to the watchful eye of Jeremy Medina and the careful planning of Elizabeth Zajac.) Thanks too to my champions at Egmont in the UK, Text in Australia, and the other international publishers of this book.

Finally, I give thanks every day to have Nancy Hinkel as my editor. I love it when I've got wheels and you want to go for a ride.

A wakes up as a new person every day.

And that's just fine — until A falls in love with Rhiannon.

One last song. One last turn. One last street. No matter how hard you try to keep hold of a day, it's going to leave you.

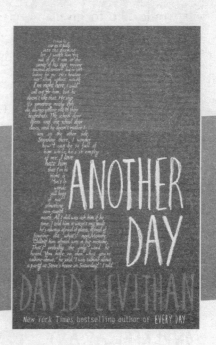

*'The best YA makes a place for its readers, and there are few writers as warmly generous as David Levithan.'*

**Patrick Ness**

TWO STRANGERS SHARE AN EPIC FIRST DATE, WITH A KILLER SOUNDTRACK, OVER ONE VERY LONG NIGHT IN NEW YORK

ANY GREAT FRIENDSHIP CAN BE AS CONFUSING, TREACHEROUS, INSPIRING AND WONDERFUL AS ANY GREAT ROMANCE

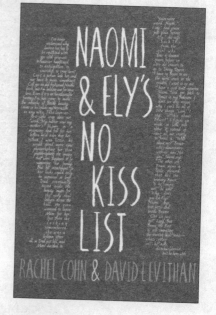

TWO

BOYS KISSING

DAVID LEVITHAN

co-author of *WILL Grayson, Will Grayson* with John Green

JUST **ONE KISS** CAN SAVE THE WORLD

ELECTRIC MONKEY

LOVE AND I ONCE
HAD A GREAT
RELATIONSHIP,
BUT I FEAR WE'VE
BROKEN UP.
IT CHEATED ON ME

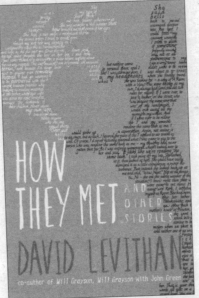

AN EXPLORATION
OF THAT WONDERFUL,
COMPLEX, SIMPLE,
ADDICTIVE, VOLATILE,
SCARY, GLORIOUS
THING CALLED LOVE

# FOLLY

## M. C. Beaton

Constable & Robinson Ltd
55–56 Russell Square
London WC1B 4HP
www.constablerobinson.com

First ebook edition published in the United States by
RosettaBooks LLC, New York, 2011

This edition first published in the UK by Canvas,
an imprint of Constable & Robinson Ltd, 2014

A copy of the British Library Cataloguing in
Publication data is available from the British Library

ISBN 978-1-78033-326-7 (A-format paperback)
ISBN 978-1-47211-291-0 (ebook)

1 3 5 7 9 10 8 6 4 2

Typeset by TW Typesetting, Plymouth, Devon

Printed and bound by CPI Group (UK) Ltd, Croydon, CR0 4YY

# CONTENTS

# ONE

Rachel walked slowly back to Brookfield House. It was a blustery spring day. Her muslin skirts blew about her body. She had been on a walk to Mannerling, her old family home, and it had distressed her to see it still lie empty and neglected. Her sister Abigail had promised her a Season in London, but Rachel was reluctant to go.

Like her five sisters, she had been obsessed with the idea of somehow regaining Mannerling, but she had persuaded herself that the stupid dream was long gone. It was only natural that she should want to see the great house she had once loved lived in again.

Now three sisters were married and gone, and

there was only she herself, Belinda, and Lizzie left. They must, she reflected, be among the most highly educated females in the land, for their mother, Lady Beverley, still retained the services of an excellent governess, Miss Trumble, although the girls had overgrown the services of one. Lady Beverley's real reason was that the governess miraculously knew how to soothe her frequent headaches and did not seem to notice on quarter-day that her mistress had 'forgotten' to pay her.

Rachel entered the back garden of the house by a circuitous route. She did not want anyone to know she had gone out walking without a maid.

She went up to her room and changed out of her walking clothes. Lessons were now reduced to two hours in the afternoon. Lizzie bounced into her room, her red hair flying. 'No lessons,' she crowed. 'We are to make a call.'

'Where?'

'Mary Stoddart – I mean, Mary Judd.'

Rachel's face darkened. The vicar's daughter had married one of the previous owners of Mannerling, a Mr Judd. Mr Judd had committed suicide, but during her brief reign as mistress of Mannerling, Mary had triumphed over the Beverley sisters.

'Why should we go there?' demanded Rachel. 'We hardly ever call.'

'She sent a note to say she had momentous news. Mama is indisposed. She says Miss Trumble must go with us instead.'

'What ails Mama now?'

Lizzie gave an unladylike shrug. 'Oh, you know. It is always this and that. In fact, she will probably brood over the accounts books.'

Ever since the late Sir William Beverley had lost Mannerling due to his gambling debts, Lady Beverley had become something of a miser. Her three elder daughters had all married well and often sent money, and it was only due to the frequent goading of Miss Trumble that the purse-strings were loosened. Miss Trumble had a way of pointing out that the Beverleys were not living in a way due to their position, which often spurred Lady Beverley on to buying new dresses for her remaining daughters and coals for the fires.

'Mary is always over-exercised about something trivial,' said Rachel. 'But it will come as a welcome break from the schoolroom. We surely do not need any more schooling. Mama says that gentlemen prefer stupid women.'

'And Miss Trumble,' pointed out Lizzie, 'says that the only gentlemen worth having are the ones that appreciate a woman with a brain.'

'Miss Trumble is unmarried,' countered Rachel. 'When do we leave?'

'In ten minutes. Miss Trumble has been looking for you. Where were you?'

She looked at Rachel's muddy pattens, lying discarded in a corner of the room.

'I went for a walk to Mannerling,' said Rachel defiantly. 'Don't you dare tell Miss Trumble. She'll start fretting that I am still in the grip of the old

3

obsession when I was only prompted by a natural curiosity.'

'Was there any smoke from the chimneys? Any carriages?'

'No, still deserted. And there were weeds growing at the side of the drive. The lodge was deserted. So many lost their employ when the Deverses left.'

'The servants were very cruel to us.' Lizzie tossed her red hair. 'We should not mourn their bad luck.'

'I have often thought the servants had reason to dislike us,' said Rachel. 'Do you think this bonnet will do? Oh, why am I bothering about what to wear on a visit to the vicarage? I mean, we treated them like machines, the servants, that is.'

'They were well-housed and well-fed,' pointed out Lizzie. 'I think they behaved very badly. I must prepare myself or Miss Trumble will come looking for me.'


Barry Wort, the odd man, who acted as general factotum, was driving the small Beverley carriage when they set out with Miss Trumble sitting beside him. It was an open carriage. Behind sat the Beverley sisters, Rachel, fair and blue-eyed, Belinda, dark-haired and beautiful in a placid way, and fiery-haired, green-eyed Lizzie.

What would become of them? wondered Miss Trumble. Rachel, the eldest of the three, had grown even more beautiful since the marriage of her twin, Abigail. Her fair hair was almost silver and her eyes large and blue. Abigail had always been the more spirited of the twins, but since she had left and Rachel was no longer in her shadow, the girl seemed more confident, more animated. But how could any gently born miss succeed in the marriage market with only an insignificant dowry? Lady Beverley constantly refused to discuss Rachel's dowry and whether she had increased it from a few hundred pounds. Rachel's three elder sisters' successful marriages made her feel that the Beverleys' luck in that direction had surely run out.

'Why cannot we have a closed carriage?' complained Belinda, holding on to her hat. 'I swear, with the funds Mama must be getting from our married sisters, we could well afford one.'

'Oh, you know Mama,' sighed Rachel. 'But it is a bore, for it means on wet days we cannot use the carriage to go anywhere. I wonder what Mary has to tell us.'

'Perhaps she has somehow gained the acquaintance of the mysterious Duke of Severnshire,' said Lizzie.

'I doubt it.' Belinda clutched at her bonnet again. 'The duke is reported to be travelling abroad and is considered to be a bit of a recluse. No one has seen him. When Papa was alive, he and Mama – at Mama's instigation, of course – pretended a strap on the carriage had broken, although Mama got the coachman to cut it conveniently outside the gates of his palace.'

'Oh, I remember,' laughed Rachel. 'Mama was monstrously offended. The duke's servants

5

repaired the strap, the housekeeper served them tea. They were informed his grace was not at home, and yet Mama swears that when they left she saw him looking out of the window.'

'If he is such a recluse, how is it that Mama knew what he looked like?' asked Lizzie.

'Because there was a rather bad portrait of him on display at the town hall at the time.'

'Did she say whether he was handsome?'

'He was accounted very handsome before the visit and nothing out of the common way after it.' Rachel pulled a shawl closer about her shoulders. 'We are nearly there. Miss Trumble,' she called to the erect figure on the box, 'we need not stay long, need we?'

'Not very long,' Miss Trumble called back. 'The sky is getting dark and I fear it might rain.'

'I hope the vicar is not there,' muttered Lizzie. 'He was detestable when he used to oil around us at Mannerling and he is now equally detestable when he patronizes us.'

But only Mary was there to greet them, Mary dressed in black and with her black eyes shining with excitement. Mary still wore mourning, not out of grief, but because a tipsy gentleman at an assembly had happened to remark that she looked well in black.

After the ladies were settled in the vicarage parlour, Mary said, 'What news!'

'Well, *what* news?' demanded Rachel crossly.

'Why, Mannerling has been bought.'

'Bought,' chorused the three sisters, their eyes shining while Miss Trumble looked at them with something like dismay on her lined face. 'Who has bought Mannerling?'

'Do let us have some tea,' said Mary, ringing the bell. The sisters waited impatiently while she gave orders to the servant.

'The new owner,' said Mary, 'is a general, retired, of course, General Sir Arthur Blackwood.'

'Retired,' echoed Lizzie in dismay. 'Then he is old?'

'Very old, I believe, and widowed.'

'Might do for Miss Trumble,' muttered Lizzie and then was quelled by a look from that lady.

'But he has a son,' said Mary. 'A widower.'

Their eyes brightened but Mary, infuriatingly – and, Miss Trumble shrewdly thought, deliberately – chose that moment to serve tea and cakes.

'So?' demanded Rachel at last after they had all been pressed to choose and praise seed-cake.

Mary's black eyebrows went up in query. 'The widower,' prompted Belinda.

'He is Charles Blackwood. His wife has been dead these past two years, leaving him with two children, a boy aged eight years and a little girl of six. Mr Blackwood, the son, was a major in the Hussars, but sold out on the death of his wife. He is accounted very rich.'

'How do you know all this?' asked Miss Trumble curiously.

'His agent was residing at the Green Man at Hedgefield and was engaging servants. They are to take up residence next month.'

'Did you find out how old Mr Blackwood is?' asked Belinda.

'I believe him to be middle-aged, nearly forty.'

Three faces fell. A widower of nearly forty with two small children did not seem in the least a marriageable prospect.

Mary saw she had lost their interest and said, 'Mr Blackwood has been seen in Hedgefield and is accounted very handsome.'

But 'nearly forty' had sounded the death-knell of their hopes, for although none of them would admit it, each sister privately held on to that old dream of marrying some owner of their old home and so getting it back.

A few fat drops of rain struck the window-panes. 'We really must leave.' Miss Trumble got to her feet.

'Such a pity you only have an open carriage,' mourned Mary.

'Just like you, Mary,' said Rachel, adjusting her shawl about her shoulders.

When they had climbed into the carriage, Barry produced umbrellas but the wind had risen, driving the rain into their faces.

Rachel felt very low. It was silly to hang on to the dream of Mannerling, she knew that. But logic warred with emotion in her brain. Nearly forty! A great age. She should write to Abigail and accept the offer of a Season in London. Among the whirl of balls and parties, she would forget Mannerling.

The days grew milder and the first leaves began to grow on the trees, and still Rachel had made no move to go to London. News of the new occupants of Mannerling began to filter to Brookfield House. The gardens were quickly being restored to their former glory and the temple which Mr Judd had blown up out of spite and then repaired had been taken down and a new Greek temple, a folly, had taken its place. Rachel felt obscurely insulted by this. Everything should be left as it was. Somehow it was the thought of this folly which drove her into going back to Mannerling, just for one look, just to see if it looked like the old one and whether things were about the same as she so fondly remembered them to be.

One sunny day when Miss Trumble had gone into Hedgefield with Barry, and her sisters were playing battledore and shuttlecock in the garden, Rachel slipped out the back way and then set out for Mannerling.

Fluffy clouds sailed across the sky. As she walked along, Rachel wondered for the first time why Miss Trumble had not encouraged her to go to London. Miss Trumble, who would normally have done anything in her power to remove at least one of them from what she called the house's malign influence, was strangely silent on the subject.

As she walked along under the tall trees which

9

arched over the road, with light-green leaves fluttering in the wind, she decided that one last look at Mannerling would be enough. Then she would go back home and send an express to her twin. Only look how deliriously happy Abigail was in marriage, she thought. Perhaps in London there would be a young man waiting for her, someone to love. Her eyes filled with dreams. People called them the unlucky Beverleys, and yet Isabella, the eldest, then Jessica, and finally Abigail had all made successful marriages. 'To men much older than they,' said a little voice in her head.

But Rachel was nineteen and had no intention, or so she told herself, of marrying someone old enough to be her father.

She retreated back into a dream about that young man who was waiting for her in London and was surprised to come out of it in front of the gates to Mannerling. There was smoke rising from the lodge-house and she suddenly did not want to be seen. She walked along the edge of the estate wall to where she knew there was a broken part, but new stone faced her. It had been repaired. She frowned. It had been a convenient way of getting into the estate without being seen. But now she was actually there, it was unthinkable to retreat. She looked up and down the road, but no one was in sight. She grasped the wall firmly and began to climb up. She then balanced on the top, seized hold of a tree branch on the other side, and dropped to the ground.

She made her way silently through the trees,

nervous now in case a gamekeeper should come across her. She had heard the new folly was on a rise above the ornamental lake.

The Mannerling park was very large, and as she emerged from the shadow of the trees a warm sun struck down on her back and she began to feel tired. But ahead glittered the waters of the lake.

She rounded a stand of alder and there, stretched out in front of her, was the expanse of the lake and on a rise stood the folly. It was a Greek temple made of white marble with slender pillars and a domed top. She had to admit it was even more graceful than the original and was amazed it had been built in such a short time. She looked cautiously about her but there was no one in sight. Rachel walked across the springy turf starred with daisies and entered the temple, which was open all round like a gazebo. There were charming views in every direction.

And then she stiffened, suddenly aware she was not alone. She turned around.

Two children stood there, hand in hand, solemnly surveying her.

The boy had a mop of black curls and large brown eyes. The girl had the same black curls and brown eyes but was younger and smaller. The boy was slim and the little girl still retained a babyish plumpness.

Rachel found she was blushing guiltily. This, then, she thought, must be the Blackwood children.

'Are you from the house?' she asked.

11

They both nodded.

'Then you must not betray me,' said Rachel. 'I am trespassing. I am Miss Rachel Beverley and I live over at Brookfield House, but Mannerling used to be my family home. What are your names?'

'Beth,' said the little girl shyly, 'and this is my brother, Mark.'

'Are you happy here?' asked Rachel.

She sat down on a stone bench in the middle of the folly and the children sat down on either side of her.

'It is a very grand house,' said Beth tentatively.

'It is the most beautiful house in the world,' said Rachel firmly.

'I don't like it,' said Mark. 'Not at all. It's haunted.'

Rachel gave an indulgent laugh. 'It was never haunted.'

'It is now,' said Mark fiercely. 'By a man who looks like a fox with sandy hair and green eyes.'

Rachel felt a shudder of pure superstitious dread. The boy had described the late Mr Judd. But then there was a portrait of the late owner, who had committed suicide, hanging in the Long Gallery.

'But you must not tell Miss Terry or she will beat us,' said Mark.

'Is Miss Terry your governess?'

They both nodded.

'And does your father know she beats you?'

Two small heads shook in unison.

'But why not?'

A look of almost adult weariness crossed Mark's

face and he gave an unhappy little shrug. 'Father has nothing to do with us.'

Rachel was suddenly sorry for them. 'I used to take a boat out on the lake,' she said. 'Is there still one there?'

Beth's eyes lit up. 'There is a blue one but we are too small to handle the oars.'

'Come along,' said Rachel, standing up. 'I will take you.'

They walked together out of the folly and down the grassy slope to the lake. The small jetty was still there and moored to it was a rowing-boat.

'Are we really going out on the water?' asked Mark, his eyes shining.

'Yes, of course. It's a lovely day and I will make sure you don't fall in.'

She helped them into the little rowing-boat, cautioning them to be careful and sit down gently, and then she took the oars and began to row out into the middle of the lake. The two children sat, enrapt, Mark trailing a hand in the water. The sun was very warm. Rachel shipped the oars, removed her bonnet, and then took up the oars again. She reflected that the children were unnaturally well-behaved for their age.

'I should really take you back,' she said after a while. 'I do not want to be caught trespassing.'

'Oh, just a little longer,' pleaded Mark. 'We are not in the way of having fun, you see.'

Rachel smiled. 'In that case, I will gladly risk disgrace. A little longer.'

The children seemed content to sit there, side by side, facing her as she rowed backwards and forwards across the lake.

And then she saw a look of fear in Mark's face and saw the way he grasped his little sister's hand tightly. 'What is it?' she asked sharply.

'Papa is arrived,' he said in a whisper, 'and Miss Terry.'

Rachel began to row towards the jetty, feeling fury boiling up inside her. The children looked so scared and vulnerable.

As she approached she saw a tall man standing on the jetty, with a thin, bitter-looking woman beside him. Charles Blackwood and Miss Terry.

Charles Blackwood was dressed for riding in a black coat, leather breeches, and top-boots. He had thick black hair, fashionably cut, with silver wings at the sides, where his hair had turned white. He had odd slanting eyes of grass-green in a strong, handsome face. He had a tall, powerful figure.

Miss Terry had a crumpled little face, as if years of spite had withered it like a fallen apple. Her eyes were a pale, washed-out blue. Her thin shoulders were bent as though in false humility, but there was nothing humble in her glaring eyes.

Rachel helped the children out onto the jetty and then climbed up after them, aware, despite her temper, of her flushed face and tumbled hair. She realized she had left her hat in the boat.

'You bad, bad children,' exclaimed the

14

governess. 'How dare you escape me! You know what this means?'

They stood before her, heads bowed, hands clasped.

Rachel forgot about Mannerling, forgot about her trespass, and threw back her head, her blue eyes blazing.

'I am Miss Rachel Beverley of Brookfield House,' she said haughtily, 'and yes, the children know what you mean. You will beat them as you have no doubt done many times before.' She rounded on Charles Blackwood. 'Oh, it is not unusual for children to be beaten, but it goes to my heart to see them so white and frightened. Shame on you, sir, for your most abysmal neglect of them. They are charming children and deserve better. They deserve parental love and kindness. Good day to you, sir.'

She marched off, her head high. Temper carried her straight to the drive and down it between the bordering lime-trees, where new leaves as green as Charles Blackwood's eyes fluttered in the wind, to the lodge where the lodge-keeper stared at her in surprise as she opened the little gate at the side of the great gates and stepped out onto the road.

Rachel was too upset to feel dismayed when, as she approached home, she saw her own governess, Miss Trumble, walking to meet her.

'Why, Rachel!' exclaimed the governess. 'What are you doing, walking unescorted and without your hat?'

15

So Rachel told her about the children and about what she had said to Charles Blackwood and then waited for a lecture. But, to her surprise, Miss Trumble gave a gentle laugh and said, 'Why, I declare you are become a woman of principle at last. We will say no more about it.'

Rachel decided to write to Abigail and say that she would go to London. The hold Mannerling had held on her had gone. It belonged to a family now, another family, and the fact that it was an unhappy family had nothing to do with her.

But in the morning when she went out to find Barry Wort, the odd man, to give him the letter, she experienced a strange reluctance to hand it over. She tucked it in the pocket of her apron instead. Barry was weeding a vegetable bed, sturdy, dependable ex-soldier Barry, whose common sense had proved of such value in the past.

'Good morning, Barry,' said Rachel. He straightened up and leaned on his hoe and smiled at her. 'We've been getting some uncommon fine weather, Miss Rachel.'

'I went to Mannerling yesterday, Barry,' said Rachel abruptly.

'Well, now, miss, there do be a strange thing. I would have thought you cured of wanting the place.'

'I went for just one last visit.'

'Reckon that place is like gambling, if you'll forgive me for saying so, miss. It's always one last time.'

'I meant it this time. But wait until you hear of my adventure.'

Barry listened carefully to the story of the children and the confrontation. 'You did well,' he said, not betraying that he had already heard the story from Miss Trumble. 'There are beatings and beatings and those motherless children could do with a bit of kindness. What was this Mr Blackwood like?'

'He is a very fine-looking man,' said Rachel slowly. 'I had heard he was nearly forty and had expected – well, a middle-aged-looking gentleman.'

'Mr Blackwood already has a good reputation in Hedgefield,' said Barry. 'But any gentleman who settles his bills promptly gets a good reputation. He's caused quite a flurry in the district among the ladies.'

'The widows?'

'No, miss, all the young ladies do be setting their caps at him. He is reputed to be a fine-looking fellow, he has Mannerling and, they do say, a fortune as well.'

The thought flicked briefly through Rachel's mind that she too might set her cap at the master of Mannerling, but then she remembered that grim face and the unhappy children. 'I will not be of their number,' she said lightly. She turned and walked away, and it was only some time later that she realized she still had that letter to Abigail in her pocket.

'You never talk to us any more.' Belinda and Lizzie confronted Rachel later that day. 'Are you going to London? For if you do, you must ask Abigail to invite us as well.'

'I have not made up my mind,' said Rachel loftily. 'And I do talk to you. I am talking to you now.'

'Where were you yesterday morning? You just disappeared and Miss Trumble went out looking for you,' said Lizzie.

'I simply went for a little walk across the fields. Good heavens,' exclaimed Rachel. 'Must I report to you every minute of the day?'

'But what of Mannerling and what of this new owner?'

'You know as much as I do. He is nearly forty, a widower with two children.'

'Do you think he means to entertain?'

'I don't *know*,' snapped Rachel. 'We promised Miss Trumble, if you remember, that we would put all ambitions of regaining Mannerling out of our heads. Why? Would you have me entertain romantic thoughts of a man nearly in his dotage?'

'I suppose it is silly,' said Lizzie. 'But it would be wonderful just to go to Mannerling again.'

Rachel looked at her uneasily. The loss of their home had affected Lizzie more than her sisters, so much so that she had once tried to drown herself. She remembered the little boy, Mark, saying that the house was haunted, and wondered if there was something supernatural about Mannerling that kept them all in its spell.

Betty, the little maid, piped up from the bottom of the stairs, 'A carriage from Mannerling.'

They ran to the window. Their former coachman was driving a carriage. There were two footmen on the backstrap and Rachel recognized in one of them the unlovely features of John, who had once worked for the Beverleys.

'You had best go downstairs,' urged Lizzie, 'for Mama is indisposed.'

'I shall change my gown,' decided Rachel. 'Send Betty to me quickly.'

Miss Trumble received Charles Blackwood in the little parlour, regretting, not for the first time, her mistress's parsimony in leaving the drawing-room unheated.

'I am sorry Lady Beverley is ill,' said Miss Trumble after studying his card. 'I am Miss Trumble, governess to the Beverley sisters.'

His harsh face lightened as he looked down at her from his great height and Miss Trumble wondered rather sadly whether her poor old heart would ever learn to stop beating faster at the sight of an attractive man.

'Then you are the very person I need to see,' he said.

'Indeed? Pray be seated, sir.'

He sat down in an armchair by the fire and looked around him with pleasure. The room was full of feminine clutter – bits of sewing, books, and magazines. There was a large bowl of spring flowers by the window on a round table.

'Were you aware,' began Charles, stretching out his long legs, 'that I met one of your charges

19

yesterday? She left her hat. I brought it back and gave it to the maid.'

'Yes, Rachel. She told me about it. She should not have been trespassing, but she misses her old home.'

'I was grateful to her for bringing to my attention the fact that my children had been subject to harsh attention from their governess. Excuse me, Miss Trumble, but there is something faintly familiar about you. Are you sure we have not met before?'

'Oh, no, sir. A governess such as myself, immured in the country as I am, hardly moves in the same circles as such as yourself.'

'Still, there is something . . . Never mind. The reason I am come . . .'

The door opened and Rachel came in, followed by Lizzie and Belinda.

Charles Blackwood got to his feet and bowed. Rachel was very beautiful and seemed even more so than the first time he had seen her, her fair looks contrasting with Belinda's dark-haired beauty and Lizzie's waiflike appeal.

They all sat down.

Charles turned to Rachel. 'I was just beginning to explain to your governess that after your visit yesterday I told Miss Terry, my children's governess, to leave immediately. I am looking for a suitable lady to tutor them and am come to you for help.'

'I think I can help you,' said Miss Trumble, adjusting the folds of a very modish silk gown.

20

Rachel looked at that gown. It was one of Miss Trumble's best, almost as if she had been expecting such a call. 'My girls' schooling has been cut back to a mere two hours in the afternoon, and time lies heavy on my hands. With Lady Beverley's permission, of course, I could offer to tutor your children if they were brought over here every day. My girls could help in their education, and company younger than mine would benefit them.'

'I would be most grateful. Are you sure Lady Beverley will allow you to do this?'

Miss Trumble rose to her feet. 'I will ask her now.'

She left the room with her graceful gliding walk.

'An exceptional lady,' said Charles to Rachel after the door had closed behind the governess. 'Where did your mother come by such a treasure?'

Rachel laughed. 'Our Miss Trumble has certainly made an impression on such a brief acquaintance. What makes you think her a treasure?'

'She has great style and dignity. And I am sure I have met her somewhere before.'

'There is a mystery about Miss Trumble,' said Rachel. 'She appeared one day, without references, references which she swears she will produce if she can ever find them. But she so quickly made herself an indispensable part of the household that none of us can bear to think of her leaving. I trust you will not lure her away from us, sir.'

'Please don't,' put in Lizzie. 'Miss Trumble swore she would stay with us until I am married.'

'And when will that be?' asked Charles. His odd green eyes were full of laughter. Rachel looked at him in surprise. He was certainly changed from the grim-visaged man of the day before.

'I will need to be very lucky,' said Lizzie solemnly. 'You see, none of us has much of a dowry.'

'Lizzie!' hissed Rachel furiously.

'It's true,' said Lizzie defiantly. 'The whole district knows it to be true and Mr Blackwood will hear it sooner or later.'

'It is not ladylike to discuss money,' pointed out Belinda.

'We talk of nothing else in this house,' muttered Lizzie rebelliously.

Meanwhile Miss Trumble was saying evenly to Lady Beverley, who was reclining on a day-bed in her darkened bedchamber, 'As you say, my lady, I am employed by you. But only see the advantages in my helping Mr Blackwood with his children. While he is paying me for my services, you need not. Of course, it would probably mean your being invited to Mannerling again and that might distress you. I shall leave you now and tell Mr Blackwood that I cannot help him – unless I decide to leave you and move to Mannerling. Perhaps that might be a good idea.'

Lady Beverley's face was a study. She was well aware that this elderly and dignified governess not only lent her status but ran her household. She forgot, too, that she had neglected to pay Miss Trumble any salary last quarter-day and said

22

faintly, 'Stay. My poor head. You must realize I am not well and am unable to deal with decisions. But if your heart is set on it, yes, I agree.'

Miss Trumble curtsied and quickly left the room before her employer could change her mind.

When she returned to the parlour, Charles Blackwood looked cheerful and relaxed and Rachel was telling him about an assembly to be held in two weeks' time in the Green Man. 'But perhaps a country hop is too undignified for you, Mr Blackwood.'

'I have not really engaged in many social entertainments since the death of my poor wife,' he said. 'But yes, I shall probably attend. I hope I can remember how to dance. Ah, Miss Trumble, good news, I hope?'

'Yes, sir. If it is convenient, I think you should bring the children tomorrow morning and we can start as soon as possible.'

He rose to his feet and bowed all around. To his secret amusement, it was Miss Trumble who walked out with him to his carriage, quite like the lady of the house, he thought.

'Perhaps nine o'clock?' said Miss Trumble.

Although she was only a governess, he found to his surprise that he was bowing over her hand.

'Until then.'

John, the footman, let down the carriage steps. Charles climbed inside. John raised the steps and shut the carriage door and turned and gave Miss Trumble a pale, curious, calculating look.

If I gain any influence with Charles Blackwood, thought Miss Trumble, I will tell him to get rid of that gossiping, plotting footman. For she knew that John dreaded any Beverley getting a foothold in Mannerling again because he knew he would lose his job, for he had gone out of his way to be horrible to them.

Inside the house, Rachel was facing her sisters' angry questions. 'You are become secretive, Rachel,' said Belinda. 'Not to tell us you had been to Mannerling and had met the owner. And he is vastly handsome.'

'But a widower with children and much too old,' said Rachel. 'I have no desire to wed a man old enough to be my father.'

Belinda twisted a lock of hair in her fingers and sent Rachel a sideways look. 'I would not find such a man too old,' she said.

Rachel looked at her, startled. Belinda had grown even more beautiful. Her black hair was dressed in one of the fashionable Roman styles which Miss Trumble could create with all the deftness of a top lady's-maid. Her cheeks were smooth and pink and her wide eyes fringed with heavy lashes.

What effect had such beauty on Charles Blackwood? Surely no man could look at Belinda and remain unmoved.

'You are too young, Belinda,' she snapped.

Belinda gave a quiet little smile. 'We'll see.'

'But we promised Miss Trumble that we would put Mannerling from our minds,' protested Rachel.

'Only look at the vulgar reputation we sisters gained in the country by trying to marry previous owners or sons of owners.'

'One son,' corrected Belinda, thinking of the rake, Harry Devers, son of the previous owners, who had caused the Beverleys so much heartbreak. 'Anyway,' she said with a little shrug, 'if Mr Blackwood has not heard the gossip about us, he soon will, and he will fight shy of us for fear one of the dreadful Beverley girls is going to ensnare him for the sake of his home.'

'Such old gossip,' said Rachel. 'I doubt if he will hear a word!'

# TWO

*The strongest friendship yields to pride,*
*Unless the odds be on our side.*

JONATHAN SWIFT

Charles Blackwood rode over the next afternoon to
pay a call on Lady Evans, an elderly widow, accompanied by his father. The old general had known
Lady Evans for years and was pleased to learn she
resided in the neighbourhood, in Hursley Park.

Lady Evans, a formidable dowager with a
crumpled old face under a gigantic, starched
cap, welcomed them with enthusiasm. 'General
Blackwood,' she hailed Charles's father. 'I declare
I have not seen you this age, and you are grown
more handsome than ever.'

The general, a genial gentleman with a portly
figure and a high colour, bent gallantly over her
hand and kissed her fingertips. 'The minute I
learned we were to be neighbours, Lady Evans, my
poor old heart beat much faster.'

'Silly boy,' she giggled, rapping his shoulder
with her fan. 'Now do be seated and I will ring for
tea. How do you go on, Charles? So sad about your

26

dear wife. You have two young children, I believe. Well, I hope?'

'I am arranging matters better for them. I have been too distant from my children and it has only just been brought to my attention that their governess was dealing too harshly with them.'

'Children must not be spoilt,' said Lady Evans. The tea-tray was carried in, the spirit stove lit. Lady Evans prepared the tea herself. 'A good beating never harmed a child.'

Charles smiled. 'We must not quarrel on matters of discipline. But they are now in the hands of an estimable governess at Brookfield House.'

'Miss Trumble,' exclaimed Lady Evans. 'She is still there? Why does she not call on me?'

The general looked at her in some surprise. Lady Evans was known to be very high in the instep and it was most unlike her to be pining for a call from a mere governess.

'Miss Trumble was governess to the children of a friend of mine,' said Lady Evans quickly. 'She is out of the common way.'

'I agree,' said Charles.

Her old eyes suddenly narrowed. 'But why does she not reside at Mannerling? Why Brookfield House with those Beverleys?'

'Miss Trumble did not seem anxious to move, so the children are to be taken there every day. A comfortable arrangement. In fact, it was one of the Beverley girls, Rachel, who brought their plight to my attention.'

'You became quickly on calling terms with the Beverleys.'

'It was by accident. I found Miss Rachel rowing my children about the lake.'

'At Mannerling?'

'Yes, ma'am.'

'But she was not there by invitation?'

'No, but Mannerling is her former home, so I could not really chastise her for trespass.'

'I have something I must tell you,' said Lady Evans. 'The daughter of friends of mine, Prudence Makepeace, was here on a visit. I had hoped to make a match of it for her with Lord Burfield, but he was tricked and ensnared by Abigail Beverley in a most degrading way.'

'You fascinate me. Go on.'

'Abigail is the twin of Rachel. Rachel was to marry Harry Devers, son of the previous owners of Mannerling. She took fright, and on the day of the wedding Abigail, who looks much like her, took her twin's place. But on her wedding night she took fright as well – or so she *says* – and ran away from him and was found in Lord Burfield's bed. The scandal! Of course he had to marry her after that, which was more than any of those penurious, grasping Beverleys deserves. Miss Trumble is all that is excellent, but I want you to be on your guard against the Beverleys. They have but one aim in life – to reclaim Mannerling, and they do not care how low they stoop to do it.'

'They are all too young for me,' said Charles mildly.

'They are serpents all, and your years will not protect you from their wiles.'

'Good heavens!' exclaimed the general. 'Perhaps it would be better to make other arrangements for Beth and Mark.'

Charles Blackwood sat silent, his thin black brows drawn down. Then he said, 'If this Miss Trumble is such a precious pearl, such a lady, such an estimable governess, then what is she doing with this wicked family of Beverleys?'

'She is fallen on hard times, obviously, and must earn her bread somewhere.'

'But with a powerful patroness such as yourself, she could surely find a better position.'

'More tea, General?' Lady Evans refilled his cup. 'Ah well, truth to tell, she does seem unfortunately attached to them. Perhaps she feels if she abandoned them they might end up on the streets.'

Charles's face darkened. 'I feel you go too far, Lady Evans. From what I have seen of the Beverley sisters, they appear high-spirited but I would not describe them as sluts.'

'Let us talk about something else,' said Lady Evans. 'The subject depresses me. So how goes the world, General?'

The general talked about mutual friends and after a while he and his son rose to take their leave.

'So what did you think of all that, my boy?' demanded the general as their carriage rolled out through the gates of Hursley Park.

'About the Beverley girls? I do not know. But it is

29

very simple to clear up the matter. I will ask Miss Trumble.'

'What! The governess? Remember your position, Charles.'

'You will come with me as well. Miss Trumble is not in the common way.'

When they approached Brookfield House, they could hear sounds of laughter from the garden. As they drew nearer, they saw the Beverley sisters and Mark and Beth playing a noisy game of blindman's buff in the garden. Little Beth had a scarf over her eyes and was tottering this way and that, trying to catch one of them.

Charles felt a stab of conscience. He realized he could not remember the last time he had heard his children laugh. He dismounted from the carriage and scooped Beth up into his arms. He removed the blindfold and she cried, 'Papa!' and threw her chubby arms about his neck.

'Enjoying your studies?' he asked, seeing Miss Trumble rise from a chair at the corner of the lawn and walk towards them.

'Oh, Papa, we are having such larks,' said Beth.

He set her down on her feet. 'Then run along and have more larks. I wish to talk to Miss Trumble. A word with you in private, if you please, Miss Trumble.'

She curtsied and led the way back into the house. When they were in the parlour, Charles introduced his father.

The general surveyed this governess curiously.

Although he judged her to be as old as he was himself, she carried herself with a sort of youthful grace. The brown curls under her lace cap did not show any signs of grey and her eyes in her lined face were large and sparkling.

'We have been on a call to Lady Evans,' began Charles, after they were seated.

'How does Lady Evans go on?'

'Very well, Miss Trumble, and desirous of a call from you.'

'It would hardly be fitting,' said Miss Trumble equably, 'for a woman in my position to call on Lady Evans.'

'Lady Evans appeared to think very highly of you.'

She bowed her head.

'Warned us against those Beverley girls,' put in the general bluntly.

'Oh, dear. Lady Evans has reason. She was desirous to make a marriage between a young lady, a Prudence Makepeace, and Lord Burfield, but Lord Burfield married Abigail Beverley.'

'This is awkward,' said Charles. 'But Lady Evans did alarm us by telling us about how that proposal was brought about.'

'Did she also tell you that Lord Burfield was and is deeply in love with Abigail? No, I thought not. Sirs, you must have heard the scandal. Prudence Makepeace had to flee the country after conspiring with Harry Devers to abduct Abigail on the day of her wedding to Lord Burfield.'

'We must have been abroad at the time,' said Charles.

'You were also not told,' went on Miss Trumble, 'that burning ambition to reclaim Mannerling was at the root of the Beverleys' schemes. They no longer harbour such ambitions. But do you blame them?'

'Well, yes,' said the general, amazed. 'Very unwomanly.'

'Exactly. Had they been men, you would have found their ambition laudable. Think on it, gentlemen. How many men do you know in society who have married heiresses to save their estates and not one breath of scandal sticks to their name? You must not be anxious. There will be nothing in their behaviour to alarm you. I promise you that. If, on the other hand, you do not trust me, then you must take your children away.'

A burst of happy laughter sounded from the garden.

'No,' said Charles slowly. 'I am too old for any of the Beverleys in any case. Is Lady Beverley not at home?'

'My mistress is indisposed. Lady Beverley is often indisposed.'

'I was going to invite the Beverleys to Mannerling, but if Lady Beverley is unwell . . .'

A gleam of mischief shone in the governess's eyes. 'Should you issue such an invitation, then it would go a long way to restoring her ladyship to health.'

Charles smiled. 'Shall we say tomorrow? You could all come to Mannerling in the carriage with the children.'

'I am sure they will accept. If you will excuse me, gentlemen, I shall go to see if Lady Beverley considers herself fit.'

'Fine lady, that,' said the general when the door closed behind Miss Trumble.

'Very fine,' agreed his son. 'Too fine to be a governess. Miss Trumble has the air of a duchess.'

'And what must we think of the girls now?'

'Harmless. Only dangerous if my heart was in danger, and you alone know that is hardly ever to be the case again.'

'Poor Sarah,' said the general. Sarah was the late Mrs Blackwood. 'She seemed such a merry little thing.'

'Too merry to confine her attentions to her husband,' said Charles harshly.

'Well, well, I always did have a soft spot for little Sarah. And she is dead now. Water under the bridge.'

Charles reflected that 'water under the bridge' was too trite a phrase to describe his fury and heartache when he found his wife had been unfaithful to him with the first footman.

'Shh,' he admonished. 'I hear our governess returning.' Both men stood up.

Miss Trumble entered and said demurely that Lady Beverley thanked them for their invitation and would be pleased to attend.

'Restored to health, hey?' demanded the general with a twinkle in his eye.

'Oh, yes, your kind invitation was very beneficial.'

'I say,' said the general as they moved to the door, 'come as well.'

Miss Trumble curtsied with grace. 'You are too kind.'

'There now,' said the general in high good humour, 'got to keep my grandchildren in line, what?'

Miss Trumble smiled and led the way out to the garden.

Charles paused for a moment on the threshold. Rachel was throwing a ball to Mark. Her fair hair gleamed in the sunlight. It had escaped from its pins and was tumbling about her shoulders. Her face was pink and her large blue eyes shone with laughter. He felt a tug at his heart and then gave a rueful smile. He hoped he was not going to start lusting after young girls at his age!

The next day Miss Trumble found herself left to school and entertain the Blackwood children on her own. The Beverley sisters were preparing for their visit to Mannerling. It saddened her that they should betray so much hectic excitement. Would that wretched house which appeared to have a malignant life of its own ever let them go?

Now that Mark and Beth were at ease with her after their first day of drawing and games, she began formal lessons, enjoying the quick intelligence they showed.

'You have done very well,' she said at last. 'Now I will read you a story.'

'Not one with ghosts in it,' said Mark.

'No ghosts. You are not afraid of ghosts, are you, Mark?'

His expressive little face turned a trifle pale, and he nodded.

'Come here and sit by me. You have seen a ghost?'

Again that little nod.

'At Mannerling?'

His small hand slid into hers for comfort. He gulped and nodded again.

'And what did this ghost look like?' Miss Trumble never jeered at the fears of children.

'Foxy,' whispered Mark. 'Sandy hair and green eyes.'

Miss Trumble felt cold. Judd had looked like that. 'There is a picture of a man in the Long Gallery who looks like that.'

'He was in my room,' said Mark in a low voice.

Miss Trumble's gaze sharpened. 'Do you mean he was clear, like a real person?'

'Oh, yes.'

'Have you told your father of this?'

'No, miss, I have not been in the way of talking to him.'

'I think we both should say something. Now, I will read you a story about pirates.'

His face brightened and he went to sit beside his sister again. As Miss Trumble read the words of

35

the story, her mind raced. She remembered her own fear when that chandelier on which Judd had hanged himself had started to revolve slowly, just as if there were a body hanging from it, and there had been no wind that day. And yet a real-life ghost that this little boy had been able to see and to describe! She could not believe it.

She finished reading, promising to read more the following day, and sent the children out to play in the garden. Then she went in search of Barry Wort.

'Such excitement,' said Barry, tossing a bunch of weeds into a wheelbarrow. 'You would think they had Mannerling back again, the way they are going on.'

'I am beginning to regret not moving to Mannerling to look after those children.'

'You, miss? You would never desert us!'

'It is tempting. Let me tell you. The boy, Mark, swears he has seen the ghost of Judd.'

'Could it be, miss, because the boy was frightened and unhappy with that governess? Children do be very fanciful.'

'No, Barry, I do not think it is fancy in this case. If he had talked of a spectral figure or anything that sounded like a Gothic romance, I would have put it down to imagination. But he saw a real figure. Do you think perhaps that someone is playing a nasty trick on him?'

'With your permission, miss, and that of Mr Blackwood, I would suggest that maybe I spend a few nights with the boy, on guard, so to speak.'

Miss Trumble smiled. 'What would I do without you?' Barry coloured with pleasure. 'You are always so sensible. I will discuss the matter with Mr Blackwood.'

Two carriages from Mannerling arrived. Miss Trumble and the children went in the smaller one and Lady Beverley and her daughters in the larger. Lady Beverley was showing no signs of illness and was dressed in a modish gown of blue silk with darker-blue velvet stripes and a bonnet embellished with dyed ostrich plumes. Rachel noticed that her mother had adopted the haughty, grand manner she had shown when she was mistress of Mannerling and wondered uneasily if Lady Beverley considered Charles Blackwood as a possible husband for one of her daughters.

Rachel was wearing a blue muslin gown which matched the colour of her eyes. It was high-waisted and puff-sleeved and had three deep flounces at the hem. But she considered that Belinda with her black curls and pink gown looked prettier and wondered whether Belinda really meant to set her cap at Charles Blackwood and in the same moment persuaded herself she did not care.

Soon they arrived at the tall iron gates of Mannerling. The lodge-keeper sprang to open them. He was a new face to the Beverleys. Lady Beverley insisted on telling the carriage to stop while she lowered the glass and quizzed the lodge-keeper in a high autocratic voice as to whether he was happy in his new employ. Rachel's heart sank. She privately hoped this would turn out to be the first of many visits, but if Lady Beverley started ordering around the Mannerling servants and criticizing any changes to the house, as she had done in the past, then Rachel feared this might prove to be their first and last visit.

She felt a tug at her heart as the great house came into view, its graceful wings springing out, as they had always done, from the central block of warm stone.

Then down from the carriage and into the hall, where the great chandelier glittered above their heads, and up the double staircase behind the stiff back of a correct butler.

'Remember your place, Miss Trumble,' hissed Lady Beverley, 'and sit in a corner of the room.'

Miss Trumble smiled vaguely but made no reply.

The general and his son rose at their entrance. Rachel was struck afresh by how handsome Charles looked with his black hair and odd green eyes. His legs were superb. She suddenly blushed as if he could read her naughty thoughts.

Miss Trumble curtsied and moved to a chair by the window.

'Miss Trumble,' cried the general. ' 'Pon rep, you must not hide yourself. Come and sit by me.' He patted the cushion on the sofa beside him.

Lady Beverley's pale eyes shone with an unlovely light but she refrained from saying anything.

'So what do you think of the place, hey?' the

general asked Miss Trumble. 'Many changes since your day?'

Lady Beverley found her voice. 'Miss Trumble was never at Mannerling,' she said. 'She came to us after The Fall.' By this she somehow implied that Miss Trumble was part of the Beverleys' loss of fortune and face.

'The Fall?' asked the general curiously.

'We were once one of the most powerful families in the land,' said Lady Beverley. 'My poor husband incurred debts and so we were driven from Mannerling, from our rightful home.' She took a wisp of handkerchief and dabbed her eyes.

There followed an awkward silence. Then Belinda said brightly and loudly, 'I see the pianoforte there and Lizzie has come along in her studies. Do play us something, Lizzie.'

Lizzie rose obediently, having been schooled by Miss Trumble that when asked to play, she should do so without forcing anyone to persuade her.

Soon Lizzie's fingers were rippling expertly over the keys. When she had finished playing a brisk rondo, the general begged her to play the tune of a popular ballad. Miss Trumble's end of the sofa where she was seated was next to Charles Blackwood's armchair. She leaned forward and said gently, 'I would like a word with you in private, sir.'

'Gladly. Come with me.' They both rose and, under the curious eyes of the others, left the room together. He led her into the small drawing-room, used by the Beverley sisters on rainy days when Mannerling had been their home.

'Now what is this all about?' he asked.

'I am worried about Mark.'

'What's amiss? Is he slow to learn?'

'Not at all. He has a quick intelligence.'

'Then what can it be?'

'He has seen a ghost – a ghost at Mannerling.'

'I hope I have not been mistaken in you, Miss Trumble,' said Charles gravely. 'All children usually have such fancies, and they should not be encouraged in indulging them.'

'I am not in the way of indulging children's fancies,' said Miss Trumble so sharply and with such an air of hauteur that Charles immediately felt like a naughty child himself.

'Forgive me. Explain.'

'Mark has given me a graphic description of Mr Judd, one of the previous owners who hanged himself. He claims to have seen him. Had I really believed he had seen a ghost, or rather, had I thought that the boy thought he had really seen a ghost, I would have done all in my power to reassure him and to talk him out of his fancies. The thing that troubles me is that I have an uneasy feeling that Mark may have seen a real person.'

He looked at her in amazement and then said, 'But why? Why would anyone try to frighten a child? We have no enemies.'

'I really do not know. I may be wrong. But to make sure, our odd man, Barry Wort, has offered

40

to guard the boy's room. He is a strong and honest man. He is not of the Mannerling staff. With your permission, I will smuggle him up the back stairs this evening. I told him to call.'

'Very well.' He looked at her doubtfully. 'And how long is this experiment to go on?'

'A few nights, that is all.'

'I will have a truckle-bed set up in Mark's room.'

'Not by your servants,' said Miss Trumble quickly.

'You suspect my servants? They would not dare.'

'Humour me, Mr Blackwood.'

'Oh, very well. I will attend to the matter myself.' He rang the bell. John, the footman, answered the summons. 'Fetch my son here,' ordered Charles.

After a few minutes, Mark appeared.

Charles studied the boy's expressive and sensitive face, feeling a pang that he had never really tried to get to know his own son.

'Sit down, Mark,' he said gently.

'A moment.' Miss Trumble moved quickly to the door and jerked it open. John was standing outside.

'Go about your business,' said Miss Trumble.

'I was simply waiting at hand to see whether the master wished any refreshments,' said John huffily.

'The master does not. Go away.'

She waited until John had gone off down the stairs, his liveried back stiff with outrage.

She closed the heavy door and then sat down.

'Mark,' began Charles, 'what is all this about a ghost?'

The boy threw a reproachful look at Miss Trumble.

'I am not usually in the way of betraying confidences,' said the governess. 'But I think this ghost of yours is something to be taken seriously. Your father will not laugh at you.'

'Tell me about it,' said Charles.

'It happens sometimes during the night,' said Mark in a rush. 'He stands at the end of my bed and he is a foxy man with sandy hair and green eyes.'

'If it was night-time and dark, how were you able to see him so clearly?' asked Charles.

'The first time it was just a black figure,' said Mark. 'So I left a candle burning after that. Miss Terry found out and whipped me for burning the candle, but I was more afraid of the ghost than I was of her.'

'See here, Mark,' said his father, 'we are going to play a game. Do you know . . . er . . . what is the name of the Brookfield servant?'

'Barry Wort.'

'Oh, I know him. He is capital. He taught me how to make a sling.'

'Now this is to be our secret, Mark,' said Charles. 'This Barry Wort is going to sleep in your room for a few nights. You are not to tell anyone about this arrangement, not the servants, not anyone.'

The boy's eyes shone. 'No ghost would dare to appear if Barry were there.'

'We shall see. I shall call on you before you go

42

to sleep. Is there still a truckle-bed in the powder-closet in your room?'

Mark nodded.

'So take some sheets and blankets from the linenpress when the servants are not around and make a bed for Barry.'

'In the powder-closet?'

'No, that would not serve. In the corner of your room. You may leave now.'

Mark rose and bowed and walked to the door. Then he turned and ran back and threw his arms around the startled Miss Trumble's neck and deposited a wet kiss on her cheek. 'Thank you,' he whispered. And then he ran out.

'Shall we return to the company?' asked Charles stiffly. His conscience was hurting him. To see his own son run with gratitude to a stranger had shown him how very afraid and ill-treated the boy must have been.

They returned to the drawing-room in time to hear dinner being announced. Lady Beverley rose and shook out her skirts. 'I am sure the servants' hall will provide you with something, Miss Trumble,' she said.

'Can't have that,' exclaimed the general. 'Told Miss Trumble to come. Guest.'

'How very kind,' said Lady Beverley with a thin smile. 'Your arm, General. It is such a long time since I have been on the arm of such an *attractive* gentleman.'

Rachel cast a covert look at Miss Trumble

and she in her turn took Charles's arm and Miss Trumble gazed blandly back before slipping away to guide Barry into the house.

What is Mama about, to behave so stupidly? wondered Rachel, as Lady Beverley flirted with the general over dinner.

The general tried to address several remarks to Miss Trumble, but Lady Beverley treated each remark as if it had been addressed to herself.

And then Rachel surprised a mocking, rather speculative look on Charles Blackwood's face as he looked at her mother. Then he said, 'I had the pleasure of calling on an old friend, Lady Evans. You are acquainted with her, I believe?'

'We have had that pleasure,' said Lady Beverley and then remained comparatively silent for the rest of the meal.

So that was it, thought Rachel. He had heard of the vulgar, ambitious Beverleys, and although he thought his own age saved him from being a target, the mother had decided to set her cap at his father. Rachel felt herself blush with shame, her appetite fled and she picked at the food on her plate.

Her mother is embarrassing her dreadfully, thought Charles. He set himself to talk to her, asking her many questions about the neighbourhood and about the market town of Hedgefield until he felt her begin to relax.

'What did Miss Trumble wish to speak to you about?' she asked finally.

'Something to do with Mark's education,' he said. 'But you must ask her if you wish to know more.'

'I do not know what we would do without our Miss Trumble,' said Rachel with a little sigh.

'You should soon be making your come-out,' he said.

'My sister, Abigail, Lady Burfield, has invited me to London.'

'And when do you go?'

'To tell the truth, I have not made up my mind.'

'But why? A young lady like yourself should be enjoying balls and parties.'

'We have balls here in the country.'

'Ah, the local assembly. But can it compete with Almack's?'

She smiled. 'I have not known much of the grand life of late. I should probably feel sadly out of place and provincial.'

'With your appearance and Miss Trumble's schooling, I do not think you have anything to fear.'

And Rachel, who would have accepted such a compliment with flirtatious ease before the revelation that he had called on Lady Evans, found all she could do was stare at her plate and wish the dinnerparty were over.

After dinner, the general suggested they promenade in the Long Gallery. 'I see you have placed the portraits of yourself, your son, and your own ancestors here,' exclaimed Miss Trumble.

'Why not?' demanded Charles Blackwood

crossly. 'You could hardly expect us to hang the Beverleys. They are in the attics, I believe.'

'I meant that there is no portrait of Judd,' said Miss Trumble quietly.

Rachel saw Charles look at Miss Trumble with dawning realization on his face. So little Mark must have confided in his father and governess about the sighting of the ghost. Rachel herself had assumed the boy had seen that portrait and his imagination had done the rest. But perhaps he had been in the attics. Children loved poking around in attics.

'As to your ancestors,' said Charles, turning to Lady Beverley, 'I cannot understand why the previous owners held on to them. If you wish, I will send them over in a fourgon tomorrow.'

'That will not be necessary,' said Lady Beverley. She raised her quizzing-glass to study a portrait of the general.

'May I ask why? I thought you would be delighted to have them back.'

'They belong at Mannerling,' said Lady Beverley.

There must be something about this place that deranges people, thought Charles. I am glad I have not felt it. To him, on first viewing the property, it had seemed peaceful and beautiful with its great hall and painted ceilings.

They moved to the Green Saloon, where the general promptly sat next to Miss Trumble and engaged her in conversation until Lady Beverley could not bear it any longer. She raised her voice.

46

'Miss Trumble! I have left my fan in the carriage. Pray be so good as to fetch it.'

'Your fan is on your wrist,' said Rachel sharply.

'Oh, so it is. You have some pretty pieces and ornaments here, General. Do tell me how you came by them.'

'Here and there. I am not the artistic one. You must ask my son.' And the general turned his attention back to Miss Trumble.

Lady Beverley fell silent while her mind worked busily. She must get rid of this governess who was taking up so much of the general's attention. But if she gave her her marching orders, then Miss Trumble would simply move to Mannerling. How dare Miss Trumble adopt the manners and attitudes of a duchess. She simply did not know her place. Hitherto Lady Beverley had been too grateful to have a governess so cheaply that she had not wondered overmuch why Miss Trumble's promised references had never arrived. Her eyes sharpened. There must be some mystery. There was something in Miss Trumble's past that lady did not want her to find out. She would demand those references and then write to Miss Trumble's previous employers and then she would know all.

The Beverley sisters were very subdued. Belinda was so ashamed of her mother's behaviour that she had made no attempt to flirt with Charles. Rachel looked awkward and uncomfortable and kept looking at the clock, as if she thought the evening would never end.

So much for the scheming Beverleys, mused Charles ruefully. The sisters were certainly not interested in engaging his attentions, and Rachel almost seemed to find him a bore!

At last Lady Beverley announced they must leave. She could hardly wait until they were home so that she could confront Miss Trumble.

She did not know that the shrewd governess had anticipated the summons and was already making plans, so that, when Lady Beverley asked her for a word in private, Miss Trumble acquiesced with every appearance of calm, a calm that did not desert her when Lady Beverley said she must now insist on seeing those references.

'I will arrange for them to be sent directly,' said Miss Trumble. 'But why this sudden concern, my lady?'

Lady Beverley paced up and down the room, showing no sign of the recent ill health she had claimed to have suffered from.

'The reason is,' she said haughtily, 'although I consider it impertinent in you to ask my reasons, that because of your position in this household you are tutoring the Mannerling children. It is up to me to make sure you have perfect references should the general ask to see them.'

And all that translated into, thought Miss Trumble, is that you see a chance of marrying the general and do not want me to get in the way and you are hoping to find some fault in my past and therefore have a reason for dismissing me.

Miss Trumble curtsied. 'Will that be all, my lady?'

Lady Beverley looked at her, baffled. She had been hoping for some sign of worry or distress. 'That will be all,' she said grandly.

Miss Trumble paused in the doorway. 'Perhaps I should mention one little thing.'

'Go on.'

'Now that the Mannerling children are here every weekday and dine with us, perhaps the food supplied could be more appropriate fare for the children of Mannerling.'

'The food is good and nourishing.'

'I heard Mark telling his grandfather that he had sat down to rook-pie for the first time. I just thought I would mention it.'

Miss Trumble smiled sweetly and left, closing the door very quietly behind her.

Lady Beverley could not know her governess had been lying and that Mark had said nothing of the kind. She turned pink at the idea that the Blackwoods might think her parsimonious or, worse, poor. Josiah, the cook, must be ordered to spend more money on his cooking.

Lady Beverley thought about getting out the accounts books to see if the extra money required could be pared from some other household expense but she caught the reflection of her face in the mirror over the fireplace. She thought she looked faded and tired. Lady Beverley had once been a great beauty, but lines of petulance, added to the lines of age, had given her face a crumpled look. She must start using proper washes and lotions. Her hand reached for the bell. Miss Trumble would know what to do. Then she hesitated. With any luck, Miss Trumble would soon not be around for very much longer, so it was better to get used to doing without her.

In her room, Miss Trumble sat down before her travelling writing-desk and began to write busily. While she wrote, she decided to call on Lady Evans the following day.

'Letitia!' exclaimed Lady Evans the following afternoon as Miss Trumble was ushered into the drawing-room of Hursley Park by the butler.

'You look a trifle guilty,' said Miss Trumble, stripping off her gloves, 'as well you should.'

'What can you mean, my dear? Come, be seated and tell me your news.'

'My news is that General Blackwood and his son, Charles, called on you and you saw fit to warn them against the Beverleys. Considering the totally criminal behaviour of your little friend Prudence Makepeace, I am surprised at you.'

'You must admit, Abigail Beverley's behaviour in snaring Lord Burfield was disgraceful.'

'The thing you will not admit is that Burfield was and is madly in love with Abigail.'

'Pooh, love is all a fancy.'

'It seems to me that you must think so. I, on the other hand, love my charges dearly and do not want anything, or any malicious gossip, to stand in their way.'

Lady Evans bridled. ' "Malicious" is too strong a word. The general is an old friend. Even you must admit, Letitia, that the Beverleys have been guilty of blatant plotting and manipulation to regain Mannerling.'

Miss Trumble gave a little sigh. 'That is in the past.'

'And so it should be. Charles Blackwood is too old for any of them. Come, let us not quarrel. I swear I will not say a word against the wretched girls again. There. You have my promise. Are you still bent on keeping on such a demeaning job, one which is well below your position in life?'

'No one knows about me except you, and no one must.'

'Oh, very well. But it is all very strange.'

'Lady Beverley is demanding my references.'

'Awkward. Do you want one from me?'

'No, I have written to several ladies who will supply me with the necessary letters.'

'Why should she ask for them now?'

'I do not know,' lied Miss Trumble, who had no intention of telling Lady Evans that Lady Beverley was setting her cap at the general and did not want competition.

'I saw you arrive and driving yourself! Where is that servant, Barry?'

'Oh, he is on an errand,' said Miss Trumble vaguely, and then began to wonder again how Barry was getting on.

Barry was bored. He had slipped down the back stairs and had hidden on the grounds while the maids came in during the morning to clean the boy's room. He planned to creep back when the coast was clear and get some much-needed sleep, for he had been awake all night long, without the sign of a ghost or even hearing a creaking floor-board.

He wandered over in the direction of the lake and went and sat in the folly, smoked his pipe, and admired the view. If there was no sign of the ghost the next night, he would beg leave to return to his duties at Brookfield House.

When he finally decided it was safe to return, he strolled back by a circuitous route, keeping all the while out of sight of the many windows of Mannerling. Then he sprinted out of the shelter of some concealing shrubbery and ran for the back door. If any servant surprised him on the stairs, he would say he had a letter to deliver to Mr Charles Blackwood personally. With a sigh of relief, he gained Mark's bedchamber, drew the truckle-bed out from its hiding place in the closet, lay on top of it, fully dressed, and fell promptly into a deep sleep.

He was awakened in the early evening by Mark leaping on top of him and crying, 'Wake up. Miss Trumble read us some more about pirates. We could play pirates on the lake. Please!'

'Keep your voice down, young man. I'm not supposed to be here.'

The door opened and Charles Blackwood came in carrying a tray of food and a tankard of beer. 'You must be very hungry,' he said ruefully to Barry. 'I had forgot you could not even go to the kitchens.'

Barry scrambled to his feet and gratefully took the tray. 'I do be sharp set, sir. Most good of you.'

'Papa,' pleaded Mark, 'I learned all about pirates today and would like Barry to come to the lake and play with me.'

'And what about this ghost?'

'Oh,' said Mark in a disappointed little voice. 'Perhaps I imagined it.'

'We'll see,' said Charles. 'One more night and then we will review the situation. You may go and play with Beth and leave your guard here to enjoy his meal in peace.'

Mark ran off. 'Do you think he imagined the ghost, sir?' ventured Barry.

'He described his ghost most vividly. As I said, we will try again tonight.'

Charles left and Barry settled down to enjoy his meal in peace, noticing that Charles had made sure there was enough food for a very hungry man. Barry did not want to see any of the Beverley girls ever again plotting and scheming to get back to Mannerling, but there was no denying Mr Blackwood was a fine-looking man. He must have married late, for the children were young. He wondered what the late Mrs Blackwood had been like.

\* \* \*

Back at Brookfield House, Rachel was wondering the same thing aloud as she sat with Miss Trumble in the parlour. 'For it suddenly occurred to me that there were portraits of Mr Blackwood and his father in the Long Gallery and a charming portrait of the children, but no portrait of Mrs Blackwood, although there was one of the general's wife. There were various portraits of ladies but in such old-fashioned gowns that they must have been the ancestors.'

'Well, unless he volunteers to tell us about her, we can hardly ask him,' said Miss Trumble. She herself had forgotten to ask Lady Evans about the late Mrs Blackwood. The governess looked speculatively at Rachel. 'Mr Charles Blackwood is a good man and his children are delightful. If he ever marries again, I would hope it would be for love.'

Rachel sighed. 'Apart from my lucky elder sisters, love does not seem to enter into fashionable marriages.'

'Better to make an unfashionable marriage than a loveless one.'

Rachel smiled. 'I would have thought a sensible lady like yourself would not have believed in love in a cottage.'

'It need not be a cottage. Anywhere but Mannerling, in fact.'

Lady Beverley came in at that moment, a letter in her hand. 'Such news,' she said. 'I had this letter from Isabella this morning, but did not read it all until now. She is returning with her husband to Perival.' Perival was Viscount Fitzpatrick's, Isabella's husband's, English estate, which lay near them on the other side of Mannerling.

'Splendid!' cried Rachel, elated at the news of the return of the eldest Beverley sister. 'Does Mrs Kennedy accompany them?' Mrs Kennedy was the viscount's aunt.

'That hurly-burly Irishwoman! I trust not,' said Lady Beverley. 'Mrs Kennedy was a vulgar influence on you girls.'

'How can you say that, Mama? Mrs Kennedy was kindness itself.'

'In any case, Isabella says nothing of her.'

'When do they plan to arrive?' asked Miss Trumble.

'In a month's time.'

Rachel slipped out of the room and went in search of Belinda and Lizzie to tell them the great news.

Lizzie clapped her hands. 'We will see our nephew and niece. Let me see, Margaret must be two, and Guy, three years old. Have you told Barry? He was always monstrous fond of Isabella.'

'I cannot find Barry. Where is he?'

'All Miss Trumble will say is that he has gone off on an errand, but whatever errand it was, it has taken him away for quite some time.'

Barry stifled a yawn and sat up on the truckle-bed. Better to get up and sit on a chair in case he fell asleep. It was so tempting to close his eyes. Mark had been a cheerful and happy child before he fell asleep. Barry was sure that this ghost did not exist.

He had left the shutters on one window open, and a shaft of moonlight fell across the boards of the floor. Mark's little bed was a modern one with a canopy, rather than a four-poster with curtains that could be drawn round it in the night, which was why he could claim to have seen a ghost standing at the end of his bed.

Barry's eyelids began to droop. He had not managed to have enough sleep during the day.

And then those eyes jerked open. He heard a soft shuffling movement in the corridor outside. He felt on the floor beside him for his stout cudgel and tensed, waiting.

The door slowly swung open. The corridor outside was in darkness but he could dimly make out a tall figure standing in the doorway, a thicker piece of darkness.

The figure walked forwards and stood at the end of the bed. Barry had told Mark not to light a candle.

Barry fought down a sudden superstitious feeling of pure panic.

Then he heard the scrape of a tinder-box. The figure had moved to the side of the bed and was lighting a candle.

Barry's moment of panic fled. Ghosts, Barry thought firmly, easing himself to his feet, did not light candles.

But as the little flame sprang up, he suppressed a gasp. Surely this was Judd. He was dressed all in black, with a long black cloak, but the hair was sandy and the foxy features were familiar.

'What are you doing here?' shouted Barry.

The figure swung to face him and at the same time raised his cloak to hide his face and let out a sepulchral moan. Mark started up and began to scream.

The 'ghost' made for the door. 'I'll give you something to moan about,' cried Barry and lashed out with his cudgel.

The man ducked and the cudgel caught him a glancing blow on the side of the head. He fell heavily, but quickly rallied and staggered out into the corridor. Barry stumbled over one of Mark's toys and fell headlong. He scrambled back to his feet and ran out into the corridor. But the 'ghost' had gone. Barry ran through the corridors of the great house, shouting and yelling. Cries came from the downstairs, where sleepy servants, roused from their beds by the noise, stumbled out into the great hall.

Charles Blackwood appeared wrapped in a magnificent silk banyan. 'What is it, Barry?'

'The ghost,' said Barry. 'I struck him a blow on the head but then I fell over something on the bedroom floor and he got away.'

'So the boy was telling the truth.'

Charles ran down to the hall and gave orders to the servants. For the rest of the night the house was searched from top to bottom, and the gamekeepers, grooms, and gardeners searched the grounds.

At last they met again in the dawn light, all gathered in the hall.

Charles addressed them. 'Someone has been trying to frighten my son. If any of you is responsible, then I shall take them personally to the nearest round-house. I want two guards to be on duty from now on outside my son's door at night.'

He did not want any of the newly hired Mannerling servants. He had not chosen any of the servants he had brought with him for fear they, too, would gossip. But he now realized that they would never be part of any plot to harm his son. He selected one groom and one stablehand and gave them their orders. They had been in his employ for some time and appeared to be trustworthy.

He then turned to Barry. 'You have done well. I doubt if our ghost will materialize again.' He handed Barry two guineas, which Barry swiftly pocketed.

The odd man said he would walk back to Brookfield House, as the morning was fine. He felt very tired. But something was nagging at the back of his mind. He had scanned the servants' faces when they were gathered in the hall, looking for anyone with the same type of features as Judd, but he could not see one. It suddenly struck him that there was one face that should have been among the crowd, a face that was absent.

He was still mulling it over as he walked up the

short drive to Brookfield House. He walked round the side of the building and round the back to the kitchen door. He was reaching up his hand to the latch when the door suddenly opened and Miss Trumble stood there.

'What news, Barry? I had a restless night and rose early. I saw you arrive.'

'I chased the ghost.' Barry described what had happened.

'But who would do such a thing, and why?'

'That I do not know, miss, but there do be something troubling me. When we was all gathered in the hall, all the servants, indoor and outdoor, I looked round the faces to see if I could spot anyone who might have tried to dress up as Judd, someone who looked a bit like him, but I couldn't see anyone. Then, as I was walking back home, I came to the conclusion that someone was missing out o' that gathering, but I couldn't guess who it could be.'

'John,' said Miss Trumble bleakly.

'John?'

'The footman. He is tall and thin. His eyes are pale green. He could have worn a sandy wig.'

Barry scratched his head in perplexity. 'But John is a milksop, a cringing, mincing man-milliner.'

'Forget his character and try to imagine him in a sandy wig.'

'Could be,' said Barry reluctantly. 'What should we do?'

'If you are not too tired, hitch up the carriage

and we will go back to Mannerling. You say you struck John.'

' 'Twas but a glancing blow, miss.'

'Nonetheless, his head must be examined and his quarters searched.'

'I'll get the carriage right away.'

Charles Blackwood, roused from a late sleep, heard their suspicions. 'You did right to come to me direct,' he said, cutting across the governess's apologies for having awakened him.

He rang the bell. A footman Miss Trumble did not know answered it promptly.

'Send the footman, John, to me,' commanded Charles. He turned to Miss Trumble and Barry. 'Now we shall see.'

After some moments, John appeared and stood meekly before them.

'Come here,' ordered Charles, 'and kneel before me.'

John flashed a sudden look of venom at Miss Trumble, quickly veiled. He knelt in front of his master. Charles whipped off the footman's white wig and then felt carefully over his close-cropped head.

Then he replaced the wig and said, 'Stand.'

John did as he was bid. 'May I be so bold to ask what this is all about?' he asked.

'In a minute. After the search for this ghost, when the servants were all assembled in the hall, you were not there.'

'But I was, sir. I was standing at the back with Mrs Jones, the housekeeper, and Freddy, the pot-boy.'

'Bring them here,' ordered Charles.

They waited in silence until the housekeeper and the pot-boy were brought in by John.

The housekeeper was small and stout, encased in black bombazine, keys at her waist and an enormous starched cap on her head. Her face had a high shiny glaze and her little eyes held a look of perpetual outrage.

Gin, thought Miss Trumble.

The pot-boy was undersized and had a loose wet mouth and moist black eyes. He gawked about him with bovine stupidity.

'John, here, says he was at the back of the Great Hall this morning at dawn after we had all given up the search for the man who tried to impersonate the late Mr Judd. Is that the case? Was John with you?'

'Yes, sir,' said the housekeeper. She had a deep hoarse voice. Definitely gin, thought Miss Trumble.

'You are sure?'

'Oh, yes, sir. John says to me, he says, that it might have been a real ghost after all.'

'And you, boy?' said Charles to Freddy.

Freddy tugged his forelock. 'I seed 'im as plain as day, sir.'

He looked to the housekeeper for approval.

'You may go,' said Charles. 'Not you, John.'

When the housekeeper and pot-boy had left, Charles said, 'You are the only servant who could have impersonated the late Mr Judd, because of your looks. But obviously I was mistaken. You may go about your duties. But remember and tell the other servants – if I find the culprit, I will deal with him first before I hand him over to the authorities.'

# THREE

*She likes her self, yet others hates*
*For that which in herself she prizes;*
*And, while she laughs at them, forgets*
*She is the thing that she despises.*

WILLLAM CONGREVE

Somehow, the sisters had expected the excitement of a visit to Mannerling to go on forever. But
rainy days set in and although the children came
daily during the week, neither Charles nor his
father came with them. There was only the local
assembly to look forward to, and that, the sisters
privately thought, would be the usual dull affair.
Of course, Isabella would soon be with them and
that was at least something exciting. But the damp
dreary days made the hours drag by. Barry began
to worry about getting them safely to the assembly and in an open carriage, too, for thick fog had
started to shroud the countryside at night, along
with the persistent drenching rain.

Lady Beverley was once more victim of one of her
imaginary illnesses and demanded 'absolute quiet',

so there were not even Lizzie's tunes of the pianoforte to enliven their days. And then, just when it
seemed to the sisters that they would be locked in
this rainy, foggy, silent grave of Brookfield House
forever, the day before the assembly the morning
sun appeared and burnt through the fog, leaving
the countryside glittering and shining under a
clear blue sky.

And Mark and Beth arrived with a letter from
the general to say he and his son would be at the
assembly, for friends of theirs had come to stay at
Mannerling and were anxious to sample the 'local
excitements.'

Belinda and Lizzie took out gowns and feathers
and lace. A party from Mannerling might include
some young men!

Rachel said it would amuse her now to go and
see all the ladies trying to ensnare the owner of
Mannerling.

A package arrived in the mail for Miss Trumble.
She opened it and took out several letters and
read them with a smile. Then she went in search
of Lady Beverley. Her mistress was up and about
and looking over several gowns. 'What do you
think I should wear, Miss Trumble?' she asked
when she saw the governess. 'I wore this plum
velvet for half-mourning, but I fear it looks sadly
démodé.'

'There is a pale-blue silk here, very grand, and a
good line,' said Miss Trumble, picking up the gown
from the bed and shaking out the folds. 'With an

overdress, the one you have, you know, of darker-blue sarsenet, 'twould be very fetching.'

'Perhaps you have the right of it.'

'My references, my lady.' Miss Trumble held them out.

'Put them on my desk over there. Oh, and Miss Trumble, it will not be necessary for you to accompany us. I do not like to leave the house empty.'

'The maids will be here, and Josiah.'

'Servants are not responsible people.' Lady Beverley crossed to the glass and studied her own reflection critically. 'I need you to prepare a pomade and one of your washes for my face, Miss Trumble.'

'Alas, I have mislaid my recipe book and fear I cannot.'

Both women eyed each other. Lady Beverley knew that the governess would now punish her for having been forbidden the assembly. There would be no more lotions, pomades, powders, washes, and, above all, magic draughts for those tiresome headaches.

'On the other hand,' said Lady Beverley, 'I suppose Josiah is protection enough for this poky little house. You may accompany us.'

'I do believe I left my book in the kitchen with Josiah. I will go directly and look for it.'

When the governess had left, Lady Beverley eagerly scanned those references. Her face fell. There were three letters, all from ladies of impeccable rank and lineage, and their praise for Miss Trumble was of the highest order.

Lady Beverley gave a petulant little shrug. What chance had a mere governess with such as the general? Such a man would not lower himself to wed a governess!

To the sisters' delight, their mother hired a closed carriage and coachman to drive them all to the assembly. The assembly, from being damned as a tiresome village affair, had become enchanted in their eyes because the owner of Mannerling was to be there.

Rachel did not want to arrive late but her mother did, Lady Beverley liking to make an entrance. She fondly imagined the general and his son being bored by the dismal country company and how their eyes would light up at the sight of the Beverley family.

Mary Judd was pinning up a stray lock of hair in the anteroom provided for the ladies when they arrived. Miss Trumble, resplendent in gold silk and with a Turkish turban to match on her pomaded curls, noticed that Mary's little black eyes were shining with malice and wondered why.

'Just arrived?' asked Rachel.

'No, I have been here this age,' said Mary. 'So passé to arrive late, do you not think?'

'I wouldn't know the ways of the world, any more than you,' retorted Rachel. 'Out with it, Mary. Your eyes are full of secrets. Is the party from Mannerling here?'

'You will see for yourself.' Mary flitted out.

'I suppose Mr Charles Blackwood has turned

up with a beautiful lady and she thinks we will be disappointed,' said Lizzie, and they all laughed at the joke.

They could hear the jolly strains of the local band playing a country dance. The air was full of the smells of scent and pomade, wood-smoke, wine and beer. They pushed open the double doors which opened into the assembly room.

It was a long room at the side of the inn, with a fire burning at either end. The band played in a little gallery which overlooked the room. At first Rachel saw only familiar faces and then the crowd of watchers in front of her parted and she could see the whole ballroom.

In the centre of the room, his height topping the dancers, was Charles Blackwood, partnered by a very tall, very beautiful woman. Her hair was as fair as Rachel's and her eyes of a very intense blue. She had high cheek-bones, a long straight nose, and a statuesque figure, slim but deep-breasted, and she was nearly as tall as Charles Blackwood. She was wearing a gown of silver gauze over an underslip of white satin. Diamonds sparkled in her hair and round her perfect white neck.

Rachel stood there, feeling small and diminished. This Amazon was a sort of grander Rachel, taller, more assured, with bluer eyes and a sophisticated, commanding presence.

'Oh, dear,' whispered Lizzie. 'Who can she be?'

'I fear that is our Mr Blackwood's house guest,' said Rachel. 'Perhaps her husband is here.'

'From the way she is looking at Mr Blackwood and he at her,' said Belinda, 'I fear there is no husband.'

The general had seen them and came bustling up. 'Capital,' he exclaimed. 'You are looking very fine tonight, Miss Trumble.' Lady Beverley glared daggers. 'And you, too, dear lady,' said the general hastily. 'Ah, the dance is finishing. You must make the acquaintanceship of our guests.'

They followed him in a little group to where Charles was bowing before his partner at the end of the dance. 'Charles, my boy,' cried the general. 'They are come at last.'

Charles smiled at them. 'Lady Beverley, may I present my friend, Miss Minerva Santerton. Ah, and here is George, Mr Santerton, Miss Santerton's brother.' He introduced brother and sister to the Beverleys and Miss Trumble. George Santerton was as tall as his sister, with the same fair hair, but his eyes were a washed-out blue and held a vacuous look and his chin receded into his high, starched cravat.

'Charmed,' he drawled. 'Didn't expect so many beauties at a little country dance.'

Minerva smiled, a small, curved smile. 'But you must have heard of the famous Beverley sisters,' she said. 'Even I have heard of them. Your fame is known in London.'

Her voice hesitated a little before the word 'fame', as if she had been about to say 'notoriety'.

Rachel felt a tug at her arm and found Mark

looking up at her. 'May I have the next dance, Miss Rachel?'

Minerva smiled indulgently. 'Shall we find some refreshment, Charles, and leave the children to their dance?'

She put a proprietorial hand on his arm. A flash of irritation crossed Charles's green eyes, but he bowed and led her away.

Rachel performed a dance, another country one, with Mark, trying to remind herself that children always came to dances at these country assemblies, but feeling gauche and awkward and wishing she had a handsome partner to restore some of her wounded vanity. She and her sisters had been used to being the most beautiful women at any country affair and she felt their lustre had been sadly dimmed by this visiting goddess.

As if in answer to her wishes for a handsome partner, no sooner was the dance over and the supper dance announced than a gentleman was bowing before her. Rachel hesitated just a moment. She had expected to be led into supper after this dance by Charles. Perhaps, she thought furiously, if Mama had not arrived so late, there would have been time for Charles to have asked her. She realized the gentleman in front of her was looking at her quizzically and waiting for her reply.

She dropped a low curtsy and said, 'I am delighted, sir.'

And then she took a proper look at him. He was a stranger to the neighbourhood; she had not seen him before. He was of medium height with thick brown hair fashionably cut, which gleamed in the candle-light with red glints. His square, regular face was deeply tanned.

Suddenly mindful of the conventions, Rachel said, as he led her to the floor, 'We have not been introduced, sir.'

'I thought such conventions were only for London balls.'

'No, I assure you.'

He led her to the Master of Ceremonies, Squire Blaine, and said, 'Pray introduce me to this beautiful lady.'

'Certainly,' said the squire. 'Miss Beverley, may I present Mr Hercules Cater, whom I met earlier today. Mr Cater is a sugar planter from the Indies. Mr Cater, the star of our county, Miss Rachel Beverley of Brookfield House.'

'There we are,' he said gaily, leading her to the centre of the floor. 'Now we are all that is respectable.'

The dance was a quadrille, which many people in the county still did not know how to perform, and so there was only one set: Rachel and Mr Cater, Charles and Minerva, the general and Lady Beverley, and Belinda and George Santerton.

It gladdened Rachel's heart to notice how ungracefully Minerva danced. Her own partner, Mr Cater, danced with ease and grace, drawing applause from the audience by performing an entrechat, quite in the manner of the bon ton who employed ballet masters to teach them elaborate steps.

Miss Trumble watched the dancers. She was glad the general was dancing with Lady Beverley. For had the general chosen her, Miss Trumble, for the supper dance, then, the governess knew, her mistress would have done everything in her power to ruin the evening for everyone else.

And then she noticed Lady Evans sitting in a quiet corner and made her way there.

'Ah, Letitia,' said Lady Evans, who was wearing an enormous turban instead of one of her usual giant caps. 'Come and sit by me, for I am become bored.'

'You must not call me Letitia in public,' admonished Miss Trumble, sitting down beside her. 'If it bores you so much, why do you come?'

'Curiosity. I was anxious to see Miss Santerton with my own eyes. I have heard so much about her.'

'Indeed! I am so out of the world, I have heard nothing at all. How old is she, would you say?'

'I know her exact age. She is one of the Sussex Santertons. Good family. Minerva is twenty-eight.'

'So old, so beautiful, and not married! No money?'

'The Santertons are as rich as Croesus.'

'So what is the problem?'

'Minerva Santerton is a widow.'

'Then why is she called Santerton?'

'It is a dark story. She married Sir Giles Santerton,

a first cousin. They were married only a little over a year when Sir Giles was found drowned in a pond on his estate. Now, he had been heard quarrelling with Minerva – evidently they fought like cat and dog – on the morning of the day he died. Also, when his body was pulled from the water, he had a lump the size of an egg on his head. There were a few nasty rumours.'

'Such as?'

'Such as that his wife had hit him on the head and pushed him to his death. But Giles's father was and is the local magistrate and shuddered at the idea of scandal, and he had not been overfond of his son in any case, and so nothing more was said about the whole business and the rumours died away. My friend, Mrs Tullock, who knows the family and is of Sussex, went to the funeral and said Minerva cried most affectingly and even fainted at the graveside.'

'But she was introduced to the Beverleys as *Miss* Santerton!'

'The death took place four years ago. After a period of mourning, Miss Santerton appeared once more on the social scene. She seems determined to be regarded as a débutante.'

'At her age, and apparently never having been married, she is in danger of being damned as an ape-leader.' Spinsters were still believed to be damned when they died to lead apes in hell.

'I think she is still in a way out for revenge on the dead Giles by acting as if the marriage never happened,' said Lady Evans.

72

'Why did she marry him if she hated him that much?'

'Her mother was dead and her father, considerably older than the mother, mark you, was an awful old tyrant. He arranged the marriage, he and Giles's father.'

'But a first cousin . . .' protested Miss Trumble.

'Oh, they were married by a bishop, and one can always bribe a bishop. Now take that fellow dancing with Rachel. He is a Mr Cater, a sugar planter, and said to be enormously wealthy. Good parti.'

'All these people arriving out of nowhere,' murmured Miss Trumble. 'And I had the stage so nicely set.'

'What's that, hey?'

'Nothing of importance,' said Miss Trumble sadly. 'Nothing important at all.'

Rachel found Mr Cater pleasant company at supper. She judged him to be in his mid-twenties, certainly nearer her age than Charles Blackwood. 'And what brings you to Hedgefield?' she asked.

'Curiosity. I met someone out in the West Indies who spoke of the beauties of Mannerling, and finding time on my hands, I decided to travel into the country and perhaps see the place for myself.'

'Mannerling,' echoed Rachel, her face lighting up.

'You know the place well?'

'Of course; it was our family home until some years ago.' Her large eyes shone. 'It must be the most beautiful place in the world.'

'I have already spoken to the present owner, Mr Charles Blackwood. He has kindly allowed me to visit Mannerling and see for myself.'

'Oh, it is so wonderful. Such an air of peace and elegance. I miss it so much. We were happy there. Who told you of Mannerling?'

'An elderly gentleman, Lord Hexhamworth.'

'Ah, yes, he was a friend of my father and was always invited to our balls. We had wonderful balls.'

'Mr Blackwood seems much taken with Miss Santerton.'

Rachel looked down the long table to where Charles sat with Minerva.

'Yes,' she agreed, but impatiently. For some reason she wanted to forget the existence of Charles Blackwood and the glorious Minerva, who made her feel small and provincial. 'The last ball we had at Mannerling,' she went on, 'was the finest. The walls were draped with silk, and a double row of footmen lined the grand staircase, each man carrying a gold sword.'

'That is extravagance to rival the Prince Regent!'

'It was so very fine.' She gave a little sigh. 'But we have accepted our new life and are relatively happy.'

'Perhaps Mr Blackwood can be persuaded to let you show me the delights of Mannerling.'

'That would not be fitting. Besides, I would feel like an interloper.'

'And yet your beauty in a beautiful house would surely be fitting.'

'Thank you, sir, for the compliment. Do you stay long in England?'

'Several months. I have not been home this age.'

'Tell me about your life in the Indies.'

At first she listened, fascinated, to the tales of hurricanes and heat, of hard labour and the rewards of being a plantation owner. But when he began to complain of the laziness of his black slaves, Rachel began to feel uncomfortable. Miss Trumble had lectured them on the evils of slavery. And yet she had up until that point found the company of this easygoing Mr Cater pleasant.

'You obviously do not believe in all this talk of freedom for slaves,' she said at last.

Something flickered through the depths of his eyes and he said with a light laugh, 'It may seem brutal to you here, in your sheltered world of England. But you would soon change your views were you in the West Indies. Sugar must be harvested and white skins are not up to labouring in the sun.'

'Possibly,' agreed Rachel. 'But slaves!'

He smiled indulgently. 'You are a very modern young lady. But tell me more about Mannerling.'

And in her enthusiasm in describing her old home, Rachel forgot for the rest of the evening about those slaves.

Charles Blackwood had to admit to himself that he was becoming quickly fascinated by the beautiful Minerva. He had not invited either Minerva or her brother to stay; they had invited themselves. At first he had been irritated, for the acquaintanceship was slight and they had not asked if they could stay, had simply sent an express to say they would be arriving. George Santerton was a bore and a fool, but the glorious Minerva more than made up for her brother's deficiencies.

The intense blue of her eyes, the gold of her hair, the swell of her bosom, and the way those magnificent eyes lit up with laughter went straight to his heart. He had planned never to marry again, but Minerva would make such a beautiful ornament in his beautiful home.

But there were Mark and Beth to consider before he even thought of presenting them with a new mother. His fury at his late wife's infidelity had made him neglect them. He realized that now and he was immensely grateful to Miss Rachel Beverley of Brookfield House for having brought that neglect to his attention. His eyes strayed to Rachel. She seemed to be enjoying the company of that stranger, Cater. If the man was as rich as rumour already had it, then perhaps yet another of the Beverley sisters would make a good marriage. He hoped she would find someone worthy of her. He could not in his heart blame the Beverleys for their reported machinations in trying to reclaim their home. The girls were very young and the plunge from riches to a sort of genteel straitened circumstances must have been hard. There was a soft glow about Rachel when she was happy that seemed to make Minerva's charms, by contrast, look like hard brilliance. He gave himself a mental shake. Minerva was speaking. 'I quite dote on your children,' she said. 'I feel it is a great tragedy that I have none of my own.'

'Perhaps you may yet have children,' he said lightly. 'You may marry again.'

'When one has made a bad mistake, or rather, one's father has forced one into an unhappy marriage, then one is not anxious to marry again.'

He looked at her with quick sympathy. 'I understand what you mean. But there are good people in this world.'

Her eyes caressed his face. 'I am beginning to think there are.'

He felt a little chill, a sense of withdrawal. Like all men, he wanted to be the hunter, not the hunted.

'How long do you plan to stay at Mannerling?' he asked abruptly.

To his horror, those beautiful eyes of hers filled with tears. 'Alas,' she said brokenly, 'I told George we had been too forward in coming. We will leave as soon as possible.'

He immediately felt like a brute. 'My dear Miss Santerton, you and your brother are welcome to be my guests for as long as you wish.'

She dabbed at her eyes. 'Too kind,' she said. 'I must do something to repay you. Your poor children, I am sure, would appreciate some feminine company. I would be prepared to spend some time with them.'

'As to that, although I do thank you for your offer, the matter is attended to. Mark and Beth go daily to Brookfield House to be educated by the governess there, an estimable woman, and they also have the company of the Beverley girls.'

'Ah, yes, the Beverleys,' she said in a low voice. 'You do not think the many scandals attached to that unfortunate family will affect your children?'

'I have heard all the scandals and no, I do not. They are very happy.'

'Mmm. Oh, well, if you are satisfied . . . I mean, I trust the girls are not using the children to ingratiate themselves with you.'

'Hardly. Miss Rachel gave me my character over my neglect of Mark and Beth.'

'We shall see,' said Minerva. 'We shall see.'

The ball wound to its close. Rachel had not been asked to dance by Charles Blackwood and she felt it was something of a slight, for he had danced with both Lizzie and Belinda, a Belinda who, Rachel thought, had flirted quite outrageously.

She felt suddenly tired. The room was overwarm, faces were flushed, and quite a number of the gentlemen were drunk. But she knew her mother would not leave the ball until the general did. Rachel reflected that she had never seen her mother look so animated before. She still had a handsome figure and a neat ankle. She had rouged her face with two bright circles, despite Miss Trumble's advice to the contrary, in an effort to banish the pallor caused

78

by long bouts of imaginary illness when she was mured up in her bedchamber. But Rachel noticed how the general's eyes kept straying to where Miss Trumble sat against the wall, and feared ructions ahead. Lady Beverley would have been shocked could she have guessed that the general's reason for not taking Miss Trumble up for a dance was because he feared she might make life difficult for her governess.

At last Rachel, dancing a second dance with Mr Cater, saw the Mannerling party leave and knew that they could now go home. Mr Cater sought out Lady Beverley and gained her permission to call.

'He would do very well for you, Rachel,' said Lady Beverley in the carriage on the road home.

'You go too fast, Mama,' pleaded Rachel wearily. 'I know very little about the gentleman except that he owns sugar plantations in Barbados in the West Indies. He employs slaves.'

'I should be very surprised if he did not, my child. How else is the sugar to be harvested?'

But Rachel did not feel like entering into an argument on the rights and wrongs of slavery with her mother. The next day was Sunday, so there would be no visit from the Blackwood children, although they could expect to see the Blackwoods in church.

When Rachel was brushing out her hair before going to bed, Miss Trumble quietly entered the room.

'You look worried, Rachel. Was Mr Cater not to your liking?'

'He is a very pleasant man. But he keeps slaves. The slave-trade was abolished, or so you told us.'

'The Abolition of the Slave Trade Act was passed in 1807,' said Miss Trumble. 'But this act, be it remembered, did not abolish slavery but only prohibited the traffic in slaves. So that no ship should clear out from any port in the British dominions after May the first, 1807, with slaves on board, and that no slave should be landed in the colonies after March the first, 1808.'

'So why is there still slavery?'

Miss Trumble sat down with a weary little sigh. 'The product is now home-grown, just like the sugar. Slavery has been going on so long that there are black children growing up into slavery.'

'It distresses me,' said Rachel in a low voice.

'Many things in this wicked world distress me,' said the governess. 'But you are not going to reform a plantation owner. Should you marry him, all you could do would be to see that the slaves were well-housed and fed and not ill-treated. With the education I have given you, you would be well-equipped to educate them. But in order to go to such a situation on the other side of the world, you would need to be very much in love. Arranged marriages often work out quite comfortably in England, but it would be different there. There would be so many stresses and strains.'

'It looked very much tonight as if our Mr Charles will make a match of it with Miss Santerton.'

'I do hope not.'

80

'Why do you say that?'

'A feeling, that is all. I think there is an instability of mind there.'

Rachel gave a little shrug. 'Where such beauty is concerned, I am sure a little madness would not even be noticed.'

'Perhaps,' said Miss Trumble.

At church in the morning, with the congregation heavy-eyed after the ball the night before, Rachel noticed that the Santertons were there, Minerva and Charles looking very much a couple. Mr Stoddart, the vicar, preached in a monotonous voice. 'I do wish that little man would end. Is he going to prose on forever?' Minerva's voice sounded in the church with dreadful clarity. Mr Stoddart flushed, but smiled down at the Mannerling party in an ingratiating way and brought his sermon to an abrupt close.

Outside the church, where ladies clutched their bonnets in a frisky, blustery wind, Mary took hold of Rachel's arm in a confidential way. 'It looks as if Mannerling will soon have a new mistress. And so suitable!'

Rachel felt irritated and depressed at the same time. At that moment, the wind came to her rescue and whipped Mary's straw bonnet from her head and sent it scuttling off among the tombstones, with Mary in pursuit.

At least Isabella will soon be with us, thought Rachel, her eyes straying to where Charles

Blackwood was escorting Minerva to the Mannerling carriage. Charles had not spoken to her or acknowledged her presence.

She did not know that Charles had had every intention of speaking, not only to her, but to various other parishioners, but that Minerva's hand on his arm had been like a vice and that, outside the church, she had instantly claimed that the sermon had given her a headache and that she wanted to return 'home'.

As his carriage drove off, he saw that new fellow, Hercules Cater, approach the Beverley family and saw a smile of welcome on Lady Beverley's thin lips.

Though he was finding Minerva a heady and enchanting beauty, she was beginning to annoy him. He did not like the unspoken and yet calm assumption of brother and sister that he should propose to Minerva.

Lady Beverley had invited Mr Cater back to Brookfield House for a cold collation. Miss Trumble had planned to find out as much as she could about the young man, but Lady Beverley was annoyed that Charles had not spoken to her and blamed the presence of the governess. Lady Beverley always had to have someone to blame. And so she gave Miss Trumble several tasks to perform, telling her that her presence was not needed in company. Miss Trumble went in search of Barry.

'I suppose Mr Cater will be deemed suitable for Rachel,' she said as Barry straightened up from weeding a flower-bed. 'I suppose one cannot expect all the Beverley girls to marry for love.'

'He seems a pleasant-enough young man, miss. Sugar plantations, I believe.'

'Rachel is troubled by the fact that he keeps slaves.'

'They all do, in them parts. One young miss can't change the way things are done.'

'No, but she would either need to become hardened to the situation, which I would not like, or become distressed by it. I cannot think Mr Cater is suitable, and yet he is surely better than some elderly gentleman with a great deal of money, for I cannot see Lady Beverley balking at anyone at all who is in funds.'

'It amazes me, miss,' said Barry, 'that she is not throwing Miss Rachel at Mr Blackwood's head.'

'Ah, that is because my lady plans to wed the general and so secure Mannerling.'

'Any hope there?'

'I should not think so. Lady Beverley was once a very great beauty but I do not think she ever had the arts to charm. She probably relied on her beauty and fortune and felt she did not have to do much else.'

'I did hear tell that Miss Santerton is of outstanding beauty and people are already saying a match is expected.'

'Perhaps. She is certainly amazingly handsome. But tall, very tall. I always feel such a lady is to be admired from a distance, like a statue. She lacks human qualities. I have written to an old friend for the full story of the Santertons. I will let you know when her reply arrives, although it should be some days because I wrote the letter last night and cannot post it until tomorrow.'

Barry gave her a sly grin. 'It always amazes me, if I may say so, miss, that a lady like yourself would gossip with an old servant like me.'

'That is because I am an old servant myself.' Miss Trumble gathered her shawl about her shoulders, nodded to him, and walked away.

As she approached the house, she could hear a burst of laughter from the dining-room. Mr Cater appeared to be keeping the company well-entertained.

Only Rachel wondered at Mr Cater's conversation. He spoke of Barbados, of the climate, of the flora and fauna, of the tedium of the long sea voyage home, of the plays he had seen in London before travelling to the country, and yet he revealed nothing of his private life, of his family, or of where he originally came from and what had taken him to the other side of the world in the first place.

But Rachel chided herself on looking for flaws. To marry such a man would mean being well set up for life, of getting away from Mama, of having a household of her own. It would be adventurous to go to the Indies.

But after the meal, when Mr Cater asked her to show him the garden, Rachel irritated her mother by promptly suggesting that Belinda and Lizzie should accompany them. She described plants and bushes and all the while her errant thoughts kept straying to Mannerling. Had Charles considered his children if he was thinking of marriage again?

At that moment, Minerva was entering the drawing-room, holding Mark by one hand and Beth by the other. 'We have had such sport,' she cried. 'I quite dote on the children. Playing with them makes me feel like a child myself.'

'Come here to me,' said Charles to the children. 'What have you been doing?'

'Playing with stick and ball,' said Mark in a low voice. Minerva had asked them whether they did not miss their mother, and he had replied, truthfully, that he could remember very little of his mother, for he had barely seen her. Minerva had then told him that he must always put his father's happiness before any selfish thoughts, and should his father decide to find them a new mother, then he and Beth must do all in their power to make that lady welcome.

And Mark did not like Minerva. Her intense blue gaze unnerved him. But he did not want his father to retreat back into becoming the sad-eyed, withdrawn man he had been so recently and so Mark forced himself to look pleased with Minerva. He longed for Sunday to be over so that he and Beth could return to Miss Trumble and the safety of Brookfield House.

The Santertons slept late. On Monday morning, Charles surprised his father as he was getting into the carriage to go to Brookfield House with the children.

'Feel a bit dull,' said the general. 'Thought I'd talk to that Trumble female. Very sensible.'

'I'll come with you,' said Charles suddenly. He did not know what it was about Mannerling that had suddenly begun to oppress him. Perhaps it was Minerva, and yet, had he been a superstitious man, he could have believed the house itself was turning against him. He could sense a malignancy lurking in its quiet rooms, but decided he was becoming fanciful and that the haunting of his son was putting him on his guard, for whoever had played such an evil trick had not been discovered.

When they arrived, Miss Trumble said that as the day was fine and warm, she would give the children their lessons in the garden. Lady Beverley urged the general and Charles to step into the house but, to her irritation, the general said he would like to sit in the garden as well.

The girls joined them. Miss Trumble started by reading items of news from the *Morning Post*, explaining before she did so that she liked the children to be au fait with current affairs. Then an article caught her eye and she began to laugh.

'What amuses you, Miss Trumble?' asked the general.

'I just read a few sentences. It appears to be a very good description of a Bond Street Lounger.'

'Read it to us,' urged the general.

'Come now, General,' protested Lady Beverley. 'You would not like to see the education of your grandchildren neglected.'

'I think Mark should know all about Bond Street Loungers. Go ahead, Miss Trumble.'

Miss Trumble looked inquiringly at her mistress.

'Very well,' said Lady Beverley huffily.

Miss Trumble explained. 'It begins with the necessary behaviour of a Bond Street Lounger in an hotel as he tries to establish his character as that of a man of fashion. "In short, find fault with every single article without exception, damn the waiter–" '

'Miss Trumble!' exclaimed Lady Beverley.

'Go on, do,' said the general with a laugh.

' "– the waiter at almost regular intervals, and never let him stand one moment still, but keep him eternally moving; having it in remembrance that he is only an unfortunate and wretched subordinate, of course, a stranger to feelings which are an ornament to Human Nature; with this recollection on your part that the more illiberal the abuse he has from you, the greater will be his admiration of your superior abilities, and Gentleman-like qualifications. Confirm him in the opinion he has so unjustly imbibed, by swearing the fish is not warm through; the poultry is as tough as your Grandmother; the pastry is made with butter, rank

Irish; the cheese which they call Stilton is nothing but pale Suffolk; the malt liquor damnable, a mere infusion of malt, tobacco, and cocculus Indicus; the port musty; the sherry sour; and that the whole of the dinner and dessert were infernally infamous, and of course, not fit for the entertainment of a Gentleman; conclude the lecture with an oblique hint that, without better accommodations, and more ready attention, you shall be under the necessity of leaving the house for a more comfortable situation.

' "Having thus introduced you to, and fixed you, recruit-like, in good quarters, I consider it almost unnecessary to say, however bad you may imagine the wine, I doubt not your own prudence will point out the characteristic necessity of drinking enough, not only to afford you the credit of reeling to bed by aid of the banister, but the collateral comfort of calling yourself damned queer in the morning, owing entirely to the villainous adulteration of the wine, for when mild and genuine, you can take three bottles without winking or blinking. When rousing from your last somniferous reverie in the morning, ring the bell with no small degree of energy, which will serve to convince the whole family you are awake; upon the entrance of either chamberlain or chambermaid, vociferate half a dozen questions without waiting for a single reply. As, What morning is it? Is my breakfast ready? Has anybody inquired for me? Is my groom here? And so on and so forth. And here it becomes directly in point to observe that a groom is become so evidently necessary to the ton of the present day (particularly in the neighbourhood of Bond Street) that a great number of gentlemen keep a groom who cannot (except upon credit) keep a horse; but then, they are always on the look-out for horses, and, till they are obtained, the employment of the groom is the embellishment of his master, by first dressing his head, and then polishing his boots and shoes."

'And I really think that is enough of that,' said Miss Trumble, putting down the paper.

'I think it is very funny,' voiced Mark.

'Prime,' said the general. 'Is there any more?'

'If there is,' said Lady Beverley, 'I pray you will restrain your language, Miss Trumble.'

'Perhaps later . . .'

'No, do go on,' said Rachel. 'I have seen such gentlemen when we were in London and have never heard one better described.'

Miss Trumble smiled and began to read again. ' "The trifling ceremonies of the morning gone through, you will sally forth in search of adventures, taking that great Mart of every virtue, Bond Street, in your way.

' "Here it will be impossible for you (between the hours of twelve and four) to remain, even for a few minutes, without falling in with various feathers of your wing, so true it is, in the language of Rowe, you herd together, that you cannot fear being long alone. So soon as three of you are met, link your arms so as to engross the whole breadth of the pavement; the fun of driving fine women and old dons into the gutter is exquisite and, of course, constitutes a laugh of the most humane sensibility. Never make these excursions without spurs, it will afford not only the presumptive proof of your really keeping a horse, but the lucky opportunity of hooking a fine girl by the gown, apron, or petticoat; and while she is under the distressing mortification of disentangling herself, you and your companions can add to her dilemma by some delicate innuendo, and, in the moment of extrication, walk off with an exulting exclamation of having *cracked the muslin*. Let it be a fixed rule never to be seen in the Lounge without a stick or cane, this, dangling on a string, may accidentally get between the feet of any female in passing; if she falls, in consequence, that can be no fault of yours, but the effect of her indiscretion.'

'Now, that really is enough, General,' said Miss Trumble. 'I am amusing you and everyone by this description, but at the moment such brutes, however satirized, are beyond the comprehension of little Beth.'

'Yes, I find your ideas of teaching most strange, Miss Trumble.' Having delivered herself of that reproof, Lady Beverley smiled at the general and went on, 'And how go the Santertons?'

'Abed, I should think,' said the general gruffly. Mark and Beth had been summoned by Miss Trumble to sit at a table next to her under the shade of the cedar tree, Beth to write the letters of the alphabet in block letters and then script, and Mark to study his Latin declensions.

'I regret I did not have the chance to dance with you on Saturday night,' Charles said to Rachel. 'But every time I was free to approach you, I found you surrounded by courtiers. I believe your sister, Lady Fitzgerald, is soon to be in residence at Perival.'

Rachel's eyes lit up. 'Oh, I am so looking forward to seeing her again. And her children. They are too young, alas, to be companions for Mark. The boy needs children of his own age.'

'And what would you suggest I do to remedy that?'

Rachel laughed. 'You will begin to think I am always advising you as to what to do with your children when it is none of my affair.'

'I would appreciate such advice.'

'You could give a children's party for Mark. Miss Trumble could furnish you with a list of suitable children in the neighbourhood.'

'It is his birthday in a week's time. Perhaps that is too soon?'

'I am sure Miss Trumble will be able to arrange something.'

The general had risen to his feet and was heading in the direction of where Miss Trumble sat with Mark and Beth.

'Come now, General.' Lady Beverley's voice called him back. 'I am become stiff with sitting here. Let us take a promenade together.'

The general returned to her side, throwing an

anguished look in the direction of his son which went unnoticed by Charles, for Rachel was talking about Mr Cater and Charles asked her, rather sharply, if she really knew anything at all about the man.

'As to that,' said Rachel, 'I know very little other than what he tells us about himself, that he is a sugar planter from Barbados and is here in England on quite a long visit.'

'No doubt to find himself a wife.'

'Perhaps. And yet Mannerling appears to be his goal.'

'In what way?'

'He heard it described to him by an old friend of my father's and in such glowing terms that he decided to travel here and see the place for himself.'

'Strange.'

'How strange?'

'Mostly gentlemen such as Mr Cater come armed with letters of introduction.'

'Perhaps he could not find anyone who knows you.'

'I have a large acquaintance in London and I believe he spent some time there.'

'It could be that he does not move in the same circles as you do yourself, sir.'

'Any sugar planter who appears to be as rich as Mr Cater, to judge from his clothes and carriage, could most certainly move in fashionable circles.'

Some imp prompted Rachel to say, 'Perhaps I will wed Mr Cater and travel to the West Indies.'

'I was not aware that you were so enchanted with him.'

'If you have visited Lady Evans and also remember my sister Lizzie's ill-timed and ill-judged remarks, you will know that I do not command much in the way of a dowry and so must take the best bidder.'

His face darkened and his eyes glittered like green ice. 'Does none of your sex ever marry out of affection?'

She quailed before his gaze and said, 'Yes, my three sisters, the ones who are already wed. Do not look so furiously at me, I pray. I was funning. I know little of Mr Cater and have no ambitions in that direction.'

But he still looked angry as his eyes went past her to where a carriage was turning into the short drive. Rachel swung round in time to see Minerva being helped down from the carriage by her brother. Minerva was wearing a muslin gown which clung to her form like the folds of drapery on a statue. Her hair was in a plait at the back, and falling in small ringlets around her face and shining with *huile antique*. On top of her head was a small round hat embellished on the front with three scarlet feathers which had been moulded to look like burning flames. She carried a parasol of white lace.

George Santerton was wearing a long-tailed blue coat with gold buttons, a high starched cravat, and shirt-points so high that they dug into his cheeks.

His waistcoat was canary yellow and hung with fobs and seals. He had lavender gloves and lavender shoes on his small feet. Rachel wondered if such a tall man could really have such small feet. Large feet were considered a social disgrace, as was a large mouth, and so many men thrust their tortured feet into shoes several sizes too small for them.

The two fashion plates, brother and sister, had probably planned to make an entrance, but once they had arrived and were settled in chairs in the garden, the sheer formality of their attire seemed out of place.

And Rachel became conscious that Minerva's blue gaze was often fixed on her in an assessing, calculating way. It could not be that Minerva regarded her as a rival! But Rachel began to think that was the case and it made her look at Charles Blackwood in a different light. For the first time, she really saw him as an attractive man, not just handsome and wealthy, but a man to be desired.

A flush mounted to her cheeks. Charles looked quickly at her and she dropped her eyes and twisted a handkerchief in her lap.

And Minerva looked at both of them.

# FOUR

*At ev'ry word a reputation dies.*

ALEXANDER POPE

A week later and Miss Trumble had gone to supervise the fairly impromptu party to be held for Mark at Mannerling and Rachel was being taken out on a drive by Mr Cater. Her new sharp awareness of Charles Blackwood had made her completely indifferent to Mr Cater's company and she was annoyed that this drive had been organized by her mother, without consulting her first.

Mr Cater had been to Mannerling and was rhapsodizing about it. For the first time, Rachel found all these descriptions and eulogies of her former home tedious in the extreme. She interrupted a description of the glory of the painted ceilings by asking abruptly, 'Where is your family from, Mr Cater?'

'We are from Suffolk.'

'Indeed. And when did you go to Barbados?'

'Five years ago.'

'With your parents?'

'No, Miss Rachel. My uncle bought me a passage. My parents died when I was a child.'

'And did this uncle own the sugar plantation?'

'No, he did not.'

'So how . . . ?'

'Miss Rachel, I am here in England on this beautiful sunny day with a beautiful companion. For the moment, I wish to forget about the Indies.'

'I am sorry if my curiosity offends you, sir.'

'I miss England,' he said. 'I miss the greenery. I miss the life. I am not comfortable in Barbados.'

'But I was under the impression that . . .'

'I loved the place? It is where I work. I am thinking of selling up.'

'And where would you live? Suffolk?'

'There is nothing for me there. Mannerling appears to have a sad history. You knew the subsequent owners, of course.'

'Yes, there was a Mr Judd. The poor man committed suicide. Then there was the Devers family. Such a scandal. You have surely heard all about it. The son, Harry, was killed falling from a roof in London, trying to escape the law. He was obsessed with Mannerling, as was Mr Judd.'

He shot her a sly look. 'As are the Beverleys, or so I was led to believe.'

'You *have* been listening to the local gossip,' said Rachel with a lightness she did not feel. 'Yes, in our case, the loss of our home hit us very hard. But we are become accustomed to our new life. The Blackwoods are very good owners, very suitable.'

'And you no longer desire the place?'

'I do not desire what is not possible to have.'

'Everything is possible. Even Mannerling.'

Rachel fell silent. Just suppose she wished to marry Charles. How impossible that would be! He, too, knew the tales about the Beverleys' plotting and scheming to get their old home back and would look on any overtures from her with deep suspicion. She wished somehow that she could still regard him as a much older person, not marriageable, but his face rose in her mind's eye, strong and handsome with those odd green eyes, and she was only dimly aware that Mr Cater was still talking of Mannerling.

There were eight children at Mark's party, all having a marvellous time playing games organized by Miss Trumble. The Long Gallery was being used for the party and a table with cakes and jellies and jugs of lemonade had been set up at the end of the gallery.

All went well until Minerva made her entrance, carrying a book. 'I am sure you are in need of some rest,' she said to Miss Trumble. 'I have told the housekeeper to prepare you something in the servants' hall.'

'Thank you,' said Miss Trumble. 'But I am not hungry.'

'Oh, I am sure you are. Please do as you are told.'

Miss Trumble curtsied. The children, left alone with the statuesque Minerva, looked at her wide-eyed.

Minerva pulled forward a chair and sat down and opened her book. 'Gather round me in a circle,' she ordered. She planned to begin reading to them and then ring for a servant to summon Charles so that he could see how well she got on with children.

They sat round her in a circle at her feet. She had found a book of children's stories in the library and she began to read about a little boy who had lost his mother and behaved badly to his father. As she read, she kept flashing meaningful little looks at Mark.

Mark felt his temper rising. It was *his* party and Minerva was not only ruining it but telling that stupid story about some stupid boy who was nasty to his widowed father. Minerva paused and rang the bell and told a footman to fetch Mr Blackwood and then continued to read.

With the perspicacity of the very young, Mark guessed what she was about. His father should not see the pretty picture she made reading to the children. He rose to his feet.

'Where are you going, Mark?' demanded Minerva sharply.

'I am going to get something to eat,' said Mark haughtily.

The other children rose as well.

'Come back here!' ordered Minerva.

'Do not pay her any heed,' commanded Mark. 'She don't live here. Come along.'

Mischievously delighted at the idea of disobeying

authority, the children followed Mark to the table and began to spoon jelly onto plates.

Minerva's temper flared. She marched up to the table and seized Beth, who was the nearest child, in a strong grip. 'You will all return to the reading!'

'Leave her alone!' shouted Mark, turning red in the face.

Beth gave a whimper of fright. Mark seized a plate containing a large green jelly and flung it straight into Minerva's face just as the door opened and his father walked in, followed by Miss Trumble.

'You little whoreson!' screamed Minerva, clawing green jelly from her face.

'What is going on here?' thundered Charles.

Beth, finding herself released, ran to Miss Trumble and buried her face in that lady's skirts.

Minerva began to cry.

Mark stood, white-faced at the enormity of what he had just done.

'I w-was m-merely trying to entertain the ch-children,' sobbed Minerva, 'when Mark threw jelly all over me.'

'Miss Trumble, take the children to another room,' ordered Charles. 'Not you, Mark.' He turned to John, the footman, who had entered and was avidly watching the scene. 'You, escort Miss Santerton to her quarters and fetch her lady's-maid.'

Miss Trumble took both children and book with her. Minerva left with the footman. Mark and his father faced each other.

'Well?' demanded Charles. 'I am waiting.'

Mark hung his head.

'Am I to understand that Miss Terry perhaps had the right of it and that you need to be beaten?'

Mark could not find any words.

The door opened again and Miss Trumble came in, carrying the book from which Minerva had been reading.

Charles swung round angrily. 'I think you should leave this to me and attend to your duties, Miss Trumble.'

'If you will bear with me, sir,' said Miss Trumble, 'I think I can explain Mark's behaviour.'

'That is for the boy to explain. He has a tongue in his head.'

'I think he might find this difficult to put into words. Miss Santerton was reading this story to the children, which I consider most unsuitable and it is probably what upset Mark.'

'Go on.'

'It is a story about a boy who had lost his mother and who subsequently behaved badly towards his father. It is a story I never read to children myself, or in fact anything by this author.'

'But how should this affect Mark? The boy has never behaved badly until now!'

Miss Trumble's presence and kind, understanding eyes had given Mark courage. He ran to her and clutched her hand.

'Did it upset you, Mark?' asked Miss Trumble. 'You have behaved very badly and must apologize to Miss Santerton. But we would like to hear the truth.'

'It was the way she was reading it,' said Mark. 'She kept flashing meaningful little looks at me and Miss Santerton had already said something to me about having a new mother and I knew she wanted my father to think she could fulfil that role, and I am . . . frightened of her.'

'Let me see that story,' ordered Charles.

Miss Trumble handed him the book. He studied it in silence while Mark gripped Miss Trumble's hand even harder.

Charles felt his fury abating. He had never, he realized, stopped to consider what the loss of their mother had meant to Mark. He had been wrapped in his own fury at her infidelity and then his shock at her sudden death. The boy could not be allowed to get away with such behaviour, but he could not bring himself to beat him, or order a beating.

He could not believe that Minerva had been so crude as to hint that she might be the children's new mother. He looked helplessly at Miss Trumble.

'I suggest you leave matters to me, sir,' she said quietly. 'The children are guests and are not to be collected for another hour. I suggest the party should go on. After the party is over, Mark will apologize most humbly to Miss Santerton and I can take things from there.'

'I am so sorry,' whispered Mark.

'Run along, Mark. You will find Beth and your new friends in the drawing-room.'

When the boy had left, Miss Trumble said, 'May I ask, sir, whether Mark loved his mother very much?'

Charles sighed and put the book carefully down on a console table. 'I do not think he saw much of her except for a few glimpses. He was passed to a wet-nurse immediately he was born and then to the nursemaid and then to Miss Terry. But he has grossly insulted a guest in my house and that must not be allowed to go unpunished.'

'No, I will see to that.'

Miss Trumble curtsied and went to join the party and found the drawing-room quiet and silent. The little group of scared children sat around Mark.

She clapped her hands briskly. 'This will not do. Did I tell you about the treasure hunt?'

'No!' they all chorused.

'I will hand you all slips of paper with your first clue. The treasure is hidden somewhere in the house. I suggest you hunt in pairs. Mark, you go with your little sister.' Miss Trumble paired off the rest. Soon the children were off hunting through the great house.

'Where do you think the treasure is?' Beth asked Mark.

'I really don't care,' he said. 'All I can think of is that I have got to apologize to Miss Santerton. I am in deep disgrace.'

Beth suddenly giggled. 'She did look such a guy with green jelly all over her.'

Mark hugged her. 'It would be almost worth it if Father were not so upset.'

'Will he marry her? Will she be our new mother? I should not like that.'

'It is something we may have to face. Drat! If only I could get this horrible apology over and done with.'

'We could go now,' suggested Beth eagerly.

'S'pose so.'

Hand in hand, they walked to the west wing and stopped outside Minerva's door.

Mark reached for the door handle and then stopped.

'What is it?' hissed Beth.

'There is someone in there with her. Shh!'

Mark leaned his ear against the door panels.

'Someone's coming out,' he said. He seized Beth's hand. There was a window in the passage opposite the door. He pulled Beth into the embrasure and drew the curtains closed.

He heard the door of Minerva's room open and her brother George's voice sounded clearly, ' 'Pon rep, sis, you are become over-exercised about a pair of spoilt brats. Marry Blackwood, send the boy packing to school, give the girl a strict governess, and then you need never have anything to do with them again.'

'You forget' – Minerva's voice – 'he seems too interested in them to turn a blind eye to their affairs.'

'You know how to make men love you, do you not? Get him in your wiles and the man will forget he even has children.'

'I would like to get rid of that Trumble creature. I have an enemy there.'

'Pooh, what can a faded old spinster like that do?'

'More than you think. Have you noticed the way the general eyes her? If I do not play my cards right, then that old governess will be mistress at Mannerling and I will not!'

'What are you going to do? Kill her?' George gave a great braying laugh.

'Oh, go away,' snapped his sister, 'and leave me to prepare for the great apology scene which is no doubt soon to take place.'

The children waited, hearing George's footsteps die away along the long corridor and then all was silent.

They finally crept out. 'Not now,' whispered Mark. 'I could not face her now.'

'I heard from the housekeeper at Mannerling that the place is haunted,' Mr Cater was saying to Rachel.

'It is not haunted. Someone tried to frighten the little boy by dressing up as the ghost of the late Mr Judd.'

'Are you sure it was not a ghost?'

'Our servant, Barry, managed to strike the ghost on the head. His cudgel contacted a human head and not a ghostly one.'

'You are unromantic, Miss Rachel. I, for one, am prepared to believe that Mannerling is haunted.'

Rachel gave a laugh. 'In all the time I lived there, I never saw even one ghost. There is nothing at Mannerling to frighten anyone.'

* * *

The party finished with Gerrard, a local farmer's boy, finding the treasure, which turned out to be a toy sword and a box of paints. The other children all received consolation prizes and went off happily in various gigs and carriages.

Mark was taken by his father to Minerva's apartment in the west wing, where he apologized most humbly. To his surprise, and then his dismay, instead of railing at him, Minerva drew him to her and hugged him and said, 'I should have known such a story would upset a poor motherless child like you. There. We have both apologized and now we can be friends.'

She smiled down at him and Mark felt himself trapped in that intense blue gaze. His father was looking at Minerva with a softened look on his normally harsh face.

Mark repeated again in a dull, flat little voice that he was very, very sorry and then turned to his father and asked if he could leave. 'Off with you,' said his father, 'and consider yourself a lucky young man. Few ladies would have accepted an apology for such rank behaviour with such grace and charity as Miss Santerton.'

When the Santertons and the Blackwoods had retired to their rooms to dress for dinner, Miss Trumble made her way through the suddenly quiet house to go down to the hall and wait for the carriage to be brought round to take her home.

She paused at the top of the staircase, listening to the quiet of the house. And then she realized it was not really quiet. There had always been many clocks at Mannerling and the general, who collected them, had added a great deal more.

She became aware of the restless ticking and tacking, which seemed to be getting louder as if innumerable little voices were whispering away the time. 'Hurry, hurry, hurry,' went the voices. 'You are old, old, old, and time is running out for you.'

She walked stiffly down the stairs, hearing all those time voices chattering away, feeling a sort of brooding menace emanating from the walls. She gave herself a mental shake. Mannerling was a large house, nothing more. It was unlike her to let her fancies get the better of her.

And then, as she reached the hall, the grandfather clock against the far wall boomed out five hours and from all over the house came the clamour of chimes, until all the tinkling and booming and chiming seemed to merge together in one great mocking, triumphant sound.

Miss Trumble wrenched open the great front door and went out into the sunlight and took a deep breath. The carriage swept up to the front of the house and a footman ran out and let down the steps. Miss Trumble climbed in, feeling shaken.

She felt suddenly that Mannerling was no place for those little children. Perhaps the menace she had felt came from Minerva's presence.

Her fancies apart, someone had tried to frighten Mark. What kind of person would play such a trick on a child?

Perhaps when the eldest sister, Isabella, arrived, she could arrange for the children to spend much of their time between Brookfield House and Perival, away from the menace of Mannerling.

Sanity, like a breath of fresh air, blew into Miss Trumble's worried life with the arrival of Isabella, Lady Fitzpatrick, her husband, and his aunt, Mrs Kennedy.

At first Miss Trumble thought Isabella might be a trifle haughty, but then Isabella had taken her aside and asked anxiously, 'And how goes Barry?'

'Do you mean our odd man? Very well, and a comfort to us all.'

'He was a very great comfort to me with his kindness and good sense.'

'Would you like to see him? We could take a turn in the garden.'

'I would like that above all things.'

When they were outside, Miss Trumble received another surprise, for the tall and elegant Isabella linked her arm in that of the governess in a companionable way and said, 'Barry writes to me from time to time. I hear great things of you.'

Miss Trumble actually found herself blushing for the first time in years. 'That is very gratifying.'

Barry walked across the back lawn to greet them, his cap in his hand, a broad smile on his face.

'Well, well, well, my lady, you do be a sight for sore eyes.'

'Does all go well, Barry?'

'Very well, my lady. Are the children with you?'

'They are with their nurse, but you shall visit us and see them for yourself. I do not want to deprive the excellent Miss Trumble or my sisters of your help, Barry, but I do wish you would return with us to Ireland.'

'Maybe soon, Miss Isabella, I mean, my lady.'

'You may call me Miss Isabella if you wish.'

If only my three girls could turn out like this eldest sister, thought Miss Trumble. If only they, too, could escape Mannerling.

'So I believe there is a new owner at Mannerling,' said Isabella, 'but fortunately of an age too old to tempt my sisters.'

'As to that,' said Barry cautiously, 'he do be a remarkably handsome man and don't look a bit his age.'

'Aha!' Isabella looked quizzically at Miss Trumble. 'And when I asked Rachel why she had not gone to London for a Season, she hummed and hawed and then said it was because of my impending visit.'

'Perhaps that was indeed the case,' said Miss Trumble evasively.

'And Mama seems in alt over the father, General Blackwood. Never say she has hopes in that direction.'

'That is not for me to say,' said Miss Trumble primly. 'But the carriage from Mannerling will be here shortly to collect the children and I must not be found neglecting my duties in case Mr Blackwood comes himself. Mark has extra lessons as a punishment for an impertinence.'

She curtsied and left.

'Miss Trumble is as you described her to be,' said Isabella to Barry. 'But I was not prepared to find such a grand lady. Her style and clothes are modish. Where did she come from?'

'Ah, that's a mystery,' said Barry. 'I believe she gave Lady Beverley references at last.'

'Perhaps she is of good family and fallen on hard times.'

'Now that's the puzzle, my lady, for to tell the truth, Lady Beverley often does not pay her and yet she always seems to be in funds.'

'Strange. I shall leave you now, Barry, and we will talk again. I hear the carriage arriving for the children and I am anxious to see this new owner should he be there.'

When Isabella rounded the corner of the house, she stopped short. A tall man was alighting from a curricle. He looked at her curiously and then bowed and smiled. Why, he is almost as handsome as my husband, marvelled Isabella, who never thought any man in the world could match Lord Fitzpatrick.

'Lady Fitzpatrick,' he said with a bow.

'You must be Mr Blackwood.' Isabella curtsied. 'You are come for your children. But you must meet my husband and Mrs Kennedy before you leave.'

They walked into the house together. The company was gathered in the little-used drawing-room.

Charles was introduced all round.

Isabella covertly watched Rachel. It was as if every fibre of her younger sister's body was aware of this Mr Blackwood. And yet he treated her with the same easy manner as he treated Lizzie and Belinda.

Despite his age, thought Isabella, he should be very aware of such a beautiful girl as Rachel. No man could look at her and remain indifferent.

And then the maid, Betty, came in and announced, 'Miss Santerton.'

Isabella's eyes swung to the doorway and she blinked at the vision that stood there. She did not notice the flash of irritation in Charles's eyes. All Isabella could think was, poor Rachel. This is too much competition.

Minerva was wearing a wide straw hat decorated with a whole garden of flowers. Her muslin gown was so fine it was nearly transparent and floated around her excellent body as she moved. The under-dress was very fitting and was of pale-pink silk, which gave the impression that she had nothing on underneath. Her eyes caressed Charles in an intimate way.

She greeted Isabella and her husband effusively but looked down on the dumpy figure of Mrs Kennedy and offered her two fingers to shake. Mrs Kennedy flashed the beauty a look of contempt and sat down, ignoring those two fingers.

Charles had taken a liking to the broad-spoken, warm-hearted little Irishwoman who was Mrs Kennedy and felt suddenly ashamed of Minerva. Here were the despised Beverleys, supposed to be grasping and ambitious, and yet they seemed kind and gentle to him. He had warmed towards Minerva since – what he considered – her gracious acceptance of Mark's apology, but now he began to wish she and her brother would leave. George was a tiresome bore who drank too much at dinner and then said the same thing over and over again.

Minerva was clever enough to realize her social gaffe had annoyed Charles and so she sat down next to Mrs Kennedy and asked, 'Did you have an arduous journey?'

'Sure, me dears,' said Mrs Kennedy, getting to her feet and waddling towards the door. 'I think we had best be getting off. Do come and see us as soon as possible.'

'Tomorrow,' cried Lizzie.

'Faith, tomorrow, tonight, any time you like, my chuck.'

Minerva smiled. 'My brother and I are resident at Mannerling, Mrs Kennedy. We would be pleased to call on you.'

Before Isabella could reply, Mrs Kennedy said roundly, 'That will not be convenient. We are all still mighty fatigued after our journey and wish to see only the family. Good day to you.'

'Dreadful woman!' complained Minerva to Charles on the road back to Mannerling.

'Mrs Kennedy? I found her excellent. She took you in dislike, as any lady of her standing would, at being offered only two fingers to shake. You brought that snub on yourself.'

'But how was I to know? Such a fat little creature and that quiz of a bonnet! I thought she was the maid.'

'Fitzpatrick said very clearly that she was his aunt.'

They continued the journey in silence, a silence which enlivened Mark's spirits. He could feel the threat of his father's ever marrying Minerva receding.

At one o'clock the following morning, Miss Trumble was roused by one of the maids who gasped out, 'You are to dress and go to Mannerling. A carriage is arrived.'

She handed Miss Trumble a letter. Miss Trumble got out of bed and took the candle from the maid and read it. It was from Charles Blackwood. The 'haunting' of Mannerling had started again and the children were frightened out of their wits.

'I shall help you dress, miss,' said the maid, Betty.

'No, rouse Miss Rachel and help her dress instead. Tell her I wish her to come with me.'

It was a windy night, with a small moon running through the ragged clouds overhead as the great bulk of Mannerling reared up. 'It must have been really bad for Mr Blackwood to summon you in the middle of the night,' said Rachel.

'Yes, I believe someone is out to frighten those

children out of their wits,' said the governess, 'and yet . . .'

'What were you about to say?'

'Nothing.' Miss Trumble had been about to say that at times she thought Mannerling really was haunted by some presence but she did not want to frighten Rachel.

Charles Blackwood had been looking out for their arrival and met them in the hall and led the way up the stairs.

'I am grateful to you for coming. I will take you to the children directly. Beth is in Mark's room.' He showed no surprise at Rachel's presence.

'What happened?' asked Miss Trumble.

'Sounds and moans and clanking of chains. One footman screeching he had seen a spectral figure in the Long Gallery. Ghostly voices sounding all over the house.'

'Was that footman John?'

'No, Henry, the other second footman.'

The children were lying huddled together in Mark's bed.

'I shall go back through the house with Mr Blackwood,' said Miss Trumble firmly. 'Rachel and I have brought our nightclothes. Rachel, I suggest, as Mark's bed is large enough, that you get into bed with the children and read them a story until they fall asleep.'

As if seeing her for the first time, Charles said, 'This is most kind of you, Miss Rachel. I did not mean . . .'

'I do not mind,' said Rachel quietly.

113

When Charles and Miss Trumble had left, Rachel said to the scared children, 'Well, this is quite an adventure, is it not?'

'We heard the ghosts,' whispered Mark, 'shrieking and wailing.'

'What you heard,' said Rachel firmly, 'was some monster playing a trick on you. When Barry hit that man on the head, the one who was pretending to be a ghost, his cudgel struck a real head. I am going into the powder-closet to change and then I will read to you. You may have all the candles in the room burning tonight.'

She changed quickly into a night-gown, wrapper, and night-cap, and then climbed into bed between the two children, after having picked a book from the shelves along the wall. She selected a mild fairy story after a search, wondering why children's stories were so bloodthirsty.

They snuggled up to her as she began to read, and after only a few pages she realized they had both fallen asleep.

She lay for some time thinking about Charles Blackwood, thinking how strong and handsome he had looked in his silk dressing-gown and with his hair tousled. She wondered how those green eyes would look were they to shine with love. And then she drifted off to sleep as well, a smile on her lips and one arm around each child.

After Rachel had been asleep for an hour, the door opened quietly and Charles and Miss Trumble looked in.

Rachel's fair hair under her lacy night-cap was spread out on the pillow. The children were cuddled up to her on either side.

Charles gently closed the door again. 'I am most grateful to Miss Rachel,' he said to Miss Trumble.

'Rachel genuinely likes your children,' said Miss Trumble. 'They will feel safe with her and it is very important for little children to feel safe and secure.'

'Yes,' he said slowly, thinking of the beautiful Rachel, her face soft and vulnerable in the candlelight. 'Yes, I can see that.'

'So we have interviewed the servants and they are all badly frightened,' said Miss Trumble, 'and it seems we cannot convince them someone is fooling them.' They walked to the drawing-room, where a fire was burning brightly. 'What do Miss Santerton and her brother think of the hauntings? And your father?'

'They appear to have slept through the whole commotion and I saw no reason to rouse them.'

Miss Trumble sat down wearily. 'You must now go to bed,' he said gently. 'I am most grateful to you. I will gladly remunerate you for your efforts on my behalf.'

The governess looked at him haughtily. 'There are some things,' she said frostily, 'that you do not pay for or offer to pay for, sir.'

'My apologies,' he said, half-amused, half-exasperated by this elderly governess who could so easily put him in his place.

After a silence he said, 'If we cannot find the culprit or culprits, then what are we to do?'

'I think the best thing would be to arm some of the staff, the ones you feel you can trust, a few of the grooms as well, and post them throughout the house. Give them instructions to shoot any 'ghost' on sight and tell this to the rest of your servants. Is there anyone from your past who would wish to harm you or the children, Mr Blackwood?'

'Not that I know of.'

'Strange. And yet there is something about Mannerling that appears to create a madness in certain people.'

'Like the Beverleys?'

'They are no longer concerned with the place,' said Miss Trumble firmly. 'I was thinking of Judd and Harry Devers. Is there anyone you know who might want to drive you out of here and get Mannerling for themselves?'

'No one at all.'

'What of the Santertons? What do you know of them?'

'Not very much. I knew them in the past and they claimed such friendship with me that I was inclined to believe it. No man is immune to hearing a very beautiful woman claim friendship. But they were not responsible for the hauntings, for I looked in on both brother and sister and they were heavily asleep. Miss Santerton takes laudanum, I believe, and George had three bottles of wine at dinner.'

116

'In any case, do tell the staff that any apparition will be shot.'

'I will do that tomorrow, or today, rather. Do go to bed, Miss Trumble. You must be exhausted. I hope your employer will not be too angry with me for having taken you away in the middle of the night.'

'Lady Beverley will be pleased that I am able to be of help,' said Miss Trumble, privately thinking that Lady Beverley would be delighted and would probably call at Mannerling as soon as she could.

Minerva was getting dressed by her maid the following morning when she heard the sound of laughter from below her window. She went and opened the window and leaned out. Rachel was running across the lawn with the children. At a little distance behind them, Charles Blackwood was following them. Her face darkened and she slammed the window shut and swung round to face her lady's-maid. 'What is that Beverley creature doing at Mannerling?'

'It was the hauntings, miss.'

'What are you babbling about?'

'There were ghosts haunting the place during the night and frightening the children. Mr Blackwood sent for that governess, Miss Trumble, to quieten the children, and she brought Miss Rachel Beverley with her.'

'So that's her game,' muttered Minerva. 'We'll see about that. Don't just stand there. Hurry and fix my hair and then fetch my brother here directly.'

When George Santerton trailed in, his sister surveyed him furiously. He was in his undress, a gold silk banyan and a gold silk turban and Turkish slippers with turned-up toes. His eyes were bloodshot and he looked groggily about him.

'What's to do?'

She told him succinctly of the happenings of the night, which had resulted in that 'scheming' governess's moving her chess-piece into play, namely Rachel Beverley.

George stifled a yawn. 'That old governess don't need to scheme for her charges, if you ask me. The general's potty about her. My guess is the old boy will propose marriage.'

'A man of his standing cannot marry a governess. I thought he might propose but I realized that such an alliance would be out of the question. Don't be silly.'

'When a man gets to his age, he's apt to please himself and damn society, if you ask me. And if this place is really haunted, I'm off. Spirits frighten me.'

'Really, brother, dear? From the amount of white brandy you are capable of pouring down your useless throat, I would have thought *spirits* were the last thing to frighten you.'

'Ha ha, very funny. But don't you think it deuced odd, all these ghosts?'

'No, I don't. I think when people are dead, they stay dead.'

'Comforting thought in your case, sis.'

They eyed each other for a moment and then Minerva shrugged. 'You don't believe all that rubbish that I killed Santerton?'

'Never said I did.'

'So, to return to the main point, what do I do about Rachel Beverley?'

He sat down and buried his head in his hands, knocking his turban off onto the floor.

'Oh, why am I asking you?' Minerva paced angrily up and down. 'You're a fool.'

'So everyone keeps telling me,' said George, raising his head. 'But I tell you what, I heard gossip about those Beverleys at that country dance. Damned ambitious lot and not a feather to fly with. I think mayhap Charles needs a gentle reminder that any Beverley interested in him or his children or both is only scheming to get Mannerling back. Your trouble, sis, is that you don't like children. Come to think of it, you don't like anybody.'

'That is not true. I dote on Charles.'

'My head aches. Go off and dote on your own.' George rose abruptly and left the room.

Minerva heard the sound of carriage wheels on the drive. She looked out again.

This is all I need, she thought, as she saw the squat bulk of Mrs Kennedy descending from the carriage.

Mrs Kennedy had been told of the hauntings by the servants at Perival, who had heard the news from a maid who was being courted by one of the Mannerling grooms. She was ushered into the drawing-room by Henry, the footman, who said he would let Mr Blackwood know she had arrived.

'Stay,' commanded Mrs Kennedy as the footman was about to bow his way out. 'What's this about ghosts?'

The footman turned pale. 'I saw one with my own eyes, madam, at the end of the Long Gallery, a great black figure.'

'See the face?'

'No, madam, I screamed and ran away, I was so frit. And then the voices came, all over the house, wailing and shrieking.'

'Where were these voices coming from?'

'In the air, madam. From nowheres in particular.'

'Thank you. You may go.'

When the footman had left, Mrs Kennedy sat thinking furiously. She remembered when she had been a young girl in Ireland, frightening a house party out of their wits with some of her friends. They had climbed up to the roof and had wailed and shrieked down the chimneys. She wondered if anyone had been up on the roof.

Not used to sitting still for very long, she began to fidget and then she rose to her feet and went out and up the stairs to the top of the house until she found a narrow little staircase that led up to a door which gave out onto the leads.

Moving nimbly on her feet, surprisingly so in such a heavily built woman, she began to search, clambering around the forest of chimneys on the roof of Mannerling. And then something bright at the edge of the roof lying in a bay formed by a little curved balustrade caught her attention. She walked into the bay and picked it up. It was a livery button, a silver button with the Blackwood crest of an oak tree on it. Her eyes gleamed as brightly as the button. Here was proof. Find the servant with a missing button and then ask the fellow what he had been doing on the roof where no one but a builder or repairman had reason to be. And then an arm went around her neck and a voice grated in her ear, 'Give that to me.'

She went very still. 'No,' she said. Her plump hand closed even more firmly around the button. The arm tightened around her neck. She could feel her heart thumping. She kicked her assailant in the shins. Her one main thought was to get herself away from the edge of the balustrade.

Despite her age, she was strong and she was powerful and she was used to danger, having followed her late husband on many army campaigns. She fought and struggled until she had swung round, facing into the house, and her attacker now had his back to the balustrade. One of her hands seized a hat-pin from her bonnet and she drove it into that arm. There was a yell of pain, she felt herself released, and she drove back both elbows with all her might into the figure behind her.

There was a tremendous scream, a scream that descended, a scream abruptly cut off.

Mrs Kennedy sat down suddenly and began to cry.

# FIVE

*I seem to move among a world of ghosts,*
*And feel myself the shadow of a dream.*

ALFRED, LORD TENNYSON

Minerva went out of the front door of Mannerling, her eyes narrowing as she saw Rachel, Charles, and the children approaching her across the lawns, looking like a family party.

She pinned a smile on her face. She would need to appear all that was amiable, she would need to pretend to like Rachel, and then she would try to pour some poison into Charles's ears about the plots of the Beverleys. Minerva was wearing a white lace morning gown and another wide-brimmed bonnet. Her white kid gloves were wrinkled in the current fashion and elbow-length. Her white kid shoes peeped out from under her gown. Her hat was of white straw and embellished with white silk flowers. Minerva considered that she now looked the very picture of a virgin.

She floated towards Charles, her hands outstretched in welcome.

And then Charles shouted, 'Look out!' He ran

123

towards her and pulled her roughly to one side as a long scream descended from the heavens towards her.

There was a sickening thump behind her. Rachel shouted to the children, 'Don't look,' and pressed their faces against her skirts.

Over their heads, she saw Charles stoop over the crumpled body which had fallen from the roof.

'Get the children inside,' shouted Charles. 'Now!'

Rachel hurried off with Mark and Beth.

'Who is it?' asked Minerva. 'And how did he come to fall?'

In all his fright and distress, part of his mind still registered how calmly Minerva appeared to be reacting to the whole thing.

'It is one of my footmen, John.'

'Oh, a *footman*!' said Minerva, and turned away as Miss Trumble came out of the house.

'It is only a footman,' said Minerva, 'fallen from the roof.'

Servants came running out of the house and over from the stables.

'Take the body inside,' ordered Charles. 'Miss Trumble, see to Rachel and the children.'

'I came to tell you Mrs Kennedy called, but I cannot find her.'

He gave an exclamation and strode ahead of the governess into the house.

A weak voice from the landing sounded down to them, Mrs Kennedy's voice.

'I killed him,' she said. 'I couldn't help it.'

* * *

They were finally all gathered in the drawing-room to hear Mrs Kennedy's amazing story. The general slowed up the telling of it by demanding to hear all about the haunting first and asking why no one had thought to rouse him.

'The question now is,' said Miss Trumble quietly, 'who employed him to do such a thing? And why did the house-keeper and that boy lie about him being present with the other servants when we were looking for the ghost of Judd?'

They were then interrupted by the arrival of Lady Beverley, and all the explanations had to be gone through again.

'Well, really,' bridled Lady Beverley, glaring at Miss Trumble, 'I should have been roused. I am the one most qualified to deal with nervous children.'

'You went to bed complaining of illness,' said Miss Trumble, 'and demanded not to be roused before noon, no matter what happened.'

'Miss Trumble and your daughter were a tower of strength,' put in Charles, but all that did was make Lady Beverley angrier than ever.

Charles rang the bell and asked for the house-keeper and the boy, Freddy, to be sent in.

Mrs Jones came in after quite a long wait, dabbing at her eyes. 'My apologies, sir,' she said in her hoarse voice. 'I am so overset by the death of poor John.'

Barry entered the room and bowed low. 'I have some news,' he said to Charles.

'Go on.'

'I took the liberty of examining the dead fellow's head. There was a bump on it which I do not think was caused by the fall, for he fell on his left side and the blow I struck him – for I now know it must have been John – was on the right. The bump must have come up after you examined him, sir. Also in his quarters, I found this.' Barry held up a sandy wig.

Charles turned again to Mrs Jones. 'So what have you to say for yourself? You said he was standing beside you in the hall.'

'It was afterwards that John talked to me about me standing next to him and reminded me of what he had said.'

'But you must have remembered yourself whether he was there or not!'

'I was so frightened with all the fuss, and sleepy too, sir. And I never thought John, of all people, would do such a thing. He had nothing against you, sir, only the Beverleys.'

'That's quite enough,' snapped Charles. 'You, boy, what have you to say for yourself?'

Freddy twisted his apron and looked at him dumbly.

'Speak,' commanded the general.

'It were her,' blurted out the boy, jerking a thumb at the housekeeper. 'Her told me I was to say I'd seen 'im.'

'Were you in this plot with John?' demanded Charles wrathfully.

'Oh, no, no, no,' wailed the housekeeper.

Miss Trumble's level voice sounded in the room. 'I think the poor woman was drunk and could not remember much of what happened.'

'I swear I only had a little gin and hot to soothe my nerves, sir,' screeched the housekeeper. 'It was John who told me all about standing next to me. I swear on my mother's grave. He told me Freddy was there as well, so I told the boy what to say, him being not right in the head.'

She began to cry noisily and Charles looked at her with a sort of angry pity. 'Go away and we will talk later,' he said.

When the housekeeper had made a noisy and lachrymose exit, followed by the boy, the company looked at one another.

'I think we should ask in Hedgefield whether John was seen talking to anyone,' said Charles. 'I cannot believe a servant would go to such lengths on his own behalf.' He turned to Barry. 'Perhaps you could ask around.'

Barry touched his forehead and left the room.

'This should put an end to the hauntings now that the wretched creature is dead,' said Minerva, stifling a yawn.

'Only if the malice was all his own,' retorted Miss Trumble.

'I think I will take the children outside again, if I may,' said Rachel.

'Such a good idea.' Minerva rose and smoothed down her skirts.

Charles, sharply anxious for the welfare of his

children, who were looking frightened, suddenly could not bear them to be subjected to Minerva's brand of 'motherly' concern, and said, 'Do go along with Mark and Beth, Miss Rachel. Miss Santerton and I have much to discuss.'

Minerva sat down again, a little triumphant smile on her lips.

'I will come with you, Rachel.' Miss Trumble headed for the door.

'Could do with some fresh air myself,' said the general.

Lady Beverley stood up. 'Your arm, General. We will *all* go.'

'Sit down, Father, and Miss Trumble. We shall all discuss this affair,' said Charles and then added innocently, 'but go along with your daughter by all means, Lady Beverley.'

'On second thoughts,' said Lady Beverley, 'I feel perhaps my place is here.' She sat down again.

'Well, I'm bored with the whole thing,' drawled George Santerton. 'Such a lot of fuss over a mere footman.'

'And, sure, I am shaken to the core of my poor old body,' complained Mrs Kennedy. 'I for one am going home.'

'You are a brave lady,' said the general. 'What an experience! I will escort you out to your carriage.'

Miss Trumble, half-amused, half-exasperated, saw the sudden alarm and consternation on Lady Beverley's face as the general tenderly escorted Mrs Kennedy to the door.

Rachel had already gone. Minerva kept turning that intense blue gaze of hers on Charles. Miss Trumble wondered whether Minerva's ambition to be mistress of Mannerling, for such an ambition was very obvious, would ever be fulfilled. But then, men were so silly when it came to pretty women.

Rachel walked with Mark and Beth towards the folly. She wondered what to say to them. They admittedly lived in violent times and there was death all about them on every gibbet they passed. But the sight of a body plummeting from the roof of Mannerling, to die at their feet, was enough to shake an adult, let alone two vulnerable children. Rachel was beginning to feel rather sick and shaken herself. It was not only the death of John but that he had been prompted by such evil malice. Even if someone had been paying him, it had been an evil thing to do to carry out such orders.

'We will take the boat out on the lake,' she said, 'and we will talk a little bit about what has happened.'

The children, who normally would have treated such an offer with noisy joy, followed her silently down the grassy slope to the jetty. They sat side by side, facing her as she slotted the oars into the rowlocks and began to pull steadily away from the jetty.

'You are both very brave children,' began Rachel. 'After we have spent some time on the water, we will return and have something to eat and then I think you should both go to bed. I am very shaken and tired myself.'

Beth began to cry and Mark put an arm round her. Tears welled up in his own eyes. Rachel shipped the oars, took out a handkerchief, and began to cry herself.

At last, she firmly dried her eyes and said with a shaky laugh, 'Now I feel better. But think on it, Mark, I was going to play at pirates, but we don't look very ferocious, any of us.'

With children's lightning changes of mood, both stopped crying. 'Real pirates?' asked Beth cautiously.

'Yes. I tell you what. If you want to be real pirates, you must learn to row. I know the oars are rather big, but you could take an oar each.'

She rowed back to the jetty. She changed places with the children. 'Now, you are the wicked Turkish pirates and I am your hostage.'

'You don't look like a hostage,' pointed out Mark. 'You should be bound and gagged.'

'I saw some string under a bench in the folly,' said Rachel.

She tied up the boat again. Soon she was bound with string and gagged with her scarf. The children gingerly rowed away from the jetty. At first they went round in circles because Mark was pulling more strongly than Beth, but they finally managed some sort of co-ordination.

Rachel was soon beginning to tire of playing the part of hostage, straining at her bonds and making gurgling noises from behind her scarf, but the children were so enraptured with this new skill of rowing that she did not have the heart to call an end to their play – which she very well could, for the scarf over her mouth was quite loosely tied.

And so that was how Charles Blackwood saw them as he paused in the folly and looked down on the lake. His children were uttering quite dreadful oaths and threats to the bound and gagged Rachel.

He strode out of the folly and down to the lake.

He hailed Mark, crying, 'You'd best come ashore. The sky is darkening and I think it is going to rain.'

At first they spun in circles, both children being anxious to show off their prowess to their father, but at last they managed to reach the jetty, just as Charles was joined by Miss Trumble.

'We were playing pirates,' said Mark, his voice squeaky with excitement, 'and Rachel is our hostage.'

Rachel said plaintively from behind her scarf, 'Would someone please untie me?'

Charles knelt down on the jetty and untied the scarf and then her hands, and Rachel untied her ankles.

Miss Trumble helped Mark and Beth out of the boat and said briskly, 'Come along. You will eat and go to bed, and if you are very good, I will read a story to you.'

They went off with her, still chattering excitedly. Charles helped Rachel out.

'You are very good, Miss Rachel,' he said, beginning to walk with her.

'I like your children,' said Rachel. 'We have all had a bad fright.'

A fat drop of rain struck the back of Charles's hand. He looked at the sky and said, 'Let us shelter in the folly for a little. I think it will only prove to be a shower.'

As they reached the folly, the heavens opened. They stood together, looking out, surrounded on all sides by a silvery curtain of rain. 'The children will be soaked,' said Rachel.

Charles laughed. 'Did you not notice the estimable Miss Trumble was carrying an umbrella?' Then he studied her thoughtfully.

'I do not want to distress you, Miss Rachel,' said Charles, 'but you know the recent history of Mannerling. The house appears to take hold of people in a strange way. Can you think of anyone who would go to such lengths to scare me away, or do you think that footman was deranged?'

Rachel felt guilty. For who could know better about an obsession to gain Mannerling than the Beverleys?

'It is difficult for me to speculate on the subject,' she said in a low voice. 'You must have heard the gossip about us. Mr Judd was obsessed with the place, as was Harry Devers. But both are dead and I know of no others.'

He gave her a slanting look from those green eyes. 'And the Beverleys are no longer obsessed?'

'No,' she said in a half-whisper.

'I am sorry to pain you, but it is all too evident that Lady Beverley is setting her cap at my father.'

Rachel felt immeasurably tired. She was intensely aware of his masculinity, of his attraction. But also that she did not stand a chance with such a man because of such a mother and such a reputation.

'Mama has not been quite . . . right . . . since the loss of Mannerling and is apt to be a trifle silly on the subject,' she said stiffly. 'But Mama would never do anything to hurt your children, nor would I or my sisters.'

He gave a sigh. 'It is all very strange. Mr Cater seemed much taken with the house. What do you know of him?'

'Only what he has told me, that he is a sugar-plantation owner, here in England on a visit. Yes, he wishes to settle here. But just suppose he craved to get possession of Mannerling. How would he know that John out of all the other servants would prove such an easy tool?'

'Who told him of Mannerling?'

'A Lord Hexhamworth, an old friend of my father.'

'Mr Cater resides at the Green Man in Hedgefield, I believe. How long does he plan to remain there?'

'I do not know. I will ask him, if you wish. He is a frequent caller.'

'Oho, and why is that?'

Rachel blushed.

'He is a good catch,' said Charles, looking at her with affectionate amusement.

There had still been a little spark of hope in

Rachel's heart until that last comment. Now there was no hope at all.

'It has stopped raining,' she said in a stifled voice.

'So it has, and look, over there, a rainbow.'

They walked back to the house together. He chatted easily of this and that, looking all the while curiously at her sad, averted face.

'I am sorry if I distressed you by seeming to accuse your family of being behind these hauntings. You must forgive me and realize I have been overset at what I see as a threat to my children. Come now, Miss Rachel, and smile at me. What would I have done without you to bring their plight to my attention?'

He stopped and looked down at her. She gave him a watery smile and then began to cry.

He took out his handkerchief and, tilting up her face, gently dried her tears. 'I am the veriest brute to distress you so. We both need some tea and something to eat.'

He linked his arm in hers and Rachel walked beside him, feeling the strength of that arm, her body a tumult of mixed emotions.

Minerva stood at the window with her brother beside her and watched their approach.

'Pretty picture,' sneered George.

'What am I to do about that wretched girl?' demanded Minerva.

'Why do you always ask me what you are to do? You're always accusing me of being stupid.'

'When you are not stupid in drink and all about

in your upper chambers, brother dear, you have some ideas.'

'I did hear in Hedgefield that the Cater fellow was courting Rachel.'

Minerva brightened. 'Perhaps that might be the answer.'

'Not if little Miss Rachel thinks she can get Charles and Mannerling as well.'

'A bribe to Cater might answer.'

George shrugged. 'You can try, but the fellow's supposed to be as rich as Croesus.'

'It has been my experience that no matter how much money people have, they are always ready to accept more.'

'You can try. I have had too much excitement for today. Do you join the others to dine?'

'And see Rachel making sheep's eyes at Charles and the mother flirting grotesquely with the general? Not I. I think I will search out this Mr Cater. Order the carriage for me.'

'Order it yourself,' complained her brother. 'The house is full of servants. They didn't all fall off the roof.'

Mr Cater returned to the Green Man after a brisk ride across the local countryside to learn that a lady was waiting for him.

Minerva noticed the way his face fell when he saw her and experienced a spasm of irritation.

'I beg your pardon, ma'am,' he said. 'I was somehow expecting to see Miss Rachel Beverley.'

135

Was every man besotted with that wretched girl? Minerva gave him a thin smile. 'We met briefly, if you remember, Mr Cater. At Mannerling.'

'Yes, indeed, Miss Santerton. And what is the reason for this very highly flattering call?'

'I thought we should have a comfortable coze about our ambitions.'

'I am a happy man. I do not think I have any ambitions at the moment.'

'Perhaps I am mistaken. Rumour has it you are courting Rachel Beverley.'

'If that be the case . . .' he said gently, sitting down opposite her in the coffee-room. He signalled to the waiter and then ordered a glass of shrub. When the waiter had departed, he went on. 'If that be the case, then it is not something I would discuss freely. It would be . . . er . . . my private business.'

A flash of irritation, quickly masked, crossed Minerva's face. This was all going to be much more difficult than she had imagined. 'I see I will have to put all my cards on the table.' She gave a little shrug. 'Why not? I understand you to be interested in gaining the hand of Rachel Beverley and the ownership of Mannerling.'

The waiter put a glass of shrub at Mr Cater's elbow. Mr Cater took a meditative sip.

'I can dream,' he said.

'But do you not see, it could be a reality?' Minerva leaned forward. 'And I am the person to help you.'

136

'Why, Miss Santerton? You barely know me.'

'I am interested in securing Mr Charles Blackwood for myself – in marriage.'

'And what is that to do with me?'

'Mr Blackwood is becoming uncommonly interested in Rachel Beverley and he is the owner of Mannerling.'

'In which case, Miss Rachel would regain her old home without my help.'

She gave a little click of impatience. 'You do not strike me as a stupid man, Mr Cater.' She began to gather up her reticule and pull on her gloves.

'No, stay, you interest me, Miss Santerton. If I remove the affections of Miss Rachel away from Mr Blackwood, how would that gain me Mannerling?'

'Without such competition, Charles would wed me and I would persuade him to remove from Mannerling. He is already upset about the place. I think the death of that footman might have been the last straw.'

'What footman?' demanded Mr Cater sharply.

'I cannot remember his name. Mrs Kennedy of Perival found a livery button on the roof and assumed that whoever had been haunting Mannerling was the owner of the button. This footman came up behind her and tried to seize it and she pushed him off the roof. Amazing! An old woman like that! Why, you are a trifle pale, Mr Cater. It was only a footman.'

'I do not like to hear of any man's death. There was really no reason for you to go to this trouble.

I do not anticipate any difficulty over my court-ship of Rachel Beverley. The family is in need of money and I gather she has little dowry to speak of, unless, of course . . .'

His voice tailed off.

'Unless, of course,' Minerva finished for him, 'Charles Blackwood gets there first.'

'Is there any danger of that?'

'I do not think there is any immediate danger. I heard rumours, I sense that Mr Blackwood's last marriage was not a happy one. That will make him cautious. But Rachel has a clever ally.'

'That being?'

'Miss Trumble, her governess, a sharp and scheming woman. She places Rachel like a chess piece neatly in Charles's way on all occasions. Charles's father is becoming enamoured of this governess.'

'So what do you suggest, O wise Miss Santerton?'

'I would suggest you approach the mother, Lady Beverley, without delay, and gain her permission to pay your address to her daughter.'

He regarded her shrewdly. 'What if I told you I was not interested in either Miss Rachel or Mannerling?'

Minerva smiled at him sweetly. 'I would not believe you.'

He smiled back. 'And what do I get if I do as you bid?'

'You get my help and a large sum of money.'

His eyes raked over her and he leaned back in

his chair. 'I have no need of money. Perhaps you could reward me in other ways.'

'We will pretend that was never said.' Minerva rose to her feet. 'I made a mistake.'

'No, no, please be seated. I jest, and rather crudely, too. My sincere apologies.'

Minerva sat down slowly. 'Do you know who was behind those hauntings at Mannerling?'

'This footman, surely.'

'A mere footman would not go to such lengths. Someone was paying him.'

'If you say so. I have no interest in what goes on at Mannerling.'

'Only in the house itself?'

'Yes, it fascinates me. I often dreamt of it.'

'Why? When you had never seen it till you came here.'

'Someone told me of it, in Barbados, where I sweated under the sun and dreamt of England. I came expecting the place to be nothing out of the common way and fell under its spell.'

'I have heard of the enchantment of Mannerling,' said Minerva. 'But to me, it is only a house, and one that is too far from the delights of London for my taste. So do we agree to help each other?'

He held out his hand. She took it in her own and he shook it. 'Remember the governess,' she warned. 'She will make trouble for you.'

'Why? I am a good parti.'

'A feeling. Make your proposal and we will see.'

* * *

Mr Cater dressed carefully in his best the following day and rode over to Brookfield House. The weather was warm but wet and he learned from the maid who took his hat and gloves that the young ladies were abovestairs in the schoolroom with the Mannerling children and their governess. He said he had come to see Lady Beverley.

Fortunately for Mr Cater, it was not one of Lady Beverley's many 'sick' days. She received him in the drawing-room, which smelt of damp and disuse.

'Mr Cater,' said Lady Beverley after that gentleman had refused an offer of refreshment, 'we are extremely glad to see you on this inclement day. Shall I summon my daughters?'

'Not yet. I am here to ask your permission to pay my addresses to Miss Rachel.'

'I did not expect this, sir!'

'You must have noticed that my attentions to your daughter were particular.'

'My daughters are so beautiful that I am accustomed to gentlemen paying them particular attention. Rachel is a pearl above price.'

By which she means, thought Mr Cater cynically, that there is no dowry worth mentioning.

'I am a very rich man, my lady,' he said, 'and would be able to furnish your daughter with every comfort. I understand' – here he gave a delicate cough – 'I have been warned that there is little dowry but I am not interested in mere money.'

Lady Beverley smiled on him fondly. 'Well, well,' she said indulgently. 'We must not rush matters.

We will see what Rachel has to say to the matter, but I cannot think of anything against your suit. Our respective lawyers will deal with tiresome things like marriage settlements. Excuse me for a moment.'

She swept out, leaving the door ajar. Lady Beverley met Miss Trumble on the stairs. 'Such news,' she cried. 'You must fetch Rachel immediately. Mr Cater has asked my permission to pay his addresses to her.'

Miss Trumble went very still. 'I trust you did not give your permission, or rather, not yet.'

'Are your wits wandering, woman? This is a rich planter. I will fetch Rachel myself.'

To her amazement, Miss Trumble barred her way. 'Step aside! You forget yourself!'

'No, stay, my lady, listen to me. What do we really know of this Mr Cater? He says he is a rich planter, but we have only his word for it. Rich men usually stay at private homes, having secured letters of introduction. He says that Lord Hexhamworth had told him of Mannerling, and yet he carries no letter from him. I have written to friends to find out what I can and await their reply. Do not turn him down, but tell him to give you time.'

'You silly woman. The man is richly dressed and his horses are the talk of the neighbourhood.'

'Who knows he even paid for them?' demanded the governess. 'What if your daughter wed him and then disappeared, to be never heard of again? The Beverleys have suffered enough scandal. You cannot promise your daughter to a man whose background we know nothing of and who is staying at a common inn. I only beg a little more time, my lady. Only think how you would sink in General Blackwood's esteem if you were party to a misalliance for your daughter!'

'Perhaps I have been too hasty,' said Lady Beverley. 'I will be cautious. Find out what you can.' She turned and went back down the stairs.

Mr Cater retreated quickly from the doorway of the drawing-room, where he had been listening intently to the conversation on the stairs. Damn that poxy governess. Something would have to be done.

Lady Beverley returned. Mr Cater listened as she said that she had been too hasty in accepting his proposition. Give it a little more time and get to know Rachel better, urged Lady Beverley.

Mr Cater received this with every appearance of good grace, secured a promise that he could take Miss Rachel driving on the morrow if the weather was fine, and took his leave.

After he had gone, Lady Beverley paced up and down. She did not like the way this high-handed governess kept taking matters into her own hands. She would watch the post and when any letters arrived for Miss Trumble, she would read them herself and make up her own mind about any news they contained.

Lady Evans received a call from Miss Trumble on the following day. 'Letitia!' she cried. 'You are welcome.'

Miss Trumble sat down and heaved a little sigh. 'Have any letters arrived for me in care of you?'

'Two. I planned to send them over today by the footman. Not that I mind you using this address, Letitia, but why?'

'Lady Beverley often thinks it is part of her position to open letters addressed to her daughters. I do not want her to look at mine. May I see them?'

Lady Evans went to an escritoire in the corner and picked up two letters and handed them to Miss Trumble.

'You will excuse me for a moment.' Miss Trumble opened the letters and scanned them swiftly. 'No, they do not contain news of the mysterious Mr Cater but of the Santertons. There is not much. Only that business about the late Mr Santerton having died under mysterious circumstances. Minerva is considered of flighty temperament and given to out-bursts of rage. But the general opinion is that she had nothing to do with her husband's death. All hysterical gossip fuelled by the lady's unpopularity in her county. Nothing really that I did not know already. I am awaiting news of Mr Cater.'

'Why?'

'He wishes to propose to Rachel.'

'Then she is very lucky. He is rich and handsome.'

'And unknown. And residing at the Green Man and not at a private residence. I must find out more. Have you heard the news of the death at Mannerling?'

'The footman? Yes, that Irish aunt of Fitzpatrick's was amazing brave.'

'She is an exceptional lady.'

'So what is behind the trouble at Mannerling, unless this footman was simply deranged?'

'That I do not know. Perhaps that wretched house has put its spell on the Santertons and they are trying to scare Charles Blackwood out of it, and yet Minerva obviously wants to marry him, in which case she would get Mannerling as well.'

'I heard something of Charles Blackwood's marriage,' said Lady Evans.

'Indeed? What was it?'

'Only rumours that his late wife was too free with her favours, and among her own servants, too.'

'That might explain a certain sadness and reserve in him.'

'Are you scheming to get him for one of your girls?'

'I never scheme.'

'And are you not supposed to be instructing the Mannerling children?'

'Not today. Their father has taken them to some fair. Do you think it will rain?'

'I do not think so.'

'Pity.'

'Why? You do not want to get wet on the road home.'

'I just wanted to know that someone's drive might be curtailed.'

\* \* \*

'Miss Rachel,' Mr Cater was saying, 'did your mama mention to you that I wish to pay my addresses to you?'

Rachel looked at him, startled. 'No, sir.'

'But it would not distress you?'

Rachel gazed down at her hands. Here was a chance of a good marriage to a rich and handsome man. It was unusual that her mother had not leaped at the offer. Charles's face seemed to rise up before her.

'What did my mother say?'

'Lady Beverley suggested we give it a little more time.'

'I think that is very wise,' said Rachel, her heart beginning to beat hard and her head full of confused and muddled thoughts.

'I have plans,' he said slowly, 'great plans. I have decided to return to the Indies soon and sell my property and settle in England. I need a good house, good land . . . and a wife.'

'I am very honoured – very flattered,' said Rachel. 'I realize you would like an answer before you return. Give me some time to think.'

'As you will. But may I make a suggestion?'

'Certainly.'

'I feel that spinster of a governess has too much influence on your family. I would not discuss this with her.'

'Miss Trumble is kind and wise.'

'But what can a shrivelled-up old spinster know of marriage?'

'I am sorry,' said Rachel stiffly. 'I will brook no criticism of Miss Trumble.'

'You must forgive me then. I am anxious to secure you.'

Rachel cast a quick little sideways glance at his face. Perhaps, she thought, if he had claimed to be in love with her, had taken her in his arms, she might have been swayed. But there seemed nothing of the lover about him. They had reached Brookfield House. Rachel reluctantly offered him refreshment. He was about to accept when he saw Miss Trumble come out of the house and stand on the doorstep, awaiting their arrival. Her eyes were shrewd and assessing as she looked at him. He shook his head and declined Rachel's offer.

'I have been waiting for you,' said Miss Trumble, following Rachel into the house. 'Did Mr Cater propose to you?'

Rachel nodded. 'I asked him to give me a little more time, although he appears anxious to get an answer soon. He returns soon to the Indies and plans to sell up and buy a property in England.'

'Interesting,' said Miss Trumble.

'Do you think I should accept?'

'That is for you to decide, Rachel, but we do not know anything about him, really, or his family, or his background. Perhaps we will find out something soon.'

There was a rumble of carriage wheels outside. Miss Trumble went back to the doorway and looked out. 'Why, it is Mr Blackwood and the general and the children.'

Rachel went out with her. Her heart lurched as she saw Charles. Was she really becoming enamoured of him, or was it because of Mannerling?

Miss Trumble welcomed them all and ushered them into the parlour and then went to fetch her mistress. The children were bubbling with excitement over their day at the fair. Beth sat on Rachel's lap and Mark at her feet as with shining eyes they described their day.

'Now, now,' she interrupted them at last. 'Let me remove my bonnet and gloves. I am just this minute returned from a drive.'

Lady Beverley, Belinda, Lizzie, and Miss Trumble entered the room just in time to hear Rachel's last sentence.

'Ah, you had a pleasant time with Mr Cater, I hope?' asked Lady Beverley. She turned to the general. 'Mr Cater is desirous of wedding our little Rachel, but our stern governess demands caution. But then elderly spinsters were always cautious, were they not?'

'Mama!' protested Lizzie.

Charles looked sharply at Rachel. He had always thought her a pretty girl, but far too young for him, and then that Beverley obsession with Mannerling was always at the back of his mind. But there was something so lovable about her, so vulnerable, as she sat there with Beth on her knees and Mark at her feet.

She looked up then and met his eyes and found herself trapped in his gaze. Her cheeks flushed pink.

'And did you accept the proposal?' asked Charles.

'I do not know what to do,' said Rachel. 'I think it would be better to wait a little to find out more about our Mr Cater.'

Rachel urged Beth down onto the floor next to Mark, for her legs had begun to tremble under that gaze. She was intensely aware of him and at the same time frightened to look at him again.

'So how do you go on, Miss Trumble?' asked the general. 'You should have been with us this day to keep these unruly brats in order.'

'You should have asked me to accompany you, dear General,' said Lady Beverley just as if she had never damned fairs as vulgar. 'I am excellent with children.'

As she never even looked at Mark or Beth or talked to them, the general wondered if she had even had much conversation with her own daughters.

He was irritated with Lady Beverley and he had not liked that remark about elderly spinsters one bit. 'We should be pleased to see you at Mannerling soon, Miss Trumble,' said the general. 'The gardens are looking very fine.'

'The gardens were always accounted beautiful,' said Lady Beverley before Miss Trumble could reply. 'And yes, we would be delighted to accept your invitation. Would tomorrow be suitable?'

The general rolled his eyes at his son, but Mark cried excitedly, 'Please say you'll come, Rachel. We can have such larks!'

'It is up to your father,' said Rachel quietly.

'Miss Rachel to you, Mark,' said Charles, sounding half-amused, half-exasperated. 'Oh, very well. I shall send the carriage for you all at three.'

'Unfortunately, Miss Trumble will be needed here.' Lady Beverley smoothed the folds of her gown, a hard little smile on her face.

'In that case,' said the general, 'we will leave it until Miss Trumble is free.'

'What is it that you wish Miss Trumble to do?' asked Rachel. 'Perhaps I could stay behind and help.'

'Now I come to think of it,' said her mother, throwing her a baffled look, 'it was but a trifling matter and can wait until another day. Yes, we are pleased to accept your invitation, Mr Blackwood.'

They rose to take their leave. The girls and Lady Beverley walked out to the carriage with them.

Charles took Rachel's hand in his and bent and kissed it. 'Until tomorrow,' he said. She felt a surge of sheer gladness rush through her body. She smiled at him suddenly, a blinding, bewitching smile. He smiled back until an impatient little cough from Lady Beverley brought him to his senses and he realized he was holding her hand in a tight grip.

After they had gone, Rachel went up to her room and locked the door. She wanted to be alone with her thoughts.

* * *

Mr Cater was in the drawing-room at Mannerling. 'You had the right of it,' he said to Minerva. 'She has not accepted my proposal . . . yet . . . and I know it is all the fault of that governess. Rachel don't rate her own mother very highly, but she dotes on that shrivelled bag of bones.'

'Such an *old* woman,' cooed Minerva. 'The old are so frail and subject to heart attacks, apoplexies . . . and . . . er . . . *accidents*.'

They both regarded each other for a moment and then Mr Cater gave a little nod.

Charles entered the room and stopped short at the sight of Mr Cater.

'My apologies.' Mr Cater rose to his feet and made his best bow. 'I was passing and called to see you.'

'Do not let me delay your departure,' said Charles stiffly.

'We have had such a comfortable coze,' said Minerva brightly. 'Mr Cater has proposed to Rachel Beverley.'

'Indeed,' remarked Charles, his face stiff.

'I will walk downstairs with you.' Minerva got up gracefully and looped the lace train of her gown over her arm. Minerva was very fond of trains and Charles wondered if she would ever take her leave or whether Mannerling was to be perpetually haunted by the swish of her gowns on the stairs or along the corridors.

'He looks on me as a rival,' muttered Mr Cater

150

as they went downstairs. 'I can see it on his face.'

'Then do something about that governess,' hissed Minerva. 'Leave Blackwood to me.'

She turned and went back upstairs. 'Such a charming man, Mr Cater,' she sighed. 'Rachel Beverley would do very well to marry him. Of course we all know what is holding her back.'

'That being?' demanded Charles moodily.

'I think your intimacy with the Beverleys has raised their hopes of getting back into Mannerling again.'

'I do not think that troubles them any longer.' Charles leaned with one hunched shoulder against a curtain and stared out moodily across the park.

She gave a tinkling little laugh. 'With their ambitious reputation? Do not be so naïve. If the daughter's ambition is not apparent to you, only look at the mother. She would have demanded her daughter marry Mr Cater were she not so blatantly setting her cap at the general.'

'I have things to attend to.' Charles strode from the room. But the poison she had poured in his ear worked its way into his brain. Had he not suffered enough from having been married to a jade who had only wanted his money?

But he now hated Minerva with a passion for having disillusioned him. The happiness and elation he had felt earlier were all gone. He went in search of his father and found him in the library.

'Father!'

'Hey, m'boy, you look like the devil. What's amiss?'

'I think the Santertons have outstayed their welcome and I am anxious to see them gone.'

'Difficult,' said the general. 'Short of telling 'em bluntly to get out, I don't think you'll move them. Anyway, Minerva Santerton wants you to propose and she'll hang around until all hope is gone.'

'And how is all hope to go?'

'Wouldn't fancy that pretty Rachel, would you?'

'I have no desire to realize the Beverley ambitions of getting Mannerling back.'

'Apart from the mother, I don't think they have any. Tell you what, you could tell Minerva that you are proposing marriage to the Beverley chit. Bet you she leaves prompt.'

'And what if Miss Rachel finds out from Minerva that I am supposed to be about to propose to her?'

'Well, she won't. What's Minerva going to do, hey? Ride over to Brookfield House and make a scene? Hardly. Tell her, my boy, she'll go off, and then you'll be free of the woman and her boring brother.'

Charles paced up and down. 'It might work. I think it might just work. I'll do it!'

At dinner that evening, Charles said, 'I was taken aback by your remarks about the Beverleys, Miss Santerton.'

'Minerva,' she corrected with a smile.

'You see,' said Charles earnestly, 'I myself have proposed to Rachel and been accepted.'

Minerva's eyes flashed blue fire.

'You said nothing of this!'

'There was really no reason for me to discuss my private affairs,' said Charles.

'But is this official?'

'Not yet,' put in the general. 'Rachel and Charles have got to get to know each other a little better before Lady Beverley calls down the lawyers and marriage settlements on all our heads. It's still all a secret. Pray do not say anything.'

George Santerton had been drinking, as usual, too much before he even sat down to dinner.

'May as well leave tomorrow, sis,' he said sleepily. 'Nothing for you here.'

'I do not know what you are talking about,' snapped Minerva. She had a determined chin and a Roman nose. How odd, thought Charles, that he had not noticed before how prominent her nose was.

'But,' she went on, 'I had intended to announce our immediate departure. May I wish you joy? The Beverleys will be in alt at having their ambitions fulfilled.'

'As to that, if you mean to regain Mannerling, that will not be the case,' said Charles.

'How so?' slurred George.

'I have decided I do not like the place. Is that not so, Father? We plan to sell.'

'That's it, my boy,' said the general, although the sale of Mannerling was news to him.

'And little Miss Rachel knows of this proposed sale?' demanded Minerva, her eyes narrowing.

'Yes,' said Charles, deciding to add one more lie.

'You amaze me.' Minerva picked fretfully at the food on her plate. 'I have the headache. Be so good as to summon my maid. It has been kind of you both to entertain us, but I pine for home and will repair there on the morrow.'

Charles found he was almost feeling sorry for her as she trailed from the room, another of those long trains of hers swishing across the floor. George Santerton, however, had no intention of leaving the table before he had demolished several more bottles of wine. Charles suppressed a sigh. One more boring evening, but tomorrow he would be shot of the pair of them.

But before Minerva left the dining-room, Mark and Beth, who had been listening outside the door, scampered off up the stairs.

'There you are!' exclaimed Mark when they reached the privacy of his room. 'You said it was wrong to listen at doors, but Papa is to be married, and to our Rachel! And that horrible Minerva woman is leaving.'

'We are not supposed to know,' cautioned Beth.

'Won't say a word. And selling this place! I shall be glad to say goodbye to Mannerling.' Mark lowered his voice. 'This house does not like us.'

'Pooh, that was that footman,' said Beth, but her voice trembled.

'I did not mean to frighten you. I just made that up,' said Mark quickly, proving that he could lie as well as his father.

154

The last light was leaving the sky as Miss Trumble stood in the garden talking to Barry. 'The sad thing is,' she said, 'that Rachel is very aware of Charles Blackwood and she would be good for his children, but I do not think she has much hope there. He looks on her with affection, it is true, but I fear the scandal about the Beverleys' ambitions will stop his feelings from becoming anything warmer. I told you how I counselled Lady Beverley to wait until I found out more about our Mr Cater, and yet I am worried that I might be stopping Rachel from seizing hold of a good marriage.'

'And yet there is something about Mr Cater you do not like?'

'It is not quite that. It is simply that he is not very forthcoming about his family or background. But I should hear from my friends quite soon.'

'You have many influential friends, miss.'

'I have worked in many important households. My employers were and still are very kind to me. I must go to bed now. Good night, Barry.'

Barry went to shut the hens up for the night and Miss Trumble made her way slowly across the lawn.

The night was very still and quiet. Then an owl flew out of the branch of a cedar tree above her head. She swung round to watch its flight.

And that was when she saw a black masked figure in the moonlight, racing across the garden towards her, cudgel raised.

For one second she stood still in amazement and then, with an agility surprising in one so old, she picked up her skirts and ran, screaming 'Help!' at the top of her voice.

Barry darted out of the hen-house, saw the distant flutter of Miss Trumble's skirts as she rounded the house, saw the pursuer, and with a great roar began to run, grabbing a spade as a weapon.

Miss Trumble's pursuer heard the thud of feet behind him and swung round, cudgel raised. Barry stood panting, his spade at the ready. Miss Trumble's cries could now be heard from inside the house.

The man lunged at Barry, who jumped nimbly back and then swung his spade, catching the man on the hip. He grunted with pain and turned and began to run, Barry after him. As he reached the brook that ran along the boundary of the garden, Barry swung the spade again and brought it down on the man's head. He stumbled and fell face down in the brook.

Barry stopped, turned him over, and ripped off the mask. In the brief glimmer of light before the moon was obscured by the cloud, he found himself looking down at a face he did not know.

Josiah, the one-legged cook, was making his way across the grass, holding a lantern. Barry turned. 'Bring the light here,' he called.

But just as he turned, the man on the ground leaped to his feet and ran off through the brook and over the fields beyond like a hare. Barry swore under his breath and set off after him again, but the clouds were gathering overhead and the night was black, and soon he realized he had lost him.

When he returned to the house, it was to find everyone awake.

'I lost him,' said Barry to Miss Trumble, who was being comforted by Rachel.

'Did you get a look at him?' asked Miss Trumble.

'I took off his mask. Never saw the fellow before. Must have been some footpad. I'll need to ride to Hedgefield and rouse the constable and the militia.'

'Do not be away all night,' cautioned Lady Beverley. 'You are to act as footman on the visit to Mannerling on the morrow and we will all need our sleep.'

'Really, Mama,' protested Lizzie. 'Miss Trumble could have been killed. The man may come back.'

'I'll go to the farm and get farmer Currie to send two fellows over to keep guard while I am gone,' said Barry. 'And Josiah has the shotgun primed.'

Rachel finally helped Miss Trumble upstairs to bed. 'Who would attack you?' asked Rachel. 'Did someone think you were the mistress of the house?'

Miss Trumble sat down wearily on the bed. 'I do not know.' For some reason she kept remembering urging Lady Beverley not to accept Mr Cater's proposal, remembering now that she was sure she had heard footsteps from the drawing-room downstairs, retreating from the door. But to think that a rich gentleman such as Mr Cater would pay some thug to attack her was surely far-fetched.

'Tell me, Rachel,' she said, 'what do you think of Mr Cater?'

'He is all that is pleasant and he is extremely suitable, and yet . . .'

'What is it?'

'Just something. Perhaps the thought of going abroad and leaving you all. He talks of selling up in the Indies and returning here, but perhaps that might not happen. Do you think I should accept him?'

'I cannot give you an answer yet. Give me a little more time. I would like to know more about him. I will do very well now, child. Go to bed. Lady Beverley will want us all to look our best for the visit.'

Rachel went to her own room, wishing she did not feel so dragged down, wishing somehow that she could accept Mr Cater's proposal, for she was sure she would never receive another.

Certainly not one from Charles Blackwood!

# SIX

With the exception of Lady Beverley, who was in high spirits, it was a subdued party who set out the following afternoon.

Miss Trumble was heavy-eyed and Belinda and Lizzie worried. Rachel was thinking about seeing Charles Blackwood again and willing herself to discover that he was not out of the common way so that she could settle her mind and marry Mr Cater.

It was a fine day, with large fluffy clouds sailing across a blue sky. To Rachel's delight, she recognized the carriage from Perival outside the porticoed front of Mannerling.

Mark and Beth ran out to meet Rachel as she descended from the carriage, their eyes shining with excitement.

'Well, you two look very happy,' said Rachel, stooping to give Beth a kiss.

'It's our secret,' crowed Mark. 'And the Santertons have left.'

'When?' demanded Lizzie.

'This very morning.'

'I wonder what made them finally go,' mused Belinda.

'Rachel knows,' said Mark with a grin.

Rachel looked at him sharply. 'No, I don't!'

Mark put a finger to his lips. 'Nearly forgot. Big secret.'

They went into the house and up to the drawing-room, where Isabella and Mrs Kennedy were already seated with Charles and the general.

'And how do you go on?' the general asked Miss Trumble.

Before the governess could speak, Rachel said, 'Poor Miss Trumble. She was nearly killed last night.'

'Hey, what?' demanded the general, looking startled. There was a babble of excited questions. Lady Beverley frowned majestically, not liking Miss Trumble to be the centre of attention.

Miss Trumble told of her adventures in a calm, level voice.

'But who would dare do such a thing?' demanded the general.

'We live in troubled times,' said Miss Trumble. 'The constable and the militia are scouring the area. I believe Mr and Miss Santerton are left?'

Mark let out a chuckle of laughter and Beth said, 'Shhh!'

'Yes, they had been here for some time,' said Charles easily. 'I believe Miss Santerton missed the delights of London.' He turned to Mrs Kennedy. 'And how are you after your adventures?'

'Very well,' said the Irishwoman. 'But, faith, it's not every day I kill a man.'

'I doubt if we shall ever get to the bottom of that mystery,' said Charles with a sigh.

'And how is Mr Cater?' asked Mrs Kennedy.

'I do not really know the man,' remarked Charles, his eyes resting for a moment on Rachel's flushed face.

'But Miss Santerton knew him.'

'I believe she knew him slightly. Miss Santerton met him when he came here to see the house, and then she entertained him one day recently when he called when I was out.'

'And they were seen together having a long conversation in the Green Man,' pursued Mrs Kennedy.

Charles looked at her in surprise and the Irishwoman's shrewd eyes twinkled back at him. 'Ah, well, sure she's gone and didn't get the proposal she expected, but she must have lost hope, and I thought that one would never lose hope.'

'Oh, but she learned Papa is to marry someone else,' burst out Mark and then turned red in the face as his father glared at him.

Had it been left at that, the subject would have been changed, for Lady Beverley so much wanted to draw the general's attention to herself, but the general said crossly, 'You must not tell lies, Mark.'

161

Mark looked at him miserably. 'I don't tell lies! I don't! I was passing the dining-room door with Beth last night and I heard him tell Miss Santerton that he was to wed our Rachel.'

'I am afraid you must have misheard us,' said his father coldly.

Beth sprang to her brother's defence. 'But I heard you too, Papa, and we are in alt to have Rachel as a mama. You did say so.'

Lady Beverley sat opening and shutting her mouth.

Charles groaned inwardly.

'Perhaps I had better explain how such a misunderstanding came to arise. Your arm, Miss Rachel.'

Rachel's heart seemed to have gone straight from heaven to hell in one sickening lurch.

For one dizzying moment, she had thought it might be true, that Charles meant to propose to her, and then she had seen the look on his face and his voice saying he must explain how the misunderstanding had arisen.

'One moment.' Lady Beverley arose. 'You cannot take my daughter away for a private discussion without her being strictly chaperoned.'

'I am sure Mr Blackwood means to take Rachel for a walk in the garden,' said Miss Trumble quickly.

'Yes, indeed, Mama, I shall do very well. Come along, Mr Blackwood.' Rachel felt she was in for enough misery without her mother adding to it.

They walked together down the staircase. A footman was up on a tall ladder polishing the crystals of the chandelier in the Great Hall. The sun shining down from the cupola cast the footman's elongated shadow across the hall. The crystals tinkled as he worked among them; they sounded in Rachel's ears like a sort of unkind, mocking laughter. It was in that moment that all her old love of her former home left her. Mannerling stood for Beverley misery and Beverley humiliation.

They walked slowly across the lawns in the direction of the folly. 'How do I begin?' said Charles at last. 'You must understand my distress and increasing dislike of having the Santertons resident under my roof. It was not only obvious to me but to everyone else that Miss Santerton thought she had only to wait at Mannerling for as long as she could and a proposal of marriage would be inevitable. Last night my father suggested a ruse to get rid of them. He suggested I tell them that I was betrothed to you in secret. The plot worked, but my wretched children were listening at the door. Please accept my humble apologies.'

They had reached the folly and stood together looking down at the waters of the lake.

'You have been a good friend to my children,' Charles went on when she remained silent. 'And when we leave Mannerling for a new direction, I will write to you, if I may, and tell you how they go on.'

'By all means,' said Rachel in a voice husky with unshed tears. Then she looked at him, startled, as the full import of his words sank in. 'You plan to sell Mannerling?'

'As soon as possible.'

Rachel gave a little shiver, although the day was warm.

Then she said bravely, 'I accept your apology, Mr Blackwood. I am glad this misunderstanding has been cleared up. I do not plan to tell my fiancé of it.'

It was his turn to look startled. 'Your fiancé?'

'Yes, Mr Cater,' said Rachel. 'I have decided to accept him.'

'I hope you will be very happy. Shall we return to the house?'

The grass was starred with daisies and Rachel felt she had counted every one in her path, for she kept her eyes firmly on the grass, frightened that if she looked at him, he would see the hurt and loss in her eyes.

Her fair hair was almost silver in the sunlight and a tendril of escaping hair curled on her neck. She looked young and vulnerable.

'Will you be happy going to the Indies?' he asked.

'It will be an adventure, sir.'

'And when is the wedding to take place?'

'As to that, there are lawyers to consult. Marriage settlements, all that sort of thing,' said Rachel miserably.

The children flew across the lawns to meet them. 'Is Rachel to be our new mama?' cried Mark.

164

'No,' said Charles. 'As I explained, it was all a misunderstanding. Miss Rachel is to marry Mr Cater.'

'She cannot!' said Mark passionately.

'Behave yourself. Both of you go to your rooms and stay there until I decide what to do with you,' roared Charles.

Hand in hand, they trailed off.

'They are only children,' protested Rachel. 'Please do not be harsh with them.'

'I am still embarrassed over my silly lie. I will not be angry with them any more.'

'Such a *silly* lie,' echoed Rachel dismally. She pinned a bright smile on her face and said with as much cheerfulness as she could summon up, 'Do not tell anyone about my engagement to Mr Cater. I would rather keep it secret until it is official.'

'You may depend on me.'

They walked slowly up the staircase. So Rachel Beverley would wed the suspicious Mr Cater. Charles scowled suddenly. He did not trust that man. But surely, when all the lawyers got together, the facts about Mr Cater would emerge. But why should he think that? England abounded in crooked lawyers. Rachel with the delicate features, the blue eyes and fair hair would be transported to the other side of the world, and he would probably never see her again. He had shied clear of her because of the tales of the Beverleys' ambitions to reclaim Mannerling. And yet, she had received the news that he was about to sell the place with no

165

protest, no reaction. Perhaps, he thought cynically, she was hoping a new owner might prove easier prey. And then he thought that unworthy. What was up with him? He wanted to shake her. And, at the same time, he wanted her to shout at him and berate him for having lied about their engagement. He could not guess from Rachel's apparently calm exterior that all she wanted to do was to run away somewhere and cry her eyes out.

When they entered the drawing-room, everyone promptly stopped talking and gazed at them inquiringly. 'I have apologized for any silly misunderstanding,' said Charles with a lightness he did not feel. 'My children should not listen at doors.'

'Where are they?' asked Miss Trumble.

'They have been sent to their rooms.'

'I will go to them.' Miss Trumble rose.

'Might come along as well,' said the general, heaving himself out of his armchair.

Lady Beverley gave an audible click of annoyance. 'Please do not trouble, General,' said Miss Trumble quickly. 'I think they will need a talk from their governess.'

Isabella covertly studied Rachel's face. Rachel was now laughing at something Mrs Kennedy was saying. Isabella, who knew her husband's aunt very well, realized that Mrs Kennedy was telling one of her tall Irish stories to amuse Rachel and let her keep her countenance. But had Rachel been wounded, thought Isabella, through the loss of Mr Blackwood, or because of the loss of hopes of Mannerling?

Miss Trumble found the children together in Mark's room. 'Now you are in the suds,' she said cheerfully. 'Listening at doors, indeed.'

'But we were so excited when we thought Papa would marry Rachel,' said Beth dismally. 'Now he won't, and he will perhaps find a lady like Miss Santerton instead.'

'Now, you both must have guessed that he did not like Miss Santerton one bit.'

Mark nodded dismally and then said, 'But why does he not like our Rachel?'

'You cannot force your father to wed someone just because you like that person. Were you listening at the dining-room door?'

Beth and Mark exchanged glances and then Mark said defiantly, 'We are sorry. It was all my fault. But it is a bad habit I was wont to indulge in when Miss Terry was our governess. She was always complaining about us and I wanted to know what she was saying.'

'Do not do such a thing again,' said Miss Trumble.

'No, I won't,' promised Mark, 'or Beth either. But it is such a pity Rachel is to marry Mr Cater.'

Miss Trumble went very still. 'Where did you come by that idea?'

'Why, Rachel must have told Papa, for he told us so in front of her and she did not correct him.'

Miss Trumble smiled bleakly, her mind racing. She felt she could see it all: Rachel, learning that

167

she had simply been used as a ruse to get rid of the Santertons – for the general had explained the game when Rachel was out walking with Charles – had said she was engaged to Cater to counter her humiliation, had probably even decided to accept Mr Cater.

Miss Trumble became anxious to escape to Lady Evans and find out if those letters for her had arrived.

She promised to read more about pirates to the children after their lessons on the following day and returned to the drawing-room.

Lady Beverley, hearing of her governess's desire to leave because of a headache, would normally have protested, the ailments of servants being no concern of hers, but she was anxious to remove Miss Trumble from the general's orbit and so agreed, and a carriage was ordered for Miss Trumble.

Once clear of Mannerling, Miss Trumble told the coachman to drive to Hursley Park instead, the home of Lady Evans.

But no letters for her had arrived. Miss Trumble left feeling dejected. She must talk to Rachel as soon as the girl arrived home and beg her to wait a little longer before making her decision.

After their guests had left, the general and his son sat in silence. The lamps had not yet been lit and long shadows fell across the drawing-room.

'Well, that's that,' said the general at last. 'I'm sorry, you know, that you did not settle on little Miss Rachel.'

'Just as well,' said Charles gloomily. 'She is to marry Cater.'

'Have a knack of securing rich husbands, those Beverleys. If we're selling this place, maybe Cater will buy it. Seems monstrous keen on Mannerling.'

'And I will always be haunted by the fear that this man none of us knows much about paid my footman to haunt us.'

'Any way of finding out?'

'Watch and wait. In fact, I have a mind not to sell Mannerling until the fellow takes himself off, just to make sure.'

'Hey, my boy, what if your suspicions are correct? Rachel Beverley deserves better.'

'I cannot interfere and stop the marriage. I have no right to interfere in her life.'

A footman came in and began to light the oil-lamps. The general waited until he had left. Then he cleared his throat and said, 'I've been thinking of getting married myself.'

'Miss Trumble?'

His father nodded.

'Normally I would protest strongly at the idea of you marrying a governess, but Miss Trumble is exceptional. She would be very good for Mark and Beth.'

'Just what I thought,' said the general. 'So I have your blessing?'

'Yes, but a word of caution. There is something very grande dame about Miss Trumble. Do not be surprised if she refuses you.'

'Why should she? She's old like me and cannot go on working forever, and that Lady Beverley don't strike me as the sort to take care of an old servant.'

'If she does refuse you,' said Charles, 'see if you can beg her to leave those Beverleys and come to us. The girls are all too old for a governess.'

'I'll do my best, but she'll accept me. No doubt about that!'

The Beverleys had almost reached home when the Mannerling coach lurched to a halt. Lady Beverley let down the glass. 'Why, it is our Mr Cater,' she cried, recognizing the planter, who was driving his curricle. 'Do you care to come to Brookfield House and take some refreshment, sir?'

'Thank you, my lady,' said Mr Cater. 'Perhaps I might have the honour of escorting Miss Rachel home?'

'But it is near dark and the carriage-lamps have been lit!'

Rachel gathered up her reticule. 'I will go with Mr Cater,' she said. 'It is only a short way.'

Lizzie watched wide-eyed as Rachel left the Mannerling carriage and was helped into Mr Cater's curricle. 'Never say she is going to accept him, Mama!'

'And why not?' asked Lady Beverley. 'He is a good parti.'

'But she would be so far away and we would not know how she fared,' wailed Lizzie.

'Tish, letters arrive from all over the world.'

'So you have given up hopes of Mannerling?' asked Belinda.

'Not I,' said Lady Beverley with a little smile.

'But you heard Mr Charles,' protested Lizzie. 'If he had any interest in Rachel at all, he would not have used her in that heartless way to get rid of Minerva and then tell her it was all a hum.'

'That was certainly bad of him,' said her mother. 'But I cannot be at odds with my future stepson.'

'Mama.' Lizzie looked at her uneasily. 'You surely do not believe the general is going to propose to you.'

'I am very sure. I have noticed the way he looks at me.'

Belinda said cautiously, 'But have you not noticed how he favours Miss Trumble?'

'Pah, a man of the general's standing would never propose to a mere governess. No, my chucks, we will soon be back at Mannerling.'

Lizzie noticed that they were now passing Mr Cater's curricle. Rachel and Mr Cater could be seen in the light of the carriage-lamps sitting side by side, talking earnestly. She gave a little shiver of dread. Mannerling had made things go wrong again. Mannerling had turned against them. Lizzie always felt Mannerling was a living presence.

'I am delighted you have decided to accept my proposal of marriage,' said Mr Cater. 'And delighted at your news that Blackwood is to sell Mannerling.

I shall make him an offer and beg him to wait until I sell my property in Barbados.'

Rachel felt she should ask him about himself, about his family, but a great weight of depression had settled on her shoulders.

'Shall we discuss this with Lady Beverley tonight?'

She realized he was asking her. 'Oh, n-no,' stammered Rachel. 'Not tonight. I am tired. Perhaps tomorrow afternoon?'

'I shall call on you at three o'clock,' he said, 'and then we shall both drive over to Mannerling and get a promise on the property.'

And Charles would think that was the only reason she was marrying Mr Cater, thought Rachel dismally. And that was when she realized that she did not want to marry Hercules Cater.

Mr Cater decided to drive back to Hedgefield, rather than be entertained by Lady Beverley, and Rachel was glad to see him go and to escape him after having to endure only a kiss on her hand.

'Rachel!' cried Miss Trumble, who was waiting in the small dark hall for her.

'No,' said Rachel vehemently. 'Not now! I do not want to talk now.'

Charles Blackwood sat in a chair by the window of his bedroom and looked out over the moonlit lawns. Rachel's face kept rising before his mind's eye. The fact that she was to marry Mr Cater appeared to have focused his thoughts wonderfully. He could think of nothing else. What kind of man was Cater? Charles suspected there was a brutal streak in him. He clutched his hair. How could he have been so blind? Pictures of Rachel playing with his children flitted through his mind, to be then replaced with dark pictures of Rachel being initiated into the mysteries of the marriage bed by Cater.

He could not propose to her himself. Not now. He had told her quite plainly how he had used her name to get rid of the Santertons. What must she think of him?

And yet, her engagement was not official. Had she any feelings for him at all?

He was convinced she was accepting Cater because the man was apparently rich. If only he could talk to her. If only his late wife's memory had not soured him so much.

He had never thought of himself as passionate or impulsive, but now all he wanted to do was to ride over to Brookfield House, get down on his knees, and beg her to accept him before it was too late.

He shifted restlessly in his chair. Perhaps he would get dressed and walk across to the folly and let the fresh night air cool his thoughts.

He dressed hurriedly, without ringing for his servant, putting on only a thin frilled cambric shirt, breeches, and top-boots over his small-clothes, for the night was close and warm.

He walked along the corridor and so down the great staircase of Mannerling. He had come to detest this house, filled as it was with sad memories.

He walked across the daisy-starred lawns under the moonlight to where the slim pillars of the folly shone white against the still waters of the lake.

He leaned against one of the pillars, his heart heavy and sad. There was nothing he could do. He was bound by the fetters of convention. He would need to let events take their course. But how he ached for her and how he realized now what he had lost.

And then an outside sound crept into the noisy tumult of his thoughts. He heard the steady movement of oars on the lake.

He stiffened. Some poacher, no doubt, using his boat to poach fish in his lake!

He strode out of the folly on down to the water's edge.

And then he saw the glimmer of a white gown and the silver shine of fair hair in the moonlight and his heart lurched.

'Rachel!' he called softly. And then louder, 'Rachel!'

A weary little voice reached his ears from across the water.

'Alas, I am caught trespassing again.'

'Come here! Come here to me!'

The little boat headed for the jetty.

He went down to meet her.

He had meant to be polite and calm, now that he was sure he had accepted the inevitability of her marriage, but as she reached the jetty, he saw the shine of tears on her face. He bent down and took the painter and secured the boat with shaking hands.

Then he stooped and lifted her bodily from the boat, cradling her in his arms, saying, 'Rachel, oh, Rachel, do not cry, my little love.'

She gave a muffled little sob and wound her arms about his neck and he bent and kissed her mouth, tasting the salt of her tears, kissed her mouth over and over again in the moonlit stillness of the night.

At last he said huskily, 'How could I have been so stupid?' He set her on her feet and stood looking down at her, his hands on her shoulders. 'How did you get here?'

'I walked,' said Rachel. 'I could not sleep. Mr Cater is to call tomorrow to propose officially. I had not accepted him before, but I was . . . hurt . . . in the way that you had used me to get rid of the Santertons.'

'You must not marry him. We belong together, you and I. Oh, kiss me again, Rachel, and say that you forgive me, that you will marry me.'

'What am I to do?' she said wretchedly. 'Mr Cater calls tomorrow.'

'Then you must refuse him. It is not official and you are allowed to change your mind. When does he call?'

'At three in the afternoon.'

'I will wait until a little after that and then ask your mother for your hand in marriage.'

'Mama does not know you plan to sell Mannerling,' said Rachel. 'Do not tell her until later.'

175

'Will it matter very much to you if we do not live here?'

Rachel took a little breath and said firmly, 'I would like to live as far away from Mannerling as possible.'

He kissed her again and caressed her breasts through the thin stuff of her gown until she groaned against his mouth.

At last he said raggedly, 'Let me take you home before I forget myself.' Holding her hand, he led her back across the lawns to the stables. 'Quietly,' he warned. 'I'll saddle up a horse. I do not want the servants to see you.'

Soon, holding her tightly in front of him, he rode out of the Mannerling estate.

When they reached Brookfield House, he dismounted and then lifted her tenderly down from the saddle, kissing her again.

'One more day, my heart, and all will be resolved,' he murmured.

'Oh, Charles, there is one more difficulty.'

'Yes?'

'I fear Mama expects the general to propose to her.'

'Then Lady Beverley is in for a shock. My father is going to propose marriage to your Miss Trumble.'

'Oh, how wonderful. Her future will be secured.'

'If she accepts him. Go in now, Rachel, and dream of me.'

He stood with a smile on his lips as she ran lightly up the short drive and quietly opened the door and let herself in. He waited until he saw the glimmer of a candle in one of the upstairs rooms.

How would Cater take the rejection? he wondered as he rode home.


Barry walked into Hedgefield in the late morning. Miss Trumble had said she needed the carriage to drive to Hursley Park. He had no real business in Hedgefield, but it was market-day and he liked to talk to some of the locals and enjoy a pint of ale at the Green Man.

He walked among the stalls, chatting to various people he knew. He bought a pasty and a mug of salop and stood enjoying the colour and bustle of market-day.

At last he wiped his mouth and decided to go to the Green Man for that pint of ale and then make his way home.

He stood on the threshold of the tap, blinking in the sudden gloom. He sat down at one of the tables and looked around for the waiter.

A man rose from a table in the corner and made his way rapidly to the door, averting his face as he passed Barry.

And all at once Barry was sure the burly man was Miss Trumble's assailant. He got to his feet and hurried to the door. 'Hey, you, fellow!' he cried.

The man glanced over his shoulder and Barry recognized him. He had last seen that face in the brook at home.

The man began to run, with Barry in pursuit.

Through the market they raced, Barry shouting, 'Stop! Murderer!' at the top of his voice. Others joined in the chase. Out of Hedgefield ran the man and then veered off the road into the woods. Barry and the other pursuers fanned out, Barry hard behind the fleeing figure. The man was thickset but fleet of foot and might have escaped had he not caught his foot in a rabbit hole and fallen headlong.

In a trice, Barry was on top of him, pummelling him and shouting to the others.

'Now,' he said, as the man was dragged to his feet and held firmly, 'who are you?'

The man looked at him defiantly and then spat on the ground.

Barry punched him full on the nose, and as the man yelped with pain, said grimly, 'That is for a start. Let's begin again. Who are you?'

'Jem Pully.'

'So why did you attack Miss Trumble?'

'Who her?'

Barry drew back his fist again.

'No,' shouted the man, and then mumbled, 'He told me there would be five golden boys in it fer me an' I whacked 'er.'

'Who told you?' demanded Barry with a sudden feeling of dread, a feeling that he already knew the answer.

'Come on,' he urged. 'You can save yourself from the gibbet.'

'Cater,' said the man. 'He said there was this old

creature out at Brookfield House, to go and watch and wait and see if I could get 'er on 'er own, like. I went to look out the lie of the land and I sees 'er in the garden.'

'Let's take this one along to the roundhouse,' said Barry, 'and then we'll get hold of Cater.'

But when Jem Pully had been secured in the roundhouse and Barry went to the Green Man, he was told by the landlord that Mr Cater had ridden out to Brookfield House to propose to Miss Rachel Beverley and had bought drinks for everyone in the tap before he left.

Barry set out for Brookfield House at the head of a crowd of townspeople, hoping he would be in time before something disastrous happened.

Miss Trumble was staring in dismay at two letters which Lady Evans had handed to her.

'What is the matter, Letitia?' asked Lady Evans. 'You have gone the colour of whey.'

'These letters tell of Mr Cater,' said Miss Trumble in a thin voice.

'And?'

'And he is half-brother to Ajax Judd, the late owner of Mannerling who hanged himself. And listen to this. He won the plantation in Barbados in a card game with Lord Hexhamworth. Someone who knew him said that Judd had written to him often about Mannerling and he was determined to see the place sometime; in fact, he was about to go there when he learned of his half-brother's death, of the subsequent sale of Mannerling, and at the same time won those plantations.'

'The family surely did not have that much money, apart from what they gained through gambling?'

'No, and the sale of a plantation and slaves might raise enough to buy Mannerling, but what did he plan to live on afterwards?'

'The estates are rich,' said Lady Evans. 'He could raise the rents and milk quite a sum of money from them. But why would he want Rachel Beverley? Such a man would surely want an heiress.'

'Perhaps he has money from other sources.' Miss Trumble stood up. 'I have not seen Rachel since yesterday evening. I must return.'

'But why do you look so frightened and worried? The man's a gamester, that is all. Not uncommon these days.'

'Because I think he was behind the hauntings. I think he set out to frighten the Blackwoods away from Mannerling. I think he paid that footman to cause trouble, and, worse than that, I think he paid some thug to injure me or kill me, for he feared I would stop Rachel from marrying him.'

'He must be in love with the girl.'

'That is what puzzles me,' said Miss Trumble, heading for the door. 'I don't think he loves her one bit.'

Driving herself, she made her way quickly through Hedgefield, stopping only on the far side when she heard herself being hailed. She recognized Jenny Durton, a laundress, and called on the horse to stop.

'Oh, mum,' cried Jenny breathlessly, 'such goings-on!'

'I am in a hurry to get home, Jenny,' said Miss Trumble.

'They done got that man who tried for to kill you,' gasped Jenny. 'Got him and took him to the roundhouse, Barry and the men. They've all gone to Brookfield.'

'Why?' Miss Trumble clutched the reins tightly.

'Because the man, Jem Pully, he done say that Mr Cater paid him to hit you, and Mr Cater's gone to Brookfield to propose to Miss Rachel!'

'Oh, my God!' exclaimed Miss Trumble, and cried to the horse to move on.

Rachel was feeling ill. She had told her mother that Mr Cater was coming to propose to her, had told her the night before; and in the morning she had awoken her mother with the news that she was not going to marry Mr Cater. But she could not impart the glad news that Charles Blackwood was to propose to her, for Lady Beverley went into strong hysterics and all Rachel could do was retreat. Miss Trumble was out. She would need to deal with Mr Cater herself.

Mr Cater arrived at Brookfield House in high spirits. His gambler's soul told him that nothing could go wrong now. He remembered his half-brother's last letter to him, in which Ajax Judd had blamed his fall on the humiliation of the Beverleys. 'If only

181

I had married one of those girls,' Mr Judd had written, 'then Mannerling would have stayed mine.'

Like all gamblers, Mr Cater was highly superstitious. He was determined to have Mannerling and determined to have Rachel to make sure of keeping the place. Rachel would return with him to the Indies for only so long as it took to sell the place.

And yet, as he drove up the drive and looked at the house, he had a sudden feeling that something *had* gone wrong. There was an air of mourning about the house, no bustle, no chatter of voices, and the little maid who answered the door to him looked cast down.

'I will fetch Miss Rachel,' she said, dropping a curtsy. 'My lady is indisposed.'

She showed Mr Cater into the drawing-room. He paced up and down. Surely he was worrying about nothing. Lady Beverley was always ill with something or other.

He swung round as the door opened and Rachel came in.

Although she looked very serious, there was a glow about her, a warmth and colour he had not noticed before.

She was wearing a simple high-waisted muslin gown embroidered with blue corn-flowers which matched the blue of her eyes. A nosegay of cornflowers was tucked into the blue silk sash of her gown.

'I had expected to see your mother first,' said Mr Cater heartily. 'Do it right and proper.'

'Please sit down, Mr Cater,' said Rachel quietly.

He flicked up the tails of his best blue morning coat with the brass buttons.

Rachel sat on a high-backed chair opposite him and clasped her hands together tightly. 'I do not want you to think me flighty, Mr Cater,' she said, 'but I cannot marry you.'

'What is this? You promised, you gave me your promise.'

'I am sorry, Mr Cater, but I cannot marry you.'

'But we belong together. You, me, and Mannerling.'

'As to that,' said Rachel, deciding to lie, 'I do not believe the Blackwoods intend to sell Mannerling.'

His eyes blazed with fury and the veins stood out on his forehead. 'That is your fault!' he cried. 'If you marry me, then Mannerling will be ours.'

'I must repeat, I cannot marry you. I am to marry Mr Charles Blackwood.'

'You trull. You will get Mannerling and leave me to rot on the other side of the world.'

Rachel stood up and said coldly, 'It is time for you to go, sir.' She walked to the door and held it open.

But although he went to the door, he kicked it shut and locked it.

'Now, Miss Rachel Beverley,' he said, 'you are going to marry me, and when I have finished with you, you will be glad to.'

Rachel darted across the room and put a chair between them, her eyes wide with fright and with dawning knowledge.

'You're mad,' she whispered. 'It was you all along. You paid that footman to drive the Blackwoods out.'

'And a sad mess he made of it,' growled Mr Cater. He took a step forward. 'Come here.'

Rachel threw back her head and screamed.

Lizzie's voice came from the other side of the door and then the knob rattled. 'Rachel! Rachel!'

'Get Barry!' shouted Rachel. 'Mr Cater is going to kill me!'

Mr Cater grabbed the protecting chair from her and threw it across the room. He seized Rachel and dragged her against him.

And then he heard the roar outside and stared over Rachel's shoulder and through the window. Barry Wort was at the head of a mob marching up the drive.

Mr Cater rushed for the door, unlocked it, savagely punched Josiah, the one-legged cook who had been trying to hammer the door down, ran through the back of the house and out of the kitchen door. Had he run off across the fields, they would have got him, but, made cunning by desperation, he dived into the hen-house and crouched down in the gloom, hearing the pursuit come through the house and out into the back garden, hearing it die away across the fields.

Miss Trumble was comforting Rachel, Lady Beverley was demanding right, left, and centre what had happened, when they heard the sound of horses' hooves and ran to the window in time to see Mr Cater on horseback fleeing away from Brookfield House.

Charles Blackwood arrived to listen in horror to the story of the assault on Rachel. He immediately rode off in pursuit of Mr Cater.

When Lady Beverley had calmed down, Miss Trumble carefully explained who Mr Cater was and of Rachel's escape from his clutches.

'I am sure there must be some mistake,' wailed Lady Beverley. 'Are you sure?'

'There is no mistake, my lady. Mr Blackwood has gone in pursuit of him.'

'The general is such a brave man.'

'Not the general. Mr Charles Blackwood.'

'Oh, it is all such a coil,' sighed Lady Beverley. 'More scandal for my poor girls. You should have warned me of this earlier.'

'I did beg you to wait.'

'It is your job to protect my girls, Miss Trumble, and you do not seem to be making a very good job of it.'

Miss Trumble primmed her lips and did not deign to reply.

For the rest of the day and the following night, Charles Blackwood, Barry and the townspeople, the militia and the constable searched for Mr Cater without success. It was as if he had disappeared into thin air.

Rachel waited anxiously all the following day for Charles to call, but there was no sign of him. Miss

185

Trumble comforted her, saying that he was probably still searching for Mr Cater. Mark and Beth had been brought over by the general for their lessons. The general seemed reluctant to leave until Lady Beverley appeared in the schoolroom, where he was seated with Miss Trumble and the children, and said she thought it would be 'fun' for them if she took part in their lessons.

Miss Trumble surveyed her employer with a mixture of exasperation and worry. Sometimes, on one of her 'good' days, it was evident that Lady Beverley had once been as beautiful as her daughters.

But as the general hurriedly said he had to take his leave, the lines of discontent once more marred Lady Beverley's face and she flashed a venomous look at the governess, as if she were the reason for the general's abrupt departure.

The carriage and a footman were sent at four in the afternoon to collect the children, but no Charles and no general.

Rachel, disconsolate, trailed about the garden, where she was joined by Belinda and Lizzie.

'You still look very upset after Mr Cater's shocking behaviour,' said Lizzie. 'That is why you are so upset, is it not?'

'Yes,' said Rachel, a bleak little monosyllable. She could not bring herself to tell her sisters of her night-time expedition to Mannerling or how Charles had proposed, although she had told Miss Trumble. She thought of her own abandoned and passionate behaviour with a blush. Perhaps he had decided she had loose morals and was not suitable to be his bride. Miss Trumble had told her that his late wife had been considered flighty. Perhaps he thought her the same!

Then she heard the sound of carriage wheels. The colour rose in her face and she ran down the drive to the gate, her eyes shining.

But it was only the general. Lizzie and Belinda joined Rachel as the old man descended stiffly from the carriage. 'No sign of that villain Cater,' he said. 'Charles has just returned and is going to bed. He is exhausted.'

Rachel wanted to weep. He had obviously not thought to call at Brookfield House first to see her, to give her any news . . . to propose.

Then she realized the general was saying, 'I am come to see your Miss Trumble. Is she available?'

'I will see,' said Rachel, and went slowly into the house.

She found Miss Trumble in her room and told her that General Blackwood wished to see her.

'Oh dear,' murmured the governess, getting to her feet. 'I may as well get it over with.'

'I hope nothing ails the children,' said Rachel, her voice sharp with alarm.

'No, it is something else.'

'Charles is returned to Mannerling. I thought . . . I thought he would call here first.'

'And propose all muddy and exhausted? No, my child, do not fret. He will be here in the morning.'

Miss Trumble went slowly down the stairs to where the little maid, Betty, was waiting at the bottom.

'I've put the general in the drawing-room, miss,' whispered Betty.

'Very good. Give me ten minutes and then bring in the tea-tray and some of Josiah's seed-cake.'

Miss Trumble went into the drawing-room. Betty went off to the kitchen to tell Josiah to prepare the tea-tray. As she came back into the hall, she found her mistress just descending the stairs.

'Was that a carriage I heard arriving?' demanded Lady Beverley.

'Yes, my lady. General Blackwood is called.'

'Where is he?'

'In the drawing-room, my lady, but–'

Lady Beverley swept past the maid and opened the door of the drawing-room.

And stood stock-still.

General Blackwood was down on one knee before the governess, his hand on his heart.

Lady Beverley backed away quickly and nearly collided with Rachel.

'I have nourished a viper in the bosom of my family,' she cried.

Rachel saw her mother's pale eyes were beginning to bulge, the way they always did before a bout of hysterics.

'Hush, Mama. Come into the parlour and tell us what ails you.'

Lady Beverley wrestled with the desire to spoil the romantic scene in the drawing-room or allow

188

herself the relief of unburdening her shock to her daughter. The unburdening won and she followed Rachel into the parlour.

'The general is proposing to Miss Trumble.'

'It is not so strange,' commented Rachel. 'He has shown himself to be a great admirer of hers.'

'*I* never noticed!'

No, you would not, thought Rachel. She wondered whether to tell her mother about Charles's proposal. But what if he had changed his mind?

'I shall send that serpent packing as soon as the general leaves,' Lady Beverley was saying.

'Oh, I would not do that.' Rachel realized her mother did not know anything about the proposed sale of Mannerling.

'And why not, pray?'

'I would have thought you would be more inclined to be very courteous to Miss Trumble.'

'And why on earth should I be?'

'Because Miss Trumble will be the mistress of Mannerling, and if you make an enemy of her, none of us will ever see Mannerling again.'

Lady Beverley opened and shut her mouth like a landed carp while she digested this idea.

'In any case,' went on Rachel smoothly, 'we must not jump to conclusions. Perhaps your eyes tricked you.'

'We will see,' said Lady Beverley grimly.

'If you think about it, General,' Miss Trumble was saying gently, 'you will find you really don't want

189

to marry me at all. A mere governess, indeed! You must remember what is due to your position.'

The general, now seated in an armchair, said sadly, 'I thought we should suit very well, two old people like us.'

'But you are not in love with me.'

The general turned red. 'Really, Miss Trumble, we are both too old for such emotions.'

Miss Trumble gave a little sigh. 'Perhaps you are right, sir. Why I said that was to underline the fact that your heart is not broken. No one shall know of your proposal.'

The general brightened. He had begun to feel ashamed of having proposed to a servant only to be rejected. Then his face fell. 'But Lady Beverley saw me.'

'And so she did. And so we will tell her that you have decided to amuse the children by having amateur theatricals at Mannerling. You are monstrous fond of theatricals and you were showing me just how well you could play the part of the gallant.'

The general looked at her with all the old appreciation. 'Demme, ma'am, but you are a pearl above price.'

She gave an amused little nod as Betty entered the room bearing the tea-tray, followed by Lady Beverley.

'I am not interrupting anything, I hope?' demanded Lady Beverley with a thin smile.

'Not at all, my lady,' said Miss Trumble, rising to her feet and dropping a curtsy. 'General Blackwood came to consult me about the amateur theatricals he means to hold at Mannerling for the amusement of the children. He acts the part of swain very well, as you witnessed.'

'Amateur theatricals!' Lady Beverley sat down and waved one thin white hand to indicate that Miss Trumble should serve tea. 'How amusing. Do you know, General, you are so convincing that for one mad moment I thought you were proposing marriage to Miss Trumble.' And Lady Beverley gave a silvery peal of laughter.

The general stood up abruptly. 'If you will excuse me, ladies, I do not think I will stay for tea after all. My son is returned from the search for Cater extremely exhausted, and I feel I should be with him.'

'As you will.' Lady Beverley looked somewhat huffy. She walked with him to his carriage, telling him that he really ought to have consulted her on the matter of theatricals – 'for poor old Miss Trumble does not have our experience of the social scene, General.'

The general bowed without replying and entered the carriage and rapped on the roof for the coachman to drive on. He did not lower the glass to say any goodbyes. He had also forgotten to suggest to Miss Trumble that she might like to join the Blackwood household as governess.

'Such an odd creature,' murmured Lady Beverley to herself. 'But I shall have him yet!'

\* \* \*

Rachel awoke very early the next morning and spent a long time choosing what to wear. At last she selected a muslin gown embroidered with little sprigs of lavender with deep flounces at the hem and little puffed sleeves. Then she went down to the parlour and sat by the window to wait.

The sun rose higher in the sky. She was joined about noon by Belinda and Lizzie, demanding to know if what Betty had told them was true – that the general had proposed to Miss Trumble.

Rachel turned reluctantly away from the window. 'Miss Trumble says he was merely rehearsing for some amateur theatricals, but I think she said that so as to save his face and not upset Mama.'

'But she could have been mistress of Mannerling,' exclaimed Lizzie.

'There are still some sane people on this earth who do not want to be mistress of Mannerling,' said Rachel tartly. 'Do you not realize that every time one of us plots to regain Mannerling it all ends in shame and humiliation?'

'Meaning that now you know that Charles Blackwood will never propose to you,' said Belinda with a toss of her head, 'you pretend you never cared anyway.'

'And neither do I,' said Rachel. She turned wearily back to the window, her shoulders drooping.

'The children have not come this morning either,' said Lizzie.

Belinda joined Rachel at the window. 'Why,

there is the carriage from Mannerling now. But it is only Mr Charles, not the children. Oh, I hope the Blackwoods have not been offended by Miss Trumble and decided not to bring the children any more. I enjoyed their visits.'

They then heard Charles's voice in the hall, demanding to see Lady Beverley.

'There you are,' said Lizzie. 'He has come to complain about Miss Trumble.'

Rachel wanted to protest, to say that he had called to ask for her hand in marriage, but a super-stitious fear kept her silent, as if long black shadows were reaching out over the fields from Mannerling to touch her very soul. Perhaps the house would have its revenge on her, and Charles would turn out to have called simply, as Lizzie had suggested, to complain about Miss Trumble.

She picked up a book and pretended to read. How the minutes dragged past.

And then the door swung open, to make her start and drop the book.

Lady Beverley sailed in.

'You are to go to the drawing-room, Rachel,' she said. 'Mr Blackwood is desirous to pay his addresses to you. Oh, my dear child, you have suc-ceeded where your sisters have failed. We will all soon be home again.'

But Rachel had already left.

She stood for a moment at the entrance to the drawing-room, looking shyly at Charles.

He silently opened his arms and she flew into

them. He crushed her against him and kissed her passionately. Betty, the maid, outside the door, gave the couple a shocked look and quietly closed the door on the scene.

'Oh, my little love,' said Charles finally, 'you have not changed your mind?'

'No, but I feared you had when you did not call yesterday.'

'I was muddy and exhausted, in no state to propose marriage. My heart, I will keep Mannerling for you, if you wish.'

'Oh, no,' said Rachel with a shudder. 'I do not want the place. Just you, Charles.'

Which made him kiss her so passionately that when they finally surfaced, both of them were breathing raggedly.

He sat down and pulled her onto his knee. 'I must tell you now about my late wife. Had I not been so bitter about her flighty behaviour and so suspicious of every member of your sex, I swear I would have proposed to you that very first day, when I found you with my children at the lake.'

'You quite frightened me.'

'Am I too old for you?'

'No, beloved. Kiss me again.'

They finally broke apart when the door opened and Lady Beverley gave a loud cough. They stood together hand in hand as Lady Beverley came in, followed by Lizzie, Belinda, and Miss Trumble.

'Congratulate me,' said Charles. 'Rachel is to be my bride.'

Lizzie and Belinda gave cries of joy and ran to hug Rachel.

'And you will live at Mannerling,' cried Lizzie.

Rachel shook her head and smiled. 'Not Mannerling. We will live elsewhere.'

'Have you gone mad?' shrieked Lady Beverley.

Miss Trumble gave a little sigh and backed away and made her way through the back of the house and out into the garden.

She hailed Barry, who came over to join her. 'Such news, Barry,' said Miss Trumble. 'Rachel is to marry Charles Blackwood and they are so very much in love.' She sat down on a garden chair suddenly and, taking out a handkerchief, dabbed at her eyes.

Then she blew her nose firmly and went on, 'Dear me, I am quite overset. Such success! The fourth Beverley sister to marry well.'

'I did hear,' said Barry, looking down at her, his expression veiled, 'that the general proposed to you.'

'I have put it about that he was merely rehearsing a play, Barry, but yes, he did propose and I refused him.'

'Why, miss? You could have been set for life!'

'You mean, for what's left of it,' said the governess with a rueful grin. 'I am afraid I am one of those tedious romantics. I could not marry for anything other than love. Ridiculous at my age, is it not?'

Barry bent his grey head and pushed at the grass

195

with the toe of one square-buckled shoe. 'Well, now, I do reckon that I am of the same mind, miss, or I'd ha' been spliced this long since.'

Miss Trumble rose. 'You are such a comfort to me, Barry. Now I must go and tell Betty to look in the cellar and see if we have any champagne left.'

She moved away across the grass and Barry stood for a moment looking after her before returning to his work.

# SEVEN

*Whilst I have nobody but myself to
please, I have no one but myself to be
pleased with.*

MISS WEETON,
'JOURNAL OF A GOVERNESS 1807–1811'

Minerva Santerton read the announcement of
Rachel's forthcoming wedding in the *Morning Post*
and threw the newspaper angrily across the breakfast table at her brother.

'Rachel Beverley and Charles are to wed,' she
hissed.

He tossed the paper on the floor and looked at
her blearily. 'He told us that.'

'But I had begun to think it was all a hum, that
he only said it to get rid of us.'

'Even if that had been the case,' pointed out
George, 'then it stands to reason he didn't want
you.'

'Those brats of his turned him against me. I hate
children.'

'Just as well then that you ain't got any.'

The butler entered. 'There is a person called to see you, Mrs Santerton.'

'Miss,' said Minerva crossly.

'Don't know why you don't call yourself "Mrs". Silly, I call it,' complained George, 'particularly when it looks as if you won't marry again and folks will forget you ever were married and think you're a spinster.'

Minerva ignored him and turned to the butler. 'We do not see persons,' she said. 'Tell whoever it is we are not at home.'

The door opened and Mr Cater walked in.

He was travel-stained, his eyes were red with fatigue, and he strolled forward and sat down at the breakfast table.

Minerva nodded dismissal to the butler. 'What are you doing here?' she demanded. The scandal had not reached the newspapers in Sussex and she did not know Mr Cater was being hunted down.

'I was in the neighbourhood,' said Mr Cater, grabbing a fresh roll from a basket on the table and wolfing it. 'Remembered you had a place here.'

'I do not feel like guests at the moment,' said Minerva. 'You will find a good inn in the village.'

'This is no way to treat a fellow conspirator.' Mr Cater rose and began to help himself to kidneys from the sideboard.

'Hey, what's all this about?' demanded George.

'I think you'd best leave Mr Cater and me to have a private chat, George. Do run along.'

'All right, but send him on his way as soon as

you can,' remarked George over his shoulder as he reached the door. 'He looks deuced odd.'

Mr Cater, between gulps of food, told Minerva bluntly of how he had tried to have Miss Trumble harmed and then his rejection by Rachel and his subsequent flight.

Minerva listened, cold-eyed, until he had finished. Then she said, 'What I cannot understand is that if you wanted Mannerling, why did you not just make the Blackwoods an offer for it?'

'I thought if I wed one of those damned Beverley girls, the house would be securely mine. Judd, a previous owner, the one who killed himself, was my half-brother. He said had he married one of the Beverleys, the house would not have turned against him and his luck at the tables would have held.'

'Mad,' commented Minerva icily. 'Quite mad.'

'Anyway, I want to rack up here for a bit until the hunt dies down and then make my way to the coast.'

'I don't want you here.'

'If you don't put me up, sweeting, I'll write to Blackwood and tell him you were in the plot to get rid of that governess.'

She tightened her lips and her eyes flashed blue fire. 'You may stay a few days, that's all, and then go on your way.'

He looked down at his muddy clothes. 'I'll need some duds.'

'George has enough peacock finery for all the men in Bond Street. He will furnish you with something. After a few days, get you hence.'

Mr Cater grinned. He had every intention of staying as long as possible.

To the further disappointment of Lady Beverley, Charles and Rachel refused to be married at Mannerling. Rachel and her family were to travel to London and stay with Abigail; Charles, the general, and the children would reside at their town house; and the pair would be married in London. Mannerling was already on the market for sale.

Belinda and Lizzie were to attend balls and parties during the Little Season, chaperoned by Abigail.

Miss Trumble believed she had fought another battle with Mannerling and won. As she helped with all the preparations for the journey, she felt the whole menace of Mannerling would soon be removed from their lives. All she had to do was to find husbands for Lizzie and Belinda.

She did not know that Belinda and Lizzie often wondered if anyone had made an offer for Mannerling. They were cross with Rachel because she refused to give them any information on the subject.

Rachel's reason for this was that Charles had told her that a certain Lord St Clair had made a handsome offer. He was the son of the Earl Durbridge, only twenty-four and not married. 'I shall keep that information from the girls and Mama,' Rachel told Charles. 'They will find out sooner or later, but I would rather it was later.'

But Lizzie and Belinda decided to call on Mary Judd, the vicar's daughter, one day shortly before they were due to go to London. Both detested Mary, but Mary was a good fund of gossip.

Mary gushed her usual welcome, but the smile on her lips never melted the hardness of her black eyes.

After various bits of chit-chat had been exchanged, Mary said, all mock sympathy, 'Such a pity Rachel is not to live at Mannerling. She must have been very disappointed.'

'On the contrary,' retorted Lizzie, 'Charles would have kept Mannerling if Rachel had wanted it, but Rachel wanted to live elsewhere.'

'Dear me! How odd! After all the Beverley ambitions.'

Belinda's beautiful eyes hardened. 'I trust you will not keep talking about the Beverley ambitions, Mary. That is in the past.'

Mary gave a little smile and poured tea. 'Then you will not be interested in the identity of the new owner.'

'A new owner already!' exclaimed Lizzie. 'Tell us. Who is it?'

'Oh, I am sure you are not interested.'

'Don't be infuriating, Mary,' said Belinda crossly. 'Who is buying Mannerling?'

'Perhaps it is a secret. I mean, apparently Rachel has said nothing to you . . .'

'Do not trouble,' said Lizzie airily. 'Rachel will tell us. Do tell us instead the recipe for these cakes. Quite delicious.'

Mary gave her a baffled look and then said sulkily, 'It's a certain Lord St Clair. Twenty-four and unwed. He is the eldest son of Earl Durbridge, and Mannerling is a present to his son. The earl is vastly rich and wishes to expand his property and possessions.'

To her disappointment, both Belinda and Lizzie affected indifference to this news and went on to beg for that recipe.

They had walked to the vicarage. When they left, Belinda and Lizzie sedately made their way along the country road under the turning leaves, but as soon as they were out of sight of the vicarage they stopped and clutched each other with excitement. All Lizzie's doubts and fears about Mannerling had left. Ambition had them in its grip again.

'It is your turn, Belinda,' said Lizzie fiercely. 'It is up to you.'

'Perhaps we can find out more about this lord in London,' said Belinda. 'We can ask Abigail. And we will be going to balls and parties and we can ask there. A rich young lord must be often talked about.'

'And let us keep this news to ourselves,' urged Lizzie, 'for if Miss Trumble thinks we have any interest in Mannerling, she might persuade Abigail or Rachel to keep us in London!'

Isabella and Rachel were walking in the grounds of Mannerling. 'I am so glad you and Fitzpatrick are to be here for my wedding,' said Rachel, 'and

Mrs Kennedy, too. I trust she is recovered from her fright.'

'She appears to be well,' said Isabella slowly, 'but do you know, she says she fears Mannerling. I tried to persuade her that the house only seemed haunted because of the machinations of that dreadful man, Cater.'

'There is no news of him.' Rachel looked uneasily around. 'I keep expecting him to return.'

'He would not dare! He has been exposed as a villain. Miss Trumble has found out more about him. As you know, he won those plantations of his at the gambling table, but the man he won them from was ruined as a result.'

'I am so glad none of us has the gambling fever,' said Rachel. 'Oh, there goes Mama, pursuing the general. I wish she would not. She is torturing the poor man. Mama hopes to secure him and persuade him not to sell. But Mannerling belongs to Charles. I have told her that many times, but she will not listen.'

'Did you tell her Lord St Clair was to take the place?'

Rachel shook her head. 'I would not dare, nor Belinda or Lizzie either. They might not even go to London, anxious to stay rooted to the spot in case the new owner arrived when they were away.'

'Mama I can understand, but surely Belinda and Lizzie have grown out of that nonsense.'

'So they assure me and then they run off and whisper together, the way I used to run off and whisper to Abigail so that no one would guess our ambitions were still rampant.'

Isabella laughed. 'You should get a coat of arms and put on it two Beverleys rampant, with Mannerling in the middle. Here come your children. I will leave you to your play.'

Rachel ran to meet Mark and Beth. Isabella stood for a moment watching them and then walked slowly back to the house. If only Lizzie and Belinda could find happiness as well.


'Is that Cater fellow never going to leave?' grumbled George Santerton.

'You do something about it,' snapped Minerva, looking moodily out of the windows of the drawing-room at the dripping trees in the gardens. The autumn weather was chilly and wet and the good summer only a dim memory.

'By the way, the head gardener wants to get men in to lay a new path down to the pond.'

'Why?'

'That, sis, is where your late husband slipped, banged his head, and fell in the pond. Such unhappy memories.'

'Not unhappy. I am well rid of him. I never walk there and neither do you.'

'The present path, nonetheless, is slippery and precipitous.'

'And this, I may remind you, is my property and I am not going to any unnecessary expense.'

'As you will. Where's Cater now?'

'Out somewhere. How do we get rid of him? Think of something.'

'Shoot him?'

'Something sensible. The servants are already gossiping about our so-called Mr Brown who arrived on a tired horse and with no luggage.'

Minerva suddenly swung round, her eyes shining. 'I have it. I will simply tell him that unless he goes, I will write to the authorities and tell them he is to be found here.'

'And they will wonder why we didn't tell them before.'

'We will say we did not know anything about it until now. But it is only a threat. But it will shift him.'

'You told me that he is wanted for an attack on the governess and an assault on Rachel Beverley. You were not part of the plot by any chance, were you?'

'Don't be so stupid.' Minerva had suddenly realized that Mr Cater had no proof that it was she who had suggested he put the governess out of action. Her blue eyes were shining with malice. 'I will go and find him and tell him now.'

'Do that, but take a gun with you.'

An undergardener weeding a flower-bed volunteered the information that 'Mr Brown' had last been seen heading in the direction of the pond.

Minerva hesitated, but then set out towards where the pond lay. She walked across the wet lawns, the rings on her pattens making soggy imprints on the grass. She then entered the woods and walked on along a winding path where tall trees sent down showers of raindrops onto the calash she wore over her bonnet, until she could see ahead of her the gleam of water of the pond.

Ahead of her, Mr Cater stood at the top of the precipitous muddy path which led down to the pond. So this was where the late Mr Santerton had met his death. And no wonder. Why such a treacherous, steep, and muddy path should have been left on such an otherwise well-ordered estate puzzled Mr Cater.

His mind worked busily. A couple more months here of free food and board and he would make his way to his bank in London before heading for the coast. He had not *killed* anyone. He shrewdly guessed that neither the Blackwoods nor the Beverleys would be anxious to keep the scandal alive.

What a dreary day! A thick mist was coiling around the boles of the dripping trees. And the days seemed long and tedious. He would try again that very evening, when George was in his cups, to get him to play a game of piquet. So far, George, even stupid with drink, had refused to gamble.

He shivered. What was he doing stumbling down this muddy path to view some dreary pond, not even an ornamental lake?

He half-turned to go back and his foot slipped. Cursing loudly, he slipped down and down the slippery path and plunged straight down into the icy waters of the pond.

He struggled and fought to rise, but thick weeds at the bottom were wrapped round his ankles. He finally tore free and with bursting lungs his head broke the surface.

'Help!' he shouted. 'I can't swim.'

Minerva stopped just above the pond and heard that shout. She turned very white and began to tremble. The mist was so eerie, she was sure she was hearing the voice of her dead husband. Had she not stood just here and heard him cry for help? As if in a nightmare, she turned as she had turned then and began to hurry away, back up the hill and through the trees, the cries growing fainter behind her as they had done on that dreadful day when her drowning husband's struggles had made him hit his head on a rock before he sank for the last time. That had been the coroner's deduction at the inquest.

It was only when she had stumbled into the hall of her home that her wits cleared and she remembered that she had gone to find Mr Cater.

George came down the stairs and stopped short at the sight of his sister.

'You look as if you have seen a ghost,' he said.

'Quickly,' hissed Minerva, 'into the library.'

He followed her in and stood looking inquiringly at her. The little-used room was musty and lined with books which had not been taken down and read since the last century.

'What is it?' demanded George. 'Is it Cater? Did he attack you?'

She shook her head.

'Then what is it?'

'I went down to the pond to find Cater,' said Minerva in a dull voice. 'A gardener said he had gone that way. I was approaching the pond and I heard a cry for help, and someone shouting, "I can't swim", I turned and walked away.'

'I'd best get the men and get down there. It was Cater. He was saying the other night that he had never learned to swim.'

'Wait! It will be too late now. He will be dead, and we will need to report that death if the servants know about it. And it will come out that we have been harbouring Cater.'

'And if it does? We will say we knew nothing of the trouble at Mannerling.'

'Who would believe us? The servants will say he arrived in a state and without luggage and has been going by the name of Brown.'

George looked at her uneasily. 'You were implicated some way in those goings-on at Mannerling. You must have been or you would not have allowed him to stay. And that's what happened to poor Santerton. It was an accident and you could have saved him, but you walked away.'

'Stop going on about what I am supposed to have done. The problem is that we must get Cater's body, which is no doubt floating on the pond, and bury it. According to the servants, he has gone off and that is that.'

'I tell you, sis, I will help you, but then I will take myself off. It's like living with Lady Macbeth.'

'You always were a weakling, George!'

'Oh, God, spare me your insults. Let us see if we can still save the poor man.'

'The servants must not see us!'

'We'll just go for a little walk. It's dark now. I will take a lantern.'

Soon they set out together, George holding the lantern high as they finally negotiated the slippery path.

They stood on a grassy knoll at the side of the treacherous path. George swung the lantern in a wide arc.

'Nothing,' he whispered. 'He's probably up in my room, taking dry clothes out of my wardrobe.'

'Wait!' urged Minerva. 'Try near the edge.'

George held the lantern out over the bottom of the path and Minerva drew back against him with a little hiss.

The body of Mr Cater lay almost directly below them, his hands stretched out grasping the mud. He had obviously managed to nearly get out of the water, but cold and exhaustion had robbed him of his final strength.

'It's going to be a day's work to drag him up that path and bury him,' muttered George. 'I say we put some rocks in his pockets and push him back in the pond.'

'You do it,' shivered Minerva. 'I could not bear to touch him.'

George gave her a look of loathing. 'I'll do it during the night. Let's go back.'

At two o'clock that morning, George, with a bag of rocks and some heavy chains over his shoulder, made his way back to the pond. He worked quickly, weighing down the pockets of Mr Cater's clothes with rocks, and then wrapping the chains around his legs. He then gave the body a huge push and heard a sinister gurgling sound as it sank beneath the waters of the pond.

And then he went wearily back to the house to get well and truly drunk.

Mrs Kennedy walked about the grounds of Mannerling the following day. There was a steel-cold wind from the east. She and Isabella and Lord Fitzpatrick were to leave for London on the following day. She had been drawn to visit Mannerling one last time, to walk the lawns and say a prayer for the dead footman. She thought she would never forget John's scream as he fell from the roof.

She went to sit in the folly and look out over the black waters of the lake. The folly was the only place at Mannerling that she really liked, possibly because it had been built on the orders of Charles Blackwood and was not part of the old Mannerling.

She had kept her doubts about the two remaining Beverley sisters, Belinda and Lizzie, to herself, not wanting to worry Isabella. She sensed that neither Belinda nor Lizzie had given up their ambitions to reclaim their old home. What a passion the wretched place aroused in people! Only think of that creature, Cater.

She left the folly and walked down to the lake. The wind abruptly died and the waters were cold and still.

'It's goodbye to you, Mannerling,' said Mrs Kennedy. 'If I have my way, neither I nor Isabella will ever come here again.'

Then she suddenly felt colder than the day itself and a mist seemed to surround her. She was standing on the jetty and a white face grinned up at her from the water. She let out a hoarse scream and crossed herself.

As if waking from a nightmare, she looked around and found there was no mist at all. She looked back down at the lake again. There was no face in the water.

She turned and began to hurry back towards where her carriage was parked outside the house. She never told anyone about her experience or that the face in the water that she thought she had seen had looked like the dead face of Mr Cater.

Rachel and Charles were married on a winter's day in London in St George's, Hanover Square. Lady Beverley wept noisily throughout the service. After all, sensibility was all the rage.

Miss Trumble felt quietly satisfied. Another happy ending. She sat at the back of the church, heavily veiled. In fact, her veil was so heavy that Barry, also at the back of the church, remarked slyly that it was almost as if she did not want any of the fashionables among the guests to recognize her.

Belinda, as bridesmaid, wondered if she herself could ever look forward to such happiness. The church was cold and she shivered in her fur-lined cloak. She and Lizzie had attended a few balls and routs and also the playhouse, but nowhere had they seen the mysterious Lord St Clair. They heard of him, however, heard he was in London, and that he was regarded as one of the most eligible men on the marriage market. They also learned that he preferred town life and that his father had bought him Mannerling in the hope that a house and lands of his own would give him more responsibility and encourage him to take a bride.

Abigail had offered them a Season in London, and both Lizzie and Belinda had decided to accept. If their quarry preferred town life, then surely he would emerge at the following Season.

Beside Belinda, Lizzie was feeling uncomfortable, for Mrs Kennedy had given her a stern talking-to only the day before. Lizzie was very fond of Mrs Kennedy but had not liked being told that Mannerling was a wicked place. She quite forgot that she had thought that very thing herself not so long ago. That old ambition was burning in her veins. Belinda must somehow manage to marry Lord St Clair. Lizzie went off into a dream of sunny days at Mannerling, back home again, and only came out of it as she realized her sister, Rachel, was well and truly married and the bells were ringing out in triumph over the sooty buildings of London.

The wedding breakfast was held in the Blackwoods' town house, which had once been the Beverleys' town house. It was to be sold as well. The Blackwoods would not be returning to Mannerling again. They had cleared out all their possessions from the place. The town house did not have too many memories for the Beverley sisters, for they had spent most of their time at Mannerling. Only Isabella had made her come-out from the town house, remembering, as she sat next to her husband, what a disaster that had been. She had been so haughty and proud, she had thought no man good enough for her.

A small orchestra was playing sweet melodies. The room was full of the happy sound of conversation.

Rachel sat at the top table beside her new husband, happy and content. Charles was buying a property outside Deal on the coast. Until they were ready to move in, they would travel here and there on their honeymoon and end up in Ireland to stay with Isabella. The Fitzpatricks were returning there after the wedding.

She floated on a happy dream through the breakfast and the dancing afterwards, until it was time to leave.

Her sisters clustered on the pavement outside the town house to wave goodbye. She felt a lump in her throat as she kissed them one after the other, then her mother and then Miss Trumble.

Rose-petals were thrown, handkerchiefs waved.

Rachel leaned out of the carriage window and waved back until the carriage turned the corner and her past life was lost to view. She put up the glass, blew her nose firmly, and said huskily, 'I can only pray that Belinda and Lizzie will be as happy as I am.'

'As to that, I hope they will,' said Charles, 'although, if you remember, we attended Mrs Dunster's party a few weeks ago. I did not tell you then, for I did not want to distress you, but I fear both Lizzie and Belinda were overheard asking curious questions about Lord St Clair.'

Rachel looked alarmed. 'They must know! We must turn back. I must talk to them, warn them.'

'No, my sweeting, the estimable Miss Trumble has been warned by me and will do all in her power to keep them safe.'

He put an arm around her and held her close. 'Kiss me, Mrs Blackwood. And if you ever mention Mannerling again, I shall beat you.'

'Would you, indeed!'

'Probably not. Kiss me instead.'

Rachel did as she was bid, and after a long while she said dreamily, 'I hope Mark and Beth will not miss us too much.'

'They are so excited to be going to Ireland with your sister, they have probably forgotten about us already.'

'When does St Clair take up residence?'

'I really should beat you. Five kisses for that. I do not know. It is his father who wants him to remove

214

to the country and away from the wickedness of Town. I think it will be a long time before he goes there. Now for those kisses . . .'

Lord St Clair at that moment was facing his father. He was a tall, willowy young man dressed in the latest Bond Street fashion, which made him look like an elegant wasp. His waist was pinched in with a corset and his vest was of black and gold stripes. 'Don't think I want that Mannerling place after all,' he drawled.

'What?' demanded the choleric earl. 'Most beautiful place in the world, and you turn your nose up at it.'

'My agent went to look at it,' said Lord St Clair with a weary sigh. 'Man, very reliable, my agent. Stout fellow. Says the place is haunted.'

'Pah! Fustian. Been at the brandy, that's what he's been doing. Get rid of him.'

'He went down to sort out the servants, you know, which to keep and which to send packing, and a lot of 'em told him the place was haunted by some chap who hanged himself from the chandelier and, worse than that . . .'

'Oh, do tell, you popinjay! A headless horseman?'

'No, a drowned man.'

The earl took a deep breath. 'Now listen to me, m'boy, you are not going to spend your life racketing around London. You can get yourself a suitable gel at the next Season, move to Mannerling, and set up your nursery, or I will disinherit you!'

Lord St Clair took out a scented handkerchief and waved it in front of his painted face, as if perfume could sweeten his father's temper.

'You wouldn't do that,' he protested.

'Oh, yes, I would. It's Mannerling and a bride, or nothing.'

St Clair uncoiled himself from his chair and headed for the door. 'As you will, Father,' he said in a mournful voice. 'As you will.'

He strolled round to Bond Street to comfort himself and fell in with two equally elegant cronies.

'You look like the deuce,' said one. 'What's amiss?'

'Got the threat of the country hanging over me,' mourned St Clair. 'Father says he'll disinherit me if I don't get meself a bride at the next Season and move to that place Mannerling he's bought me.'

'Do as he says,' counselled the other. 'Move to Mannerling and take the Town down with you, big parties, good friends, good bottles, and a complacent wife, and as soon as she's produced the heir, take yourself back to Town.'

'Jove, the very idea,' said St Clair, brightening. 'The countryside will never have seen anything like us. Mannerling it is!'